CRYSTAL RAIN

CRYSTAL RAIN

TOBIAS S. BUCKELL

A Tom Doherty Associates Book **TOR®** New York

SF

CRYSTAL RAIN

Copyright © 2006 by Tobias S. Buckell

This book is printed on acid-free paper.

Book design by Jane Adele Regina

Map by Jeffrey L. Ward

A Tor Book
Published by Tom Doherty Associates, LLC
175 Fifth Avenue
New York, NY 10010

www.tor.com

Tor® is a registered trademark of Tom Doherty Associates, LLC.

Library of Congress Cataloging-in-Publication Data

Buckell, Tobias S.
    Crystal rain / Tobias S. Buckell.—1st ed.
      p. cm.
    "A Tom Doherty Associates Book."
    ISBN 0-765-31227-1 (acid-free paper)
    EAN 978-0-765-31227-3
    I. Title.
    PS3602.U2635C79 2006
    813'.54—dc22

                                                        2005016722

First Edition: February 2006

Printed in the United States of America

0 9 8 7 6 5 4 3 2 1

For Emily

my first reader and then girlfriend,
fiancée, and finally wife as I wrote this book

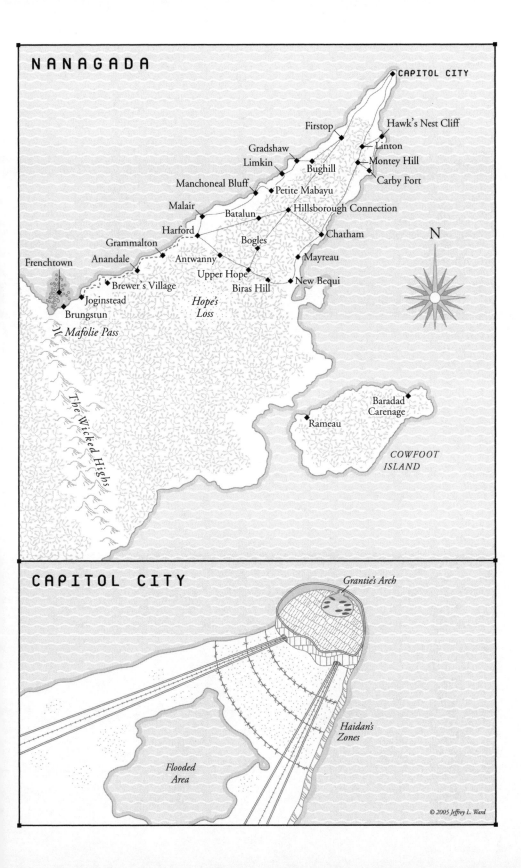

CRYSTAL RAIN

PROLOGUE

Brown vines dried and crumbled along the village Refojee-Ten's edges. Everything thirsted for the impending rainy season: the dry jungle, the hard-packed dirt roads winding through the village, the two wells, and the drooping emerald ears of corn.

Wiry elders sat hunched over rickety tables outside playing cards, their eyes scanning the late-afternoon sky as they shuffled and dealt.

In the distance over the green fringe of the treetops, the hazy Wicked High Mountains cut and shredded dark clouds, forcing them to release sheets of rain several days' walk away from Refojee-Ten. The elders flicked their cards, flashed their gums, and licked lips as they eyed the pictures in their calloused hands.

Rainy season tugged at their joints. It made them feel older, creakier, and yet thankful life was about to return because soon the jungle air blowing into the streets would be wet, the roads muddy, and the corn so fresh you could hear it grow at night in the fields.

Yes, rainy season would burst in any day now.

So no one jumped when the thunder cracked the sky. They looked up and nodded, wise to the land's regular cycle proving itself for yet another year, as it had all the many years of their lives before.

But the thunder did not die and give way to fat raindrops. It continued to boom louder and louder until mothers ran away from their wash-lines to grab their children. Men stopped and looked up at a fiery smoke trail that crossed the sky.

The elders dropped their cards and stood up, shielding their eyes to watch in awe as a white-hot fireball flew over the village. The ground shook as it disappeared into the jungle with a distant explosion. Panicked birds swirled into the air to create confused patterns of bright plumage above the trees.

The smoky trail remained in the sky until dusk.

By that time the greatest hunters in Refojee-Ten had taken up their rifles and walked off into the dangerous night with torches to see what this curiosity was.

Two days later the hunters found a section of the jungle where the trees had been blown down like mere sticks.

Cautious, they followed the destruction inward. To walk over the hot ground, they bound their feet with aloe and arm-sized leaves. They choked from the smoke. When they could walk into the destruction no longer, they turned around and found a weary-looking man sitting on a steaming metal boulder.

He wore a top hat, a long trench coat, and black boots. His eyes were gray, his dreadlocks black, and his face ashen. It was as if this man had not seen sun in all his life, but was born brown once.

He spoke gibberish to them, then touched his throat several times until the hunters understood his words.

"Where am I?"

Near the village of Refojee-Ten, they told him, which is as far from the north coast as it is from the south coast, but a week's walk from the Wicked High Mountains.

They asked him if he came down from the sky, and how he did it.

The man ignored their questions. He leaped from the metal boulder and landed among them. He pointed at their rifles.

"These weapons, you got them where?"

They told him they traded with northerners for them: bush hunters and merchants. It was an infrequent trade, but enough to let the villagers understand the world outside the jungle's depths. The rifles, they knew, were made in a place called Capitol City.

"And how would I get there?"

Go north through the jungle, they said, to Brungstun, and then use the coastal road. Or wait for a northerner to come trade with us and go with them.

This satisfied the stranger. He seemed harmless, tired, and thin. He looked much like a pale insect one might find in the mud, so they took him back to the village. On the way back he ate their dried foods and acted as if they were the finest meats.

He only stopped eating once: to stare at a bush by their side. A jaguar leapt out, and the stranger grabbed its throat and slung it across the road. The hunters watched the cat drop to the ground, neck twisted at an odd angle.

The stranger stayed in the village for a week. He ate anything offered to him and gained strength. When he left, his muscles bulged. His skin looked like earth now; a proper and healthy color for a man.

He chose, against all their protestations, to walk north through the dangerous jungle to go find the rest of the world. He asked one last question while among the Refojee-Ten villagers. "How long do I have until carnival?"

They told him the number of months. Though, they knew, some towns celebrated carnival on different days throughout the land. When they asked him why he wanted to know about carnival, the man smiled.

"I'm looking for an old friend, one who never misses carnival." And that was all he said.

After he left, the hunters talked at length about what they had seen and wondered who he was. But the elders shook their heads over their cards. Not who, they said to the hunters. What.

When pressed for further details, they shook their heads and turned back to their cards, waiting for rainy season to start.

PART ONE

THE WICKED HIGHS

CHAPTER ONE

The Wicked High Mountains loomed around Dennis and his men as they skirted house-sized, reddish slabs of rock jutting from the soil, avoided deep, echoing chasms, and paused at a tiny stream to fill their canteens.

Above the tree line the air cooled enough that Dennis could see his own breath. Yesterday he would have been amused. Today his huffing betrayed how fast he moved over the crumbling ground.

Dennis looked around at his men. Mongoose-men. Nanagada's best bush warriors. They hopped from rock to rock with grunts. Some had long dreadlocks down their backs and full beards. Others had short, cropped hair. They came from all over Nanagada, and despite being smeared with mud and colored chalk to help them blend into the shadows, they had skin ranging from mountainside and Capitol City soft brown to south-coast dark black.

Each man dressed in gray: heavy canvas trousers, long-sleeved shirts, and floppy wide-brimmed hats. All over this dull uniform sticks and leaves jutted out, glued on in random patterns.

Out of the jungle and on the rock they stood out like shaggy gray-and-green creatures.

Still, this was the quickest way to Mafolie Pass.

The second moon rose. A dim double-lit darkness would be far better than the blatant daylight they'd been running in. Dennis glanced at the sky. They'd be less likely to get spotted by an Azteca airship at night.

Earlier, many miles downrange of Mafolie Pass, they'd captured an Azteca scout. Much to their surprise, the Aztecan knew several code phrases. The mongoose-men had few spies among the Azteca. It was a rare encounter.

Most Azteca who came over the mountains fled for Capitol City: Nanagada's farthermost northeastern point. As far from their past as they could get.

This Aztecan said his name was Oaxyctl. *O-ash-k-tul*. His teeth chattered. He had barely made it over the mountains. Shivering, hungry, and hardly understandable, he told them Mafolie Pass was under attack.

"That happen sometimes," the mongoose-men replied. Azteca threw various-sized attack parties at the pass randomly to test the thick walls and Mafolie's perfectly placed guns, but the pass remained impenetrable. The mongoose-men based Nanagada's defense from Mafolie Pass.

"Not from the pass," the spy hissed, his back against the rough bark of a turis tree, his legs in the mud.

"Mafolie Pass the *only* place any big army able to cross," Dennis objected.

The spy wiped his face with a dirty sleeve. "They dug a tunnel," he spat. "You understand?"

They blinked. "A tunnel? Under the whole mountain? We would know about that."

"Nopuluca," the spy cursed at them. "Azteca dug for a hundred years now. They fooled you into thinking they were still testing the pass while always digging. But they're here. Believe me. We are dead men."

He'd begged water and food off them. They'd told him where the next low-mountain station was. Then the strange spy scrambled off down the mountainside.

"If we all done dead," they called after him as he clambered down into the thick greenery, "why you come here? Where you think you going?"

But he had already disappeared into the bush.

Dennis and his mongoose-men broke their camp after a minute's consultation, leaving anything they couldn't carry where it sat, and started the run for Mafolie Pass.

The heavy morning mist made it impossible for Dennis to see more than a few trees ahead. Small animals skittered around them, noises amplified in the dimness. The mongoose-men relaxed a bit, back in the jungle now. They were still three hours from Mafolie Pass. Better they relax now and not fray their nerves before getting closer.

A twig snapped. Dennis signaled stop by flicking his wrist.

The group's rifle barrels rose in quiet unison.

"Pddeeett?" chirped a voice from deep in the mist. It sounded birdlike enough to fool any townie.

"Pass?" Dennis called out.

"Plain porridge," came the answer. "No sugar."

Everyone lowered their rifles. Their best runner, Allen, had dropped his packs and gone ahead yesterday to scout. Now he pushed through a pricker bush, sweat dripping from his forehead, and grabbed an offered canteen. He splashed water on his face.

"Come follow me." Allen wiped his face on his sleeve, smearing dirt over his cheeks and breaking a leaf off his hat.

"Azteca?" Dennis asked.

Allen nodded.

No one slung their rifles.

Allen led them down through a ravine, then back up the other side. They followed him, leaning into the sharply angled ground, arms loose, zigzagging up. A small dirt road cut through the bush at the top. Next to it a stone sentry-house perched on the ravine's edge. Thick moss clung to the cracks in the wall and dripped with condensation.

"You had see anything?" Dennis asked.

Allen shook his head. His baggy canvas shirt was stained with sweat over the chest and armpits. "It real quiet now," he said. "Come."

Together they walked forward. Allen pointed at a dead animal beside the sentry-house. Flies buzzed around it. Dennis walked over; saw a pair of hands bound with rope. "Look upon that." He pushed the flayed body with his boot. He managed to roll it over, breathing through his mouth to avoid the smell. He pulled his machete free from its scabbard strapped to his lower leg. "See that?" He pointed at the ragged hole between the corpse's second and third ribs.

"Them cut through for him heart," a mongoose-man said.

"Warrior-priest in a hurry, don't want cut through no breastbone," Allen added.

Dennis didn't see an eagle-stone imprint. Some passing Azteca warrior did this in a hurry without the usual Azteca equipment. Typical of a small hunting party come over the almost impassable Wicked Highs . . . but this was here in the heart of the mongoose-men's world.

Allen pointed to the sides of the dirt road. "See that crush-up leaf and footprint? I guess a thousand come through. At least."

A thousand. No small hunting party. A full invasion swing toward Mafolie Pass, but on *this* side of the mountain. Just as the spy had said.

Dennis glanced down the road, imagining the tightly packed throng of bright feathers and padded armor marching down the mountains and into Nanagada. If they destroyed Mafolie Pass, Azteca could come over the mountains with ease. With enough time and supplies they could march anywhere in Nanagada. The Azteca would rule everything if no longer held back by the mountains.

"Got some decisions for we make." Dennis squatted by the road. He leaned forward on the machete's handle for balance. The dark blade dug into the dirt. "You all ready for some heavy reasoning?"

The mongoose-men stood in a loose circle around him. Two stood up on either side of the road, looking around the curve for any surprises.

"Mafolie Pass probably already run over," Dennis said. "We late. So what next?"

Allen shuffled in the dirt. "No wheel imprint here." He looked up at everyone. "These Azteca all moving on foot, seen?"

"Make sense, wheel don't do you much good in the mountain."

"They have no supplies with them. They moving light, moving quick. But they go have to get supply coming behind them if they want eat."

Dennis thought about the hungry, tired spy. How much food could these Azteca carry? A few days' worth at the most.

There had to be supplies on the way.

"Yeah. More Azteca go be coming down the mountain," Dennis agreed. "We could choose to run down the mountain to warn people, or we can slow down Azteca supply."

"Could do both, if we split up," Allen said.

Dennis cleared his throat and looked around, an unspoken question in the air. Who stayed to face more Azteca, and who got to run down the mountain to do the warning?

They drew straws. Four men would split with Allen to run down the mountains and find the nearest station with a working telegraph. If all the wires were already cut, they would do their best to make it through the jungle to warn any towns they came across.

"*Pddeeett!*"

Dennis looked up. One of the men doing watch down the road. "Yeah?"

"Azteca!"

"Supply or warrior? How many?"

"Jaguar warrior party, no supply-men," the lookout yelled back. Dennis's stomach churned. A supply group would have been easy to ambush. "A hundred. They got clubs and packs and guns. A bunch of regular-looking warrior coming behind as well."

Allen looked at Dennis and unslung his rifle. Dennis shook his head. "Leave. Now. We go hold them down a bit. You run. Get the word out. Hear?"

Allen nodded and shook Dennis's hand. Then Dennis pushed Allen away and picked up his rifle. He jogged toward the bend as Allen grabbed his pack, strapped it on, and disappeared down the ravine with four mongoose-men following him.

Dennis slowed and inched his way up the roadside, using the heavy bush as cover. The lookout scrabbled his way over on his elbows and carefully parted a pricker bush for Dennis to look through.

Azteca feathers and standards flapped animal likenesses in the wind. The first scouts appeared down the road. Then the first row of regular Azteca marched out, a dust cloud rising around them.

"Some say a cornered mongoose the most vicious," Dennis said. "We go be even more ferocious."

The rest of his handful of men crawled into the bush near him. They dug around for the best hiding positions. One mongoose-man monkeyed up a tree, his feet kicking off loose bark.

Dennis raised his gun and sighted the lead banner carrier. "When you ready."

A rifle cracked from up in the tree. The Azteca line slowed. The mongoose-men opened fire and the first row of Azteca dropped to the road. Dennis fired. The gun bucked into his shoulder. He blinked his eyes clear and reloaded, levering the still-steaming spent cartridge out with a practiced flick.

The Azteca return fire ripped through the bush around him. Pain exploded down Dennis's arm. He grabbed his shoulder, trying to stop the blood spurting into the leaves around him. Feet pounded the ground as Azteca slashed through the branches at them.

Dennis heard more shots from his men, branches snapping, grunts, gasps, and screams as Azteca and mongoose-men fought hand to hand.

A light-skinned warrior jumped past Dennis, smacking him in the head with a club.

He struggled to raise his rifle with one hand, but it was knocked free. Two Jaguar scouts grabbed his legs and pulled him out onto the road. They aimed their weapons down at him.

Dennis lay there and looked up into the sky.

The mist had cleared away. Between the blotchy green leaves and branches he saw that a strong wind was pushing clouds rapidly through the sky, far above him.

Against the sound of the pitched jungle battle, the two rifles above him fired, one just after another.

CHAPTER TWO

John deBrun sat in a canvas chair and doodled on a piece of paper with his good hand. His left hand, a simple steel hook, rested with the tip dug into the chair's wooden arm. He drew a semicircle on one side of the paper with a swoop of his quill. He did the same on the other side to form an egg. Then he shaded shapes onto it. Wicked spikes. Shadows in the crevices. John added water dripping from the spikes, a slight déjà vu moment flitting through him, and then held the piece of paper back at arm's length.

Just a spiked sphere. That's all. He set the paper on the floor.

Several other sketches lay on a varnished table in the basement's corner. A giant metal bird with a beak that writhed into a human face. A half-finished sketch of a woman melting into a fiery sun.

The largest painting hung from the ceiling. John often lay beneath its chaotic blue ocean-wave landscape. When salt spray drifted in through his shutters, John recalled sailors' screams and water streaming across the deck. Cold, frigid water.

Half-sunk into the earth, his house remained nice and cool, despite the heat outside. Wonderful protection as dry season came to the lowest slopes of the Wicked Highs. After all day fishing the Brungstun reefs, John often retreated down here. But even at the basement's coldest, it never compared to the chills he got when looking at the painting.

"Hey," said a familiar voice. The twenty-year-old memories of his sail north fled. John turned. His thirteen-year-old son, Jerome, sat on the stairs. "Mamma done cooking. You go come up to eat or what?"

"What'd she cook?" John didn't sound Nanagadan. He'd spent enough years listening, but he kept to his own strange language patterns. Despite his son's teasing. Or the in-laws'. It was the only thing he had from his past.

"Saltfish stew. Rice-n-pea," Jerome said.

John loved Shanta's cooking, but could never find enthusiasm for her weekly dose of saltfish. Just rice and peas for him today, then.

He leaned forward and stood with a grunt. The scars down his legs ached. Jerome grinned and ran up the stairs.

"He coming, he coming," Jerome yelled, headed for the kitchen.

Shanta leaned around the corner, then turned her attentions back to the iron skillet of rice. Coal burned in the square stove's bin, heating the kitchen's confines. Her white dress shifted against her curved hips.

"What take you so long?" Shanta berated him. "I call you already."

John sat down at the scarred table. A plate of fresh johnnycakes still glistened with oil in the middle of the table. John reached over and speared one with his hook.

Jerome turned in his chair. "He using he hook to eat he food." Jerome grinned as he told on his dad. Shanta turned around and gave John a look. John avoided her eyes and pulled the fried dough off his hook.

Shanta set the skillet on the table. "Quit playing," she warned.

Father and son exchanged meaningful mock glares, blaming each other for drawing Shanta's irritation.

"You want to go into town with me, tomorrow?" John asked Jerome. Jerome scrunched up his face and thought about it.

"Yeah. Where?"

"I need to go out to Salt Island." The salt bin had reached the halfway mark last week, and John needed to make some extra fun money as well; carnival started in two days. He didn't want to be broke during the food fair. It was his favorite time of year. "If you help me, I'll give you some money for carnival."

Shanta filled Jerome's bowl with saltfish stew and then nudged the pot toward John. He shook his head. She sighed and handed him the skillet of rice and peas. "Be back before dark. You know how I get when you out late."

John nodded. It would be Jerome's first sail out of the harbor. "We'll be back in time." Jerome kicked him in the shin and John winced. "Don't do that," he warned in his best "danger" voice. It was halfhearted. Jerome had been a surprise after six years of marriage. Shanta had been thirty-six and they both had worried throughout the pregnancy. John doted on his son as a result. The strong emotions still sometimes startled him.

Later, once Jerome slept in his room, John helped Shanta with the dishes. She cleaned. He rinsed and set them on the rack.

"He excited," Shanta said.

"Yeah, he'll enjoy the trip out." John's hook hit a pot and clinked as he balanced the last wooden bowl on the other dishes. Shanta flicked the water off her hands. John moved up close to her when she turned. "Hello, Miss Braithwaite."

"Mr. deBrun. How you doing?"

"Fine. Fine." John kissed her and held her close; his tanned and weathered skin against her deep brown. "I thought about you when I was fishing today."

"What you think?"

"How much you would have liked to salt those groupers we netted."

"Hey! Man, why you tease me so?"

" 'Cause I love you."

"Ah." She leaned into him. Then: "John?"

"Yeah?"

"When you painted . . . you remember anything?"

"No." He kissed her hair and noticed several gray streaks. More and more had been appearing. Yet she never commented on the fact that when she'd met John, he'd looked older than her, and now he looked younger. "Don't worry about it." He loved her for caring. Shanta didn't talk much about the gap in John's memory. Yet sometimes it seemed to him she secretly worried about it more than he did. Did she want him to stop thinking about it because it always tore him up so? Or did she worry about some past secret that might be exposed that would tear them apart?

Shanta grabbed a towel and dried her hands. "I don't want Jerome going sailing much after this."

"Why not?" John took the dish towel from her hands and hung it up on a peg. "What harm is there in it?"

"I remember when they pull you up out the water. Twenty-seven years, John, but I remember. You all wrinkled. Strapped to some floaty thing . . ."

"You were young." John remembered her standing on the beach. Then he remembered the gray streaks in her hair and regretted saying it.

"Huh," Shanta snorted. "Twenty-two. Old enough to give you plenty grief."

John had struggled with the fact he couldn't remember anything before he had washed up on the beach. He had taken his name off the silver necklace around his neck with the name *John deBrun* written on it. Even though he didn't speak like everyone else, he understood Nanagadans. Which meant he must have been exposed to the land before.

John stayed to sail boats in Brungstun, hoping to regain his memories. He could picture maps in his head as if they were before him. He could navigate by stars, sun, map, and with his eyes closed. But he started out a horrible sailor. He had known nothing about winds or the tides or the waves and weather around Brungstun.

"He won't be like me," John said. "None of that adventuring spirit. He'll grow up, be respectable. A town banker, right?" Shanta mock-punched his arm. "He won't break any young girls' hearts," John teased, continuing. "Won't leave for Capitol City . . ." Shanta's grin disappeared.

After six years learning the sea with local fishermen, John had trekked to Capitol City with a small group of mongoose-men led by Edward, a bushman who became a close friend for the trip there.

Shanta stepped away from him. "Don't talk about Capitol City, John. Not tonight. I never slept when you was sailing the ocean. I don't want ever think you was dead again. You know how horrible—"

"I'm sorry." John pulled her back to him in a hug. "I'll shut up." During the trip John had looked for clues to his past in other towns on the way north, and in Capitol City itself. He'd been offered a chance to join a trio of ships as navigator. The expedition was to see if there was land to the north, but in the dangerous, icy waters of the north seas John had found nothing but death, and some fame as he navigated the single surviving ship back to Capitol City. He'd been forged into a captain and a leader during that horrible trip back to Capitol City from the icy north. Or maybe that had been something always in him. "I came back, right? I'm here now."

Shanta shrugged. She spun away from him. "No excuse for all that."

"Let's quit being glum. Carnival's almost here." He turned around with a large grin.

Shanta sighed. "You and carnival. Look at you. You like a little boy, all excited."

John extended his good arm and danced a quick circle around her. "Just a couple days." He smiled.

"Come on." She smiled back and pulled him along. John followed her down the hall to their room. Shanta paused at the doorway. "It really cold there up in the north, like you say?"

"You could see you *breath*." John imitated her accent to make her laugh and, at the same time, remembered that the cold had almost killed him. He helped Shanta unstrap the hook. She didn't need help with his loose shirt, and by now he could undo the back of her dress with one hand.

"Please don't go adventuring north again," she whispered.

"Once was enough. Never again."

They made love. She chased the chill out of him.

For the night.

CHAPTER THREE

Oaxyctl ran through the jungle toward Brungstun in the double-shadowed light of the twin moons that peeked out from between a break in the rain clouds. He was so close to safety since making it out of the mountains, skirting well wide of Mafolie Pass and a few mongoose outposts along the way. He'd come too far not to make it now.

The padded cloth strips wrapped around his feet pulled loose. Round trellis leaves slapped him and left conical stickies and dripping sap down his chest. Oaxyctl slowed down and hopped, pulling one foot up to his hands. He tore the last piece of dirty white cloth off his right foot and threw it into the trees. The movement tripped him up, and Oaxyctl pitched forward.

He threw his hands up and slid through sweet-smelling, half-decayed leaves. He scrambled over a root, caught his balance again, and wiped away dirt stuck to his forearms.

He knew he was easy prey. He left tracks. Tracks all over the place: the footprints, the cloth, the broken twigs, and the dirt falling from his arms. Even if he left nothing to betray him, *it* would still follow. This was a desperate dash for freedom. Oaxyctl leapt over vines twining themselves over the ground and twisted past tree trunks he couldn't put his arms around.

Any magical abilities inside the tall, domelike ruins he'd stumbled on a few hours back had failed centuries ago. The men who had grown the buildings' rock outer shells had died not long after, and no one would think to occupy a building of the ancients this deep in the jungle. Oaxyctl had hoped just to shelter from the rain for a night in them. But when he'd pulled himself over the glassy, slick stone and looked down, he'd seen flesh and metal hanging from a hook forced into the wall beneath him. A wall that he could have shot a gun at and not chipped. Two hearts lay tossed in the mud underneath. Oaxyctl had looked at the broken saplings and torn vines throughout the courtyard, claw marks in the mud, and known exactly what he saw.

A Teotl, a god, was surely here.

He had let go and slid down the side, not even noticing as he banged his chin against the lip, and run back into the forest.

Now Oaxyctl burst out of the steaming, cool rain forest and into a copse. Mud stretched out before him for two hundred yards. Beyond that he could see tamarind trees waving in the gusting wind. Rain fell, and then poured down, in sheets. It spattered into tiny pools that collected in kidney-bean shapes across the sea of brown.

He looked down at his bare feet. Cold freshwater rushed in to encircle them as his feet sank down into the mud.

Footprints, Oaxyctl gibbered to himself. Footprints everywhere! In his mind's eye he could see the long line of prints leading across the muddy copse he would leave as he ran.

"Sweet, sweet, Quetzalcoatl." He dug at his left hand with a fingernail. He scratched until blood trickled down into the skin between his index finger and thumb. Quetzalcoatl didn't accept blood sacrifice. Many others demanded it, though, and Oaxyctl had to try *something*. He scratched and scratched until the blood flowed freely and mixed with the rain.

"This is not even my land," Oaxyctl said. "But I would fertilize it with my own blood for mercy."

A trellis tree snapped and shook in the wind. Oaxyctl jumped. He looked around, his eyes wide. The wind died. The world fell silent. In the distance a frog let out a long belching croak, then shut up.

Oaxyctl broke from the protection of the forest and sprinted across the mud. The ground threatened to slip out from under him. He flailed his arms to keep balance. Hyperventilating and sloshing through puddles, he got halfway across the two hundred yards before he heard a long, sharp whistle in the air above him.

He froze.

The Teotl landed in front of him with a wet explosion of mud that plastered Oaxyctl from head to toe and threw him backward from his feet. Oaxyctl sat up and huddled forward. He shook with fear and averted his gaze.

He wasn't scared of dying. No. He was scared of far worse. Oaxyctl feared the pain that was sure to come.

"Notecuhu," he whimpered. *My lord.* "Please, it is a great honor." He crawled forward, not taking his eyes off the mud that almost touched his nose.

Squelch, squelch. The sound of the clawed feet slushing forward sent shivers roiling down Oaxyctl's gut. He tasted bitterness coming up his throat and his nose flared as he smelled rotted flesh. Face this like the warrior you are, he urged himself. Be noble. Meet an honorable death and give your heart willingly. He thought these things even though some deeper instinct in him raged to fight tooth and nail to the last gasping second.

But that would accomplish nothing, Oaxyctl knew. His body tensed like rope about to fray and snap, and Oaxyctl steeled his soul.

"Amixmähuih?" the deep and raspy voice of the Teotl asked.

"I am not afraid," Oaxyctl said.

"Cualli." Good. The Teotl wrapped two sandpapery thumbs around Oaxyctl's neck. The four fingers rested on his spine. *"Quimichtin.* Spy. Traitorous creature, we know of your betrayal. But we are not done with you."

The Teotl cupped Oaxyctl's chin with its other hand. It drew a long bead of blood up his neck with its second thumb. The hand was ribbed with tatters of pale, blue-veined skin.

"I was found out." The Nanagadans had caught him and sent him back over the mountains to work for them. "What could I do?"

The Teotl ignored his rationalization of double treason. "What you will do now is what I bid you. You know where other *quimichtin* are here, ones that you have not betrayed just yet. Give them away. The black human warriors that live on this side of the mountains will trust you and let you walk among them if you give them this information, and if you fight on their side."

Oaxyctl dared to look at the Teotl's legs. External bones ran down the midnight black cartilage of its thighs. On each side of the Teotl's hip, rain and pus quivered along the joints of tentacles, one of which stirred, coils shifting to reveal tiny jaws.

"I will do so." Oaxyctl looked back down.

The Teotl shifted its grip and pulled Oaxyctl out of the mud. Oaxyctl struggled for air as two thumbs pressed down on his chest and the Teotl's fingers on his back pushed his shoulder blades in. He dangled above the mud. Oaxyctl faced the god and panted. Here stood a being whose kind dwelled in Aztlan's sacrificial pyramids. It wore a cape of flayed human skin, the empty, floppy arms knotted around the Teotl's neck, feet twined around the tentacles by the god's hip.

It shook rusted locks of hair and looked at him through oval steel eyes.

"We hunt men who may stop this invasion. Now we hunt the man who will try to go north," it hissed. The silver jaw and gray gums did not move as the Teotl spoke. The whisper wormed its way past from deep in the fleshy throat. "You are to find a man, here. He has great secrets within him. You must get codes from him. Then you will kill him."

"The man who goes north?" Oaxyctl gasped. "I don't understand."

The hand holding Oaxyctl's chin up caressed his cheek. Blood ran down the sides of his neck and collected in the V of his chest.

"He will try to leave the land for north. This man is dangerous. But important." The god puffed wet air. "Any moment now . . . we will push in greater numbers over these mountains. We will have men sacrificed before us in this land. We will destroy their gods, our ancient enemies. But we must have this man."

"So how will I know him?" Oaxyctl croaked. His vision danced as he tried to pull a full breath.

"His name is John deBrun, and we think he lives near this town. We are sure of it. We smell it faintly. He has the secret codes that set free the *Ma Wi Jung*. Torture them from him or bring him back to us alive. That is your choice, for you can walk among the *nopuluca* as I cannot. He must not die before releasing the codes to the *Ma Wi Jung*."

"Lord," Oaxyctl shook in fear for his impudence. "May I have Jaguar scouts to help me capture him during the invasion?"

"You do this *now*. Only days remain before we begin to march again, and there are those who do not want to risk this man living, no matter what we may reap. They give no orders to save him, as I wish. They are weak-minded and miss potential. So we charge you with this mission. As we all invade, you find this man. Keep the human alive and obtain his secrets. Do well, you will be rewarded well. Fail . . ."

The god did not finish but let go with a snort of steam. Oaxyctl dropped into the mud, his legs folding painfully under him.

"Remember." The god turned around. "The *Ma Wi Jung* codes. I will be near you again."

Oaxyctl inhaled deeply and watched the Teotl walk back into the forest. Somewhere near the trees it slipped into the shadows and Oaxyctl was alone.

He lay back into the mud. Without thinking he put a hand over his heart. It still thudded. He was alive. He'd thought he was dead when he'd crossed the mountains and the mongoose-men captured him, and he'd thought he was more dead when the god had landed in the mud in front of him, yet he was somehow still alive.

It was almost the end of rainy season, but the heavy clouds opened up anyway. Oaxyctl lay still in the downpour and began shaking. Several hours later a Brungstun mongoose-squad circled him. Their guns hung easily by their sides, dangling from leather straps, and their canvas clothes dripped rain. Their unshaven but quite human faces looked down at him with suspicion. Oaxyctl cried with relief to see them.

But even now he realized there was still nowhere to hide. The Teotl could walk almost anywhere, Jaguar warriors would be coming over the hills any day now. The gods still commanded him. There was nothing he could do against this.

Nothing.

The mongoose-men tied his hands and dragged him off to Brungstun. Oaxyctl shook all the way there.

CHAPTER FOUR

John sat at the table the next morning, buckling his hook's metal cup tight onto the stump of his hand. He levered the straps until they bit into his wrist's calluses and looked up to see Jerome in the doorway.

"Hey, Son." John smiled.

Jerome blinked. He picked up a piece of bread and some cheese from the counter by the stove. He had something on his mind. "You always have to do that?"

John nodded.

"You wrist all scar up. It hurt?"

"Sometimes."

Jerome took that as a good enough explanation.

"You ready for a good sail?" John asked, changing the subject.

"Yeah, man." Jerome waved the bread in the air. "Ready for sure!"

"Good." John packed a bag with extra bread and cheese wrapped in wax paper, added a bottle of ginger beer, and picked up a heavy canvas bag, brown and stained with use, from the stairs. Dry salt crusted the two loop handles. "All right, let's go."

They walked out and waved at Shanta, hanging clothes up to dry on the line in the yard. Shirts and pants flapped in the wind.

"Take care," she called. "And bring me back plantain to fry up."

The walk to Brungstun took twenty minutes, the footpath passing by boulders near where John sometimes watched the ocean below explode up into the air, spraying and hissing as it turned into a tangy mist when it reached him. Then the rock under their feet turned to dirt, and then into a shiny rock road made by the old-fathers that followed the coast's curve through Brungstun to Joginstead, where it stopped. Brungstun houses, pink and yellow with sheet tin roofs, lined the road's edge.

Brungstun nestled in a carved-out nook in Nanagada's coastal cliffs that dipped down into a natural harbor. The rocky trailing edge where the Wicked High Mountains entered the water protected the small village from the ocean's worst, and the jagged offshore reefs made a natural breakwater that made a large area around Brungstun safe for fishing. The Wicked High Mountains themselves protected Brungstun and the rest of Nanagada from the Azteca.

John and Jerome passed a farmer selling fruit along Main Street, and Ms. Linda waved at them and asked Jerome if they had any sweet tamarind. She would bring some by, she said. The post master told John the telegraph was down, yet again, and he hoped it would be back up soon. He asked John to pass the message on if he was going to Frenchtown. It took another twenty minutes just to walk down the slope of Main Street to the boats as people chatted with them. Five thousand people lived in Brungstun, and they all knew John.

"Here we are, finally," John said. "Jetty number five."

His small boat yanked at the pier cleats while the ones out at anchor bobbed, their masts swaying. Water stretched out for miles beyond the harbor, dark in some places, light in others that indicated reefs just under the surface. In the hazy distance, rock chimneys jutted above the water.

Jerome dropped the two bags he'd carried with him. "It windy."

"No worry," John replied, stepping into the fifteen-foot wooden boat, *Lucita*. Water splashed around the bottom. He leaned over and grabbed the calabash-gourd bailer. As he scooped out the water lapping over the floorboards, he continued, "It's a good day for a sail. Sharp and steady."

Still somewhat dubious, Jerome said, "We won't capsize or nothing?"

John held up his hook as he walked forward and put the two bags under the bow's lip where they would stay dry. "I swear by the hook."

Jerome laughed. He sat down on a wet seat. "Okay then."

The snappy wind leaned *Lucita* over. They passed through the forest of anchored boat masts. The harbor steamer paddled by, going the opposite direction. The passengers on their side waved at John and Jerome. Jerome held on tight to his seat and didn't move. He jumped at every unusual crack of the sail and squeak of floorboards.

John skirted some smaller reef, then sailed north. Eventually he tacked and turned northwest for Frenchtown.

After half an hour he tacked again, pushing the tiller over and ducking the boom as it flew by his head, ropes and blocks rattling. It snapped taut and they continued forward. John shifted to the higher part of the boat.

The water lightened into aquamarine. John let the sails out with his good hand controlling the mainsheet, his hook on the tiller, and *Lucita* slowed. Another reef. He dodged the boat left toward darker blue, and thus deeper, water. Jerome relaxed, leaned over, and trailed his hand in the water. "How far Frenchie Reef?"

"Not too far." People who didn't sail needed patience. John sighed. You didn't just get in a boat and show up somewhere.

In the distance a long line of white breakers roared. John skirted them and followed another reef line, edging up against the wind until palm trees magically rose from the clear water. Frenchtown, Salt Island.

John closed his eyes and looked at his mental map of the area around the *Lucita*. Sharp, clear, and in his mind's eye he could rotate it around to examine it from different directions. The Wicked High Mountains rose to John's left in the west, splitting the continent in half as they ran north and south. They trailed off into the sea to make a commalike curve of rock chimneys and reef. Inside that protective curve lay Brungstun. Among the reefs were the flat islands the Frenchi lived on.

It was all an impassable, jagged maze. No ships ever got out from this protected area into the ocean. No ships got in. In this safe basin the Brungstun and Frenchi fishermen existed.

"Mom say the water dangerous. Story does say that old metal airships from the old-fathers fell into the harbor water. We could wreck on them."

John opened his eyes and nudged the tiller to adjust their course. "I've never seen that. Just the reefs I need to watch out for."

Nanagada's coasts were too rocky and clifflike to land on. Except for fishermen in Capitol City's great harbor, a few traders from Baradad Carenage on Cowfoot Island on the continent's other side, and the fishermen in this protected area, no one sailed the ocean. The towns settled on inland lakes or rivers. Safe, with calm weather and easy wind.

John smiled as a gust leaned the *Lucita* over. They didn't know what they were missing.

Lucita pulled into Frenchtown's flat, still water. Huts clustered on the beach's edge, and bright-colored fishing skiffs lay canted on the sand.

The water depth shortened to three feet. John moved forward and pulled the daggerboard up. It sat in a little well just behind the mast and dripped water as it slid out. John could see water, and the sand beneath it, passing under his boat. Without the extra ability to point into the wind, *Lucita* skittered sideways.

John ran back and grabbed the tiller. He expertly wobbled the boat the rest of the way to shore and dropped the sail as the *Lucita*'s bow hit the beach.

Then he grabbed Jerome and threw him into the water.

"Hey, man!" Jerome stood waist-high in it, dripping wet.

"Hey, you." John jumped in after him. Jerome splashed at him as John pushed the boat as far up the sand as he could.

"DeBrun, that you?" someone called.

"Yeah."

Troy, a fisherman, sat in his boat with a paint tin. Troy's white skin flaked from sunburn. His straight blond hair hung down to his shoulders. No locks, just limp strands. "Where you been all this time?"

"Busy fishing. Have to make a living."

Troy laughed.

John couldn't help looking at the bad sunburn on Troy's pale skin. Frenchies could put on an accent so strong he had trouble understanding them. But they were very white. That was uncommon. On Cowfoot Island off Nanagada's southeastern coast, and northeast up the peninsula in Capitol City, yes, he had seen some white people. But that was it. John reached over the prow and pulled out the canvas bag.

"More paintings?" Troy asked.

"Yes."

"Good." Troy put down his brush and hopped out onto the sand. He looked down at the canvas bag. "I go trade with you."

Jerome wandered down the beach toward several Frenchie children. His darker skin color stood out, oddly enough. He joined them kicking a leather football down the beach, laughing when it hit the water and stuck in the wet sand.

John smiled and followed Troy in toward his small beach store. Two old, wizened Frenchies sat on the porch smoking pipes. They nodded as he passed, then continued playing dominoes, enthusiastically slapping the ivory pieces down with sharp bangs. Once inside, John set the canvas bag on the counter. Wooden shelves of tinned food lined the back wall. A few burlap sacks leaned against the counter's foot.

Troy opened the bag and pulled out the two paintings.

"I like this. Is a righteous picture," he said. A ship listed at sea, mast broken. Giant waves smacked at it. "This other one"—Troy pointed at a sketch of the Brungstun cliffs—"I sell me cousin that."

"Those took a lot of work," John said.

"I won't go thief you, man." Troy reached under the counter and pulled out a gold coin.

John sucked his breath in. "You're too generous." Frenchies dove along the reefs to supplement their fishing. Sometimes they found strange machines that had fallen from the sky in the days of the old-fathers and would strip them for any precious metals they could find. "You're making carnival very sweet."

"Is a time to enjoy." Troy smiled.

"You coming to town?"

Troy laughed. "I know I go see you there, right?"

John chuckled with him and looked at the sacks on the floor. "I'm going to need some salt."

"I get you a sack. Hold up." Troy disappeared and came back out with a hefty bag he dropped on the counter. John made to go pay for it, but Troy held up a hand. "You coin no good with me." He smiled.

"Thank you." John grabbed the sack as Troy cleared his throat.

"John . . . the painting. They ever help you memory yet?"

John looked down at the burlap between his fingers. "No. Not yet." He wondered if Troy bought his paintings out of pity. "Maybe they never will. You still buying?"

"Anything for an old friend, John." Troy smiled.

John hefted the sack. "Thanks, Troy. See you at carnival."

"See you at carnival, John."

When John stepped back out of the shop, he paused. The two old men had stopped playing dominoes and stared at the sky over the water off the Wicked Highs. Three bloated metallic slivers crept their way back toward the Azteca side of the Wicked High Mountains, circling around the mountain chain over the reefs and rock chimneys.

According to legend and some older folk, Nanagadans once lived on the land on the other side of the Wicked Highs. The coast over there was just as inhospitable, so no Azteca ships ever took to sea. But small airships could climb over the peaks, and larger airships sometimes skirted out over the ocean to fly over Nanagada. Dropping spies into the jungle here, no doubt. John usually saw one a month when out fishing.

The old man nearest to John harrumphed and slapped down a domino.

"They running more and more of them things these days. I already see five this month. Watch and see if Azteca warrior don't soon start walking over the mountain to cause trouble."

"Them feather-clot won't be coming over the mountain anytime soon," his partner said. "They had a whole army that try that once on Mafolie Pass. The mongoose-men gun them down something wicked."

"Yeah. Maybe that true. Hey. You lose you game."

"What?" The other old man was startled.

John walked out onto the sand. He knew he lived close to the mountains and that the Azteca lay on the other side. It took something like this to remind him how close the Azteca were. Sometimes, when John wondered where he'd come from, he imagined he was a Nanagadan spy who had been trying to escape from the Azteca at sea and been shipwrecked.

That was just a fantasy, though. Thinking about Azteca made him nervous. "Come on, Jerome," he said. "We have to go now."

Seeing the Azteca blimps stole any positive feelings from the day. He wanted to go home.

CHAPTER FIVE

People peered out their windows to see the excitement as Dihana and thirty ragamuffins marched the two blocks to Capitol City's waterfront. A drunken fisherman paused at the street's corner, swayed, then retreated back into the alley's shadows when he saw them.

The ragamuffins slowed down in front of warehouse fifteen. A trio of mongoose-men guarded the large doors, deadly long rifles held in the crooks of their arms. They surveyed the street and the ragamuffin force with cold calm.

"Is better you wait up some," the first mongoose-man said.

Dihana shook her head. "I am the prime minister of this city, with all the rights and responsibilities that entails." Over a hundred thousand people lived inside Capitol City's walls and she accepted responsibility for them all. "You tell me I can't go *where*?" She'd learned that particular verbal tone from Elijah, her father, well before he'd died and she inherited the position of prime minister.

The mongoose-man nearest the door cleared his throat. "Let she through. Alone."

The rusty side-access hinges squealed as the mongoose-men pushed the door open. Dihana walked through, her skirt filling out and brushing the sides of the doorframe with the motion.

In the middle of an empty expanse of dirty concrete floor, a man stood over five dead bodies. Blood settled in several footwide pools underneath each victim. Knife strokes had left tattered and sliced shirts on both the dead and the alive.

One corpse's throat still seeped blood from a bullet puncture.

"General Haidan." Dihana kept an artificially calm composure. The mongoose-men's leader usually stayed out beyond the city's immense walls. "What the hell have you done here?"

"Repaying a debt, as an old friend of Elijah." His dreadlocks had grayed, and his face looked more leathery. A man who always braved the elements. A man who had always stood by her father. "You go listen?"

Dihana bit her lip. This was irregular. "Okay. Go ahead." She did her best to ignore the death by her feet.

Haidan turned to the mongoose-man by the inside of the door. "Bring them two we got over here." He folded his arms.

Dihana shook her head, impatient with his cryptic approach. "Last time we met, Haidan"—just after Elijah had died and she'd been struggling to handle her new responsibilities with no time for grieving—"you said you'd honor the contract between the city and the mongoose-men. That you always would protect us. Why couldn't you have just asked me what you needed done in the city. It's suspicious when mongoose-men start just showing up in the city in numbers." A mongoose-man pushed two men with burlap sacks over their heads through the door.

"Shut the door," Haidan ordered. The door squealed and slammed shut. Dihana flinched. She'd made a mistake, gotten trapped. The Haidan she knew as a child would never have done this. But things changed. Hundreds of mongoose-men had actually come *inside* the city tonight. Maybe alliances were being made in the dark behind her back.

"The ragamuffins know where I am," Dihana said. Haidan had encouraged her when she'd struggled to run the city after Elijah had died. She wanted to say she felt sorry he no longer felt she was the best choice for prime minister. She hoped this new Haidan would exile her somewhere pleasant, and that the bush hadn't changed him enough for him to kill her.

Haidan frowned. His locks swayed as he shook his head. "Don't be silly," he growled. She'd read him wrong. "Them man can't even test with me mongoose. I don't want the city, we protecting it. Me and you, we go have to reason things out. Things happening."

Dihana almost shuddered with relief. Deep inside, she hadn't believed, couldn't believe, that Haidan would do such a thing. The mongoose-man stopped in front of them and ripped the burlap sacks away from the two men's heads. Dihana stared at them.

"You're familiar," she whispered. She hadn't seem them since she'd become prime minister. Councilmen. They'd all abdicated the Council, disbanding it when she came to power, leaving her confused and without any help except for Haidan. They'd hoped she'd fail, she knew, and that they could return to run Capitol City.

But she hadn't failed. And they'd remained in hiding all this time.

Dihana looked down more closely at the corpses. Two she recognized as other Councilmen from her father's circle. The other three: poorly dressed farmers. Or maybe shopkeepers in work clothes. Haidan caught her eyes when she looked back up. The two Councilmen shuffled nervously.

"Them two claim they was here to meet a Vodun priestess," Haidan said.

"She a trap for we," the nearest man said. He glared at Dihana, and she looked back at Haidan.

"This ain't no Loa doing." Haidan shook his head. "Is Azteca."

"They don't look like Azteca," she said.

"When you promise a desperate man gold, land, woman, power, whatever, he would do anything. Even against his own people. This ain't the first Councilman we find dead. Seen many more outside Capitol City." Haidan looked at the two nervous Councilmen. "More go die if them keep try hiding."

"Why?" The Councilmen had hidden themselves well enough all this time.

"Azteca activity like nothing before. And we lose communication with Mafolie Pass. Them dead quiet. Street whispering say any Councilman head go be repaid in it own weight in Azteca gold. So them Councilmen need you, Dihana. They ain't go say so, but they need you bad." He looked at her.

Dihana let the pause hang between them all. Let them stand and fidget for a few seconds, she thought. Haidan folded his hands over his belt buckle and waited. He could be fully trusted, she thought, though she wondered why he hadn't come to talk to her before any of this. Dihana turned to the two Councilmen. "Get to the Ministry building. We have space for you. Call all the other Councilmen you can in."

They stood still. Maybe they thought there was some negotiation to be hammered out between them.

"If you smart," Haidan ended any such thought, "you go do it."

The two Councilmen looked down at the dead men by their feet. "We accept," the one nearest Dihana said, the words forced. "But we expect to stay in the East Wing rooms." The best rooms in the Ministry.

"We'll see what we can do," Dihana said as Haidan shouted orders to reopen the doors. Two mongoose-men and some ragamuffins led the Councilmen down the street from the door.

Haidan turned to Dihana. "Still got time?"

"Yes." Dihana looked down at the bodies. "But not here."

"Fair enough," Haidan said. "Ministry?" Dihana noticed, for the first time, the powder marks on Haidan's right hand. He looked down, rubbed the hand against his thick pants, and shrugged.

"Yes. Yes, that would be good," Dihana said.

Capitol City's walls towered above the rooftops, taller than anything anyone in the city could build. A reminder, always, of the secrets Dihana's ancestors died with. Only they could have built something like Capitol City. The great amphitheater-shaped city perched on the rocky peninsula's end created a natural harbor inside its protective walls and housed Dihana's hundred thousand fellow city dwellers. Just outside, an ever-shifting population tended to farms and grain depots that supplied Capitol City. To secure a fast and constant supply of food, Dihana had presided over the construction of train tracks, the Triangle Tracks, that extended out 250 miles from the city. She wasn't sure how many villages or towns had sprung up along those tracks, but one of her projects included a new census that would start among the towns and villages along the tracks and into the bush, all the way down the dirt roads and coasts to the Wicked Highs. But the planning for that was just beginning.

The Ministry building had the only real park inside Capitol City, a long, rectangular green spit that extended until it stopped in front of the waterfront warehouses. Dihana and Haidan walked the road back to the Ministry building, the park with its shadows and shifting trees on their right. On their left the city's buildings blazed with lights from their windows, supplied from the proliferation of electric cables that draped between them like jungle vines.

They walked two blocks in silence. Haidan's mongoose-men remained at the warehouse taking care of the bodies, and Dihana had ordered the ragamuffins back to their nightly patrols.

Haidan nodded at the two ragamuffins standing watch when they passed through the Ministry's gates.

"Someone waiting for you," the ragamuffin on her right said. "By the step them."

"Mother Elene," Haidan said, pointing out the Vodun priestess who sat waiting for them.

Mother Elene stood up, her shaved head gleaming in the light as she raised her chin. Gold earrings flashed near the knotted handkerchief around her neck. "Thank you, General, for your warning."

Haidan nodded, then stepped back, watching both Dihana and Mother

Elene with interest. "Me, Mother Elene, and them Councilmen were invite to come talk at that warehouse."

"We think the Azteca were hoping to set we against you, Dihana," Mother Elene said. She smiled and glided past Dihana with a rustle.

"And now you're leaving, just like that?" Dihana had clenched her hands into fists. She opened them.

Mother Elene paused just behind her. "Maybe time come for we speak again. The Loa wish it. You?"

The city's gods, the Loa, had opposed Dihana's leadership along with the Councilmen. Only instead of hiding as the men had, they had continually critiqued and opposed her decisions through their priestesses all throughout the city. They had opposed the expedition she'd created to explore the north lands, and they'd resisted her creating the Preservationists, who scoured the city and the lands for insight into their past, and the past's technologies.

"Why the change?" Dihana finally asked, but got no answer. Mother Elene had left.

Haidan put a hand on Dihana's shoulder. "Come." Instead of heading for the large steps up to the storm doors, he turned right. "I want show you something where the light don't shine so."

"I used to do that with Dad."

"Yeah. Back then." Haidan followed the hibiscus bushes inside the wrought-iron gate. "A lot change since then."

Dihana sighed. "You don't think I did things right?"

"Dihana." Haidan shook his head. "The airship you sell me mongoose, that alone worth all the trouble you stir up." He stopped. "You know Elijah and I disagree a lot, back then?"

"No," Dihana said. "It would have been nice to have heard that, at some point." Haidan sat down on a stone bench. Dihana sat next to him and folded her arms. "You left me just like the Councilmen did. But at least you didn't hide." Haidan had continued taking the mongoose-men defense taxes, purchased weapons from the city, and sent telegrams from wherever he hid in the bush. The Councilmen had just disappeared. "I had to deal with the Loa alone—"

Haidan interrupted with a snort. "Dealt? You cut them out of any chance to direct the city. Instead of keeping them close, you push them away. Now they doing everything from deep in the dark where you blind."

"They lied to my father, Haidan." She'd had every right to deny the manipulative Loa their demands that she cease building airships, or their order that she stop helping fund a fishing fleet, or that she shouldn't allow villages and farms to grow along the tracks. The Loa agenda was to keep them stuck in a fallow state.

"You think he didn't know that? Girl—"

"I am *no* girl, mongoose-general." Dihana glared at him. Haidan rubbed his nose and looked down at the ground. "The Loa promised him things they could not deliver. Could never deliver. And they strung him along with those promises."

"I know, Dihana." Haidan stood up with a grunt. "I tell him so, often enough. But Elijah say that using old metal technology would doom us, like it had doom everyone in his time. He insist the only way for we survive is for we adapt the Loa organic knowledge. We had to *grow* we weapon, not hammer out the metal."

"I changed that." Dihana had created the Preservationists, a society of people who dug up everyone's past and investigated it, found things. "It was not a mistake. We have better rifles, better airships, steam, all no thanks to the Loa."

"I know. I had ask you dad for something like what you doing now." Haidan took her arm and she stood up. "Even though I was Elijah's closest man, he never agree with me there."

"Dad's closest man." Dihana closed her eyes. "How come you were never mine?"

"Trust me, Dihana, you did fine. I had mongoose-men to look after, I had to make sure we was strong, that Azteca couldn't cross the Wicked Highs, couldn't mess with the city. I couldn't be here the same for you as I had for you father. Until now."

"Now?"

Haidan put his arm around Dihana's shoulder and turned her around, pointed up into the sky at the Spindle. "It's changing, Dihana. Did you father ever tell you about that? What that mean?"

"Yes." Dihana looked down at the grass. Her father had taken her out on this same piece of lawn once and told her about the Spindle. "The two jets that come out of either side have stopped. No one can see that with their naked eye yet." When Elijah had taken a young Dihana outside, he'd explained that no one in Nanagada understood the stars anymore. All that knowledge had been lost and he couldn't re-create the science. The Loa had counseled him not to.

But he'd been insistent that she understand something about the Spindle. It wasn't just something pretty in the sky, he said. It had been the path to Nanagada from all the other worlds, as legend hinted.

"Elijah tell me if the Spindle ever shrink, all hell breaking loose," Haidan said. "He said Azteca believe gods go come through it when it 'stabilized.'"

Dihana nodded. "He told me that too." That was why she had Preservationists scanning the Spindle with telescopes.

"I been preparing all the mongoose for fighting."

"I increased the size of the ragamuffins."

Haidan looked back down at the garden. Dihana looked around at the hibiscus bushes and their shadows. They seemed to hide dangerous things now, and she wanted to go back inside.

"I go stay here in the city." Haidan walked her back toward the building. "We all need to work together. We go need to figure out what the Azteca doing. What trouble they causing."

"I've been ordering more things built," Dihana said. "Airships, larger guns . . . ever since I realized."

Haidan gave her hand a brief squeeze, and Dihana remembered Haidan picking her up and holding her in the air when she was a girl. "I should have come and talk to you sooner."

"Yes," Dihana said.

"We probably need the Councilmen too. See if we can figure out what they have the Azteca want."

"We need more of your men back here in the city. If you can't contact Mafolie Pass, that might mean Azteca are trying to attack it right now."

"I know," Haidan murmured. "Trust me, I know."

As they reached the steps, Dihana looked at Haidan. "Are you worried?"

Haidan tapped his boots on the stone. "Wicked nervous. Something dangerous going on. I feel that in me bones. But at least we ain't go work across each other." He sighed. "Got a lot of thing for me arrange, moving headquarter back this direction, getting more fact-them out the bush, but I go be in close touch, okay?"

"Okay."

"And, Dihana?"

"Yes?"

"You know me long enough to call me Edward, you know?" Haidan turned around and walked off toward the gates.

"You haven't quite earned that back just yet," Dihana said. But he was too far away to hear her.

CHAPTER SIX

Jerome was having trouble getting to sleep, so Shanta sat by his bed. "A tale? Is a tale you want?"

"Yeah, yeah."

She smiled. John melted back into the kitchen and made a sandwich.

"Okay then," Shanta said. *"I see, I bring, but I ain't responsible."* Her voice dropped, and her accent thickened a bit. The way Brungstunners spoke was fluid. It changed depending on whom they talked to, and how they felt. John sounded different. People in Brungstun called him north-sounding, yet that wasn't it. Up north in Capitol City everyone still sounded like people in Brungstun, just not as heavy, whereas John sounded as if he'd grown up away from them all. Though, the longer he was around Shanta, the more he sometimes tried to sound like her. Usually it was when he was relaxed, not trying to.

Shanta began her tale.

"A long time ago, all we old-father them had work on a cold world with no ocean or palm tree. It was far, far from this world. It was far, far from them own world, call Earth! They had toil for Babylon. In return, Babylon oppress many people. And eventually them Babylon-oppress people ran away looking for a new world, a world far from any other world so they could be left alone.

"All sorts of people left. Some pale-looking man like Frenchi and Bridish come. And there was Afrikan. And there was Indian. Carib. Chinee. All of them had join up for the long, long voyage. All color of skin leave. Year and year and year them travel till they had discover this sweet world we live on, just like all the original island on Earth. Here were some cool wind and easy sun.

"Them old-father had some massive power. They find a worm's hole in the sky between all them other world to get here. And when they wiggle through them hole, they had fly down from the sky to land here and begin a new life, free from oppression.

"But the evil *Tetol* come in from other worm's holes that had been all around for long time. You see, the Tetol is dangerous, nasty things, who want to rule and own we all. But some other great being, the Loa, weren't evil, but help and guide we against the Tetol . . ."

The *original* ragamuffins would save the day, John knew. The ancestors of the ragamuffins of today who policed towns and kept civil order. The raga-muffins flew out in giant airships to destroy the worm's holes and cut this world off from further Tetol invasion. Yet the ragamuffins had not been able to destroy the Tetol on the ground. The Tetol created the Azteca and made them a fearful warrior race.

Thinking about the Azteca's masters wandering unchecked over the world disturbed John. It reminded him of their airships flying near Brungstun. He stepped out onto the shaded porch and watched the sun slip behind the brown boulders.

Shanta tiptoed out behind him and lit a lamp. "Good day?"

John nodded and slipped an arm around her waist. "Yeah. Looking for-ward to carnival tomorrow."

Shanta chuckled. The final sliver of sun slipped behind the boulders in time with a faint scraping noise from behind the house.

"Thunder?" John asked. The eaves blocked their view.

Shanta shook her head. "No." She stepped off the porch and lifted her skirt above her ankles. "Something different. Come."

John followed her out and around behind the house, where the Wicked Highs loomed large over the tall trees. The sound got louder. Branches snapped and cracked. Three seagulls flew away with loud protests. John won-dered if he should get a machete, or maybe one of his guns from the cellar.

"Shanta," he yelled. She'd already reached the edge of the bush around the house. Her determined form stepped barefoot around the pricker bush and hibiscus. "Damn." He picked his way around the same bush. Mud oozed up between his toes.

"John. Up in here."

He followed her voice to a large mango tree and looked up. Silver fabric draped between the branches. A small airship lay spread over several mango tree canopies, the tip poking out through the tree closest to their house. A harness dangled from between a nook in the branches farther back, a man struggling in it.

"Is he Azteca, or is he one of ours?" John asked.

Shanta gave him a withering stare. "That don't matter."

Chagrined, John looked up again and saw the man turn in his harness to face them. He had tight curly hair, and a black face. Not an Azteca spy, then.

"Hey," Shanta yelled upward. "You have to hang on. We coming."

John shuffled to his left. "The branches up that high look weak, but I bet I can reach him."

"I go get a machete. We could hack he out—" Shanta got halfway through saying that when the man groaned. He fumbled at his waist.

"Hey!" John and Shanta warned together. The clasp clicked open and the man dropped. His leg caught on a branch. It spun him around and he hit the ground by the mango tree with a thump that scattered leaves.

"Shit!" They rushed forward. The man wore heavy clothing to keep him warm in the high air. He had an air bottle strapped to his thigh, and the hose ran up to his neck, where it was fastened to a necktie soaked in blood. The man had been shot. In the chest, and in the side, maybe some other places, it was hard to tell.

The aviator groaned and stirred. He opened bloodshot eyes. The skin around them creased with crow's-feet. "Help," he whispered.

"We go do what we can," Shanta said. "But it look like you done lose plenty blood, and you fall . . ."

The man slowly turned his neck to look at them. "I dead," he said, words just audible. "Been shot seven time. I come for warn you, and any mongoose-men here, any ragamuffin that near."

"We'll get someone," John said, trying to calm the man and get him to relax. "What's your name?"

"Allen." The low hiss of his voice turned urgent. "Listen *now*. Or you all dead. All of you. Hear? Dead." The man took a long, deep breath, shuddering as he did so. "Azteca coming down the side of the mountain. Understand? Azteca. A lot of Azteca."

He closed his eyes.

"He still alive?" John asked.

"I think," Shanta said. "I won't go move him like that, though. He need a stretcher. And Auntie Fixit."

John stood up. "I'll wake up Jerome and have him run for your aunt, then. I'll come back with a piece of board we can strap him to."

"Yeah."

When John stood up and looked around, he realized it had gotten much darker. The bush and the trees around him hid in shadows and shifting leaves. They rustled in the dark and threw shadows all around him. Too many scary stories, he thought. Most by Shanta.

*   *   *

Jerome tried to get back under his blankets and pretend to be asleep. John didn't bother berating his son. He pushed the lighter button on the gas lamp. It took three tries before the spark caught and the room slowly filled with yellow, flickering light.

"I need you to fetch your aunt Keisha."

Jerome's eyes widened. "Auntie Fixit? What happen? Mama okay?"

John nodded. "She's fine. Just go for your aunt." Keisha's house lay a mile between town and John's house. Jerome could make it in seven minutes. He could sprint like the wind. "Be careful, it's dark."

Jerome nodded. "I gone." He reached under his bed for his shoes.

Azteca coming down the mountain . . . "And Jerome?"

"Yeah?"

"Tell Harold to bring any Brungstun ragamuffins he can get with him." John debated for a second whether to tell Jerome to stay at Harold's house, closer to town and safer, but then realized that the safest place would be next to Harold, a ragamuffin himself.

"Okay."

"Go then."

John jogged down the steps to his basement. He found a plank he'd planned to use for a bench but had never got around to building. It would do. He held it with his good hand and steadied it with his hook. He hurried back through the rear door into his yard, stopping by the kitchen to grab some linen strips.

"Here," Shanta called. She squatted in the muddy ground next to ripe, red mangoes and dead twigs. John handed her the board. "Careful." They grunted and slowly rolled the aviator onto the plank, John careful not to gouge the man with his hook. He handed Shanta the linen. She ran the straps under the board and tied the man down as John lifted first one end, then the other, with his one hand.

"Okay."

John had gauged the board's length just right; they each had a good two inches on either end. They picked up the makeshift stretcher and walked back toward the house. They paused halfway there while John shifted his grip, using his other forearm to rest the weight on.

"Kitchen?" John asked.

"Yeah. For now."

They got the stretcher in, placing it on the kitchen table. Shanta washed and dried her hands, opened the valve on the gaslight, then pushed the lighter button. It clicked. Darkness fled from the room, remaining only in the corners and behind cupboards.

"Come." Shanta took out a pair of scissors and began cutting away the man's thick overcoat. John removed the man's air canister and necktie. When Shanta cut away the shirt, she sucked her teeth in annoyance. Neat, round holes punctured the skin. Blood oozed from them. "He lucky he still alive."

Lucky, John thought. Or determined. He remembered the Azteca airships flying over the sea and wondered what had happened.

He looked at the bullet holes. Azteca coming? How? In airships, or maybe they'd shot this man before he'd gotten in an airship?

John left Shanta with the dying man and went down into the basement. He paused in front of the large oak chest, then walked under a large beam. With a hop he jumped up and grabbed the brass key off the top of the beam and knelt down at the chest.

The large padlock snapped open, and John tossed it aside. He opened the lid and looked inside at two rifles and a pistol.

He took the gun out with his good hand and looked it over. Then he put it down. He broke open two airtight cases of ammunition, using his hook to pry open the edges, and awkwardly loaded the breech, swearing silently as he almost dropped the gun.

If Azteca came and he had to defend his family, it would not be much of a battle, but at least with the aviator's warning he could get ready.

CHAPTER SEVEN

Hooves clip-clopped down the packed-dirt road. A horse snorted. Keisha and her husband's concerned voices floated in. Seconds later Keisha herself burst into the kitchen. John stood at the basement door, keeping out of the way and holding the rifle like a staff, the butt resting on the top wooden step.

"What happen?" Then Keisha saw the kitchen table, the bloodied man, and gritted her teeth. "Where he come from?"

Jerome pushed into the kitchen from behind her and started at the man. "He fall from he airship all stuck up in we mango tree."

"Get from here," Shanta ordered. "This ain't for children." Jerome dallied, still staring. "Now," Shanta said. Jerome retreated.

Two mongoose-men came in with Harold, Keisha's husband. John walked over, leaned the rifle against the door, and shook Harold's large, calloused hand. "I didn't realize there were any mongoose-men here."

"Several of we came in town a few days back," the first man said. "Been working outside and around town with an Azteca who's mongoose. He help us flush out a couple informers, but now he and a couple we men missing, so we came in town to see if anyone seen him. We worried. And General Haidan go be mad if he missing. Azteca mongoose-men hard to find."

"Haidan? Edward Haidan?" John had left Brungstun for Capitol City with a young Edward Haidan, a mongoose-man, years ago.

"Yeah."

"He's still in Capitol City?"

"Sometimes. Let's get out the way here."

"Yeah. Living room." John dropped the line of inquiry and moved them away from the wounded man on the table. He had seen enough torn bodies in the north seas. Rotted toes and blackened fingers that had to be cut off. People crushed by equipment or hanged by ropes as they fell from the rigging. He didn't like facing such horrors in his own home.

The four men pulled up chairs and spoke to each other in whispers after John relayed the aviator's warning.

"If a hunting party coming down the mountain, we should find them. You sure he didn't say how many?"

John shook his head. "He was scared. Must have been a large group."

"Twenty Jaguar scout could wreak some serious havoc," Harold said. "Carnival starting up next morning. What you think I should do?"

"Don't take any risk," the mongoose-men advised. "It might be a small group, but get you ragamuffin to tell anyone outside town to come in for carnival. Keep ready for anything. We need to try and contact Mafolie Pass anyway, something wrong with the telegraph."

"That telegraph thing hardly ever work," Harold noted. "You could wait a day and see if it down for sure."

The mongoose-men shook their heads. "We going now, just to make sure. And if Mafolie okay, we go ask them for men to go out and scout."

Harold nodded and turned to John. "You could come stay with us for carnival."

"Thank you," John said. "Can Shanta and Jerome leave with you right now? I'll follow tomorrow, but I want to pack some things up and take them with us, in case this stay ends up being long." He wouldn't risk returning to the house until they knew for sure that they were safe. This, along with the strange Azteca activity in the sky, turned John's thoughts toward finding a small place to stay in town for a while.

"No problem, man." Harold stood up.

Keisha had been leaning against the doorframe. "Sound like a good idea. I don't feel safe out here, and I don't want me sister here either." She took a deep breath. "The man dead. Sorry."

"Damn," John and Harold said together.

The mongoose-men stood up and walked over, jaws clenched. "We go find who did this and make them pay."

John cleared his throat. "We can bury him here, I have a plot out in the jungle. If you need."

The man's burial was a simple, somber affair. John and Harold stood by as the two mongoose-men dug a shallow grave. Keisha and Shanta packed a few changes of clothes back inside the house.

One of the mongoose-men reached in his pocket to retrieve a medal. It glinted in the moonlight, and after driving a sharp stick in the ground, the man hung the medal from it.

"Least a man can do, seen?"

John and Harold nodded. Leaves shook and stirred softly as they walked back inside, boots clumping up the stairs.

*   *   *

Shanta wasn't thrilled John was staying behind. She hefted a bag full of clothes. "Why you can't just come with us now?"

"It could be long," John explained. "When we were out with the Frenchies we saw airships flying over the reefs. Maybe more Azteca will be harassing people inside the towns. We need all our stuff."

"Be careful," she warned. "Please be careful. If you hear anything, just leave as quick as you can. You hear?"

John kissed her on the forehead. "I'll be careful."

"I thought I lost you when you left for north. Don't leave me again."

"I'll be there before lunch tomorrow. I'll join you at carnival, okay?" They hugged, then Shanta got onto the buggy behind Harold and Keisha. Jerome perched next to her.

"Hey, Jerome," John called out. "We'll have some fun tomorrow. I'll buy you any lunch you want, okay?"

Jerome smiled, though his eyes were a bit bleary. "You think you go find me during carnival?"

"What, you have plans?" John asked.

"I go be hanging with me boys," Jerome said. "We go get a good seat to see carnival."

"I'll hunt you down." John smiled. Harold looked over. John nodded.

"Hah!" The horse looked back at Harold, turned around ever so slowly, then picked its way down the road. John stood and waved until they turned a bend and disappeared.

The two mongoose-men stood at his door.

"I have extra rifles for you, and I can pack you food and water." John smiled. "Don't worry about taking them"—he held up his hook—"they're damn hard to fire with one of these."

"Thanks, man," they said.

He supplied the two mongoose-men with food and watched them disappear straight into the jungle, not even bothering to use the road. Then John walked around, finding valuables and packing them onto a cart. He stopped only once, to hold up a pendant he'd given Shanta just after they'd married. He smiled at the chiseled engravings of scudder-fish hanging from the silver chain. Then there were Jerome's toy boats, and illustrated books, to pack.

Outside the open windows the bushes shook in the wind, constantly rustling as John packed their lives onto the cart, making decisions about what to leave so he could pull it down to Brungstun in the morning. As John walked around the house, turning off all the lamps one by one as he retreated down into the basement, he lingered at each room's doorway. He loaded the pistol lying in the bottom of his chest, an easier task than loading the cumbersome rifle. He held it in his good hand and slept on the basement floor next to the chest.

A sound woke him. A single footstep creaking the kitchen steps.

John sat up, looked down at the pistol, and wiped the sleep from his eyes with his good hand.

The kitchen door creaked open.

John tiptoed quickly across the basement past his easel. He stopped at the far window, on the other side of the house from the kitchen. Mouth dry, he slowly opened the window and pulled himself up onto the sill with his elbows. They scraped along the concrete, leaving skin. John wiggled through onto the grass and pulled his legs through, then closed the window.

Another door creaked inside, and he heard whispers.

He jogged across his lawn toward the road, keeping as low as he could. The bushes to his right rustled.

"*Ompa. Ompa, nopuluca!*"

Shit. John ducked and fired at the voice. He fumbled, trying to hold the gun to his chest with the hook and reload it as he ran.

"*Nian,*" the voice screamed.

John shook the spent cartridge out and got the new one in. As he turned, a lead weight smacked him in the face. Netting draped around his feet and hands. His vision watered and his nose dribbled salty blood.

He stumbled and fell, unable to see through his tears. The netting tightened around him as he struggled. Slow down, he told himself, listening to feet pounding closer. He still had one shot. John blinked the tears free. The first moon lit up the area enough for him to see that three Azteca surrounded him. Younger warriors with sandals, simple loincloths, and painted from head to foot. They yanked on the net, pulling John through the grass.

He aimed the pistol and they froze. Three more warriors stepped up and pointed rifles at John's head. They pointed their chins at his pistol and jabbed the rifle barrels at him.

John let go of the pistol. They snatched it from him, fingers grabbing in between the netting, then kicked him in the side.

Every Azteca horror tale flicked through his head as the warriors laughed with each other and dragged John across his own lawn in the moonlight. He didn't understand a word they said.

John yanked at the netting. All it did was snag his hook until he couldn't even move his arm. He screamed, but the Azteca only laughed. He grabbed the netting with his good hand and pulled his back off the ground so he could see his house one last time, then he let go and slumped into the netting.

At least Shanta and Jerome were safe, he told himself.

CHAPTER EIGHT

Jerome had been annoyed to have to pick a few favorite toys and clothes before the ride to Auntie Fixit's house. Uncle Harold was okay, he'd given Jerome a cookie before he'd rushed off for town. But Auntie Fixit insisted he go to bed right away. No one in the house slept, though, least of all Jerome. The adult voices kept him up, so after a few hours he went out and opened the door to the kitchen. His mother looked tired, and Auntie Fixit's dress was still stained with blood.

"Could I get something to eat?" Jerome asked. "I can't sleep."

Auntie Fixit sighed. "Okay. Help you-self."

Jerome found some bread, then took a red velvet pillow from the couch in the living room. He walked out onto the porch so they could keep talking without him. He sat on the wooden porch bench and looked at the stars. The Spindle was out tonight. So was the Triad, the Eastern Cross, and Brer Rabbit.

His mom came out and sat next to him. "You okay?" she asked.

"Never seen no man all shot up before. Make me feel sick."

"Me too." She hugged him. "What you doing, watching the stars?"

"I thinking about that one story you tell me. Ten mirror."

"Ah. Ten mirror. Ain't too late already for stories?"

"No!" Jerome wiggled around and laid his head on her lap.

"Well, remember, I see, I bring, but I ain't responsible—"

"You always say that," Jerome interrupted.

"It mean the story change sometime when we tell it," Shanta said. "And that sometime the thing people do in it may not be right. It's just what it is. No more, no less. Okay?" Jerome nodded. She continued, "See, them old-father realize Nanagada was too cold to live upon. So they build great big mirrors, ten of them, to fly up in the sky and heat the ice. That was when they had fight the Tetol hard, but was losing."

"That's where the ragamuffin had come in," Jerome said.

"Right. Most of the ragamuffin already dead, trying to stop the Tetol. So the ragamuffin Brung thought hard for a real-real long time. Then he crack the sky in explosions and killed all the magic machine the Tetol was using, and destroy the worm's holes. But he also kill all the magic machine our old-father in Nanagada use.

"For a long time people struggle to live, but you could still see them ten mirror in the sky. But then they began to fall and burn. Most landed in the ocean. But one time a mirror fell into the middle of Nanagada, by Hope's Loss. It left great slivers in the forest that would twinkle at night. One day a little girl lost in the forest—"

"Hope's Loss?" Jerome squirmed.

"East, in the middle of Nanagada, where the Tetol dropped rocks from the sky and destroyed the land. They say the land still poisoned today, and no one can live there."

"Oh. That why the Triangle Tracks don't go through there to come here to Brungstun?"

His mom looked over at him. "No," she said sadly. "No train tracks come from Capitol City to Brungstun because of the Azteca. If they ever came over the Wicked Highs, they could get back to Capitol City before people had time to prepare."

Mentioning Azteca ended the tale for the night. They both fell silent, looking west back toward their house. Jerome got off the bench and stretched. His mom grabbed his waist and looked Jerome straight in the eye. "You dad been all over the world, first by road all the way along the coast to get to Capitol City, then by boat to sail the north seas. He go be okay just getting stuff out the house." She smiled.

Jerome nodded. But he wasn't sure whom she was reassuring: him, or herself. "I know, Mom. He fine."

He left her out on the porch, looking out at the stars.

Dad better be in town by lunch. Jerome would look him up and make sure he bought him a big, tasty meal. And maybe Jerome would show him where he was going to watch carnival from. Dad always loved carnival; he'd like the place Jerome had found to watch carnival from.

CHAPTER NINE

Someone knocked on the door. Dihana looked up from an expanse of opened letters. The city's landlords were refusing to board the hundreds of mongoose-men Haidan had in the city unless they got upfront payment.

"Come in."

A Councilman cautiously walked in. "Prime . . . Minister." He choked on the words.

Dihana stood up and extended an ink-stained hand. "Mr. Councilman. This is a pleasant interlude in a long day." The man looked at her with suspicion. "I trust," Dihana continued sweetly, "you are adjusting well to your accommodations on the Ministerial Grounds?"

"You talking strange," he said. "You mocking me?"

Dihana cleared a swath of space on her desk. A few letters fluttered to the floor beside the desk. She thickened her accent, easy to do with all the bottled-up anger in her. "It was unpleasant when you had all run away like a bunch of yellow-belly when Elijah die and left me to be prime minister. I ain't too sympathetic, seen? And I remember your name, Councilman: Emil. Sit."

Emil sat. "You ain't strong enough to protect we. Elijah couldn't protect himself, how better you go do? We too important to sit in the open just to help *you*." He folded his hands and bit his lip. "We been here since the beginning. We go still be here long after you die."

Dihana ground her teeth. The Councilmen were hundreds of years old, just as her father had been. They should have worked with her. She could have done great things with their ancient knowledge.

Maybe she still could.

"You think because you have Nana in your blood you're superior," Dihana said. Emil looked startled. Yes, Dihana knew what kept the Councilmen almost immortal. Elijah had tried to explain Nana, but the young Dihana had been hurt and confused when he'd said she didn't have them. "Why not?" Dihana had demanded. "Why can't you give me Nana as well?"

Elijah had sat stiffly on the other side of the minister's desk. "I wish I could," he had said. "The Loa say they can, but I don't think they're right, though they promise me—" She wondered later how painful it must have been for him to live knowing he'd see her die.

"So then *we* should do it, we should try to make Nana again, like the old-fathers did," Dihana had said.

That had brought a dangerous glint to Elijah's eye. "No. We can't."

And that was how that remained. Always. Until he died. Shot through the heart by an Azteca assassin.

"Nana wasn't enough to save him," Dihana told Emil. "A bullet for him was like a bullet for anyone else."

Emil shifted, maybe reminded of his own mortality. "We know."

Dihana stopped moving the letter opener from hand to hand. She pointed the silver point at him. "Why did you run? With all the knowledge you have? You could have helped."

Emil crossed his legs and grabbed his knees. "You bring electric light here, right? You and the Preservationist know how it work. But you think the people in the city using it know? All they know is they turn the switch on or off, or replace a bad bulb."

Dihana understood. "You're ignorant. In the middle of wonders, you just accepted them, never understood them. And when they were taken, you didn't know how to bring them back." Strung along by her father's promises of technology from the Loa and giving him their full support. Dihana now saw them through adult eyes. "Do any of you know anything useful?"

"Of course." Emil straightened his back, insulted.

Dihana picked up an opened letter and started folding it to keep her fingers busy. "What things?"

"History, real events, explanations. We remember the real thing, not any legend," Emil said, talking up his percieved importance.

"Okay," Dihana said, trap set. She put the paper down. "Talk with the Preservationists. Have them come here to you. Tell them everything you know. *Everything*. And I'll be reading their notes."

Emil nodded. He didn't get up though.

"We have a favor to ask," he said. "We missing a man. He out with the Frenchi. We want mongoose-men to bring him back."

"Why?" And why did they need mongoose-men to fetch him? Were the Councilmen pushing at her more? She bit down the impulse to automatically refuse them their request.

"He ain't a Councilman, but he know all of we. If the Azteca catch him, they go know who we all is."

They were hiding something. She wanted to reach over, smack the superior look off Emil's face, and find out what. "How many mongoose?"

"Fifty."

Fifty mongoose-men for one man? "I'll think about it." Dihana crumpled the paper under her hand into a small ball. Now to worm out what it was. "But . . ."

Her door opened. No knock, but Haidan stood silhouetted in the corridor light and she bit back an annoyed order to be left alone. Haidan kicked the door closed with his bootheel. He grabbed the back of Emil's chair.

"Hey . . . ," Emil protested. "This an important talk."

"Not any longer." The veins stood out on Haidan's forearms. "Mafolie Pass been take by Azteca. Some mongoose-men from the Wicked Highs used a courier blimp to fly to Anandale. They say it a whole invasion. Brungstun and Joginstead both cut off the telegraph line. Azteca coming over, Dihana. A whole army."

"Oh, God," Emil whispered. "Oh, God."

Dihana pitied Emil for just a brief second. Azteca in Brungstun might capture this important man the Councilmen worried about. Now they really depended on her protection. Any other day this would have drawn a smile out of her. Right now she put it aside. "Okay. What now?" She felt numb. This was crisis mode, she would show no shock, but silently she kept thinking: Azteca are coming over the mountains. Azteca are moving toward the city. Azteca.

Haidan's locks fell forward off his shoulders. "I order back all the mongoose into Capitol City. We need recruit more. The Loa, the Councilmen, you, me squad-leader, the head of Tolteca-town, and several other go all need meet. As soon as possible."

"Meet with the Loa? After that last encounter?" Emil stood up. "We refuse. We ain't stupid." He fumbled open the door and slammed it behind him.

Dihana shook her head. She was living in a three-hundred-year-old nightmare. *The Azteca loose in Nanagada.* Not just spies and scouting parties, but hordes. The thought brought a clenching sourness to her stomach. One hundred thousand people were now vulnerable in the city. How many more in towns along the coastal roads before the Azteca ever got to Capitol City? After Joginstead came Brewer's Village, and then Anandale, and then . . .

"I headquartered in the city," Haidan told her. "A house from back when I had live here. Where should I put the mongoose-men coming in?"

"Let them camp in front of the Ministry while I try and find places," Dihana murmured. Details, just details against the fact that she would probably see Azteca camped outside the city walls. "How long before the Azteca get here?"

"Don't know." Haidan looked tired. Bags under his eyes. "Five or six week. Maybe more, maybe less. Depend on how much food they carrying, if any. How long they stay at each town. And how we try stopping them. But once they reach Harford and get on the Triangle Tracks, it go be quick."

"We need to know," Dihana stepped back from the edge of despair. It felt like falling, but inside her head. "There's a new steamship the Preservationists are finishing. In the harbor. I was planning another expedition north into the ice with, but you could use to scout the coast." It wasn't much.

"May be useful," Haidan said. "We need everything. Councilmen, businessmen, fishermen, ragamuffin, Loa, we all need to plan together. We need to agree on how we release this information. We need calm while getting organize before the word get out."

Dihana sighed. "You're right. But, though I hate agreeing with Emil, I don't want to involve the Loa in any discussion."

Haidan let go of the chairback. "If you all can't use the Loa like the Loa use you," he ground out, "then you might as well just wait for the Azteca to come and rip you heart out on a stone in market square." He backed away. "You tell me when that meeting go happen, okay? Or I take all me men and head out deep into the bush, become a mongoose biting the heels of the Azteca, because this city the only place we can break that tide for sure."

The door slammed shut.

"Haidan?" He was angry. Maybe a bit scared. And that made her even more scared. Dihana swept every single letter off her desk. None of that crap mattered right now.

Azteca were coming.

CHAPTER TEN

Down Brungstun's Main Street one of the town's few steam cars pulled a large float coated in strips of multicolored cloth. Men on top drummed steel pans, the music echoing off the sides of the houses and warehouses they passed. Horses pulled more floats behind them, and costumed dancers followed.

Along the sidewalk wooden booths sold patties. Or curried chicken. Or johnnycake. Or sandwiches. Jerome could buy bush tea, maubi, malt . . . the list went on.

Jub-jub pranced down the street, covered in black paint, demanding money from the crowd. Along the procession's side Jerome spotted moko jumbies on their tall stilts. One rested against a balcony, taking a break from his frenzied dancing down the street and talking to some women watching the parade.

Too bad Dad wasn't here yet to enjoy it. Mom said he'd show up for at least some of the celebration later this morning.

Jerome bought a brown bag of tamarind balls and popped one in his mouth. The sweet sugar coating dissolved. He puckered his lips as he sucked on the sour part and wandered along. A woman danced right past him, stiff feathers from her peacock costume sticking out all over from her back, bouncing around as she shook herself down over the cobblestones. She headed for the waterfront toward the judges.

Jerome wasn't going with the parade toward the waterfront. Jerome had a goal in mind: the tall four-story warehouse and store called Happer's. From the top he and his friends could see the whole town.

A piece of patty hit his shirt, staining it brown. Jerome brushed off meat flecks and looked up. "Why you got to be always testing me?"

"Easy target, man. Easy easy." Swagga's cheerful face looked over the edge of Happer's, way up on the roof. He looked proud. Jerome picked up a nice oval pebble lying by the street side and pocketed it for when Swagga wouldn't expect it.

Happer's had an iron fire-ladder on the alley side. Jerome grabbed the first rung and pulled himself up carefully, checking to make sure the rungs wouldn't pull out from the green concrete wall, and climbed up to the rooftop.

"Finally." Swagga gave him a hand up and over. Jerome looked around. Other friends, Schmitti from school and Daseki from half a mile down the road, sat on a tablecloth. They had ham-and-cheese sandwiches and a pitcher of lemonade.

"That you mum's cloth?" Jerome asked Schmitti.

"That he bumba-clot," Swagga yelled. They all burst out laughing. None could cuss more wicked than Swagga.

"You want a lemonade?" Daseki asked.

"Yeah." Jerome walked over. The unpainted concrete rooftop already shimmered with heat. But the view made up for the lack of shade. Daseki poured a glass of lemonade. Jerome sipped it and walked over to the other side of Happer's so he could see the carnival parade. "You won't believe what all happen to me last night."

"What?"

Jerome held the lemonade between both hands and told them about the mongoose-man who'd died in his kitchen, and how he'd run to get Auntie Fixit. By the time he was done the lemonade tasted way too sweet. He looked at the bottom of the glass and saw clumps of sugar.

"Man," Daseki said. "Everything cool happen to you. You father have a hook, you mom cook well, and someone fall into you garden last night."

"The post master had tell my dad the telegraph ain't working before we had gone sailing, so we can't warn anyone in Joginstead that some Azteca scout around. And everyone has to stay in town," Jerome finished.

"Yeah," Schmitti said. "We staying here tonight with me cousin."

They compared notes about how many Azteca might be around. It seemed weird. Unreal. But the adults didn't seem to think it was too much of a threat. They said scouting parties were all that could come over the Wicked Highs, and if everyone stayed in town, the mongoose-men and ragamuffin around town and in the bush would protect them. Carnival went on. In the distance the raucous clash of four or five different steel-pan bands playing different tunes floated up. Most of the parade had already turned around and was making the final leg down the waterfront to pass in front of the wooden stands the judges sat in.

Schmitti held up a leather bag. "You want go play some marble?" Schmitti had taken Jerome's best marble last week. "I be easy on you."

Daseki snorted. "Don't fall for it, he too good."

Jerome noticed a pillar of smoke rising from the forest outside Brungstun.

Someone burning space for a new farm, he thought. That time of year. Had to be. He sat down to lose his next favorite marble.

"Swagga, you go play?" Daseki asked.

Jerome pulled the pebble from his pocket. He winged it, hard, and it struck the wall along the edge. Swagga jumped into the air and everyone laughed. "That's for the patty you throw down on me shirt," Jerome said. "And you lucky I didn't aim at you. You coming to play?"

Swagga shook his head. "No. Come over and look at this here, man."

Daseki sighed elaborately and they all went over to the edge.

"What you see?" Schmitti asked.

Swagga pointed. Jerome looked down. The man Swagga pointed out walked down Hilty Street into Brungstun from the south. He wore a long coat. Shoulder-length dreadlocks straggled out of a black top hat.

"You ever see him before?" Daseki asked. "He look real serious."

"No. He look Frenchi, though."

The man had light brown skin. Not as light as a Frenchi, but definitely not like that of anyone in Brungstun. It reminded Jerome of his dad.

"I bet you he from up near Capitol City," Schmitti said.

"Then why he coming in from the south on Hilty road, uh?" Swagga asked. Schmitti sucked his teeth loudly.

"Man, don't schoops me like that," Swagga said. "He ain't from here: he looking all around them building like he new."

The man looked up at Happer's, and they all dropped down to the ground as one. Daseki's eyes were wide. "You think he see us?" They weren't supposed to be up here. Their mothers would get real angry.

"I dunno," Jerome said. "I hope not." The man in the top hat and coat made him nervous. He looked around. The heavy wooden trapdoor down into Happer's was bolted shut from the inside so thieves couldn't get in. And neither could they. The only way down was by the fire ladder.

"Someone look over," Swagga ordered. Jerome bristled. Swagga was a friend, but sometimes . . .

Swagga sighed. "You all yellow-belly." He pulled himself up over the wall and glanced over, real quick, and crouched back down. "He coming up the ladder!"

"We in trouble! He got tell we parent we was up here and we all go get in trouble!" Schmitti started shivering. His dad was famous for a good hiding. Swagga grabbed the bag of marbles and gave them to Jerome.

"You have the best throw," Swagga said. "Maybe if you hit he hard, he go leave to look and tell someone we up here instead of coming up and seeing who we is. Then we can run."

"Yeah." Jerome swallowed.

Daseki nodded and whispered, "Bust he in he head good, Jerome."

Jerome took a deep breath, then leapt up. He leaned over the edge. The brim of the man's hat wasn't even ten feet below him. Jerome leaned in and threw the leather bag as hard as he could.

The man's head snapped up and he caught the bag in his left hand. Jerome looked down at gray eyes as the marbles made a scrunching sound.

"Oh, man," Jerome said, jumping back from the small wall. "He go kill we dead." Something cold in the man's eyes made him stop worrying about his parents finding out and made him wish he were anywhere but on the roof of Happer's.

Schmitti started to cry. "Swagga, what we should do?"

Swagga backed away from the wall, going the other direction from Jerome. "Split you-self up. Maybe he only catch one of us, and the other three can run down the ladder."

Jerome's heart thudded, he could hear everything: his leather shoes crunching as he walked over pieces of gravel, Schmitti sniffling, Daseki's wheezing breaths. A gust pushed dust into the air, making him blink.

And just like that the man leaped over the wall. His coat swirled out around him, then settled down. He threw the bag of marbles out in front of him and took his hat off.

"Hello," he said to Jerome. "I think you dropped something."

He sounded northern. Almost like, Jerome made the comparison again, his dad. This man had a weathered face too. He looked old, but in a young body. His muscles filled out the coat. When he moved his arms, Jerome could see his biceps through the heavy cloth sleeves.

"Who you is?" Swagga demanded. "You the Baron?" Swagga was right, Jerome gulped. This man dressed fine, like the Baron Samedi, Death himself. Top hat, coat.

"The Baron?" The man frowned. "Samedi?" He snorted. "That's good, but I'm not that kind of legend, no." He smiled at the four boys. "Call me Pepper." He walked forward, boots clicking on the concrete. "The view up here is very good. I like it."

Jerome nodded, trapped. Behind Pepper, both Daseki and Schmitti ran to the edge of the wall and climbed down the ladder. Pepper looked over his shoulder at the disappearing boys and turned back around.

"I'm not going to hurt you," he said to Jerome and Swagga. "This is just the best lookout in town. But since you two are here, I was hoping you could help me. I'm looking for John deBrun. I know he never misses carnival. I've been in the jungle for weeks trying to get here before carnival. Do any of you know John deBrun?"

Dad! Jerome shot a look at Swagga. Say nothing, he willed his friend. For once in his fool life, Swagga kept his mouth shut, still looking at Pepper with wide eyes.

"Why?" Jerome asked.

"We're old friends from a long time ago," Pepper said.

Yeah, right, Jerome thought. And Dad wasn't in town yet anyway. Maybe Uncle Harold could handle Pepper and figure out if he was a friend for real.

"I could take you to someone who know him," Jerome said.

"I'd appreciate that," Pepper said. "See, I only just arrived after a long, long journey. I've been spending a lot of time looking for old friends all over Nanagada, and if John deBrun is here, I would love to see him again." The words sounded cheerfully fake.

He pulled what looked like binoculars covered in bumpy rubber out from his coat and looked east toward the Wicked Highs.

"There usually that many airships in the air over there?" he asked. Five sliver-shaped ships floated in the air above the mountain slopes.

Jerome shook his head. "Never seen five all together before."

Pepper put the strange binoculars away. "Odd," he murmured. Then he looked at Jerome. "Let's go see this man of yours who knows John." He indicated that Jerome lead the way.

As Jerome led Pepper down Gregerie road toward the waterfront, and Uncle Harold, Swagga pulled close and whispered, "You think he really you father friend?"

"I don't know."

The sound of steel pan increased, and the few people along the street's side this far from the real crowd down Main Street at least bounced to the rhythm, if not outright danced. Jerome turned left heading home, east for half a mile, to dodge the worst of the crowd. Almost no one was here. The music faded away. Jerome figured they could pick up the waterfront from farther down and come back up on the judging booths easier this way.

A scream echoed down the street at them.

"You hear that?" Swagga asked.

"Yeah," Jerome said.

"Sound like a jumbie, man." Swagga turned back around. "I'm going back this way." He ran off toward the crowds.

"He has the right idea." Pepper sniffed the air, like a dog.

Jerome kept walking. "We just need to get around the corner here. We can cut through and end up on waterfront." He turned into an alley, and Pepper trotted past him. Jerome could see the harbor past the cobblestones and a green fishing boat that bobbed out at anchor. All they had to do was turn and walk the waterfront down to the crowds.

"Come on, child, quick." Pepper looked up and down the waterfront.

Jerome turned the corner after him. Distant song and the nearby lapping of harbor waves against the waterfront's concrete edge mixed in the air. Jerome hurried to keep up with Pepper. He almost smacked into the man when Pepper froze, looking into the shade of Harry's bar, empty since it was this far down the waterfront. The BEST SPIRIT IN TOWN sign squeaked. It hung from a wooden roof that shaded the tables on the sidewalk, propped out over them at an angle by poles.

"*Tlacateccatl,*" Pepper whispered. Jerome squinted. And saw.

An Azteca warrior stood inside. He wore a bright red cape that came to his waist, feathers braided into his hair like one of Jerome's aunts, and leather bracelets. Blood ran off the grooved mace in his left hand. It was crowned with several black metal blades.

The warrior looked up from his work, smiled with full, black-colored lips, and moved to unsling the large gun strapped to his back. Pepper's left hand ducked beneath his coat. He pulled out a gun not much bigger than his hand.

It spat, not nearly the loud bang Jerome expected. The Azteca warrior staggered back into the bar with a bloody hole in his chest. Pepper walked in, gun still in hand. He fired three more times, looked down at the man on the ground, then walked back out.

He carried the Azteca's long gun with him.

"Come on," Pepper said. "You need to introduce me to this man who can find John deBrun. There seems to be an Azteca problem here. We don't have much time to dally."

Jerome trembled. "Uncle Harold said ragamuffin and mongoose-men would be out guarding the edge of town. He said it were just a scout party. How that warrior get in?"

He could have died. Right there. And he'd just seen Pepper kill that Aztecan without missing a beat. Again Jerome found himself trying to puzzle out what kind of person Pepper was.

He had to be a soldier.

And should he tell him the truth about his dad?

"I ran into Jaguar scouts coming out here," Pepper said. "I'm getting to know more about these Azteca than I want. That warrior was a *tlacateccatl,* he commands many warriors. Not a good commander, he's too far ahead of his men, even if he is a scout. An unblooded warrior. Probably got too excited about making sure he got a couple captures before the general attack. Either way, seeing him, my guess is that a whole army is creeping into this town." Jerome almost jogged to walk as fast as Pepper. "They would have just secured the town's border after I got here," Pepper said. Jerome kept as close to Pepper as he could. He was more scared now than when he went out at night and the wind made his skin prickle. Right by Pepper's side seemed to be the safest place right now.

What about Dad back at their house?

Everything around them, the shadows the cheerfully painted buildings cast, the gutters, the faceless windows, everything seemed sinister and dangerous. It destroyed the comfortable feelings Jerome had about Brungstun. And even though Pepper had saved his life, he still scared Jerome. Even more so now, as Pepper's face hadn't even changed when he'd killed the Azteca.

The waterfront curved out in front of them, menacing and dangerous.

CHAPTER ELEVEN

The Azteca had dragged John deeper into the bush that night until they reached a clearing with a large black stone in the middle. This wasn't a small scout party. John saw enough different Azteca to guess that hundreds of Azteca warriors crept around the bush near Brungstun. Maybe more.

Three sleeping men lay tied next to a downed mango tree. Blood and dirt caked their clothes, but John recognized them as mongoose-men.

John had been shoved against the tree, his cheek scraping bark. A few deft kicks to his knees and stomach dropped him to the ground, and the Azteca scout by his side had bound John's hands and feet together, then roped him to the mango tree. A warrior clubbed John's head to knock him out for the night.

It still throbbed when he woke up late in the morning.

John now wriggled his back up against the tree and looked across at the awake mongoose-men.

"What are your names?" he whispered, but they remained silent. "My name is John deBrun. I'm from Brungstun, who are you?"

The man with a battered face next to him looked off in the distance. "Is best we don't know each other. Trust me."

"We *have* to get free," John said. "No one could expect this many Azteca. We have to warn Brungstun that so many are here."

"Shut up, man, just shut up," a second mongoose-man hissed. "We ain't escaping, and you ain't making this easier."

John's thighs cramped underneath him. "What do you mean?"

The man next to him, the first to speak, shifted. "Make you peace. Because soon we go die."

A faint sob, a cough, and silence fell again.

Peace? How? He didn't remember who most of himself was. He'd settled, taken a family, and been happy. But now that he'd had the barrel of a gun pointed down at him, he felt soft, mushy, unprepared.

Frustrated.

The white-hot feeling made him jittery. Frustrated that with only a few hours left of his life, he still could not remember a thing from before that singular moment when he'd washed up on the Brungstun beach.

A single thing.

At least the men around John had an entire life to regret, or miss. He was going to die not even knowing who he really was. And how selfish, he berated himself, that this frustration ate at him almost as much as the helplessness of being unable to run out and be by his wife, his son.

Azteca moved and shouted. Last night's captors surrounded the tree and pointed at the four captives, coming to a decision. They sliced the ropes free and made two mongoose-men stand up. To his shame, John felt relief.

As the two men stumbled off, John turned to the man next to him, the only one to talk to him. "Please," John begged. "Tell me your name."

The man closed his eyes. "Alex."

"How many will they take?"

Alex shrugged. "It varies."

The two men were dragged off around the tree's branches, out of sight toward the black stone at the center of the clearing. For several minutes only a few jungle birds fluttered and cawed into the silence.

Then the screaming began. It stopped after a high-pitched hiccup, a groan, and a joyful shout in Azteca.

A minute later the second man started screaming.

When that stopped, John and Alex sat with their backs to the mango tree, avoiding each other's eyes. They remained silent, waiting for the Azteca to come back for them.

CHAPTER TWELVE

It took forever to get closer to the carnival crowd by following the waterfront. All around the gentle U of Brungstun's edge the warehouses and shops clustered, and then behind them, inching up the coast's steep slope, the residential areas of town jutted out in cheerful colors highlighted by the drab roads cut into the bright green brush and jungle. Jerome jumped at every sudden noise.

They encountered the edge of the carnival crowd: a couple kissing near a doorway, someone selling fruit on a table where the juices had leaked out and stained it black in patches. Five fishermen milled about, talking about their boats.

Jerome slowed down. "We should warn them," he said to Pepper. He yelled, "Azteca coming! The Azteca coming!"

No one paid him any attention as they moved farther into the thickening crowd. The more people around, the more the shouting and jumping of carnival drowned out Jerome's voice. They pushed their way toward the large wooden scaffolds by the bank building and post office.

Jerome couldn't see Uncle Harold up in the sheltered judges' benches. Half the judges were gone. Was it because most of the judges were Brungstun ragamuffin and off investigating the gunshots?

Another scream floated over the chaos of carnival. Jerome shoved and elbowed through to the street. He couldn't see Pepper anymore, but the peacock-costumed woman he'd seen earlier came proudly walking down the street. Behind her a band of women costumed as birds twirled batons with streamers on the end.

Shots echoed from the alleys. People paused. Steel pans fell quiet as three parrot-costumed women at the end of the street turned around. Fifteen men with blue-feathered bamboo masks and stiff cotton pads marched toward them.

"Azteca," Jerome screamed into the still.

The masked men pulled out clubs and nets. The first one to reach a parrot-costumed woman knocked her out. The two behind him threw a net over her and pulled her down the road, back toward other Azteca stepping into the street. Jerome whirled around. Azteca warriors trickled out from between buildings at the far edges of town. Both sides of the waterfront were blocked. Azteca shadows stood in the alleys. Everyone in Brungstun stood corraled on the waterfront as hundreds of Azteca poured out. They moved into the edges of the crowd, knocking people out with clubs and carrying them away in nets, working at the edges with quick, practiced calm, and stopping anyone from running away. People screamed and babies wailed while everyone shoved at everyone else. The air smelled sour.

Just a few hundred feet from Jerome two farmers with machetes ran forward to slash at one Azteca before getting shot. Blood ran along the cobblestones. A moko jumbie on fire ran toward the pier. He wobbled on his stilts and then fell to the ground. He didn't get up.

The crowd surged as several thousand people tried to pull back from Azteca nets and weapons. Jerome fought to keep standing.

A hand grabbed Jerome's collar. He screamed.

"Quiet." Pepper picked Jerome up, tucked him under an arm, and started running through the crowd. Jerome's feet slapped against people as they passed, and Pepper paused once to pull out his silent gun to shoot a lone Azteca who had pushed too far into the crowd. The Azteca grabbed for ankles as he fell. People trampled and kicked him.

Pepper ran down to the docks toward the steamboat, but Jerome twisted around. "Take that sailboat," he yelled, pointing at *Lucita*. "The steamboat take too long to warm up."

Pepper dropped him to the dock and Jerome staggered for balance. A splinter caught his heel before he stopped, but he barely noticed it as he jumped into his dad's boat.

The mast swayed a bit.

"Mr. Pepper," Jerome yelled. "What about me mother?"

Pepper threw the aft painter into the cockpit. The rope's end stung Jerome's cheek. Pepper ran along the dock and grabbed both the bow and mid painter in his two hands. He yanked on them hard and the cleats ripped free with an iron-nailed shriek.

"Pepper! I need to find her." Jerome's hands trembled. He grabbed the mast. "She out with the Azteca. What they go do?"

Pepper pushed the boat out from the dock and leapt in, bringing the rear down. Jerome caught his balance. Several others in the crowd were leaping to boats. A crowd had gathered on the steamer and a small trickle of smoke wafted over the boiler.

Jerome ran to *Lucita*'s stern and grabbed the gunwale's wooden lip. Pepper found the oars, shoved them into place, and began to row. Each strong pull shook them forward away from the dock.

"You have to do what you have to do," Pepper finally said. "Now would be a good time to jump."

The oars hit the water, slap, then drained as he lifted them into the air. They bit back down into the water again.

"I'm scared." Jerome sat down on the rear seat, ready to cry, holding his stomach. His eyes burned.

"Drop the tiller and steer us," Pepper said.

Jerome turned back around and loosened the rope to the oval-shaped rudder. It splashed down into the water.

Several Azteca in stiff cotton lined up on the waterfront and aimed guns at them. Pepper stopped rowing. His gun huffed a few times and three Azteca fell, one into the water. Others ran for cover, feathers bobbing.

"You know how to get the sail up?" Pepper asked.

"Yeah."

"Do it."

Jerome hustled to get the sail unlashed from the boom while staying out of Pepper's way. Pepper pulled at the oars like mad, pointing them into the wind. Bits of the sail draped over the boat's side, some dragging alongside in the water.

Dad would have yelled at him.

Jerome cried silently, wiped his eyes on his sleeve, and pulled the sail up as far and as tight as he could while the wind yanked hard at it. The boom swung around and banged. When Jerome tied it down, Pepper pulled in the oars and took the tiller with the mainsheet in his hand. He pulled it in, bringing the boom and sail in closer to the boat.

Lucita tilted over and picked up speed. Pepper, still calm and serious, sailed them away from the waterfront.

The sun beat down on them. Pepper hadn't said a word in the last twenty minutes; he lay against the side of the cockpit, one leg steering them upwind, one arm in his jacket, the other trailing in the water. They weren't really going anywhere, just making three legs of a triangle around and around some imaginary spot in the ocean.

Occasionally Pepper would take out his rubber binoculars and look back at Brungstun.

At one point they'd come near the light water of Severun's Reef, but without needing a warning, Pepper had tacked hard, the boom swinging violently as the wind eased up on it. He must have known the harbor well.

A dark knot inside Jerome kept threatening more tears. He'd left his mother in Brungstun to die and his dad trapped at the house. He'd seen people die! Get shot. Captured by Azteca. He shivered. The image of blood dripping into the street sewer grate as if it were only so much wastewater, that image he felt he would never shake as long as he lived.

He couldn't do anything. He had never felt so helpless as he did now.

"How you do it?" Jerome asked Pepper.

"What?" Pepper blinked his gray eyes and looked around.

"Stay calm like that."

"Damned if I know," Pepper muttered. "The only other choice is running around screaming." He scanned the horizon. "Doesn't look like anyone else made it out of the docks."

That was what they had been waiting for.

Pepper shifted and adjusted the tiller. *Lucita*'s tiny bow aimed for Frenchi Reef.

"Where you from?" Jerome asked. "Out by Capitol City?"

Pepper shook his head. "Further."

"How much further?"

"What did you learn about in school about where we all came from?"

In school? School taught him the same tale his mother told him.

"We came from the worm's hole, up in the sky," Jerome said. "You come from the worm's hole?"

Pepper nodded. "We came from different places. Some settled in orbit. Others settled up north. Many people from the Caribbean came here to Nanagada, looking for some nice equatorial sun and peace. We were just a tiny bunch of refugee camps and lake fishing villages, hoping we could hide in this far-out corner and be left alone." Pepper stretched, and the bench beneath him bowed slightly. He eyed the water, then continued, "Very few on Earth knew we were here. Hell, some people in orbit didn't even know about all the islanders along the coast and jungle. Better times," he sighed. "Before the wormhole was destroyed."

Pepper talked as if he had seen these times firsthand.

"They say the old-father didn't survive them times, just like the machines," Jerome said. "How come you here?"

"They lie," Pepper said. "Those of us well protected, those who knew what was about to happen, survived while the Pulse, nukes, and engineered diseases took everyone else. A few survived: some Teotl, Loa, and others like me. Many marooned in hardened escape pods. Three hundred years of floating in space, though, that'll screw you up." He snorted. "Here's the result around us. Mostly only on-planet islanders survived."

"And Azteca."

"Yes, them too. When I left, the Azteca were religious fanatics who worshiped the Teotl. Who started breeding and using them as cheap, savage troops. The Teotl love using our weaknesses against us." Pepper shook his head. "I hope you all have the resources to buck them off the mountains."

The conversation had returned to things that made sense to Jerome.

"Most of the mongoose-men up in Mafolie Pass, or back around Capitol City them," he said. This was common knowledge. There were squads scattered all throughout the mountains and lands.

Pepper leaned over and splashed some salt water on his face.

"What we doing now?" Jerome asked. "Hiding on Frenchi Island?"

"No. I'm dropping you off. Giving myself some time to think. Then I need to start looking for John."

Jerome swallowed. Pepper had saved his life, and he seemed to be honest. "Mr. Pepper." Pepper raised an eyebrow. "I fibbed you. I know where John deBrun is."

"You seemed to be holding something back."

"He . . ." Jerome's voice quivered. "That's my dad, see? He in the house, outside town, last night." Jerome looked down at the brackish water sloshing about the boards by his feet.

Pepper hit the seat with a fist "That complicates things."

"I'm . . . sorry."

Pepper leaned forward and looked at Jerome, straight in his eyes. "I never would have taken John for the settling-down kind."

Jerome avoided the gray eyes. Maybe he should tell Pepper about his dad's memory loss. Dad and his mother did their best to hide it from him, but he picked it up from their whispered conversations when they thought he wasn't listening. And the way she looked at Dad's paintings sometimes. As if they scared her.

But that was something personal. Jerome figured his dad and Pepper could sort that out if they ever met.

If his dad was alive.

Pepper adjusted the tiller. "Tell me what your dad looks like. Describe him to me. I haven't seen him in a long time."

Jerome struggled. Dad was just dad. But he did his best and told Pepper about Mom, Dad, his family, and the airship that had floated into the trees behind their house. When he finished telling Pepper about Dad's hook, Pepper turned his attention back to sailing, which relieved Jerome. He wanted to go sit on the bow and pretend he was alone on the boat.

Frenchi stood waiting when *Lucita's* bow struck the sand. Troy walked forward. "Something wrong?" he asked. "Ms. Smith say she see smoke from Brungstun when she was out fishing."

Pepper splashed into the water, his coattails floating on the surface. "Azteca attacked Brungstun. They're moving along the coast now towards Capitol City, is my best guess."

Troy had a shotgun behind his back. He pulled it out and aimed it at Pepper. "I know Jerome, here. I don't know you."

Pepper held his hands in the air. "Easy. I'm not staying. I'm dropping the kid off." Jerome bristled at being called a kid. Pepper walked backward. "Jerome, jump off."

Jerome leapt onto the sand, and Troy put an arm around his shoulder. "You okay?"

Jerome nodded.

"I'm going to leave," Pepper explained. "I have things to do. But I would appreciate some food. Preferably salted."

One of the men behind Troy asked, "You going back to fight Azteca?"

Pepper nodded. Then he frowned. "You look familiar," he told Troy.

Troy ignored him. "Give he all the saltfish and jerky he need. And some johnnycake." He put down his gun. "That man hard," he told Jerome. "A killer. Better we help he leave." He walked back up to his store.

Jerome stood shakily on the beach, his feet sinking into the sand as the occasional wave washed up and wet them.

Troy and one of his cousins helped pack several canvas bags for Pepper, placing them in *Lucita's* forward stow-hatch. Pepper told the Frenchi that they needed to have somewhere to run to, or some defense against the Azteca, as they would eventually come.

"There is reef we can hide behind, sand and coconut trees, we boat them to run in."

"You can last a month or two like that, maybe, if you were well prepared," Pepper said. "What then?"

They smiled. "That go be long enough to see what happen. Any longer, and all Nanagada done for anyway."

"True." Pepper nodded.

Jerome watched them all nod as despair rolled over him. What he wanted to tell Troy and everyone else was that it wasn't worth it. The Azteca would come for them all anyway, and they could do nothing to stop that. They could only make a stand and fight, he thought. Bash them back something wicked. But running was futile.

He looked out over water and clenched his fists. He felt utterly unprepared in any sense for the new shape of the world that had dropped on him.

Pepper waited until the sun started slipping beneath the far-off reefs and breaking waves before he seemed ready to leave. He walked down the beach to where Jerome sat alone by a coconut tree.

"You leaving?" Jerome said.

"Yes."

"I want to go with you."

"And do what? What skills do you have that I need? I know what I need to know, I have the boat. It is up to me to track down your father, if he's still alive."

Jerome banged his head against the tree's rough bark. "What I can do?" he cried. "What?"

"You can tell me this." Pepper loomed over Jerome, dreads dangling down like snakes. "Did John ever talk to you about the *Ma Wi Jung*?"

Jerome shook his head. "I dunno."

Pepper grabbed him by his shirt and picked him up. He pushed Jerome against the coconut tree, hard enough that Jerome's spine hurt when it scraped against the bumps in the trunk.

"Look right here at me," Pepper hissed, "and tell me if your father ever told you anything about the *Ma Wi Jung*."

Jerome squirmed, scared at the sudden ferocity. He had no doubt that Pepper could snap his back against the tree and leave him for dead.

"I swear," Jerome wailed, a tear rolling down his cheek.

"No coordinates? No secret rhymes that give its location that you've sworn never to tell anyone?"

"No! Never." Jerome sobbed, scared for his life again, scared of Pepper. In a night his world had been flipped. What was once safe had become dangerous. And people he had thought safe were dangerous.

Pepper dropped Jerome to the sand. "I'm sorry. If I see your father, I will tell him you are alive. Tell Troy I'll sink any boats in Nanagada; make it harder for the Azteca to come out here."

That was it.

Pepper had that calm face Jerome remembered. When he'd shot the Azteca. Jerome watched Pepper walk down the beach to the *Lucita*, coat swishing. He pushed off, pulled the sail up, and never looked back.

Jerome sat by the coconut tree, watching the sail grow smaller back toward the Nanagadan coastline, where a long, black pillar of smoke, lit orange at the base, snaked up over Brungstun. Somewhere at the foot of that fire Schmitti, Swagga, and Daseki were alone with Azteca. Along with his mom, they would die, or be savaged by the Azteca, or . . . he didn't know what.

Jerome could not take his eyes away. He didn't move until Troy came over with a wool blanket, picked him up, and carried him back to one of the shacks by the beach.

CHAPTER THIRTEEN

John stood up and rested his wrists on the mango tree to hold himself up. His leg muscles cramped. The Azteca holding the rope to his neck tugged a warning. John glared at him. The Azteca hollered and walked up to him, the rope drooping to the ground between them.

"What?" John spat.

He got a solid punch straight to the face. Spitting blood, his upper lip throbbing, John stared right back at his captor. The Azteca smiled and pointed his head at a point just past the tree. Seven Azteca warriors stood waiting. A handful more stood around the clearing's edges watching the scene. Campfire smoke trailed over the trees nearby. Another couple hundred Azteca nearby?

"*Ompa.*"

John looked in the direction of the black rock. The two bodies from earlier in the morning lay next to it.

"We dead," Alex said, next to him. "We dead."

The stone was soaked black with dried blood.

"Will they kill *everyone*?" John coughed as he was pulled forward.

"Not everyone." They shuffled around the fallen tree's branches and leaves to approach the sacrificial stone. "Healthy people first. They save women and children for later. Some end up slave."

The Azteca standing by the stone took off his mask. Extra feathers swung from his unbraided, clumped hair as he walked forward and pulled out a long, black knife. It soaked up the late-afternoon sun.

The warriors around John backed away reverently.

"Warrior-priest," Alex whispered.

The warrior-priest walked forward. He grabbed Alex's head and pricked his left earlobe with the obsidian knife. Blood ran down Alex's neck. He jerked back, trying to kick at him, but the warriors stepped forward and hit him until he stopped struggling.

I can't just watch this, John thought.

He took a breath and ran backward until the noose choked him. The Azteca stepped forward and beat him to the ground with fists, quickly and calmly, accustomed to the antics of those about to be sacrificed.

Gasping and bruised, John watched from the ground as they untied Alex's hands. Four warriors stepped forward and threw Alex to the ground. They grabbed his hands and feet, picked him up, and carried him up onto the stone. They crouched as they pulled on his feet and his hands, keeping Alex still and giving room to the warrior-priest.

"Nopuluca," one chuckled.

The priest straddled Alex, looked up into the sun, then plunged the knife deep into the supine man's ribs. Alex screamed. He screamed as the priest cut and snapped bone, and he didn't stop until the priest grunted with satisfaction. The tearing sounds continued until a final whimper, and then the priest held Alex's dripping heart up toward the sun.

The clearing erupted in Azteca cheers as the priest shoved Alex's limp body off the stone and two warriors grabbed John's hair. He felt tugging on the back of his wrists as they untied him. Before he could move, warriors had his hand, his hook, and his two legs in firm grasp. They swung him up into the air and then downward. John's back slapped against the sacrificial stone.

It was warm.

He looked up at the fluffy clouds above him, the sun off to the right. This was the last thing he would see. His frantic straining and pulling couldn't dislodge the sinewy hands holding him down. He was trapped. Helpless. Waiting for the knife.

When the priest stood over him, John fought the desire to shut his eyes. He tried to stare down the priest. One last tiny act of defiance.

Someone in the distance shouted.

Something hissed. The priest turned and then crumpled to the ground, impaled by a four-foot-long spear. The warriors froze, stunned.

They let go of John and reached out toward the priest. Only one warrior paused to scan for the spear thrower, shock still on his face.

Waste no opportunity, John thought.

He sat up and swung his hook into the belly of the closest Azteca. It punctured thick cotton and finally skin with an extra shove, then a pop. The warrior hiccuped and looked down.

John yanked the hook out to disembowel him.

The man's ropy intestines slithered out onto the ground. John rolled off the sacrificial stone to grab the dying Azteca's gun.

Another spear hissed through the air. Another Azteca was pierced and thrown backward. John pulled the gun barrel up with his bloodied hook and fired point-blank at the only Azteca on his side of the stone.

Not sure how to reload Azteca-designed guns, he threw it aside and picked up the one dropped at the impaled warrior's side.

With a scream an Azteca leaped over the stone. John blew a good-sized hole in the man's chest, then turned and ran. He heard a scream and a thud, another spear no doubt, and kept running.

He tasted sweat. It burned his eyes, but he didn't slow down from his full, zigzagged sprint until pricker branches started slapping his face and he tripped over a vine.

His right knee popped when he stood back up. He ached all over, and a good nick on his shoulder must have come from a close bullet.

But he was alive.

If it wouldn't have spelled death, he would have shouted with elation. But the Azteca who had been watching from a distance would start tracking him or calling their brothers nearby to come help.

John hobbled through the bush, getting deeper in.

After a good half an hour, he slowed down and rested against a tree. He used a large leaf to clean the blood from his hook. Then he used the hook to cut at the rope around his neck. He threw the strands onto the ground.

"You are lucky to be alive," said a voice.

John jumped up.

"Easy." The man stood just behind John with a spear pointed down at the ground. He looked unmistakably Azteca, with high cheekbones and smooth brown skin. He wore his hair brushed forward, the neat trim bordering his forehead.

But he wore mongoose gray, complete with pieces of glued-on bush.

"My name is Oaxyctl." *O-a sh-k-tul,* he pronounced it. He looked down at John's hook, then back up.

"You threw the spears?" John asked, eyeing the barbed point near the dirt and leaves. His hook remained by his side, ready to try to knock the spear aside if needed.

Oaxyctl nodded.

"Who are you?" John asked, alert. Carelessness meant death. Then it dawned on him. "The mongoose-men in my house last night said they were looking for you."

"What'd they say?"

"They were worried. You went missing with some other mongoose-men."

"Yes. We were attacked. I made it. They didn't. I work for the mongoose-men. I teach them about Azteca and sometimes spy for them." Oaxyctl looked back past John toward the clearing. "You did well back there. They get confused if you get the priest first. But scouts will be coming quickly. We need to move out of here if we want to live."

"Okay." John dropped his hook slightly. "But thank you, thank you for intervening."

Oaxyctl smiled tightly. "I'm sorry I couldn't rescue the men with you." He edged forward. "Now, what did you say your name was?"

"John. John deBrun."

"Ahh. Good. A very good name. Good." Oaxyctl sounded relieved.

The Azteca-turned-mongoose-man trotted between the trees, and John followed him. "I'm from Brungstun."

Oaxyctl used his spear to push aside a branch for John. "Brungstun is occupied. If we go south, and then east, we can skirt the invading army and make our way towards Capitol City. It will be safer there."

The words sucked the elation of being alive from John. Brungstun gone? Shanta, and Jerome, dead or slaves? His chest hurt. He followed Oaxyctl numbly, trying to organize his thoughts. Going to Brungstun would just kill him as well, as cold as it sounded . . .

Capitol City. "I would like to travel there with you," John said.

At Capitol City he could join any fight to push the Azteca back, recapture Brungstun. Oaxyctl was his best chance to live.

"Good." Oaxyctl sounded pleased with that.

CHAPTER FOURTEEN

During a small pause to catch their breaths, John watched chitter-birds swoop around the trees in sudden bursts, moving from one tree branch to another. In the distance a monkey chattered angrily from the treetops. Shadows crept out as twilight approached.

"How did you end up near the clearing?" John asked, voice low.

"I was skirting Brungstun looking for the *quimichtin* who killed my friends," Oaxyctl said. "Then I heard the screams."

"Quimichtin?"

"Spies," Oaxyctl whispered. "Like me, but that look like you."

John crossed his arms, chest still heaving. "I didn't realize there were so many." He wondered who among the familiar faces he'd seen on the streets, or on fishing boats, had been a spy that had helped the Azteca.

Oaxyctl shrugged. "Lots of spies here. Not many in Aztlan." He sat next to John and unfastened a tin water flask from his hip. He opened it and drank, water dribbling down the corners of his mouth, but didn't offer the flask to John.

"That's understandable." John fingered a buckle around his wrist. "I'm sure Azteca over here would rather not go back."

"You think Aztlan is that detestable?" Oaxyctl took another swallow.

"If life there is anything like what just happened to me, yes. Fucking savages." John spat. "I have a family in Nanagada. My wife, her name is Shanta, and my boy is—"

"Dead," Oaxyctl said calmly. "They are all dead. Even if they still breathe this second, they are prizes, slaves, or gifts to hungry gods. They will be sacrificed to help the crops grow, or for battles to swing in Azteca favor, or even just because the gods demand it."

Each word struck John like a pelted rock. He raised his hook and pointed it at Oaxyctl. "Are you trying to goad me, Azteca?"

Oaxyctl capped his flask and returned it to his hip.

"Quiet or you'll kill us," he hissed. "I'm not Azteca anymore, John. I'm a mongoose-man. I fight by their sides to kill Azteca spies. I betrayed my own kind. You are a just a townsman. I did not have to stop and save you when I heard the screams of the sacrificed on the eagle stone. I did not have to risk my life to save yours. And I certainly did not do all this for you to call me or my people savages."

"The blood spilled speaks for itself," John growled.

"It does. But speak ill of just the Jaguar scouts, not all Azteca. Or maybe I will kill you."

John took a deep breath. "I don't understand you."

"Maybe you should try," Oaxyctl snapped. "The mongoose-men lie with their hearts ripped out. That could be you, or me. So here we are together, John deBrun. Let us both live with it."

John let his hook fall slowly down to rest beside him. "I was better at hardships before I married Shanta. My son and my wife are a part of me now, understand? This is like losing half your body."

"What makes you think that I didn't leave my family behind when I came over the mountains?"

John wasn't sure yet how to judge Oaxyctl. It was usually an easy thing for him to decide whether he trusted someone. But John sensed many different muddled things in Oaxyctl that sometimes didn't feel right.

He'd saved John's life though, that meant something.

Oaxyctl held up a finger, then carefully picked up a sheaf of five-foot-long spears and slung them over his back with the leather strap. "We must move." A long rod with a notch at the end dangled from Oaxyctl's right hand, ready to fit in a spear and throw it.

"Azteca?" John asked.

"Maybe. Not sure."

John stared into the forest. Why had he been arguing with the man who had just saved his life? He had to snap out of himself.

"Capitol City is a long way from here," John whispered, looking around the large, shady leaves for attackers. "Weeks by a good road." Oaxyctl had a large pack of supplies. But John knew it wasn't enough food and water to last a walking trip all the way to Capitol City.

"I don't plan on walking there," Oaxyctl whispered back. He stepped toward the leaves and led them farther into the heavy jungle, quietly aiming down a nonexistent path south, away from the coast. John followed just as carefully. The more miles they walked, the more he could try to erase the feel of the sacrificial stone, warm and smooth against his back.

*   *   *

The deeper into the jungle, the less they could count on any paths. Oaxyctl sliced his way through the thick bush, sure of his direction even as night fell and they continued on. Neither of them were interested in stopping due to the dark. Not with scouts behind them. And both knew it was stupid to fashion a torch that would give them away.

"The nearest town to Brungstun is Joginstead." John had visited Joginstead on occasion. It was due east from Brungstun. "Are we going there after we go south to avoid Azteca?"

"We'll get close," Oaxyctl said.

Eventually Oaxyctl gave John his flask for water as they continued in silence. But Oaxyctl mainly kept to himself, and John focused on strengthening his mind for the long voyage ahead.

Survival. The instinct bubbled from deep inside him, past the nonexistent memory. John knew he was good at that. And when he was stronger and more prepared, there would be revenge. As much death as he could bring back on the Azteca. It felt comfortable to think that way.

Maybe he'd been a soldier before he'd lost his memory.

CHAPTER FIFTEEN

Dihana held on to the door's top edge as the steam car turned hard into one of Capitol City's angled streets. She tried not to yawn despite its being late morning already. She'd just finished a live telegraphing session with the mayor of Brewer's Village, Roger Bransom. The telegrapher on her side had translated her request into stutter, and the telegrapher in Brewer's read the stutter out loud to the mayor. After a pause the machine in Capitol City would chatter, and the telegrapher would read the reply to Dihana that had been spoken 370 miles away down the coast.

Dihana had asked Mayor Bransom several questions based on the mayor's last visit to Capitol City to verify his identity before talking about any particulars of the impending invasion.

The open vehicle bounced through a pothole and she winced.

So now she knew Brewer's Village had not been overrun. Brewer's was sixty miles away from the several days' silent Joginstead. According to Haidan, that meant Brewer's Village had three to six days to prepare for an invasion. Dihana and Mayor Bransom agreed that he had to immediatly send the village's women and children up the coastal road to Anandale.

She'd had similar live "conversations" with mayors in Anandale, Grammalton, and Harford. They'd decided to send women and children up the coastal road while the men remained to fight. They'd head south into the bush if the Azteca army proved unstoppable.

Which it would. Eventually Capitol City would be packed with refugees who would be unable to fight a siege.

Something else gnawed at her. She didn't pay much attention to anyone on the street waving or saying hello. Her telegrapher had told her that her secrecy was pointless. Word buzzed on the street that an Azteca army had got past Mafolie. The announcement was supposed to be released by papers the next morning so that Dihana would have more time to coordinate with mayors throughout the Triangle Tracks before panic broached, so this was a problem.

Lines were starting to form at banks, people changing city notes for gold. Speculation was spreading, mutating, and turning dark.

The steam car lurched to a halt as a ragamuffin with an unbuttoned shirt waved them down. They had stopped in the middle of Baker's District, although Dihana hadn't seen any bakeries on this block since childhood.

Crowd noise one street over surged. People shouted. Glass broke.

"What's going on?" she asked while the ragamuffin caught his breath.

"We found a dead man," he said. "Sacrifice, Azteca-style, heart torn out and all."

They had stopped just outside Tolteca-town, where most Azteca immigrants clustered. Dihana's mouth dried as she saw a brown-skinned man stagger out from an alley holding a bloody rag to a gash in his head. "City people out in that street?" she asked the ragamuffin.

"People standing around, trying to get in to see the body. Word spreading."

Dihana tapped the driver on the shoulder. "Get back for more ragamuffins." She opened the door and got out. The driver looked at her. "Go. Now."

"Just four ragamuffin here," the ragamuffin standing by her said as the car hissed and groaned, then lurched away.

"Take me there."

It was the hair Dihana noticed. Fifty or sixty men with black, straight hair cut in a fringe across the forehead, clustered on the street around an abandoned building. They faced the crowd, their backs surrounding four ragamuffins who nervously held their rifles in a semiready position before a broken-in door.

"They found it inside this old store. Flies coming out got people suspicious." Xippilli, an Azteca nobleman Dihana knew well, pushed through his fellow men and approached Dihana. The Capitol City crowd gave them room. The words *prime* and *minister* fluttered through the crowd. "When we realized what we had, we sent for ragamuffins," Xippilli continued. "And the pipiltin"—Tolteca-town's Azteca nobility, Dihana knew—"ordered me to round up as many men as I could find to stand guard so nothing got meddled with. What should we do next?"

Dihana walked Xippilli back into the Azteca crowd and leaned in close. "What am I supposed to do, Xippilli? We offer Azteca—"

"Tolteca," Xippilli interrupted.

"—sanctuary in this city. Even despite the fact we know this allows spies in."

"We are Tolteca," Xippilli said. "Tolteca spurn the worship of the war god. It is only Quetzalcoatl who deserves our attentions. And not with people's lives. We left that behind. We ran from it. I climbed the great mountains myself, my child strapped to my chest, to leave that behind."

"I know that, Xippilli, I swear to you I understand. The Loa opposed me on this, many opposed me on this, but I worked hard to convince the city to allow Tolteca-town. But no matter what you choose to call yourself, *Tolteca* or *Azteca,* you came from over the Wicked Highs to live here. You were once Azteca, and that is all that matters to these people in the street right now. They're understandably suspicious, and nervous. And on top of all that, the news is breaking around the city that the Azteca have crossed over the mountains." Dihana had told the pipiltin herself the same night she'd found out. "I don't want to go in, I don't want to see this."

Xippilli turned and rested his back against brick, looking out at the murmuring crowd. Maybe a few hundred milled about right now, Dihana guessed, facing them as well, to Xippilli's fifty men and the five ragamuffins with rifles.

"What would you have us do, Prime Minister? Go back out into the open land? Where Jaguar scouts will find us? We face the same horror you face now. You now are in the nightmare we have feared ever since any one of us has slipped over the mountains for what we thought would be freedom." Xippilli sagged and looked down at the deteriorating cobblestone sidewalk.

"I will do what I can to help, Xippilli, but the solutions may be hard. This is bad. Both these things together, bad. I'll have to get Haidan, we'll need to coordinate a plan to patrol Tolteca-town."

"Do you have any idea who broke the rumor?"

Dihana shrugged. "Could have been anyone. A telegrapher, a newsman, a Tolteca."

Someone pushed up close to the Azteca cordon shouted, "What did they do to that man in there? We have a right to know what they did!"

"We don't know anything yet," Dihana shouted back at him. "Have some respect. Let the ragamuffins do their job."

"How raga go protect all of we if the Azteca live in the middle of everything?" someone else yelled.

"The same way they protect you from any other criminal," Dihana returned.

"We want justice!"

"You get justice by hunting down the man that did this," Dihana told the crowd. "Not by kicking out your neighbors. We don't even know if an Azteca did this." She ended the conversation by turning her back to the crowd and facing Xippilli.

Xippilli leaned closer. "Do you know for sure Azteca march at us?"

Dihana pulled back and stared at him. "What do you mean?"

"When you met with the pipiltin, you said Mongoose-General Haidan gave you the evidence that the Azteca were coming. Did you verify it with anyone else?"

Dihana's stomach churned, making her feel light-headed. She couldn't talk about her father's warnings about the Spindle, it would seem ridiculous. But, "Brungstun and Joginstead don't reply to any messages."

"Did they report an Azteca invasion before going quiet?" Xippilli's dark eyes seemed like dark wells. "Any raids by Jaguar scouts in Brewer's Village yet?"

She shook her head. "No."

"I will say this, and then hold my tongue. If I wanted to take over this entire city, with a smooth transition, I would snip the telegraph wires to the first two towns along the coastal roads, station patrols to stop anyone in them from walking up to Brewer's Village. Then I'd convince the prime minister to invite mongoose-men into the city to prepare for the invasion. And suppose there's a riot as a result of the Azteca rumor. I could get the prime minister to invite more mongoose-men in quickly. I would have them position themselves all over the city in the name of preventing rioting."

"If Haidan wanted the city he could take it," Dihana said. "He has thousands of mongoose-men to my hundreds of ragamuffins."

"I never named names. Haidan could be just as fooled as you are." The crowd's muttering pitched higher; a scuffle developed down at its end as more people joined and jostled for space.

"You know something I don't, Xippilli?" Dihana hissed.

"All I know is that the mongoose-men are incredibly talented." Xippilli remained calm, as if chatting about tea. "And Mafolie Pass is impregnable. The mongoose-men own the Wicked Highs, Dihana, trust me, I *personally* know how hard it is to get over. How did the Azteca do it in large numbers?"

Dihana shook her head. "Even if you're right . . . no. I can't consider this right now." Why was he trying to sow so much doubt in her mind? Was Xippilli a spy, trying to confuse her? Or maybe he was just right.

"The crowd is getting larger. We have retired warriors amongst us," Xippilli said. "Maybe you should deputize some of us."

"No. I can't afford to have a war start inside the city over that." The scuffling at the edge of the crowd increased: ten mongoose-men and a pair of ragamuffins arrived, yelling at people to move aside. "Xippilli, the man inside. What is he?"

"What do you mean?"

"You know what I mean."

Xippilli bit his lip. "He isn't Azteca."

"Prime Minister. Rubin Doddy." The first mongoose-man joined them and shook her hand. "We got a car coming in quick with ten more mongoose."

"What about ragamuffins?" Dihana asked.

"We nearest. Ragamuffin coming, just not here yet," Rubin said.

The crowd, now maybe five hundred up and down the street, filled the air with discontent. "There's a body in the shop. Give the ragamuffins what time they need to investigate. Then we need to wrap it up and get it out of here as soon as possible. Get your men to clear out this crowd."

"Heard." Rubin turned around and signaled his men. They fanned out. The car of promised extra mongoose-men steamed down the street, and ten more mongoose-men leapt out and added themselves to the cordon. The ragamuffins walked into the broken building.

"What about you, Prime Minister?" Rubin still stood next to her.

"Where is Haidan? I need to talk to him."

"Down the Triangle Tracks now, in Batellton."

"Doing what?" Dihana asked. He hadn't told her he'd leave the city.

Rubin looked at her if she were crazy. "Preparations. Prime Minister, the word is spreading throughout the city that something wicked happened in Tolteca-town." Too quick, Dihana thought. Far too quick. Most rumors were slower to spread. "Haidan didn't give orders for anything like this, but I think we can get more man out on every street corner—"

"No." Dihana knew what she was going to do. She steeled herself, projected authority, made the leap. "We're getting all the ragamuffins out on patrol."

"That don't make no sense," Rubin said. "How many ragamuffins you got?"

"Enough to let everyone know we're serious. Everyone knows the ragamuffins. For some they're family. For others, it's just the familiar uniform. We don't need outsiders patrolling the streets." Dihana looked out at the crowd. "But we need mongoose-men to lock down Tolteca-town. No one goes in, or out, unless at a checkpoint. Who do I have to talk to to get that started if Haidan isn't here?"

"Gordon is second-mongoose," Rubin said.

"Xippilli, come with me. We need to find pipiltin to come with us. We're going to quarter all the mongoose-men right here, in Tolteca-town, and get them off the Ministry's grounds."

"The city's going to explode," Xippilli said, and Rubin nodded in agreement.

"The ragamuffins will take bullhorns and read an announcement. We're going to distribute paper explanations. Tonight we're going to explain that the Azteca are coming, and that the Tolteca are helping by quartering the mongoose-men who will fight the Azteca army."

She stood in front of the two men and raised her eyebrows. They looked at each other, then Rubin whistled for the car, pointed out two mongoose-men, and leaned in. "My two best mongoose will ride with you. Get out quickly. When more come, we'll push them out. We will start securing the area. Good luck convincing Gordon."

Dihana pulled Xippilli into the car. One mongoose-man took the wheel and began pressurizing the boiler. The other sat next to her. "Keep low," he said. "You probably a target. Don't risk you own head."

She complied. Xippilli bent down and looked across at her. "I hope this works."

Dihana nodded.

She did too.

CHAPTER SIXTEEN

Pepper tracked his way through the bush in the stolen cotton garb of the higher nobles: thick, starched cotton, the inner sides layered with blue and fiery-red parrot feathers. He carried a round shield with leather fringes hanging from the bottom. He'd ripped off the gold decoration. Gold was universal currency, he could use it later.

He could barely see out of the heavily stylized wolf's-head mask. It hadn't been made to fit him, but it hid his dreadlocks, and the original owner didn't need it anymore. Yesterday Pepper had waited offshore until night before he landed. He had found the high-class warrior guarding the docks and killed him, then destroyed all the boats in the harbor with explosives taken from the Azteca's own stores.

Disguised as this warrior, Pepper had visited the town's center to find records. The Azteca loved documentation. They had a whole class of scribes dedicated to it. And the scribes were busy: all around Brungstun, Azteca lords were taking inventories of food supplies and farms. Some moved into the nicer houses, while the empty barracks at the end of the wharf had been filled with Jaguar scouts. Brungstun children milled about in pens surrounded by barbed wire.

Pepper found deBrun's address and lit all the records on fire.

He'd be damned if any Azteca used them to hunt any Brungstunners hiding from them still.

He killed three Azteca with their own macuahuitl on his way out, dashing their brains out against the whitewashed wall with the effective wedge-shaped clubs. Then he climbed up a wall in the nearest alley, walked over several roofs, and jumped back down to the ground.

He walked out of town unchallenged.

Fifteen minutes out of Brungstun, Pepper found the smoldering ruin of deBrun's house. He followed tracks from there to find a sacrificial stone in the middle of a cleared area not too far up the coastal road. The Azteca had sacrificed a few victims just before and during the attack on Brungstun, asking their gods for a good battle.

It was an odd scene, though. Several Azteca lay dead on the ground. One lay suffering from gunshot wounds.

"Great sir!" three warriors called out in Azteca when they saw him.

Though Pepper wore dark blue colors from the nobleman he'd killed, and they wore red, they looked to him as a superior. "Our priest was slaughtered yesterday like an animal by a one-handed savage. Some of our brothers have broken the orders to stay here. They chase him and his accomplice in the forest. May we have permission to join and hunt the *nopuluca*?"

Nopuluca: barbarian. Pepper grimaced behind his wooden mask. He slapped the macuahuitl he'd gained into the ground thoughtfully. He knew enough Azteca to understand what he heard, but he doubted he remembered enough to speak well. He'd last taken to learning it so long ago. He rubbed his throat, readjusting to speak Azteca.

"Gather before me," he told them.

Several frowned at his badly pronounced Azteca words and fractured grammar, but they obeyed. Pepper adjusted his pronunciation. "Describe to me about one-handed man."

An eager young warrior, looking to curry a lord's favor, spoke up. "A man with one hand killed them. We saw it from the clearing. He should honor the war god with his blood. Instead he runs. Our brothers ordered us to stay here and wait for orders, but we wish to chase the heathen."

How many one-handed men lived on the outskirts of Brungstun? Pepper wondered. The four warriors moved closer.

Time to act before they spread out enough to make this harder.

Pepper swung the macuahuitl in his left hand up with enough force to smash the nearest warrior's jaw into his skull. In the same breath Pepper fired into the group with his own gun, wading forward through the bewildered Azteca and swinging the macuahuitl in long bone-jarring arcs. Those that still stirred afterward, groping around in their own blood, he calmly executed with their own guns to save his bullets.

He saved one, wrapping a dropped net around the young man. The warrior flailed and tripped back against the sacrificial stone.

"*Tlatlauhtilia . . . ,*" he whispered. *I beg . . .* "Kill me now."

Pepper crouched next to him. "How many warriors here?" he asked in fractured Azteca.

The warrior shook his head. Pepper sniffed. He could torture the man, but many Azteca resisted torture well. This one looked young, inexperienced, so he would start with something easier. He looked the warrior in the eyes and pulled his right hand out of the netting to find a pulse.

Pepper took several deep breaths. "You number only in thousands, here to capture people for sacrifices?"

The fluttered eyelids, slight blush, negated the warrior's lying nod of agreement.

"Is this a . . . Flower War?" Pepper asked. Slight pause. Different Azteca regions, as far as he could tell from both ancient history and the tiny regional wars fought in the Azteca areas when he had last left Nanagada, waged ritual wars on each other to capture sacrificial victims. "Is this a small war?" Long pause. "A big war?"

The warrior smiled. "We will take this whole land as ours and rule it as ours. We will destroy your gods in Capitol City. We will take your machines and technologies, your—" He stopped as Pepper folded the warrior's fingers back almost flat with his wrist.

"Speak when I ask," Pepper growled. "Your warriors who move forward, tens of thousands?" That was on target. It was in the way the warrior's broad face allowed blood to heat it. All these things—flutters, unconscious gestures—told Pepper more about people than people often knew about themselves.

"Our gods command us. We march through towards your great city."

Pepper leaned close to the netting over the warrior's face. Black face paint had rubbed off onto the net's knots. "How did you get over the mountains?"

The warrior hesitated.

"By airship?" Pepper asked. No, he saw. "Boats?" Not that either. "Did you cross mountains somewhere?" The right direction. "Where?"

The Azteca ground his teeth. He would not answer this one.

Pepper pulled the man's hand forward and folded it into a fist. He cupped it in his own, large hands and squeezed. A cracking sound came from each of the Azteca's fingers as they snapped.

Both men locked eyes, not wavering. Pepper squeezed harder and kneaded until he got a whimper. "I destroy hands and feet. You will be cripple. No honor, no glory?" He wished he were more fluent in Azteca than this. "Your bones will be dust if you do not answer."

The Azteca groaned as Pepper squeezed again. "Tunnel," the warrior whispered. "Through the mountains."

"How long it take to make tunnel?"

"Many generations. The gods directed it. We obeyed."

"And Nanagada people don't know about this?"

"It is hidden from them. Their spies are few and are lied to."

Pepper dropped the man's hand and wiped the blood off his own on the grass. This was ugly. The Azteca didn't have a supply chain. He only saw warriors living off the land, pillaging for their food as they moved toward Capitol City. That was a huge gamble for the Azteca. They could starve before reaching Capitol City, could all likely die here. But many Azteca remained in Brungstun. If the Azteca kept each city and captured its supplies intact, and used the population as slave labor, they could set up a limited resupply system as they advanced up to the peninsula. Taking Capitol City would be almost impossible with an initial unsupplied mad dash, but this method would deliver the entire coast into Azteca hands. Bad news.

A grimmer thought was that the Teotl were most likely also hunting the *Ma Wi Jung*.

Three hundred years later those damn creatures were still carrying on their war against each other, with humans caught in the middle.

Pepper looked at the prints leading away from the sacrificial stone and into the jungle. "Time to think about catching up, John, isn't it?" Pepper said. The Azteca struggled, confused by the change in language. Pepper ripped the heavy mask off. It bounced in the grass. Behind the netting the warrior's eyes widened. Pepper slammed a macuahuitl down into the man's ribs.

"Die slowly." Pepper left the Azteca on the crude eagle stone gasping through a punctured lung. He followed tracks to a tree where a second pair of boots joined the original pair and then headed south. Together.

John had a friend. How interesting.

CHAPTER SEVENTEEN

A man born under the sign of Ocelotl, even if of nobility, could only struggle toward a better life through fasting, sleep deprivation, and the application of his intelligence.

So it was said.

When Oaxyctl's parents presented him as a newborn to the Calmecac chiefs at a sumptuous banquet in the heart of Tenochtitlanome, the chiefs asked his parents for his sign. Upon hearing it they gravely shook their heads.

"Children born under this sign grow to become thieves," they said. "If this child were female, we might offer you the honor of waiting until she grew hair to her waist, then place her head between two rocks and offer her to Tlaloc for a better rainy season."

Oaxyctl would not be a priest, or a judge, or a leader of warriors.

He attended the Telpochcalli instead, with dirty kids and commoners. They sang history and trained to become simple warriors. The instructors pricked his skin with thorns when he forgot his lessons.

When he grew old enough to fight, Oaxyctl left for a small village far away in Imixcoatlpetl's shadow, the Cloud Serpent's Mountains, known to most simply as the Great Mountains. Back then *nopuluca* lived on the Aztlan side of the Great Mountains. Oaxyctl captured many to gain respect, feathers in his hair, and eventually a wife.

The pipiltin of Aztlan then gave Oaxyctl the chance to become *quimichtin* and spy on the lands on the other side of Imixcoatlpetl. Since then his life had become a complicated mess of double spying, fear, blood, and long journeys over the Great Mountains. He'd turned in many spies he had once called friends. And then killed many mongoose-men who thought him a friend. And he'd repeated the cycle again in Brungstun to hunt for John deBrun.

Oaxyctl did not believe in curses, or unlucky life signs, but about now he was beginning to change his mind. Oaxyctl had once never believed in gods either. He'd assumed they were the results of men who dreamt too much. A suspicious man, Oaxyctl sneered at all mystical things. The priests in Aztlan smelled of death, were painted black, and had shaggy, snaggled hair soaked with the blood of the sacrificed. Their shredded earlobes and bitten lips caused Oaxyctl to avoid them. And what they did to their genitals with knotted ropes . . .

He'd thought them mad until the day the priests brought the chairs to his town. And inside them sat the ancient, pale, squinting gods.

So unhuman. So different. Oaxyctl shivered. If he'd been wrong about the gods, then maybe he was wrong about his life.

Maybe he needed to fast more, sleep less.

But the practical warrior in him told him that right now, those actions would lead to death. Better to stick with the application of his intelligence. And what did his intelligence tell him?

Something had worried Oaxyctl since he'd met the Teotl: the god's explanation that there were those who wanted John dead, no matter what.

Were there really other gods who might kill him for doing what he was doing as it was against *their* wishes? Did the gods argue often? He'd never heard such a thing. And how did he make sense of such a thing, him, Oaxyctl, just a mere human?

Oaxyctl wished that he'd had more time. Then he could have taken John and tortured him for the *Ma Wi Jung* secrets at leisure.

Gods. He'd barely rescued the man in time from the Huitzpochli offering, and that involved shadowing some very good Jaguar warriors and waiting for exactly the right moment. He'd prayed that it would work, offering blood from his cheeks even, that John could escape from the eagle stone as Oaxyctl struck the warriors down. He'd come so close to failing, he still shook slightly when he thought about it.

But he'd done it. Found the right man from talking to people in Brungstun, gotten to the right location, and done his god's bidding.

Oaxyctl's own countrymen still chased them. And Oaxyctl needed time to make the right potions and tools to force the truth out of deBrun. With the invasion happening, he knew time was something he didn't have.

Could he risk stopping, letting the warriors get to them, and claim he was one of them? Too risky. Suppose they killed deBrun in the process? The god said they had no orders to save deBrun, but rather to kill him.

The god *would not* like that to happen. Oaxyctl was sure he'd suffer if it did. He felt sick remembering how close deBrun had come to death.

Once deBrun released his secrets, Oaxyctl could return to Aztlan and forget this foreign wilderness in the gods' good graces. He wouldn't have to worry about whom he really spied for anymore. He could go back to a normal life. He missed having a wife.

He couldn't remember much about her; he had left many years ago to become a spy. By now she must have given him up for dead and have a new husband. Yet he still fantasized about that life. Two of them alone in a small home, cuddling by a stove fire and the small statue of a local pulque god on the wall, while a mountain fog rolled by at night.

He liked how soft women were, bringing flowers and scents into the environment. He hated mud, sticky sweat, blood, and long, long treks for his own life. He missed the way things had been, for a small time in his life when he lived on the foothills of the other side of the Wicked Highs.

John deBrun had been muttering about Joginstead and a bath under his breath, while every once in a while Oaxyctl caught the long-off look of mourning in the man's eyes.

They spent part of the early morning asleep under a tree, covered in twigs and leaves. Oaxyctl gave John jerky and dried fruit, and some water from his canteen. Both slept uneasily; John kept crying out and waking up sweating.

At noon they stretched and kept walking. But well before Joginstead, Oaxyctl veered off to the east even farther. They walked a good many miles before they came to the clearing Oaxyctl aimed for.

If John deBrun died before giving up information about the *Ma Wi Jung*, then Oaxyctl would die a horrible death. He knew this with certainty. And if any Azteca caught them, Oaxyctl could still not figure out how to guarantee that John would remain alive.

So he had chosen a different path.

Gaining himself more time.

Oaxyctl tramped through the clearing, knelt in the middle, and cleared off leaves and dirt to reveal trapdoors set into the ground. "We are here," Oaxyctl declared.

"But this isn't Joginstead," John said.

"I never said we were going to Joginstead. It is probably also occupied." Oaxyctl pulled the oak doors up with a grunt, then let them drop open on either side. He led John down the stone stairs of a mongoose-man depot known only to a few courier mongoose-men. Two of them lay dead back in Brungstun.

Oaxyctl felt for the controls set against the wall's corner, groping along in the dark. When he triggered the switches, air hissed and spit. A large hole opened above them; flush hangar doors slid aside despite the heavy weight of earth and vines carefully arranged over them. Dirt spilled down over the edges.

In the new light they could both make out a shapeless gray mass of an airship's unfilled bag. It hung in midair from ropes and nets fastened to the large cavern's underside. The Nanagadan military, *nopuluca* though they were, had some fascinating tools they'd taught Oaxyctl how to use when he'd trained with the mongoose-men once.

"We'll take this emergency mongoose-courier airship to Capitol City," Oaxyctl said. "First we need to fill it, though."

John deBrun nodded. Oaxyctl saw trust grow in the man's eyes.

Oaxyctl smiled.

With the help of spies in Capitol City, Oaxyctl could drug and take John somewhere to interrogate him. He could take the careful days he needed to slowly pull the information out of John while the Azteca warriors slowly made their way up the coast toward the peninsula.

Better dangers he knew in Capitol City than Azteca warriors here.

Oaxyctl wondered what it meant that he felt more comfortable among the Nanagadans than his own warriors.

Nothing, he told himself fiercely.

With a definite plan before him, though, for the first time in three days Oaxyctl relaxed somewhat.

He would accomplish his tasks. The gods would respect him yet.

Oaxyctl was not cursed.

CHAPTER EIGHTEEN

John watched as Oaxyctl checked the hoses leading to the gasbag, then followed them back to the cavern walls. Oaxyctl then spun the valves open. The hoses straightened and filled out, and after a slow hour the airship's bags started to visibly fill. The floppy lengths of fabric expanded and filled the cavern.

In the dusky light John cocked his head to look at the airship. Amazing. The cavern itself, a natural sinkhole, must have had its top shaped with dynamite, and the courier airship roped into its hidden hangar beneath the jungle clearing. Several netlike lengths of rope hung on the airship's dull-colored gasbag, just like rigging on a ship. Presumably to allow maintenance of the whole structure.

Oaxyctl ran around shutting valves. He yanked on small ropes leading up the sides of the hoses. They popped off with puffs and dropped away from the airship.

"Get on," Oaxyctl ordered.

"How?" John asked. The ground dropped away to darkness just a few feet in front of the steps leading in. John kicked a small pebble with his muddy boots. It jumped forward and disappeared, occasionally hitting a wall and bouncing. Finally a distant plop floated up and weakly reverberated around the cavern.

Oaxyctl pointed. A rope ladder ran from the side of one of the walls to the airship's undercarriage. "You first," he said as he looped his bundle of spears over his back.

John put a hand to the cavern wall. The rock chilled his fingers as he slowly walked along the edge toward the rope.

"Are you sure this is secure?" John looked out to the end of the rope ladder attached to the airship. The ledge beneath his feet slimmed down to mere inches.

The cavern echoed their voices back and forth between its walls.

"You scared?" Oaxyctl asked.

"No." John looked at the rope ladder. It rose upward at a slight angle and swayed slightly as a gust from above played with the airship. "I've been on rigging like this. But it was *my* rigging."

He crouched and grabbed a rung. Why this angle? Climbing straight up presented no problem, but here the ladder lay almost horizontal. John studied it for a second, well aware of the different ways the hook on his left hand would get in the way.

To lope across the unsteady ladder he kept his hook folded into his chest, straining across with just one arm and his legs. He only missed a rung with a foot once and instinctively hooked a rung with his left arm to prevent falling. He reached the undercarriage fairly quickly, grabbed the bamboo side rails, and pulled himself into the small basket.

The whole undercarriage was bamboo, he noticed.

He turned around to help Oaxyctl, watching the five-foot-long spears on the mongoose-man's back warily.

"What is that anyway?" John asked about the long handle with the notch at the end. "I haven't seen anything quite like that."

Oaxyctl took the spears off his back. He used the leather strap to tie them to a bamboo rail. "Atlatl. You launch darts with it. It triples the length of your throw."

He busied himself securing his pack. Then he used the cloth straps on the chair to buckle in. John copied him, though the buckle eluded him at first, as he had only one hand. Once he was strapped in, John looked up along the dirty fabric half a foot over his head.

A wooden panel with brass dials and knobs swayed from the undercarriage's struts above Oaxyctl's head. Hoses and pipes led away from it.

At the top of the stairs the airship had looked huge. Up close, all John could see above him was the dark expanse of airtight canvas, the light playing off the varnish over its side. All around the cavern, menacing dark edges loomed close, lit by the gap in the earth just big enough to fit the airship through.

Hopefully they wouldn't hit anything on the way out.

Oaxyctl shifted, causing the undercarriage to squeak. Even though apparently designed for two, their thighs were still mashed close to each other. John's pants had rips in several places, and it looked as if Oaxyctl had cut slits in his that allowed him to run faster.

"Ready?" Oaxyctl asked.

John nodded.

Oaxyctl held a box with a single switch on it. A wire ran from it all the way to a cavern wall. He flipped the switch up and threw the box over the side. It clanked against the rocky sides.

Sixteen ropes held the airship down. Several groaned from the strain of keeping the lighter-than-air vehicle tethered. They now snapped backward like whips in reverse.

The airship rose into the air. The cavern lip moved past them and gave John a glimpse of the clearing once more. Then they rose over the trees, the wind blowing them into the highest branches, where startled monkeys howled at them in protest.

A hot air gusted, free of the shade below. The airship skipped, then rose over a green sea that stretched before them, rolling all the way to the horizon's edge until it met the blue skies.

Oaxyctl leaned back after loosening the straps some. He grabbed a wooden handle on the end of a string and started yanking at it. Once, twice, three times.

John craned around to look.

Behind the undercarriage was a large wooden propeller blade with a flap behind it. Just like the propeller and rudder of a fast steamship, John thought. He'd seen a design like that in Capitol City. Oaxyctl yanked once more, and the engine roared to life.

John recognized the stench quickly enough. He turned around.

"Alcohol?" he yelled over the engine.

Oaxyctl nodded. He grabbed a lever with a polished brass and cherry inlaid knob between his legs. When John looked backward again, the large flap behind the propeller waggled, then turned all the way to one side.

"It doesn't have too much fuel," Oaxyctl said. "And we don't have enough power to fight the wind. But it can help guide us."

The airship slowly changed direction, though the wind still blew them off course, and Oaxyctl kept looking out at the sun to line them up properly. They were getting blown back toward the Wicked Highs to the west, not going northeast toward Capitol City.

"Will we be able to make it to Capitol City?" John asked as a cloud of blue-and-gold parrots burst from the treetops to flee before them.

"There is a great wind high over the Great Mountains that blows east. We must climb higher into the air to find it. If your ears hurt, you pretend to chew." The airship rose faster. "We don't have air tanks with us, so watch your breath. We must be careful not to choke."

John settled farther back into his seat. The horizon seemed to move farther back, but at the same time he could see more of the land all around him. A curl of smoke in the distance rose from Joginstead.

The next time he leaned over the bamboo rail and peered down, John sucked in his breath. He could no longer see branches, just a smooth carpet of green.

"How high are we?" he asked.

"Very high," Oaxyclt said. "High enough that if you fall, maybe you'd have a few seconds to flap your hands hard and pretend to fly."

John didn't find that funny.

They gained height slowly, still getting blown sideways and west. Oaxyctl began to turn the airship to face the mountains. John frowned. The Wicked Highs rose, an impassable wall before them. The air rushed them toward the jagged peaks and valleys. John could see where the trees stopped and bare rock poked into the air.

"How much have you flown machines like this?" John asked. They weren't too far up that he couldn't look down and see that they were moving quickly over the ground toward the Wicked Highs.

"Enough to know what I'm doing," Oaxyctl said.

The air played with them. John's stomach lurched as the airship dropped down, then rose up. It shook several more times, the air stirring them up as they approached.

"It will get rougher," Oaxyctl said.

And it did. One drop, the airship being shoved down against its will, almost convinced John he would die dashed against the side of the mountains in this contraption.

"Just hold on." Oaxyctl spun dials on the panel above him. Hoses leading from thick tanks lashed to the carriage's underside hissed. The airship rose faster. "Near these mountains at this time," Oaxyctl explained loudly, "the winds seem to be sucked in just above the surface of the land. Then they rise right up the side of the mountain, and then higher in the air they go the other way. We can use that."

The winds *were* changing, bearing their airship up the mountain's side. This was like sailing, in a way, John thought. But you could go up and down as well.

Oaxyctl jockeyed them higher, and when they rose as high as the Wicked Highs' top peaks, the wind changed and they flew quickly eastward, as Oaxyctl had predicted. So now they were sweeping in the right direction:

mostly east. Eventually they needed to turn north to aim for Capitol City, but at least they were being blown away from the Azteca.

Everything smoothed out, and as they flew away from the mountains, Oaxyctl stopped the engine.

Off to the north by the coast, a thick pall of smoke rose. A burning Brungstun. John looked away from it with burning eyes, looking east at the long expanse of thick-jungled land.

There was hope in this direction.

CHAPTER NINETEEN

John watched tall clouds heavy with water drop down toward the airship, blocking out light. Waves of chilly wind gusted over John and Oaxyctl and shook the airship. They both shivered in the undercarriage. Compared to the massive clouds that spread in all directions and towered up into the sky, they were nothing more than a small dot.

It rained softly for an hour. Rivulets trickled down the sides of the airship to form a miniature waterfall of concentrated raindrops that soaked them. John looked up at the dripping panel above Oaxyctl and hoped someone had waterproofed it.

Eventually the steady drenching ceased. Water randomly dripped down off the gasbag to fall far down to the ground. John shook himself to get the pockets of water on his lap off and kept shivering.

"Will you be okay?" Oaxyctl asked.

"It's cold," John said.

Oaxyctl nodded. He adjusted dials and the airship lowered. "I can't go too far down or we'll lose our wind. But let's warm up."

The sun appeared: long shafts of a welcome golden light beamed at the ground as the shower clouds dissipated. Oaxyctl maneuvered them low enough that the cold didn't pierce John's skin to his bones. The wind wasn't as strong. John couldn't tell for sure, but it looked as if they were moving over the ground at a more leisurely pace.

If he had a sextant, he could tell for sure, though the beginnings of a mental map were suggesting itself to his mind's eye, as it usually did whenever John traveled. He looked around for anything he could adapt to make sightings with, but saw nothing. He took off his shirt and wrung it out over the edge, then laced it to the bamboo handrail to dry off. The lowest edge of the gasbag's rope net swung near him.

With a mighty shiver John wrapped his arms around himself and rubbed his skin real hard to warm up.

"Food?" Oaxyctl offered. He opened his pack and dug around. Oaxyctl had more jerky. But he also had some chewy, stale johnnycake and a small jar of honey. They dipped the johnnycake in the honey as if it were dessert and sipped at the canteen as they passed over a swatch of land shaped in squares. Farmland out in the middle of the jungle. Some group forging into the virgin land.

"Do you think about your family much?" John asked, looking out for some familiar landmark. Right now every hour in the wind was an hour away from the coast most familiar to him.

"My wife." The wind lessened and Oaxyctl twisted dials. Hoses hissed. "I think about her." They slowly rose. The wind picked back up.

"My wife's name was Shanta." It hurt John to use the word *was*. He realized he had started to bottle up the black scar, his loss, into the middle of himself. Words like *was* were a first step.

What scared John was how easy it came to him. Some long-forgotten instinct allowed him to cauterize his emotions. What kind of person could do that as a matter of fact? Someone who had lived a rough life, John thought. Maybe that was why he had no memories of it.

He shivered. Not because of cold, but a sense of dread that settled in on him. A small figment of the past, and not returning in some hazy, forgotten dream.

"Necahual," Oaxyctl said, after the long moment's silence.

John shook himself. "I'm sorry?"

"Necahual was my wife's name. It's a common one. It means 'survivor.'" Oaxyctl smiled. "And for her, appropriate. She could sniff out positions that would help me earn respect with a second sense I admired. I wonder sometimes what she is doing now."

John smiled as well. It was hard to picture the hardened warrior, once bloodthirsty worshiper of human sacrifice, as having a family life.

"Do you have children?" John asked.

"Children . . ." Oaxyctl paused to check the dials above him. He cleared his throat. "No." He bit his lip. John wondered what emotions Oaxyctl struggled with. "Didn't have time for children before I had to cross the Great Mountains."

"I'm sorry."

"So am I." Oaxyctl dug around in his pack and pulled out a dirty blanket. His fingers turned white as he pulled the knot loose that bound the blanket into a small, tight package. "Here. Wrap this around your neck and head, it should keep you warm while we fly."

John did so, then chuckled.

"What?" Oaxyctl asked.

"You suddenly seem to have a soul."

Oaxyctl looked at him. "After saving your life, John deBrun, it would make no sense to let you die."

John blinked and bit his lower lip. "True. I owe you much." He settled into his seat as best he could. More questioning advice from his deepest instincts bubbled up. Did he really trust this man?

Yes. Of course.

Okay, the tiny instinct guided him. Next he needed shelter, water, food, sleep. *Act strongly only after sleep.* The mind without sleep is not geared for survival, he thought to himself.

The words and concepts made sense.

"Would you mind if I took a nap?" John asked.

Oaxyctl shook his head.

They flew on into the clear skies, moving with the wind over the land. Occasionally a bump would force John to unconsciously grab something with his good hand.

Something shook John awake. His eyes fluttered open, and he realized that his good hand clutched the straps holding him in. They chafed hard against his chest.

The airship dropped suddenly, shaken by the air. John felt as if his chest had been shoved under several feet of water; he had to suck at the air to get rid of the suffocating feeling.

"What's going on?" he asked. Wind buffeted them again.

Oaxyctl had a strained look on his face. "We're being followed."

John looked around. Many miles behind them a larger craft followed, though John squinted to make it out. Oaxyctl had sharp eyes.

"I've climbed as high as I dare," Oaxyctl said. "I have some length on them, but they gain on us."

"Why don't you use the engine?"

"It won't do us much good, not enough fuel, and we need that fuel to navigate when we get lower to the ground."

"Damnit, what *do* we do?"

Oaxyctl tapped a dial. "For now we try going higher."

The airship lay over on its side like a ship as more wind hit them. Oaxyctl led the lighter-than-air machine even higher in search of faster winds. John hoped he could handle that sort of tossing.

And not pass out for lack of air.

CHAPTER TWENTY

The Azteca airship chasing them looked larger than their own courier airship. John guessed its gasbag to be easily twice the size of theirs. Highly stylized terra-cotta-colored feathers ornamented the nose, and a pair of propellers jutted out from the sides of the canopy.

Three sharp cracks spat through the air. John instinctively ducked, then looked upward.

Oaxyctl nodded. "They're trying to drop us out of the sky. They don't want us to get north with any reports on where they are." Oaxyctl turned around and yanked on the cord. The motor coughed and spluttered, but did not start. "We're too high. We need to drop our altitude."

More shots pierced the wind's low roar. Oaxyctl grimaced and worked a lever. John heard hissing, not from the hoses, but from farther up on the gasbag. They dropped.

John turned around and looked. The Azteca airship followed.

The sound of wind passing them picked up, and John's stomach flip-flopped. They were falling fast.

"How much air did you let out?" John asked.

"Helium." Oaxyctl twisted dials and the hoses leapt to life. Condensation ran along the bottom of the black rubber tubes leading under the carriage to the tanks strapped underneath. Oaxyctl yanked on the cord behind him again. Once, twice, three times. On the fourth try the alcohol engine cleared its throat and groggily roared to life.

Oaxyctl pushed the lever throttle on the panel above him as far forward as he could. They both turned around to look through the blur of the propeller. "Where'd he go?" Oaxyctl peered around.

John looked up at the stained canvas above him. Oaxyctl followed his gaze. "Damn."

They heard another series of shots. A bullet whizzed past, too close. Oaxyctl unbuckled the straps holding him into his seat.

"What are you doing?" John asked.

"Going up the side to see where they are."

John shook his head. "You have to fly this thing." They'd fallen far out of the sky, and even with more gas in the airship, he could feel them still dropping. He yawned to pop his ears. "Do we have a gun of any sort?"

"There is no way I'll let you go up there." Oaxyctl pointed at John's hook. "I don't know who's more dangerous, you or them."

John grabbed a strap on his wrist and popped it off. He ignored the smell of unwashed skin as he pulled the rest of the straps loose to remove his hook.

"You could die," Oaxyctl said.

"We stand the best chance of surviving this way." John tried to keep the nervousness out of his voice. Heights never bothered him. But he'd never been on rigging in the middle of the sky.

And what was in Oaxyctl's deep, calculating eyes? John couldn't tell. But after furrowing his thin eyebrows, Oaxyctl nodded. "Here." He reached down beneath his seat and forced open a first aid box. He pulled out a flare gun and a cartridge of flares.

John wrapped the gun and ammo in his shirt and tied the bundle in on it-self with a knot. "Just don't make any sudden movements, okay?"

Oaxyctl nodded. He didn't look happy about this in the slightest. John would have thought anyone would be relieved to stay in the undercarriage, but Oaxyctl looked more nervous than John did.

John unstrapped himself from the chair. He wrapped a foot around the rail and leaned out. He looked down, saw the world far below his knees, and looked right back up at the distant and safe horizon. He grabbed the rope net swaying from the gasbag with the outstretched fingers of his right hand.

John held his breath and wrapped his good wrist around the thin rope. He hopped forward and hung in the air by one securely wrapped hand.

He let his legs dangle out and pushed his left arm up through netting un-til he hung from his elbow. Then with his right, John pulled himself up. Once he had his legs hooked into the netting, he could scramble up; he'd done this on ships' masts without a hook before.

John followed the pregnant curve of the airship up toward the sky.

The wind rushing past the sides of the machine pulled at him, but it didn't tug hard enough to startle him. What did make him jump were the sounds of three more gunshots. John crabbed his way along the netting and looked up to see the Azteca airship above them. Someone leaned over the side to point a rifle.

John flattened himself as close to the varnished canvas as he could. He wrapped his legs around the netting and untied his shirt.

Years of sailing had taught him to gauge the distance without a second thought. The Azteca sharpshooter, used to stable ground, couldn't aim accurately enough to hit them yet, thanks to the swaying and wind.

The Azteca airship, though, kept trying to drop down closer for an easy shot.

John laid the flare gun against his forearm to aim it as best he could. It looked small and not very accurate, but he'd used something similar to fire ropes to other ships. He didn't fire yet; he waited, getting a feel for the wallow of the airship. Just like at sea. The Azteca airship, above and slightly behind them, sank even closer. John squinted, waited for the great mass of fabric and gas beneath him to shift, and fired.

He quickly snapped the gun open and emptied the spent cartridge. It spun off with the wind down toward the distant ground.

Nothing happened. He'd missed. Yes, he saw the flare well over both airships, shining and smoking its way slowly back to ground.

John slid another flare in, snapped the gun shut, and fired again. They had given him their belly, and he took advantage by aiming for the tanks slung to the midsection of the undercarriage.

The warrior leaning over the edge started craning around. Looking for John. The Azteca aimed several more shots, but if he couldn't hit the airship, John guessed only a fluke shot would hit him. So he stayed carefully wrapped around the netting and fired again.

A fireball exploded out of the side of the Azteca airship. One of the engines caught fire and exploded, the propeller spiraling fire as it fell down through the air.

"Got them!" John yelled.

He opened the gun, slid in another flare, and fired at the Azteca gasbag. And then again. That was the last flare, but he saw it melting through a section of the gasbag.

The fire quickly leapt along the entire undercarriage. One of the warriors jumped from the edge. Spread-eagle, his pants on fire, he screamed as he dropped past John's airship. Up above, the Aztecan machine staggered in the air as numerous holes appeared in the bag. It dropped. Slowly at first, then quickly.

Shit.

John scrambled down the netting. He dropped the flare gun out into the air, not wanting to try holding on to it with only one good hand. He folded his legs around netting and let go with his hand, falling to swing upside down, his head level with the bamboo rail.

"Go go go go," he yelled at Oaxyctl. "Go right! They're coming down on us."

Oaxyctl swore in his own language, a long fluid series of vowels, then he spun dials. John jackknifed his whole body and swung out from under the airship as best he could to look up.

Flames and smoke.

Something struck the top of their airship and screamed. The whole thing shook. John tensed his leg muscles as he swung back and hit the side of the airship. An Azteca warrior slipped down the side of the netting, grabbing for anything but not succeeding.

He fell down toward the ground. Though from John's inverted point of view, it looked as if he fell upward. John pulled himself upright, still watching.

Things took forever to fall all the way down to the ground, John thought, waiting until the Azteca disappeared into the green. Oaxyctl finally coaxed the speed he needed from the airship, and they aimed down at the ground to pick up speed. John couldn't tell if his imagination was playing tricks on him, but he saw ripples race across beneath the netting.

They couldn't let out that much gas.

Could they?

No, the undercarriage swung violently as the airship tilted. They'd been struck. Hoses hissed loudly as Oaxyctl filled them with gas again. It sounded as if he'd spun the valves open as far as they would go.

They rose into the sky, now. John watched the flaming wreck of the Aztecan airship fall quickly away beneath them. As they rose, he gave himself time to let out the breath he'd been holding.

But even then he only had time for a breath before Oaxyctl yelled at him. "Check for fire!"

John unhooked his legs and scrambled up toward the top of the airship.

After several more panicked minutes, John found only smoldering netting. He used his shirt to beat it out. Once he was sure it wouldn't reignite, John made his way back down.

When John clambered into the undercarriage, hanging on with a single hand and swinging his feet in, he found that Oaxyctl did not look relieved.

"There isn't any fire," John reported.

"No," Oaxyctl said. "But we lost a lot of helium getting out of that. It will be only a matter of time now before we have to land."

John strapped himself into his chair. The once creaky and unsafe-seeming undercarriage now felt like firm ground compared to scampering around on the netting.

"How long do we have?" John asked.

"Maybe a few hours."

John looked up at the material over his head. "Is it still safe to fly, then?" he asked nervously, the image of the large Aztecan airship plummeting to the ground still strong in his head.

Oaxyctl nodded. "I will fly it until the last moments. Then we land. And hopefully we live."

Hopefully? John looked over. He grabbed the straps holding him in. At least they were far away from the advancing Azteca. A small consolation, but he would take it.

"Any landing we make that we walk away from," the Aztecan said, "will be a good landing." Then he muttered to himself, "I truly was born under an unlucky sign."

CHAPTER TWENTY-ONE

Oaxyctl had taken the airship as high into the clear sky as he could get it with the remains of the gas in the tanks strapped to the underside of the bamboo carriage. John noticed that they hadn't climbed high enough to pick back up the strong winds that would take them all the way to Capitol City. They drifted slowly, like a ship without sails.

Fortunately they still drifted toward the east. One of the two moons was out, barely visible in the daylight.

Oaxyctl swigged water from his canteen and looked over the edge. "Look at that." He pointed. A brown, arcing scar in the earth.

John leaned forward. He knew where they were. "It's called Hope's Loss."

Oaxyctl folded his right leg underneath himself. "Hope's Loss?"

"You've never been to Capitol City?"

"No." Oaxyctl shook his head. "But I know much about it. I have friends there."

"Twenty-two years ago I journeyed through the bush to Capitol City with a friend of mine. Edward. A mongoose-man. A damn good one. He wanted to investigate Hope's Loss. He wanted to see if the stories were true."

"Which stories?"

"Ah." John picked up his hook. "You haven't lived around here long enough." He slid the cup over his wrist and began to strap the hook on. The leather edges bit into his sore skin. He avoided Oaxyctl's curious gaze, lowering his eyebrows. "Supposedly, during the last days"—John grunted and levered the hook on—"evil beings rained rocks on this land, killing many people. It wasn't stopped until all machines of destruction, on all sides, were destroyed. There are other more fantastic stories, but there is one thing they all have in common." John leaned over and looked at the scars. "They say the land here around Hope's Loss is poisoned, for nothing will grow there."

Oaxyctl also leaned over and looked around. "And is it true?"

John nodded. "I held four of my friends in my arms as they died, just weeks after walking through there." John took a deep breath and let it out. "Edward, he always remained sick after that. Just the two of us arrived in Capitol City. As the people said, a poisoned land."

"Were you sick?"

"For some reason, I've always been fine."

"Lucky."

"Yes." John leaned back against his wicker seat. "Very."

"There are similar stories in Aztlan, on the other side of the Wicked Highs. About cursed lakes that are perfectly round. People from villages that try to settle them, once a generation or so, die. We share a lot of similar history and destiny."

John looked over Oaxyctl. "Tetol?"

"Teotl," Oaxyctl corrected.

"Those beings were what the legends say caused most of the trouble. They rule your people, they tried to destroy my people—"

"My 'people,' as you called them," Oaxyctl said, "are varied. Some of them know no better, as all society is dictated by the Teotl and the priesthood. They know only what is told to them: that only blood can appeal to the gods, only blood brings the food, and only blood ensures your soul's survival into the afterworld. And even then, many only follow this out of fear from the Teotl and instruments of the priests. There are the Tolteca who have fled over the mountains to live here, and there are also people like me, Azteca who have joined the mongoose-men to fight the people that were once my own."

"I'm sorry," John said.

"All our ancestors have been cast down from greatness. That is all we know for sure. All else is confused and muddied, because the Teotl, my people, your people, and the Loa that the Teotl have sworn to destroy are all in conflict. And you and I, John, are just tiny drops in that ancient storm."

The airship had lost height, but it looked as if they would pass well over the scarred land.

"Okay." Oaxyctl's outburst surprised John. He kept what was on his mind silent: no matter the madness of the circumstances, or history, for him nothing justified the pillaging and disregard for life the Azteca brought to Nanagada.

Nothing.

Oaxyctl guided the ponderous lighter-than-air machine down toward the long, rolling upper canopy of Nanagada's deep inner jungle. He started the engine as the wind pushed them backward.

"Do you see a clearing of any sort?" he asked, after several minutes of scanning the horizon.

"No clearing," John said.

"Damn." Oaxyctl looked up at the dials on the wooden panel over his head and bit his lips, seeming to wish for more lift. "We should land now, while we still float. Who knows when it will begin to fall."

He aimed them at a lower section of trees, and they sputtered along. Now, as John looked down, he could perceive breaks in the steady stream of green beneath the canopy. Oaxyctl leaned over, shifting the bamboo undercarriage, as he appraised the area.

"This is as good as anything," he said.

John nodded.

"Hang on then." Oaxyctl pushed the levers by the side of his seat, forcing the whole motor-mounting behind them to squeak and swivel upward. The airship tilted down, slowly, and then Oaxyctl gunned the engine. The airship settled down toward the trees.

The top branches, thin and laden with rich green leaves, brushed the undercarriage. It sounded like sand underneath a skiff. Only it got louder as they sank in between the branches and leaves. The soft sifting transformed into a violent scratching. A large limb snapped. The snapping continued. Like firecrackers.

The airship came to a stop.

"Can you reach anything?" Oaxyctl asked.

John looked around at the bowed branches poking through the gaps of the undercarriage. The nearest branch, one of the stronger ones that had stopped the airship, looked large enough to hold his weight. "Yes. You?"

Oaxyctl unstrapped himself. His actions were careful, he didn't move any faster than he needed. He moved to a crouch and picked up his pack and spears. "You will have to go first," he told John.

John fumbled at the straps. Steady, he told himself, reaching out. He grabbed the edge of the branch with his good hand. Then he slung his hook out over into the branches and hopped off. The branch bowed down, a good four or five feet below the undercarriage. John arched his back and got his feet up around the branch and crawled his way upside down toward the trunk. He grunted and pulled himself onto the crook and leaned his back against the bark.

"Okay, I'm here," he called out.

Oaxyctl swung off. The branch bowed again. The branch cracked. Oaxyctl looked startled and pulled himself up as quickly as he could. John gave him a hand up onto the crook. Far below them the ground peeked out from between the tiniest cracks in leaves, where the sun turned into hazy shafts of light that penetrated the cool shadows.

"It'll be hard to see the sun once we are below the trees," John said. "Do you know where we are?" John's highly visual internal map was beginning to build a picture for him.

"Not really, but that's okay." Oaxyctl lowered himself down to the next branch. John hung by his hook from an overhead branch and grabbed Oaxyctl's hand. The mongoose-man half-turned. "What?" he snapped.

"Watch your step."

The branch beneath Oaxyctl's leather boot crumbled away in a puff of rotted dust. It smashed down through the leaves, shaking loose drops of condensation, seeds, and dirt, which all trickled down through the air in a sifting shower.

"Thank you." Oaxyctl swung over to another branch. John followed him down, blinking as everything got dimmer and dimmer.

Oaxyctl paused to notch a dart into his atlatl. With a burst of energy he whipped the dart at the gasbag, puncturing it.

"That will keep it from getting into the air again," he explained, "now that our weight is off of it."

The airship, without them in it, had been struggling to rise again.

At the base of the tree Oaxyctl took out a compass, oriented himself to north by the needle, and shifted his pack and spears. "We're much further away than I wanted to be. We need to keep moving; our airship will be visible if any other Azteca airships are close and saw all that and are hoping to catch us."

He struck off, and John followed. "Would we make that much of an important target?"

Oaxyctl shrugged. "If we were an airship that had taken photographs showing the size and details of the Azteca army, and of exactly where they are, it might be worth their time to consider sending another airship and small group of warriors to find us."

Good point. John picked up the speed of his walk.

More walking, he thought, brushing aside a prickly vine draped in front of him. But in the right direction.

North to the city.

CHAPTER TWENTY-TWO

The tracks stretched on for miles, cutting a swath through the muggy green land as they headed down a gentle hill toward the end of the northern peninsula of Nanagada. The sun left a band of mist that hung over everything, giving the edge of the forest by the gray wooden trestles a gloomy feel.

Tizoc stood by the edge of the tracks, waiting for the mile-long train to thunder past. Pieces of gravel shook down the sides of the sharp slope. The wheels clicked steadily along.

Then silence fell, the last cab rushing off into the distance. Tizoc adjusted the gray cloak he wore to disguise himself and continued on.

Huehueteotl, the ancient god that commanded Tizoc's culpilli, the ancient council of leaders, had given him this task in person. As tradition demanded, ever since the Flower Wars were first formalized thousands of years ago, a warrior-priest would go before the main army to the city about to be captured and ask for its surrender, its gods, its gold, and its subordination to the superior forces of the Azteca.

Tizoc felt pride that he could walk so calmly toward his death.

He crested the gentle hill and looked out over the tracks. They led gently down toward a great hill of rock that blocked the peninsula.

Not rock, Tizoc realized, but Capitol City.

He stood and slowly realized what he looked at. This "city" of the soon-to-be-conquered was no city. The walls, giant, spread like hills across the entire peninsula.

How many people lived in there? The dazed Tizoc guessed half a million. The rock face rose into the air, and he could see embankments, even a road, along it. To think that his people could not capture this city would have been sacrilegious, so Tizoc told himself this would be a fine jewel for the crown of the empire, this Capitol City.

He had a job to do.

Tizoc shifted a gnarled and muddy walking stick to his left hand, threw off his dull gray cloak, and walked forward.

They stared at him. He stood outside the massive walls, by the vendors and stores along the street that curved along the front of the city. They stared at his feathers, the paint that covered his whole body, and the designs woven into his clothing.

Some knew what Tizoc was.

Tizoc looked at the traitors who lived in Capitol City, the ones calling themselves Tolteca, straight in the eye. These cowards who had run away from the true land to hide here, they would be first on the altar after the city fell. Their blood would start the new reign.

He walked forward in the street, until enough people stopped and stared, and the men with tangled hair down to their shoulders stepped forward with rifles.

"I am the priest Tizoc," he shouted out loud. "I am *Azteca,* and I come with words for your commanders and culpulli." He pointed at the warriors with their guns. "Take me now to your chiefs and priests. I am to deliver the terms of your surrender."

A wave of whispers rippled through the crowd along the side of the street. Heads turned to face him. Someone spat into the street at him.

"Who you think you is?" yelled a woman selling yams piled in a cart across the street.

Tizoc repeated his words. A rock smacked the back of Tizoc's head before he could finish. He fell to his knees, but didn't grab the wound. It throbbed, but he let it bleed freely down his back. A gift for Huehueteotl, he whispered.

A small crowd rushed in on him. Tizoc did not try to cover his face from the blows. He tasted blood, felt it trickle down the sides of his neck.

They broke his arm and then a leg by stomping on it.

I am for you, he told the sky. Any real civilization would have taken him to their leaders, talked the terms, and arranged either a tithing or a proper battle. Not this savagery.

But he expected little of them, as they kicked him across the street. Bones cracked.

Their plainly dressed warriors moved in between the crowd, pushing people aside forcefully to get to Tizoc. They used the butts of their guns to knock the most vicious aside. Tizoc found himself dragged by his broken arms across the road. He could barely see. He wished he could whimper.

He was forced to his knees. Black, polished boots hit the ground, throwing dust into Tizoc's eyes. A hand grabbed his chin, and Tizoc's broken jaw seared the inside of his throat.

"We are mongoose-men. You have terms?"

Tizoc worked his mouth, blood draining out the corners. "Are you the leader of the mongoose?"

They shook their heads. "Tell us your message anyway," they said.

Tizoc sighed. He would not even have the honor of delivering the message to the right person.

"Thirty percent of your gold, your food, your machines, and your young will be delivered as a tithe to Huey Tlatoani, the Great Speaker, and his gods."

The man in front shook his head. The solid locks shook against each other and his thick shoulders.

"I will die before that happens," he said sincerely.

Tizoc nodded. "That is how it shall be." His vision faded. Huehueteotl, honor me.

Huehueteotl?

He sighed one last bloodied breath.

PART TWO

CAPITOL CITY

CHAPTER TWENTY-THREE

The train slowed to approach the tracks leading into Capitol City's gaping tunnels. The chuffing echoed, and Haidan caught a glimpse of a family's washing hung up to dry in a balcony several hundred feet over the top of the train. Things looked more crowded than when he'd left. More stalls crammed the tracks. More weary faces looked back at him.

"I forget how good it feel to be back in the city," the old lady across from him said. "Thirty years I been gone. Now me family sending me up the tracks to be safe in the city. Azteca coming, you know?"

Haidan looked over at her and the dinged-up suitcases by her feet. The car was packed with people heading for the city. And their luggage. Crammed in every bit of free space, spilling out into the middle of the aisle. A fight had broken out at the Batellton ticket office over the last few tickets. He found it annoying that Dihana hadn't been able to keep things silent just a bit longer. Now the mongoose would find travel more difficult.

Feet thudded onto the roof above him. Daring boys raced along the top of the train shouting at each other, thin voices pitched up against the sudden hoot of the train's whistle.

So much energy.

He looked out at the smooth rock. If ever there was proof of the past we lost, reflected Haidan, it was here in this great stone monstrosity of a city, hollowed deep under the rock, raised over with buttresses and walls and courts, all created by the mysterious and powerful machines wielded by the old-fathers. There was nothing else like Capitol City in Nanagada, no town, no village, nothing. And Nanagadans couldn't create another Capitol City.

Not for a few generations yet, he thought. Maybe one day, if Dihana's Preservationists kept up their work.

And if they survived the Azteca.

"Final stop for number thirty-three engine," the ticket-taker yelled as he walked down the aisle. He sounded as if he'd come in from a town outside of the tracks, his inflection thicker than most in the city. "Capitol City Station Four. It about five o'clock. Thank you and make sure you step careful out between the car."

Brakes screeched, metal on metal, slowing them down as the smooth tunnel walls turned into a rock platform. Ticket coves lined the walls, and Nanagadans of varying skin colors, religions, and regions were leaving the other trains that had just come in under the watchful eye of ragamuffins and mongoose-men. No one was getting back on the trains to leave. Steam floated up from under the cars and obscured the jostling crowds. Haidan stood up, briefcase held tight in both hands.

"Mommy, Mommy," a young child screamed, pushing through the passengers with his elbows. His puffy hair bobbed as he ran. Haidan dodged the groin-height arms and let the kid through.

"Right here," a soothing female voice said.

Haidan stepped out from between the two cars and looked around. Three mongoose-men in dress uniform, white shorts and short sleeves, gold braids on their shoulders, stood waiting for him. He caught their glances and nodded. They moved forward. Quickly in step, today, as Haidan felt rather good. No pains in his stomach, or lungs.

"Good to see you, Haidan." The mongoose-man on the left, Gordon, sounded as if he'd grown up deep in the bush. And he had. Gordon adjusted the rim of a pair of smoky oval glasses. His bald head glittered with a sheen of sweat.

"We have an electric waiting for you," said the muscular mongoose-man on the right. "Your wire was received a few hours ago." They were definitely back in Capitol City, Haidan thought, where everyone around you sounds different from everyone else. The city was a mishmash of families that had lived here as long as could be remembered, as well as everyone else who lived in Nanagada. It was a chaotic mess.

It was a city.

"The prime minister, she need see you soon, okay?" Gordon said.

"Not yet." Haidan needed to get back and caught up with city preparations. He'd ignored building Capitol City's defenses between picking up this prize in Batellton and planning the mongoose-men's retreat to Capitol City as the Azteca advanced. "Let's go," Haidan said. The three men circled him, and together they walked through the grand sloping tunnel out of Station Four into Capitol City.

A Preservationist-designed pod-shaped electric waited for them. The whip connector stood raised over the back, ready to reach up to a track to draw power. Haidan took the driver's seat. Gordon sat next to him and unholstered a pair of pistols. He set them on his lap. "Things real tense around the city right now."

"Good thinking." Haidan tapped the charge dial and stared at the controls.

"There the power." Gordon pointed at Haidan's feet. "That how you turn it on." He pointed at a switch by the small steering wheel.

Cramped, briefcase between his knees, Haidan flicked the indicated switch forward and pressed the accelerator. They moved out into the street, Gordon looking left and then right for Haidan. They moved away from the irregular walls of the city, honeycombed with their train and subway stops, streets and offices, into a great open-air, lozenge-shaped atrium several miles in length. Capitol City itself lay inside the great walls, roads, and docks. The city's buildings were built by later generations, after the Last War. It was a consensual conflict of cultures, refugees, and out-of-control city planning.

Haidan aimed the electric into the center of an upcoming road, looking up at the wire mesh that hung just over the street between brick buildings. He dodged families on carts, horse-drawn carts, until the whip behind them bent and made contact ten feet over their heads. Sparks flew. Now they rode off the city's power, no need to worry about the battery.

"Everyone know Azteca coming. Lot a refugee coming in on train."

Haidan sighed. "I know."

"Been a riot near Tolteca-town. Things tense. Dihana asked we mongoose-men to move into Tolteca-town."

"What?" A red open-air trolley, passengers lining the sides with baskets and bags fresh from market, slowed down in front of them. People were buying too much food. Stockpiling it. Haidan swerved around. They coasted adjacent to the power netting while Haidan looked for a chance to get the bouncing whip back in.

"She came to me in the barrack," Gordon said.

"She overstepping."

Gordon shrugged. "Doing the right thing."

"Maybe." Haidan slowed down, let an old lady cross. "I don't want her thinking she could use mongoose-men anytime she want. Any more report on Azteca movement?"

"It all dead silent down by the mountain." Gordon clutched the handrail in front of him as they turned a corner. "I have more bad news. Brewer's Village: they spot Jaguar scout. Didn't say how many. I send an airship from Anandale to look."

"From Anandale?"

"Brewer's Village can't be reached anymore."

Haidan got the electric back under on another street with electrified wire mesh and accelerated. He followed the wall, making a long counterclockwise trip, the twelve-story-tall rock face to his right. "Damn," he muttered.

"Yeah," said Gordon. "Still ain't go see Dihana first?"

They passed a series of apartment blocks hewn into the sides of the wall and painted yellow. On Haidan's left a battery of wooden buildings barely got over four stories tall. He slowed the electric down, turned left, and started dogging through the streets. The mesh over their heads petered out and the electric whined along under its batteries.

"Well?" Gordon asked. He knew Haidan too well.

"Yeah." It didn't take long to reach the Ministerial Mansion. Guards in mongoose-gray and beige stood in front of the large steps. Floodlights bathed the front of the mansion in light as the sun dipped beneath the tall walls of Capitol City. Haidan stopped the electric. "Wait for me."

He got out and walked up the stairs toward the large wooden storm doors.

The conference room was cramped and lit by several expensive brass-gilded electric lamps on the table. Thick wooden shutters strained against the slats holding them shut, not even allowing the slightest bit of light through.

It felt as if someone had battened down for a storm in here.

Haidan walked down the side of the oval conference table and took a seat. Dihana sat by herself at the expanse of table.

Oh, child, what is going on now?

"Hello, Haidan." The prime minister's long, plaited hair hung over the table. Her eyes were red from lack of sleep.

"Dihana. Bring me some understanding," Haidan said. "Azteca marching up the coast. Gordon saying we can't reach Brewer's Village now. We can't be sure how many out there, or how they had get out from between Mafolie Pass, but they sacking towns and moving quick. We need Tolteca help, and it sound like you invading Tolteca-town."

"It was the best thing to do." Dihana's green eyes crinkled. "People were ready to run into Tolteca-town and take their own revenge. It would have been bad."

Haidan scratched the table. "I calling all mongoose-men to fall back to the Tracks. Once there they burn anything the Azteca can feed themselves with. Then they must tear up what track they can, destroy bridges, and regroup here in Capitol City."

"All that?"

"All that." With Mafolie Pass, in the past Nanagada only had to worry about small groups of Azteca who snuck in. Small, quick, and mobile groups of mongoose-men stationed themselves all over the slopes for this reason. They had no massive defending army. Haidan was improvising. "You still thinking wrong, Dihana. Just like me not too long past. Realize: a full Azteca army coming. The whole thing. If people ain't inside these wall, they dead. So inside these wall, things better be in some damn good shape. No sense we fighting two wars."

Dihana bit her lip. "You're right." She put her elbows on the table and held her head. "What more do you need from me?"

"More airship. Can the Preservationist help?"

"They're yours to command, Haidan."

"Good. Because I need to swear them to secrecy." Haidan released the catches on the briefcase he'd held by his side until now. He set it on the table and opened it up. "In Batellton you Preservationist digger found a *map* of the whole world."

Haidan had grown up a poor vegetable farmer in the jungle near the Wicked Highs. When he wasn't busy with chores, there were things in the old roots out around the newly cleared land that intrigued him. Ancient ruins. Buildings run over by vines and powerful trees. The hints of a forgotten past lay scattered in the ground beneath the ruins. Digging in the dirt, Haidan found small machines with rubber grips, handprints carved on them. Strange coins in a language he never understood. He made extra money taking the most interesting finds to Brungstun, to a mongoose-man called Jules, who sold them to Capitol City.

Eventually Haidan followed his trinkets all the way back to Capitol City. He'd led a group of mongoose-men and a fisherman, John, through the forest from Brungstun to Capitol City. Still interested in his trinkets, he'd participated in digs around the edges of the city wall, or in towns along the Triangle Tracks until Prime Minister Elijah forbade any further such activity.

Haidan had tried to talk Elijah out of it. The prime minister had refused, but been impressed enough with Haidan that he asked him to lead the Capitol City ragamuffins. Haidan turned it down, not being interested in being stuck in the city, and was instead promoted to lead the lesser force of Nanagadan bush scouts, the mongoose-men. In time Haidan came to respect Elijah's actions. Elijah used the Councilmen to manage the day-to-day life of the city, while Haidan built up the mongoose-men to patrol the mountains against the Azteca. Both men tried to ensure their long-term survival, balancing everything constantly against the fear of the Azteca and the demands of the once powerful Loa.

A balance that was destroyed when Elijah died. The Council broke apart when Dihana inherited the prime ministerial position. The Councilmen felt they should have voted one of themselves to prime minister, and in between their infighting over a candidate and opposing Dihana as prime minister, riots raged throughout Capitol City for two weeks. Haidan had helped her order the ragamuffins out in the streets to break the violence and hunt down the Councilmen who'd started it.

The Loa gave up on the city's leadership and disappeared into the basements of their street temples as Dihana took over. They offered her no help, and she'd handled everything on her own, with only Haidan by her side. She'd never forgotten or forgiven the Loa for that. And once Capitol City settled into calm, Haidan left for the bush, worried more about the Azteca than the petty machinations of the Councilmen or what the Loa might be up to. He regretted that focus. But right now, he didn't regret his constant interest in the past. And in maps.

In all his years of living here, Haidan had seen maps of Capitol City's streets, of the sewers beneath it, and many recent maps of the lands from the Wicked Highs on east. Haidan collected maps. Part of his rise to general was due to his well-planned ambushes and patrols. He used topography to gain an upper hand on Azteca who tried to infiltrate.

Yet none of those maps Haidan had seen were maps of the entire world.

In the briefcase a piece of paper lay sandwiched between a pane of glass and a polished square of hardwood. Haidan laid the map on the table.

"Fisherman know that far enough north it get cold like when you go up a mountain. Of three expedition you funded, only one touch the northland. We know nothing about the land west of the Wicked Highs except what the Tolteca talk about. We hardly understand the world." Haidan smiled. "But right here I got a complete map of the sea between Capitol City and the northland. Right down to the smallest little island."

She moved closer, chair creaking as she stood up to lean over. Haidan put his palms flat on the table and pushed the map toward Dihana. The lamps glinted against the protective glass behind her.

On the map's lower corner Nanagada stretched out from the Wicked Highs onward. A small dot marked the northern peninsula tip, and the words *Capitol City* had been written next to it. Down near the mountains, in even smaller handwriting, were the words *Brun's Town*.

Haidan wet his lips. "Some villager digging a well in Batellton hit a bunker deep beneath the ground. We know the old-father had make Batellton a temporary headquarter during Hope's Loss. They were getting ready for some serious battle on the ground, when all the machines stop working for everyone." Haidan looked up at Dihana. "I think this a document one of the old-father actually wrote on while settling Nanagada."

"Incredible," Dihana whispered. "But why is this important now?"

Haidan caressed the glass. He'd been hoping for detailed maps like this for a long time. His first hope had been to use them to take the fighting to the other side of the Wicked Highs. But now that Azteca marched toward them, he had something more ambitious in mind. Something based on old history few knew.

"There's something more: *Starport*," he said. "That was where we old-father land, before the Tetol froze the north and fought us away. You read what the Preservationist write. There's something there, tough like the machines sometime we find in the ocean that still work, left by we old-fathers." His voice rose. "You must trust me. There's proof, and I know how to get there. We might find *something*. We know some machine that survive come down out the sky, legends say so. They say some old-fathers could never leave because the Tetol waited above for all of them. Those machine might still work. They might still help. And I think I know where a working machine might be."

"How will you get there?" Dihana asked, leaning back in her chair. "The last expedition I sent almost starved to death, couldn't get past the ice, and then most died getting back."

"We get there quick." Haidan spread his arms. "By airship over sea. It possible with this map."

"Haidan . . . the cost." Dihana shook her head.

"Very hard right now. I know. That why I need you help."

Dihana sighed. "Plan this expedition, but nothing more."

"Good." Haidan put the map back in his briefcase. "There someone who can help." He snapped the case shut. She had been avoiding this, he knew. "We need talk with the Loa."

Dihana folded her hands over each other. Her lips pinched out a straight line. "You think that is necessary?"

"Don't got enough resources for anything we planning. The priestess and all the god them living in this city been accumulating plenty of that. The Loa exist here, they need protection too."

Dihana stood up. "How are they of any use to us in this coming battle?"

Haidan pushed his chair away and stood up as well. "Who the enemy? The Loa who withdraw and lay low when we get insistent, or the Tetol, who command in fear and blood and don't care how many die by them?"

"Okay." Dihana stood in the doorway. "I know you're right. I just don't like it." Haidan pushed past her into the corridor. "Haidan . . . if the Azteca come, we don't have much of a chance surviving, do we?"

"I been waiting for something like these maps for a long, long time. Going to the northland a long shot. Might be the only one we got, come soon enough."

"I don't know what else I could have done, Haidan."

"I going now. Plenty to take care of." Not just the planning for an airship expedition, but the large unnamed steamship sitting in the harbor needed some retrofitting with some ideas Haidan had. Another of his side projects, it was already being changed as he thought about the oncoming Azteca. "And, Dihana. About moving me mongoose-men into Tolteca-town. You should have talk to me first."

"You taught me well enough how to take command, a long time ago, when I first took this job and riots started on the street."

"Don't make it a habit." Haidan paused with her near the hurricane doors at the end of the corridor. "This could still blow up in we face."

"You want them back out?"

"No. But pay careful attention to thing down there." He left her by the doors, walking out onto the steps toward a patient Gordon.

CHAPTER TWENTY-FOUR

Three days later, and Brungstun still burned. The black pillars of smoke rose day in and day out, floating up until the wind caught them and took them down into the forest during the day. During the night the pillars drifted far out over the ocean toward Frenchtown.

Jerome stood on the beach and, like a scab that he couldn't resist picking at, watched the pillars of smoke. He dug his toes into the sand, dimly aware of the water gurgling as it settled in around his feet.

Several boats set sail from the beach. Troy ran along the shoreline yelling at people with a piece of paper in his hands. "Make sure you done get enough saltfish too," he admonished a departing boat, heavy with burlap bags stacked up to the rail. He walked over to the coconut tree by Jerome. "And you, you little pickney-child, I have something definite for you."

"I don't want help with *nothing*," Jerome said.

"You go need keep you-self busy. This moping about here ain't go help you none. Come follow me." Troy walked away. Jerome stood still. "Now," Troy said. "Or I tie you up and drag you me-self."

Jerome sighed. He pulled his feet out of the sand and followed.

Troy led him around to a small bay hidden by an overhang of rocks and fallen boulders. Nets and bamboo gates cut the bay off from the ocean around the island. Several Frenchi Jerome's age paused, chest-high in the turquoise water. Some looked surprised, others sad.

He didn't want their damn pity. Jerome stood still. "What this?"

Troy waded out until the water came to his neck. He put his mouth underwater and bubbled a rhythm. One of the kids laughed and pointed as a pair of fins broke the surface and circled Troy.

"Scudder-fish," Troy explained. He put out a hand and the creature came to a stop. A pair of funny tails wiggled from behind the scudder-fish: a smooth, fast-looking creature with a yellowish beak.

It was the strangest sea creature Jerome had ever seen. He waded into the water and the scudder-fish turned to look at the disturbance—a twisting motion so graceful and quick Jerome almost couldn't believe it happened—and it faced Jerome. It bubbled the water with its beak and moved toward him, then rubbed against his outstretched hands.

Up close Jerome realized that the scudder-fish stretched out longer than Troy, six feet long. And strong. He could feel the iron-hard muscles under the smooth skin.

"It feel like smooth cotton," Jerome said. Someone giggled.

"Look at this." Troy took the scudder-fish's two fins in his hands. It swam, and Troy's chest pushed through the water. "If you's real nice to them, they help pull you around the reef them. And you can train them to help you find stuff in the water."

Troy made a full circuit of the small bay, even diving with the scudder-fish under the surface several feet, then breaking back up through the water in front of Jerome. He let go and floated over. "I want you to join me niece and nephew them here and learn how to make friends with the scudder-fish, and dive deep. Very deep."

"But why?" Jerome asked. What was the use of all this if they were going to die when the Azteca got out here to the islands?

Troy pointed out past the bay at one of the ships sailing with supplies. "We Frenchi been breeding scudder-fish a long time. We use them to dive. If you want to stay with us, you have to learn how ride. So learn quick. There hardly much time this, you understand?"

The children all looked at each other, as if they were in on some secret. "Look," said a girl next to him, her brown hair matted to the back of her pink neck. "When you go deep, you just hold you nose like this." She demonstrated, pinching her nose. "And blow. Then you ear feel better."

"Okay." Jerome pushed off his feet toward the scudder-fish. It flicked around him and bubbled.

"We go teach you everything," someone else said.

Jerome smiled. He floated out with the scudder-fish. There was a friendliness in the scudder-fish that made his soul fly a little lighter. The gentle crash of the waves against the shore didn't jar him as much. It seemed to soothe.

He set about learning how to dive with the scudder-fish.

CHAPTER TWENTY-FIVE

Haidan sat in the study in his home perched on the left edge of Capitol Harbor, where the great amphitheater of Capitol City left the jagged peninsula to dip in the water. The city's great walls created a large protected semicircle of water where boats anchored.

The porthole windows in his study looked out over the black water of the harbor, with the breakwater side of the city wall visible from them. A gentle fog was rolling in, though.

Haidan leaned back in his chair. Stutter slips littered the floor. A large map on his wall bristled with colored pins, a quick and dirty theater map of Nanagada with his best estimates of where Azteca were coming and where the mongoose-men retreated.

He'd spent hours earlier moving around Capitol City, scouting for a better operations center than this temporary setup in his house. They'd settled on an unused warehouse on the waterfront. Mongoose-men were in the middle of moving stuff over. And now Haidan could snatch some time to pore over the rest of the briefcase's contents. The proof he'd talked to Dihana about lay inside.

They were typewritten entries with handwritten comments in the margins. A Preservationist had found them in a security box that had taken a full day to break open. It had been inside an excavated compound office deep beneath the ground, hidden away in a secretary's desk. The box was hidden inside a secret panel that had rotted away.

He'd shown Dihana the map. These he wanted for himself.

Haidan blinked scratchy eyes. The clock in his study gonged that it was morning. He coughed and dabbed at his lips with a handkerchief lying on the desk, then picked up one of the yellowing pieces of paper.

There were handwritten entries:

April 5: 1,500 moved from Starport to Center Staging. 17 dead. Haidan read the following seventeen names.

April 7: Fourth air strike. Battle-Town. 500 dead. For this entry there were no lists of names, the author of this manuscript having decided there wasn't enough paper.

April 15: Orbital 2. Nuclear strike? 2,000 dead.

May 3: Orbital 1 and 3 destroyed. Unknown how. Unknown casualties.

There were several reams of administrative records. A dry account of the original settlers of Nanagada being moved to safer areas, or being caught in the cross fire of the wars of long ago, when Nanagadan people had great powers. Haidan had a feeling that if he looked in these records long enough, he would recognize surnames that still existed in Capitol City.

He set these aside. He would study them later, match them to the history books he had, then turn them back over to the Preservationists before Dihana found out about his little indiscretion.

The real gem lay under the administrative records.

Haidan pulled it out.

He'd read it once already at the start of the train ride back up. It had fired the proposal he'd given Dihana for the trip north.

He carefully set the piece of paper on the desk in front of him.

Imagine, he told himself, imagine yourself an old-father. You been fighting the Tetol, high in the sky, looking down on this world, or even under the sea. Imagine that all your knowledge, technology, all the machines you use to fight the Tetol, died in a single day.

Everyone would be scattered all over. Some would have fallen out of the sky, drowned at sea, or been stranded. You could hear some of that reflected in the old tales still told out in the bush about those days.

Here was this letter, scratched in fading pen that Haidan's tired eyes fought to focus on, written during this time.

"Jesus, Stucky, I can't believe someone did this," Haidan read to himself.

Jesus, Stucky, I can't believe someone did this.

It hit at noon. Everything died. All my implants suddenly blipped and I couldn't get messages, hunt info, nothing. I'm using pen and paper. I've never even heard of an electromagnetic pulse like that. Who did it? Us or them? I guess it doesn't matter anymore, right?

I used Sadie's telescope last night but it's not powerful enough to see if the wormhole home still exists. We can't see any light from the orbitals so we're sure they're all dead. I wrote it down on the admin sheets. Tens of thousands, gone.

If we did this, we killed ourselves as well. The pulse killed almost everything with a microchip in it. A few hardened things work here and there but not enough. Civilization is going to die here, and they're going to be a lot of hungry people soon, and a lot of people getting cancer as a side effect, I wouldn't doubt. We watched the supply ships in orbit burn up like meteors last night. The lab peo-

ple are saying the terraforming mirrors will fall too, so we're lucky to be near the equator. When it gets cold up north, they're going to suffer worse.

This is our home planet, now, I guess.

Corporal Bradson thinks no more aliens landed on the planet besides the one ship we spotted right before the pulse. But I still wake up at night wondering if more might have gotten through.

We don't have much to defend ourselves with down here. Personal firearms mostly. The aliens won't have much either, but after they have their next generation of pupa, they'll be ready, just like at Gatrai. We're lucky we survived them this long, I guess, even if we are killing ourselves to kill them.

Bradson's leaving us unguarded here in the middle of the forest to go north. He claims the Ma Wi Jung *is up there and should still be working. We cooperated with aliens to build it for that sort of thing.*

It's a mess here, Stucky. People are dying without meds, or medic-bots. I never realized how dependent on tech we were until this happened. Would they have killed us all if we surrendered? The xeno-psychologists didn't think so, but we're talking about aliens. Who knows what they really think? All we know is they don't value human life very much.

The aid agency we came in with left enough food to cover the camp for the next few months (poor bastards were climbing back to orbit when the pulse hit), but we feel we should start making roots. Particularly since all the soldiers inside the compound are packing to go north.

Did you meet any of these refugees who came down the gravity well? A lot of them are from Earth and are engaged in small-scale farming here. I know you're from Earth too. Have you ever heard of a place called the Caribbean? They all have funny accents, I can hardly understand half of them, but they're helping us build towns. Even then, I know we're going to be decimated, and starve, and there are so few of us to begin with. Right now the only thing we can afford to worry about is feeding ourselves. I feel like we just stepped back into the stone age.

Hope you get this, hon. We're leaving for one of the fishing villages on the coast near the mountains. "Brun's Town." I know you'll want to join up with Bradson. He gave me the coordinates to the Ma Wi Jung. *And maybe if you all succeed, maybe we stand a chance.*

No matter what you choose, please return. I miss you.

It was signed *Irene.* Irene and Stucky, two ancient, anonymous, long-dead ancestors. Old-fathers. Haidan wondered what had become of them as he looked at the figures scrawled at the bottom. Coordinates to the *Ma Wi Jung*. It had to be a weapon. An ancient weapon. And even after the catastrophe his ancestors had thought it would still work.

This was something that could be used against the Azteca and the Tetol. Haidan had hinted at this earlier to Dihana. But she didn't know that he had, in his hands, the location to one of the old-father's ancient machines. One that could help them.

Yes, there were problems. Would it still work? Would they be able to control it? Sometimes machines were found that still worked, and this machine had been designed to do exactly that. On the second, he had doubts. It could take months, or years, to control the machine.

Did they have that time? Probably not.

This long-dead ancestor had called the Tetol "aliens." It wasn't the first time Haidan had seen the Azteca's masters called that. Other documents and letters collected in the museum used that old term. Haidan wondered if she made it through the jungle from Batellton to Brungstun, and if she was one of his distant relatives.

Ma Wi Jung. The name rolled back in his mind.

If they could get north across the ocean to Starport, Haidan realized, they could find it, whatever it was. This could be a useful advantage. *If* they could manage to get to it and figure out how to use it before the Azteca broke the city's walls.

An explosion echoed through the air, and the panes in the porthole windows rattled. Haidan ran from his study, down the stairs. The sudden motion made him dizzy, though, and he started coughing. Blood speckled his lips, and he wiped it clear before anyone noticed. A pair of guards stood at the door, their rifles up and pointed into the street around the open door.

"Bomb?" they suggested in unison.

"It Tolteca? Maybe it were one of the airship shops?"

Haidan looked out at the dark street.

"Azteca out in Tolteca-town causing trouble," the other mongoose-man said. "They don't like mongoose-men sleeping in their street."

"No." Haidan shook his head. "We need airship too bad. The Azteca coming know it and telling their spy to aim for that first." Airships might allow him to see how many Azteca marched against them, airships might allow him to drop bombs on them from the air, or put mongoose-men of his own behind their lines. Airships might allow them to escape. And damn it, airships might, a bold and dangerous flight though it might be, allow Haidan to find out what the ancient device in the icy north was, and whether it could be used against the Azteca. "Get any extra men to guard the airship shop. All day, all night."

But it might be too late already. Dihana would know they needed the airships for defense. She wouldn't let him send a small group of them north if airships were in scant supply.

Haidan bit his lip and looked out down the street toward the harbor.

CHAPTER TWENTY-SIX

To dive deep into the water Jerome followed the Frenchi girl's directions. After several feet his ears hurt, but by holding his nose and blowing hard, his ears went 'pop,' and he could try to dive deeper.

He wanted to try riding the scudder-fish, but everyone insisted on showing him how to hold his breath and drop to the sand in the deep part of the bay. It took almost a day to conquer his desire for air, and his fear of letting the water close off over his head.

Jerome didn't relax until the girl came back up to him and showed him how to breath slowly to ready himself for the dive, and to let out his breath to sink to the bottom.

"My name Sandy," she said. "You Jerome, right?"

"How you know?" Jerome asked, surprised.

"Everyone know you: only one who make it out Brungstun."

Jerome turned away from her and bit his lip. He'd been keeping his mind away from those memories by spending the day splashing about with them. That was what Troy had intended, no doubt. Now he thought about his mom, and Swagga, and Schmitti . . .

"But I also remember you from the time when you had visit here with you dad." Sandy saw that Jerome didn't want to talk about any of that, so she said, "Why don't you try and dive again?"

Jerome nodded. The wind blew over his ears as he took several deep breaths, then sank beneath the water. The world fell quiet, and water bubbled out his nose until his body became heavy enough to fall.

It felt wrong to blow out all the air in his lungs, but Jerome sank to the bottom. Calm descended on him as his feet and hands kissed the sand. He opened his eyes and could only make out blurry shapes around him.

Jerome listened to a steady cacophony of croaks and grunts from the ocean's far distance. The heavy rhythmic sound of the small waves lapping against the beach stirred at him. Even the indistinct voices of the splashing swimmers ten feet above him filtered down.

It felt peaceful. Time played tricks with him. It seemed as if only a minute had passed, or a long hour.

Okay, he thought, maybe not even a minute. His lungs burned. Jerome pushed off the sand and swam to the surface. For a brief moment he could see his reflection off the underside of the mirrorlike border between ocean and air, then he broke the surface next to Sandy.

"Good," Sandy said. Jerome smiled. One of the older Frenchi rode the scudder-fish around the bay with a whoop.

"Could I try and ride he now?" Jerome asked, excited.

But before she could say anything, Troy yelled from the beach that it was time to come in. When Jerome stood out of the water, he shivered from the cold wind. He rubbed his waterlogged fingers over each other.

"We all looking shrivel-up," Sandy said. Jerome looked up. Everyone had wrinkled skin from the hours in the water.

The gentle pink and orange hues of the sunset glowed in the west, the bands of color peeking over the Wicked Highs and the foaming waves breaking over the reefs. Azteca were in that direction. As if to confirm this, he noticed a small speck in the sky over the ocean. An Azteca blimp. Jerome pursed his lips and turned around. When he faced the beach and walked out, he noticed that the pillars of smoke from Brungstun were turning toward them with the beginnings of the night wind.

Jerome noticed Troy staring at the blimp in the distance.

With the sighting of the blimp the entire Frenchi community burst into even more action. Jerome was taken to dress in warmer clothes. When he came down to the main beach in front of Troy's store, he found that people had gathered around the fishing boats. Again Jerome marveled at everyone's light skin color and the red noses some had from the sun. Jerome could get sunburned, but not like that.

Troy, and the old men who always sat in front of his store slapping domino tiles, faced everyone. Overhead the smoke from Brunstun blotted out the early-evening stars.

"It now or never," an old lady from the crowd said. Everyone looked around them with sad or worried expressions.

"It just an airship, Harriet," a young man next to her said.

"Only one now. But just you wait. Soon it go be another. And when they see where we is, they go build a boat to come for we."

Another old lady walked down to the beach. "Harriet right. They already leave Brungstun to come for we. We been using one of them looking glass on top of Gaston house to see town."

The crowd gasped. Jerome wondered if he could use this looking glass the old lady talked about to look at Brungstun. Could he see people through it? he wondered.

More Frenchi trickled in. "What you had see?"

"Look like they build a few large barges and they's getting ready to pull them with an old steamer that been up on the docks for repair."

Jerome felt faint. It was going to happen. They were coming for him at last. He would die soon.

"Okay." Troy held up a hand. "Then we don't have no choice. The smoke clouds and dark go fuss with the blimp seeing where we go. Tell everyone in they house sleeping is time they wake up. We leaving."

The crowd melted away. One of the old men tapped Troy on his shoulder. "What about the boy?" he asked, pointing at Jerome.

"He go with the rest of the pickney. He hold he breath well enough."

People called out to each other, some went door-to-door waking everyone up. Many already had large sacks and bags sitting in their fishing boats. Three families pushed their small fishing boats off the sand into the water and rowed out of the harbor.

"What going on?" Jerome asked.

"We scattering." Troy stood up, his knees popping. "And some go hide in a place the Azteca ain't go find us. I want you to go stand by that boat there." He pointed at a yellow skiff with hand-painted letters on its bow. "You go leave with a group of pickney-them there."

Jerome nodded, and Troy trotted off. He yelled at several of the men, wanting to know if anyone else would go back up to Gaston's house and keep an eye on the Azteca with the glass. And he wanted to know how many working guns everyone on Frenchi Island had.

More boats rowed off into the dark waters. Jerome walked over to the small skiff, wondering what was going to happen next. If they were going to try to sail away from the Azteca, then they couldn't come back to the few small islands all the Frenchi lived on. And as Pepper said, they could last a month like this. What then?

Troy came back, crouched, and looked Jerome straight in the eye. "Now, you go have to give a big promise, okay?"

"Yes."

"You can't ever tell no one where we going, or what we go do here."

Jerome swallowed. "Okay."

CHAPTER TWENTY-SEVEN

Twelve children jumped aboard the skiff. A pair of tired-looking fishermen with leathery skin and scraggly beards pushed the yellow craft out to sea. Several of the other skiffs out on the water had been painted black, but Jerome had the impression that much of this had been planned hastily, so their skiff remained brightly colored.

The skiff was heavy, the waves lapping into the boat. One of the men handed them a pair of calabash gourds to bail water with. If an Azteca blimp saw them, Jerome wondered, would they shoot at them?

"Keep bailing water." The sails remained packed away on the floor, tied tight with hemp ropes. The men sat side by side and pulled on the long wooden oars. The bow jumped and dipped into the water, and they pulled out from Frenchi Island into the reefs.

"One, two . . ."

"Tree, fo'." The fisherman on the right had a much heavier accent than his companion. Jerome's companions sat on the floorboards, wrapped in blankets but already getting soaked. They looked tired. And scared.

"One, two . . ."

"Tree, fo'." Jerome laid his head against the side of the boat and watched the Frenchi fisherman's arms flex. The two pegs holding the oars in place creaked with each stroke.

A small figure wrapped in a patched-up blanket crawled underneath the seat between the fisherman's legs and shuffled back to sit next to Jerome. It was Sandy. She pulled the blanket around her tight.

"You know where we going?" she asked. He shrugged. Sandy leaned closer to him and pointed over the edge of the boat at a tall rock island that had once splintered off of the mainland. There were several other smaller ones around it.

Even from several miles away Jerome could see the sudden random explosions of white spray shooting up into the air as the ocean dashed itself against the sharp rocks scattered around the miniature islands.

"You can't land any boat there," Jerome said. "That mad."

"It go be all right," Sandy said. "It okay if I sit here?"

Jerome looked around. "Um, yeah, sure, I guess." She smiled a bit and pushed her face down into her blanket. Jerome stared at the water that sloshed out of the floorboards and wet his bare feet.

An entire herd of scudder-fish paced the skiff as they got closer. They swam fast circles around the tiny craft, swooping just under the hull and lying on their sides to look upward at the sides of the boat.

Jerome stood up with a smile. A set of waves boomed against nearby rocks and took it right away. He could barely see the rocks in the dark night, but he could sense how close they were.

Not even half a mile away the water foamed and hissed, defeated for the moment. The ocean lay silent after the loud explosion of water and spray, the constant draining sound overpowering the area as water rushed off the rocks and crevices to return to the ocean.

"We here," Sandy said. The men shipped the oars. The skiff bounced in the chop reflected back at them as another series of waves passed them and dashed themselves against the immovable rock faces.

Children began slipping into the oily, dark water.

"You remember all that we had teach you today?" Sandy asked over the sound of the surf. Jerome nodded, holding on to the rail to balance. "It all for a reason. Troy had want you to come with us."

"But where?" Jerome snapped. The scudder-fish surrounded the boat, jostling against its side.

"Down deep there are cave we can hide in." Sandy dropped the blanket to the floor of the boat and jumped over the rail. The splash wet Jerome. "Come in." She waved, nothing more than a small, pale blob in the black night ocean. Jerome could see stars reflected off random smooth patches of water the skiff created with its rudder.

Jerome swallowed. What was the alternative? he wondered. Go back and face the Azteca? What could he do there? He jumped in.

The cold water slapped his face. A scudder-fish pushed past him. Jerome's fingers ran over the smooth skin until he caught one of its two fins and he lurched forward. When he looked back, he saw the two fishermen jump out into the water.

"They go let the boat hit the rock. That way the Azteca go think we all dead trying to escape," Sandy yelled.

Jerome's scudder-fish surged forward toward the rocks. He held on, looking from side to side to reassure himself that everyone else followed next to him, that he wouldn't be dragged to drown against the rocks. As the next wave rose, the scudder-fish sped up over the small rising crest, flailing its two tails, and for a few seconds they surfed down the front of the wave. Then it passed from underneath them.

The waves grew bigger. A random wavelet smacked Jerome on his side, almost knocking him off. The water around them boiled, and the smashing waves made noise loud enough to pound Jerome's chest. When Jerome dared to sit up and look forward, he could see the details on the jagged spires of worn rock just ahead. Quicksilver rivulets of water dribbled down through their nooks and crannies, reflecting the moon.

"Hold you breath," someone yelled, as a wave cut Jerome off from the rest of the group. Jerome did as he had been taught earlier in the day. He took several deep breaths, and then one last final one. The scudder-fish, sensing his readiness, plunged under the water.

At first he almost panicked as the darkness closed over his head. He could feel the powerful thud of waves, but now the world around him existed only as far as he could reach out with his fingers. The scudder-fish stroked downward and Jerome's ears stabbed him with pain. He held his nose and blew them out.

But once wasn't enough. They moved downward so quickly he kept his left hand gripped to his nose and blew to keep the pressure off. The water grew colder and colder.

How long would this take? The need to breathe again hit him hard. The burning in his lungs felt odd in the cold water.

The scudder-fish banked; Jerome could feel the change in the water over his skin. He closed his eyes and leaned between the fins. Don't think about breathing. Focus. He felt everything slow down to a pinprick, just as he had on the bottom of the bay.

Calm.

It only worked for another few seconds. The burning in his lungs returned and Jerome blew bubbles. That helped some, but then soon Jerome had nothing left to blow. I go die, he thought. Right on the back of this animal. But Jerome realized he didn't want to die. He gripped the fins of the scudder-fish. Pepper was right. One could only focus on the moment, on living then and there.

Jerome focused as hard as he could, pushing back until he felt the sharp edge of blackness descend on him anyway and his grip loosened.

The scudder-fish veered upward.

They broke into air with a spectacular crash. The moment Jerome felt it prickle against his skin, he opened his mouth and sucked as much air as he could.

He hung on, panting, as the scudder-fish pulled him toward sand. Strong hands picked him up, and Jerome could see brass gaslights flickering along the side of a large cavern. Children and scudder-fish popped up behind him, everyone gasping for air.

Blankets and hot fish soup waited for them. As they huddled around the fire, matted hair and forlorn faces half-lit, Jerome realized that somewhere above him, miles out on Frenchi Island, the adults were going to fight the Azteca. More people would die to protect his life.

He wanted to live, he thought, staring at the middle of the fire. He knew this for sure.

He would avenge them. His friends, his mother, his dad. They might be dead, but he could hurt the Azteca back. Somewhere. Somehow.

But he would live, that was for sure.

CHAPTER TWENTY-EIGHT

Dihana looked up with bleary eyes at Haidan as the office door opened. "Evening." She pulled her head off the desk. "Getting sleep."

"You put this one off long enough," Haidan said.

"I know." Time to gird herself to face an old set of fears. Her hands trembled a bit as she smoothed her jacket, tucked in the blouse, and straightened the long skirt. The Loa had come up from its temple to see her. Usually they skulked in their temple basements scattered throughout Capitol City, making people come to them. No matter what happened tonight, at least she'd forced one of them to come to her. That gave her a small measure of confidence. "Let's do it."

They liked the dark, that she knew. The conference room had been buttoned shut yesterday. The corridors had been modified. Heavy carpeting hung near all the windows and along the walls.

It suffocated her just to walk into here.

Wheels squeaked down toward the conference door, followed by footsteps.

The door opened. Mother Elene pushed a wheelchair in. The Loa inside lolled between the wicker webbing, the large globe of its head held in place by a brace. Just under the papery-thin skin of the Loa's head, Dihana saw soft cracks in the skull plates. Every year a Loa's head grew larger, and the skull split and grew aside to accommodate.

"Mother Elene." Dihana stood. "It is good of you to come."

It had no legs, Dihana noticed. Pale, pasty flesh sagged in bags under the arms. It fumbled a piece of sliced apple toward its toothless mouth and chewed listlessly.

"Good you finally talk," Mother Elene said. "Though we know we last on you list."

"Will you sit?" Haidan asked.

"I go stand here by Gidi Fatra," Mother Elene said. "I translate."

"We are hoping for help defending the city," Dihana said. "The mongoose-men are good, but there are too few of them. We have weapons, and airships, and steam cars . . ."

Mother Elene raised her hand. Dihana stopped. The Loa hissed. The wicker under its pasty bulk squeaked.

"Gidi Fatra, as all Loa do, think you walk the wrong path." The Loa strained to move itself, bleary eyes scanning the room with jerks of its fleshy eyelids. "Fatra say we can't hold the city walls."

"You want the Tetol to rule us here?" Dihana snapped.

Haidan turned in his chair, a movement she caught from the corner of her eye. Dihana ignored the gentle warning while Mother Elene listened to the Loa.

"We ain't saying we ain't go help."

"What you offering?" Haidan asked, putting his elbows on the table.

"With only you men," Mother Elene translated, "it don't look . . . likely, that we go win a war. Not after we lose Mafolie Pass."

"We *can* hold them outside the city walls," Dihana said.

The Loa heaved itself to face her, eyes narrowing. She realized it could understand her. It hissed at her, spittle drooling down off its lower lip.

Mother Elene translated. "Maybe it won't take a few week them, maybe it go take many year, but without Mafolie Pass them Azteca can take all the time they need."

Haidan raised his arms and folded them. "Maybe. Or maybe there a few trick up we sleeve still."

The Loa snorted. Then it looked at Haidan.

"Over the last day or so," Mother Elene said to Haidan, "you men been buying up fur, can food, and talking to any men who been far north or up the mountain where it cold. You planning a trip north."

Haidan folded his arms. "I planning something. But not north. Why I go upset the Loa by trying for another north trip? Besides, I need all the fighting men here, not there."

Dihana glanced at him again. Haidan betrayed nothing but calmness. He kept his gaze on the Loa.

"You ain't fool we," Mother Elene said.

"The general is a man of his word," Dihana said.

Mother Elene smiled. "You go need we help to go north. You don't have no idea what up there."

Haidan leaned forward. "You saying the Loa want help we go north? They change they mind after all these years?"

Mother Elene put her hands on her hips. "Loa always got all of we best interest in mind. Always been, always go be."

To Dihana's surprise, Haidan leaned back and laughed. He shook his locks. "So what exactly up north for the Loa then?"

"Gidi Fatra, and all the rest of he order, support this thing you planning. They want update every day about it, and more regular talk with you about they place in the city. We go talk further about what we go help you with later."

"You didn't answer the general's question," Dihana said. "What do you think is up in the north that brings this change?"

Mother Elene looked to the Loa, but it hissed nothing back at her.

"You have our cooperation now," Mother Elene said. "Information go be shared later."

It was, Dihana felt, as good a start as any, and she let the matter drop with a quick glance at Haidan. He spread his arms and shrugged.

"That's it?" Dihana asked.

"For now. That is enough."

"Okay." Dihana looked at Haidan. "There have been attacks. Would you like mongoose-men stationed anywhere?" Haidan coughed, disapproving her offer, and she continued, "For protection of the Loa? They are vulnerable without armed men to protect them."

"No," Mother Elene said. "That been thought out already. None of the Loa below the street temples. They hiding good. Contact the priestess them, and the Loa will hear what you say."

"You don't trust us with your location? Not even if we gave our word to keep the location secret?"

"Your word?" Mother Elene asked. "Not yet." She walked back to the wicker chair, turned it around toward the door, and wheeled the Loa out of the conference room. She closed the door behind her carefully so it didn't catch her long, purple skirt.

"Interesting," Haidan said.

Dihana wondered what they had gained here. An order from the Loa? She wasn't her father. They weren't even going to help with the fighting. Frustrating.

"This manuscript you have," Dihana said. "I want a copy. If the Loa are after the same thing, I want to know everything I can."

"I go send you a copy, but I told you everything. It a machine. That all I know."

Dihana reached out and grabbed his forearm. "But I don't think we can afford taking away any airship just for the Loa to go north. We need them when we start fighting."

They couldn't afford another northern trip. The previous ones, although by ship, not airship, had not been successes. No, they would have to wait until they knew what future, if any, Capitol City had.

"You canceling this because we can't afford it? Or is it just that you refuse to do anything the Loa say?"

Dihana held nothing back. "You might be right about that, but how can we be sure we know what Loa want of us? What are they trying to do?"

"Survive," Haidan said. "When Azteca coming, that is about all you can do. If they holding back, is because we all building trust. But we need them. Most of this city worship them, you can't toss that aside."

True, Dihana thought. But a bad taste lingered still.

In Capitol City, Hindis prayed at their shrines, and Muslims prayed at night toward a constellation they said held Mecca. The Holy Christian Church had churches. In the bush, wary with hunter's expertise, the normally peaceful Rastafarians honed warriors with the skills that kept Nanagada safe.

But no religion held as many followers in Nanagada as Vodun, for any believer had only to walk to a church to find the Loa, pale and malformed, giving their scratchy prophecies in a holy tongue only the Mothers could translate.

Haidan was right. Though she *would* find out what the Loa thought was up north. And wanted. But now it was time to talk to Haidan about housing more people in Capitol City, about where to get the money to build defenses around the walls, and how to slow the Azteca down when they arrived.

He asked her if he could put more mongoose-men out in the streets with the ragamuffins, patrolling for trouble. The streets had become dangerous. He had street corners, warehouses, and posts already planned.

CHAPTER TWENTY-NINE

The sleeper car rocked along toward Capitol City at the end of ten other similar square steel cars under the swept column of black smoke pouring from the grimy engine's stack. In the dark, boxy confines tired bodies hunched along the drop-down sleepers. Dusty streams of early-morning light flicked in through the closed windows, strobing the inside of the car with sudden glimpses of the weary occupants.

Some were mongoose-men making their way to Capitol City. The rest were weary mothers and children, their possessions in packs around their feet. Some whispered that a few people in this car were from Brewer's Village, and that Anandale would fall within the week yet. Three days of service remained before the trains withdrew and the northern tracks were destroyed behind them by the mongoose-men. The train was crammed with people fleeing up the northern coast toward the city.

Oaxyctl sat on the hard bench seat, looking at John deBrun's hook hanging loose from the bunk above him. It moved in rhythm with the sway of the car over the tracks. With each clack Oaxyctl counted off the increasing miles between the advancing Azteca and himself. The farther they got, the more he could relax.

They'd come far in few days. Oaxyctl pushing through forest with no care for leaving tracks in his hurry to keep in front of any Azteca. John kept up with him. Both mute, hardly able to talk when pushing through the jungle, wary and nervous, alert for any strange sound, they kept on until they found the tracks and followed them to a station.

Oaxyctl's skin itched from sticky leaves, his eyes burned, and he was hungry, but at least he lived. And had his prize. In Capitol City Oaxyctl would find some *quimichtin* contacts posing as Tolteca and get the tools he wanted for this grisly task of pulling the information he wanted from John. They might even find him a soundproofed room.

He had the time, now, to do everything right. The way the god wanted. Oaxyctl relaxed. It will turn out okay, he told himself.

Or unlucky, he thought.

Best not to think about that. Oaxyctl stared at a triangular tear in the upholstery while John snored in the bunk overhead.

*   *   *

Oaxyctl had never been to Capitol City. He sat by the window, craning his head. The walls stood higher than the tallest sacrificial pyramids in Tenochtitlanome.

Mothers stirred children awake, telling them they had arrived. People shoved beds back up into the walls and moved their belongings out from under the seats.

"This we home now, Ma?" a boy several seats over asked.

"Just for a while, sweetie. Just for a while."

Next to Oaxyctl, John looked over at one of the other trains parallel to them, moving slowly out of one of the tunnels into Capitol City. Great spikes and mounds of dirt menaced the train from either side of the tracks. Defensive measures, earthworks. Oaxyctl counted ten roads leading out of the city along with the northern and southern tracks. Now he understood why it was said that all roads this side of the Wicked Highs led to Capitol City.

"We'll need to find a place to stay," Oaxyctl murmured. "I have some money with me in my pack, but not much."

"You work for the mongoose-men," John said. "I heard someone in this car saying there's temporary lodging for them all around the city."

"Yes." Oaxyctl smiled. "But after all that time in the jungle, it would be nice to find a better room. It would be quieter."

"Okay." John extended his good hand. "I owe you my life. I don't know how to thank you enough." The train slowed. "I have no money to help or repay you with. I'm going to join the mongoose-men and fight, though. Hopefully all the way back to Brungstun." John grimaced. "I hope we meet again. And that I can return the favor."

"Room with me," Oaxyctl suggested. If not, he'd have to hunt John down again later tonight.

"I was hoping to look up some friends . . ."

Friends? The last thing Oaxyctl needed was John's friends. "I insist." Oaxyctl fidgeted with a corner of his shirt. "At least this first night. We've only just arrived. You'll have somewhere to clean up and come back to if you can't find your friends. I'll go down to a mongoose station tomorrow. If you come with me, we can sign you up then." Then, Oaxyctl thought, he could tie John up in the room and get started on this.

The train chuffed to a stop inside the tunnel by the platform. John stood up, along with all the other passengers. "If it's no trouble?"

"It's no problem at all," Oaxyctl said, and picked up his pack.

Oaxyctl found himself bewildered. People of all skin shades wearing bright clothes packed the streets. Their various accents echoed off the sides of the tall rock by their side.

"If I remember," John said, "there are rooms over into the middle a bit more towards the harbor. Near Tolteca-town. Cheaper."

Tolteca. The closer to Tolteca the better. "Yes, let's try that," Oaxyctl said, as boxy wooden vehicles zipped quietly along the street next to him. Donkeys laden with baskets plodded along the sides of the streets, their bored eyes fixated on the ground. Crowds of people and goods shoved and trickled toward the streets.

Oaxyctl held his atlatl at his side as they walked on, spears strapped in a tight bundle with cord. Two men with muddied feet leading a brown donkey away from one of the train's cars looked him over and frowned. He nodded back at them, but they refused to meet his eyes.

A lady with a wicker basket of clothes on her head spat at the ground when she saw him. Something bleak and angry hung in the air. He looked around, surrounded on all sides, and felt unprotected, unsafe. John walked ahead, oblivious. Oaxyctl hurried forward.

A rock struck the side of his head hard enough to blur his vision. Oaxyctl staggered.

Five men, previously inspecting fruit on a table, walked forward and surrounded him. "Where you going, Taca-man?"

Oaxyctl stood his ground and itched to let a dart fly. "I'm a mongoose-man. Strike again, and you will have a problem."

"Our only problem you," they said. "Get back on the other side of the mountain and leave we all alone."

Oaxyctl walked forward. They didn't spread apart. When Oaxyctl stepped between them, they threw their shoulders forward to stop him. The young man on the left punched Oaxyctl in the belly. Oaxyctl crumpled. Several lightning-quick kicks and punches disoriented him.

He hunched over his atlatl darts and yanked one from the bundle.

"Hey!" John yelled as he turned back around. The group paused, unsure who he was. John walked forward. In a single motion he raised his hook and snaked it around the nearest man's neck, the point resting just a hair away from the man's Adam's apple.

"What this?" the young man asked. He kept his hands out in front of him and shifted from foot to foot.

"My hook," John said, "on your neck. This man you're beating is a mongoose-man. He spends most of his time out in the bush protecting you from the Azteca."

"Fine job he doing," someone yelled from the road.

"Shut up," John yelled. He pointed at the four other men. "Hit that man again, I cut your throats. He saved my life. Let him go. Now."

They swore and let Oaxyctl go. He stood up. "Thank you." Oaxyctl gasped for air. "Let's go." He replaced the dart, glad not to have to kill anyone in such a public place.

John removed his hook. The men walked off, cursing and swaggering as if they'd achieved something.

"Hey." A mongoose-man walked toward them. "Hey, you."

Oaxyctl and John both stopped. "I'm sorry," Oaxyctl said. "We—"

"It okay," the mongoose-man said. "I hear you say you was a mongoose-man. I here giving directions to all the mongoose fresh off the train. You have proof?"

Oaxyctl pulled his shirtsleeve up. A blue-green caricature of a mongoose, the long, thin mythical animal that hunted snakes, coiled around his arm. It was new, and still angry bright on his skin.

The mongoose-man looked suspicious. "It a bit new."

John stepped in. "That man saved my life. He is not a spy. Trust me."

"And you is?"

"John deBrun. Maybe you all remember from the—"

"Northland expedition!" The mongoose-man clapped John on the shoulder. "Yeah, man, I remember you."

Oaxyctl relaxed.

"Okay," the mongoose-man said. "You can clear that up tomorrow." He pulled out a small rectangle of stiff paper, which had his signature on it. "This scrip for a room in the city tonight. Temporary. Address for the nearest command station on the back. Wait till next morning before reporting in," the mongoose-man advised. "They getting full trying to process everybody already."

Oaxyctl took the parchment. "Thank you."

The mongoose-man nodded and looked down the street at the backs of the band of men who'd taken after Oaxyctl. "Least I can do. We been ordered to hand them out to any returning mongoose-man we meet."

John took the piece of paper and looked at it. Wind swirled up street dust and fluttered the edges. "I know where this is." He looked around the street. "But let's take a less conspicuous route."

Oaxyctl agreed.

The entry to their room was in the alleyway. Laundry hung overhead in the air, out to dry. A pair of women argued from their windows about clotheslines.

Inside, Oaxyctl limped over to lie down on the slatted bed while John washed his face in the tiny washroom. The sound of trickling water made Oaxyctl thirsty.

"It's tense here," John said. "I've never known anyone to assault someone on the street like that."

"What do you expect?" Oaxyctl looked up at the paint peeling on the ceiling. His stomach hurt. And his lower back. He'd be pissing blood tonight. He touched his jaw and sucked his teeth. "They know Azteca coming. I look Azteca. Everyone is stressed."

What could he have done? Killed the men right there on the street? It would have screwed the entire thing up. Ragamuffins would have jailed him, and the local mongoose commanders would have done the same. No, he'd chosen the right course of action. Any longer, though, and he would have had to fight from sheer desire to live.

He couldn't stand up without pain.

He would have to take care of John now.

Now? He wondered if he could quickly subdue the wiry man. Oaxyctl had noted how quickly John had wrapped his hook around that boy's throat. In this much pain thanks to the beating, Oaxyctl wasn't sure if he could avoid that hook at close quarters.

"That doesn't make it right." John sat down on a small chair by the bed. "You and the Tolteca here have just as much to lose."

"Or more." The Tolteca were the worst form of traitors. They would die slowly when the Azteca army came over the walls. Oaxyctl sat up and untied the bundle of atlatl darts. It rolled open, and he put his hand on one.

John stood back up. Oaxyctl watched his motions. Strong, determined. If he waited until John took off the hook, or fell asleep, he'd have a better chance. Oaxyctl was weak right now.

John leaned over and tightened his bootlaces.

"Where are you going?" Oaxyctl asked. John paused and stared at him. Oaxyctl swallowed. He had to be careful about the tone of his voice. "I'm sorry, I'm hungry, but wasn't sure if I wanted to go out on my own." Oaxyctl opened his pack by the corner of the bed and fished out silver coins with the Triangle Tracks emblem stamped on the front.

"I have a friend out by the harbor. I want to see if he's still there." John caught the coins Oaxyctl tossed at him. "I'll bring something back. But it might be a while."

"Okay." Oaxyctl kept his face straight. John seeing a friend. Not good. John seemed well-known around here. Someone was bound to come looking for him after a few days of silence if they knew he was in the city. But it gave Oaxyctl time to go find the things he needed from the spies in the city, and then rest when he got back.

A bead of sweat ran down the side of Oaxyctl's face. John had gone out of his way to save Oaxyctl on the street. He wondered what it would be like to face John when the man realized what Oaxyctl really was.

But such was living for the gods. He dare not disobey. There were worse things than death. The sun had to rise every morning, the crops needed to grow. And it was blood that gave all these nourishment.

The war gods proclaimed the Azteca to be the fiercest human warriors in all of time. The gods had chosen to bring the Azteca into this world to capture prisoners for sacrifice. Thus the world remained fertile.

Sometimes doubt surfaced in Oaxyctl's head. He saw the heathen Nanagadans and all their varying religions on this side of the mountains, and their crops grew well without any blood sacrifices.

But the Nanagadans would fall soon. The Azteca could not be stopped. The gods would rule everything. So doubt didn't matter. It would be over soon, and Oaxyctl could live in a city and put this behind him. *Far* behind him.

Oaxyctl watched John step out through the doorframe. John's hook glinted in the light outside, and then the door slammed shut, shaking dust loose into the air. Oaxyctl waited for the tiny swirling particles to settle before he stood up.

He took his atlatl with him and kept to the darkest alleys, where the people who would harass him could be killed with minimal effort, and few would notice.

It still hurt to walk, though.

CHAPTER THIRTY

People walking toward John avoided his eyes and brushed past. Mongoose-men patrolled the street corners, rifles slung under their arms. He stopped in front of a family sitting around a fire by the side of the street, orienting himself. The man at front looked out over the street with a blank stare.

A cold wind came in over the walls from the sea. John tasted brine and pulled his shirt around him tighter. He looked back at the family and saw the father quickly hide a knife under a rag and the daughter glancing up the street, keeping an eye on the mongoose-men.

"Babylon come soon for oppress we," a Zionist yelled from a street corner, standing on a small box that strained under his bare feet. As John walked closer, he preached toward John. "Himself streaming over the mountain. We have fall, and now we go suffer bondage in a different land. God help we, we have fall."

An explosion rocked the air. John ducked and shielded his head. Shocked, John looked around. The Zionist, his long locks swaying, did the same. He pointed at the sky, east: a thin gray trail of smoke curled over the buildings.

"Azteca spy," the Zionist spat. "Already here, among all of we."

The two mongoose-men on the street corner conferred briefly, then one walked over to the small electric parked by them and drove off toward the smoke. The Zionist stepped off the box. He pulled on a dirty pair of sandals lying on the ground behind the box and laced them up and eyed John. "Don't look too safe on these street anymore." He took his box with him as he walked off down the street.

Maybe getting back inside was safer. John didn't even know if Haidan still owned the old house he'd purchased just before John had left to return to Brungstun. But it was worth at least checking. John didn't want to put Oaxyctl through any more trouble.

He reoriented himself toward the harbor.

A pair of mongoose-men patted John down, checking for weapons, before allowing him down the street. Another pair stood at the small two-story house. They released the safeties on their rifles and stepped forward. "What you need here?"

"I'm looking to talk to Edward," John said.

"Who?"

"Edward Haidan."

The mongoose-men looked at each other. "Who you is and why you want talk to General Haidan?"

"My name is John deBrun. I'm an old friend. From Brungstun."

The mongoose-man on the left nodded. "Hold up a second." He slipped through the door.

John waited. Voices inside conferred. A tired face looked around the door. Despite the silver locks, John recognized Edward. The door swung clear open.

"John deBrun!"

"Mr. Haidan." John laughed. "Been a while."

"I give up on anyone ever calling me Edward again these day." Haidan laughed. "My God, John. I can't believe you here."

John raised his hook in front of his chest and smiled. Haidan grabbed it and pulled John forward past the doorframe into a hug. Haidan felt like a small child, bony and thin, when John hugged back. He had to be careful not to impale his old friend.

Haidan gave John a look over. "You don't look so good, man. How you get out Brungstun? I hear you marry and have you a kid. She name Shanta, right? You all come by road?"

John looked down at the doorstep. Haidan caught the motion and understood. Exuberance dried up; he reached out with an arm and touched John's shoulder. "Come in?"

John nodded. "Please."

Two mongoose-men stood by the door. Muscled, wearing coveralls, they also had daggers strapped to their sides. They put down the guns they had aimed through two peepholes. John had stood half a foot from the muzzles of two rifles.

"More guards?" John looked around. The foyer held old wooden chairs, and bookshelves on every wall. Corroded pieces of metal lined the shelves along with the books, trinkets and artifacts from below the waves.

"So far the bombs that been set off been in airship and gun factory them. Maybe the next one for me."

"Azteca spies?"

"Who else," Haidan said. "Azteca here, pretending to be Tolteca. You think, after living with the fear of death for so many years, living here would break them free. No. Still spy, still Azteca." He walked down the foyer and up to a cramped set of stairs to his study. He paused on the second step, hand on the varnished rail.

"I haven't eaten yet today," he said, as if suddenly realizing the fact. "Are you hungry?"

John shook his head.

"Okay." Haidan continued up the stairs as he yelled out to the guards. "A little bush tea and hops bread could be good, you know?"

There was a long pause. "They do that?" John asked.

"Sometime being the man running everything ain't bad," Haidan said.

John smiled. On the second floor the wooden rail looked over the foyer and main door. One mongoose-man stood with his arms folded by the door, the other off in the kitchen rustling around in cupboards.

Inside the study John sat down in a faded leather chair. "You're the man in charge of it all now, then?"

Haidan sighed. "For all the good it doing, yeah." He sat catty-cornered to John. Again, towering bookshelves covered the walls around them. A small ladder had been shoved against the wall. John realized that, except for the bookshelves, the study felt like a ship's cabin: small, cramped, utilitarian. Varnished wood everywhere.

"Don't beat yourself up. What's coming over the mountain, that's hellacious. We both know it."

"Yeah." Haidan rubbed red eyes, his lack of sleep obvious to John. "But that why I should have been working harder on defense. I spend me resources wrong. We all paying now."

"We all did what we could," John said. "What do you have in store?"

"Big airship-them. Steam car with armor. Some other thing the prime minister and I cook up. Thing that could mess the Azteca army up something serious as they move towards the city."

The sun blinded John through a pair of large portholes in the back of the study. He could see the breakwall of Capitol Harbor spanning the lower lips of the brass rings. "I want to join the mongoose-men." John leaned closer toward Haidan. "I want to fight."

Haidan smiled. "I don't want recruit you as a mongoose-man, John."

"You know I can fight." John grabbed the steel curve of his hook. "I've hacked my way through a lot of jungle just to make it here. I've seen the Azteca close up. I know what this is going to be like."

"I don't want you on the ground, John. But now I know you here, I got something I want for you consider. We got this airship expedition plan. We going north again, but quicker, safer, and by air."

John looked at Haidan. "North?" The chair his friend sat in dwarfed him, holding him in folds of soft leather and sturdy planking, built into the wall. "By airship?"

"Maybe." Haidan said. "A lot of problem with all this yet. Prime minister not with me on it yet. I still got me a backup plan, though." He waved at the window. John wasn't sure what he was getting at. "Maybe it get use that way, maybe not. Either way, I have something for you consider soon, so just hold on and wait, okay, John?" Haidan leaned forward with a cough. "But this all a change of subject, John. You just get in from Brungstun. You need time rest, you know that. How you managing?"

Haidan's eyes locked on John. John looked down at the dusty floorboards to avoid the intense gaze. "There was nothing I could do, Man. Nothing." He put his hand to his forehead. "I'm tired. Real tired. And I want someone to pay. I want to join the mongoose-men. I want to go back down with weapons. I want to fight." John raised his head. "And you're telling me to wait, you have something else in mind."

"What good you fighting on land? You a sailor." Haidan folded his legs up into the chair. "I know where I could use you."

"No."

"Come, John."

"I'm not going on the airship with you. I'm not going north again." John held up his hook. "I've already paid my price to the cold. Plus, my wife and child won't be saved by going north."

That was the most important part. He already felt ashamed for staying alive, for running through jungle *away* from the Azteca. He told himself the whole way it was regrouping, living to fight another day. And yet, the feel of the eagle stone on his back, the helplessness of being unable to even struggle free, had pushed him to run just as hard.

Haidan sighed. "I think it over. John?"

"Yes."

"Tell me what happen."

John took a deep breath and leaned back into his chair. He gripped the large flat arms, the surface rough under the tender part of his forearms.

He was halfway through recounting his journey to the city when a mongoose-men interrupted. John was glad to stop.

"They here for you," the large guard said.

John wiped his eyes dry and cleared his throat.

"I go to go." Haidan cleared his throat and dabbed at his lips with a dirty brown handkerchief. "Time for we step up more serious preparation with invasion coming. The Azteca about five days out from Anandale now. Then it go be Grammalton, and then they start taking Triangle Tracks towns and moving much quicker, even though we getting ready to break up track. So we need more weaponry and people now. Sorry we can't continue."

"Yeah."

They stood up. Haidan grabbed John's good hand. "Where you staying?"

John told him. Haidan nodded. John knew that he would not forget the address; Haidan's mind was a locked cage. Nothing escaped it.

"And how you money?" Haidan asked. When John shook his head, Haidan dug into his pockets and pulled out a pouch of coins. "Take it all. You at least need lunch, eh? I go try come visit as soon as I get you something. I go find something for you. I promise." Haidan clasped John's shoulder. "I know everything crazy. But it still good to see you. I go come to see you when I done. I want talk to you some more. Hear?"

"Yes. Thank you. For everything."

"Old friend, John. No problem at all."

The guard accompanied them down the stairs and out the doors. An electric waited for Haidan. He jumped in and took off.

The pair of guards by the door stood with John. He turned and asked them for directions to the nearest market.

CHAPTER THIRTY-ONE

Capitol City stank of everything to Pepper. Fruit in the stalls, fear in the sweat of the people walking down Main Street, heading for market. He could smell the fresh salt of the Northern Sea coming in over the rooftops, a fine mist that settled on his coat, and that had to be brushed off like flakes of dander when it dried.

The smells built up, and Pepper stood still. He let the hems of his new leather trench coat, traded for Azteca gold in one of the towns along the coastal road, flow in the breeze. People avoided him, a second instinct. They looked at him sideways, or from a distance.

John deBrun, where you is? Pepper wondered, the accent of his deepest thoughts much like the voices around him. The ancestry was the same.

No traces of John. Did he pass John and his companion at some point and get to Capitol City first? He'd roamed all over the city for the past two nights. Maybe. John would be slower in the jungle than Pepper. Pepper was made for the kind of situation, John less so.

But something else got Pepper's attention: Teotl. And Loa. Alien scents so very similar to each other. Right at the corner of Fifth Street and Main.

Pepper followed the faint traces, zigging and zagging to pick it back up where it had been trampled out by dirty shoes, manure, or dirty water.

The trail led all the way to Capitol Harbor. A small fleet of sailing vessels lay at anchor. Many more were tied up along the lower stepped piers. Pepper got on his hands and knees and followed the smells to the edge of the pier. The pier itself ran along the almost circular harbor. Only the arch leading out to sea prevented it from making a perfect circle. Tents fluttered in the wind, shelters hastily erected by the press of refugees fleeing into the city. All the buildings and farms that stretched out around Capitol City had been emptied and razed, the crops harvested and put into city storage, and the land burned. It looked as if the apocalypse had already visited the land and left it blackened and flat.

Whoever led the city defenses planned well. There was nowhere for the Azteca to hide within striking distance of the city. Trenches were being dug, no doubt to be lined with stakes or explosives and other surprises. Pepper froze, shook his head, and waited.

The point of a knife dug into his back. "Give me your coat."

Pepper looked down at the water and the edge of the pier, ignoring the person behind him. A streak of clear ooze stained the lip.

Something had been out hunting.

Pepper smiled. What he wanted now was to find out what a Teotl was doing here in Capitol City.

Hopefully not hunting the same thing Pepper was hunting.

And the fact that a Teotl had snuck itself into the city intrigued him. It must have sailed all the way to the Northern Sea and then snuck in. How? Submarine?

Pepper spun around, grabbed the knife, and held his attacker by the throat. The gaunt man held Pepper's wrists and gasped for breath. His ring finger had a mark on it. A wedding band, gone. Pawned?

"Please," the man pleaded. "Me wife, the wind chills her in we boat. Me landlord kick me out. Mongoose-men live there now. What else I go do?"

Pepper looked down at the fish-scaling knife in his hand, then let go of the man. He dug into a pocket and threw gold coins at the man's chest. "I'll keep the knife." Pepper backed away to the edge of the pier. "Consider it a bargain. Leave." The desperate fisherman nodded and ran back toward the tents.

There were spaces between the great slabs of stone that made the pier. Pepper slipped his fingers between them and flexed, then dropped his legs from their hold on the edge until he hung underneath the pier.

Slowly, deliberately, Pepper moved between the forest of pillars. If Teotl could grow submarines again, they might be growing bigger, more dangerous things. Then again, it was only one submarine and one Teotl. If a fleet had been grown and manned by Teotl, Capitol City would be dripping blood back through these sewers.

A submarine, thought Pepper, might come in handy. The *Ma Wi Jung* was buried in the north continent. If and when he caught up to John deBrun, he needed a way to get there.

Time to see what went on underneath these piers.

CHAPTER THIRTY-TWO

S mells of saltfish stew and fresh bread filled the air. The sun hung dead over the market, beating down through the heavy, thick air and warming the skin. A vendor poured a bowl full of saltfish stew from an iron pot hanging over a small wood fire. John handed over too many coins and took the small wooden bowl from the vendor. He walked over to the nearest wall at the corner of the market and held the bowl up and sipped.

Salty, nasty fish in a watery broth.

The smell hit him.

Home.

Shanta.

Someone jostled him, and stew spilled down his fingers. John looked around the square. Hundreds of stalls and umbrellas, people with baskets or wheelbarrows pushing through each other to get from table to table. And packed with desperate city people trying to buy everything. Scraggly fruit, old meat, skinny live animals, patchy vegetables, all were for sale and over sagging wooden tables. Market seemed just as tense as the streets, if not more so. Azteca were coming, and the market knew it. Mothers pushed grandmothers aside to pick at canned meats, and occasional fights were broken apart by watchful ragamuffins.

It was overwhelming.

John dropped the bowl of saltfish, stomach churning. He turned against the wall and threw up, spattering the lower part of the bright red paint.

A few more heaves and he was finished. He stood with his head against the chipped wall, eyes closed. How could he go on? Everything that balanced him was gone. No memories. No nothing. What was a person without memories?

A child.

He'd been stillborn at Brungstun and, desperate for identity, had become a sailor, a fisherman, and adventurer in Capitol City, searching for something.

No one could even begin to explain how it felt to *be nothing*. It sent him into spirals of self-doubt, and fear.

Fear: Suppose he forgot all this?

He was gripped by fear that something would happen, and everyone he knew would become lost to him again. It could happen anytime, he felt on some gut level. He could just lose everything again.

There had been dark moments before his marriage. Moments when, unable to pierce the darkness obscuring what he was, John wondered how to continue.

He was there again.

Running had been action, action that kept one away from thinking too much. Now he had time to think. It made him feel as if he were being spun apart.

John smacked his head against the wall. The pain and jarring on his forehead felt good. How could he know what to do with himself next if he didn't know what to do?

Suppose Shanta and Jerome *were* dead, as Oaxyctl claimed. What did he do with himself then?

Fade away? Because he couldn't start over again. No.

Were his new memories going too? He panicked. No. He remembered Haidan. He remembered the first time he'd met Shanta, Jerome's birth. Everything from the moment he washed up.

He had that.

But didn't have his family anymore, just their memories. And he could never trust memories, could he? John wiped his tears off with a sleeve, then punched the wall until his knuckles were bloody.

Action. Action. He had to *do* something soon, or he wouldn't be able to maintain a hold on anything. No one around him even gave him a second glance. There was an air in the market that John had never felt before, one where people seemed to be in their own space, not looking at each other. It wasn't just him, John thought, the whole place was coming apart.

He took a deep breath and turned back around. Time to find some food that didn't make him think of family and take it back to Oaxyctl.

CHAPTER THIRTY-THREE

Four muddy children and their uncle, a leathery-skinned man in rags and a straw hat, stood in Dihana's office.

"They had round everyone up in town square." The old man's voice quavered, and he put a protective arm around the small girl. "Start in from the edges, yank 'em out, drag them to a stone. Then . . ."

"They take Mum first. Then Dad." The girl had distant, wide eyes. Unflinching and calm, she stared straight at Dihana. "Cut they heart out." They had seen a thing that made Dihana's stomach churn just thinking about it. And to this little girl Dihana was nothing to fear.

The door opened, and another ragamuffin pushed in. "Papers, from General Haidan." He set the sealed packet on her desk.

Dihana regarded the unexpected intrusion. "Sabotage map?" She was expecting a map of sabotage locations and a summary of damage.

"And something else."

She looked up at the small girl, who still stared at her. "How did you all escape?" Dihana asked.

"We didn't." The oldest boy shivered. "They sent us ahead. We it."

Dihana looked up at the ragamuffin who'd brought them into her office. "We don't have much space, everyone trying to make do, but that man behind you will get you some food, and a place to stay."

They shuffled out. The ragamuffin who'd delivered the map waited for the door to close. "Brewer's Village?"

"The last from it, yes."

"They say the Azteca sacrifice over half the village."

"Yes." Dihana waved him quiet. She'd suffered hearing it from the actual survivors coming into the city, and all she could think about was seeing everyone in Capitol City die before her eyes. She unrolled the package, setting aside a clutch of letters to look at the map she wanted. "So it's not just weapons they're after," she murmured. "It's the grain." The Azteca must know that Capitol City would be a long, long siege. They were doing their best to soften it ahead of time with their spies.

"Trying to starve we from the inside," the ragamuffin said.

"Here." Dihana looked up from the map. "Take as many ragamuffins as you can, and tell the mongoose-men in Tolteca-town that this is one of their tasks from now on: block off Tolteca-town from everyone else street by street. Any Tolteca outside Tolteca-town will be picked up and returned, or jailed if they do it again."

"They go revolt."

"Haidan has the mongoose-men tearing up track, looking to destroy the couple bridges between Harford and here. But when the Azteca hit the Triangle Tracks, it won't be long before they come here. In that time the spies in Tolteca-town can do much damage. We can't afford it." On her side Dihana had gotten silos filled, helped the fishermen build new boats with armor and cannon on them to sustain them with fresh fish during the attack. She'd shut down banks, seized businesses, and declared emergency conditions. Every night handbills and criers circulated, explaining what she was trying to do, how they must all stand together.

"Okay." The ragamuffin stared straight at her.

"Someone inform Xippilli before the command goes out, though. Give him an escort to come straight here if he wants. He'll be angry."

The ragamuffin nodded and withdrew.

Dihana turned to look at the letters. The top was just a scribbled note from Haidan: *This is my little secret, and why I think the trip north is so important.*

Underneath was an older slip of paper. "Dear Stucky," Dihana read.

She almost changed her mind when she finished, wondering what *was* hidden away in the cold north of the world. A machine, a weapon . . . but what was the use of an archaeological expedition right now? They would either shatter the Azteca at the foot of their walls or fall to their knives. Trying to study the past now would take too long.

And they needed all the airships to defend the city. Haidan, of all people, should have realized that.

CHAPTER THIRTY-FOUR

Oaxyctl navigated the warrenlike streets of Capitol City in a daze. He kept to the shadows, away from people, and followed a street-by-street pattern from memorized instructions a year old until he passed into a dingy collection of buildings.

Tolteca-town.

He relaxed a bit. It was like home away from home: signs in Nahuatl, occasional snatches of familiar-sounding conversation.

It hadn't occurred to him until this moment, but he'd been the only brown-skinned person among all the darker Nanagadans. Now he didn't stand out as much with his straight fringe of black hair.

Oaxyctl stopped a woman with a laundry basket balanced on her head.

"Could you give me directions to Xippilli's house," he asked. Xippilli, he'd been told, was the most respected of the Tolteca in Capitol City and would be easy to ask for by name. The woman gave him instructions that took Oaxyctl straight to a two-story brownstone, where a number of Tolteca lounged around the front.

"I am looking for Cipactli," Oaxyctl said. "Do you know of him?"

They looked him over. "We'll take you to him."

Cipactli worked for Xippilli as an adviser, Oaxyctl determined by looking over the parchment on Cipactli's desk. Cipactli himself came into the room, dressed in a black suit with a silver tie.

He walked over and fiddled with the desk drawer, then looked up. "I'm sorry," he said with an even face, "I've never seen you before."

"I am Iccauhtli," Oaxyctl said. "New to the city. I presume to ask if you would be generous enough to show kindness to a stranger."

"I am sorry, my brother." Cipactli stopped moving papers around. "I can not . . . offer you help. But let me give you some money."

He handed Oaxyctl a few coins, and something else, feathery, to Oaxyctl's palm.

"You are generous, my lord." Oaxyctl snapped his hand shut. "I will not forget this."

Cipactli ushered him out the door.

Only farther down the road did Oaxyctl unclench his fist and look at the coins. A tiny piece of paper lay between them, giving him Cipactli's home address. Be here in thirty minutes, it said.

Oaxyctl ate the paper and put the coins in his pocket.

Oaxyctl lit a match and watched Cipactli flinch. The dim yellow light danced off the rocky walls and sturdy wooden beams. Dust patterns swirled in front of the match, disturbed by the movement.

"Greetings, fellow *quimichtin*," Oaxyctl said.

"What is your need?" Cipactli walked farther into his own basement. "I have to be careful now. Mongoose-men are everywhere. It is tense."

"A god has charged me with a mission."

Cipactli's mouth dropped. "I apologize. You have anything you need." He swallowed, eyes wide. "Do you know which god?" The match went out, leaving them in the dusky dark of the basement. Cipactli fumbled around to turn on a weak electric light near the stair door.

"I was afraid to ask." Oaxyctl didn't want to think back about the rainy forest encounter. Just get it done, he thought. Get it over as soon as possible, and get out of the city before the invasion. "The invasion is close?" Oaxyctl tried to figure out how much time he had.

"They are over halfway to the Triangle Tracks," Cipactli said. "There are delays. The mongoose-men slow them down some. But the gods prevail. Anandale will fall in a handful of days yet."

"The gods prevail," Oaxyctl echoed. He'd found paper and pen when he'd snuck in. He handed a list to Cipactli. "I need all these."

"You are honored to be charged by a god." Cipactli held the list up to the small light and read it. "Who will you be torturing?"

Oaxyctl wondered if he should tell Cipactli it was not an honor. He wasn't even sure it was safe. The fact that other gods might disagree with his god's need to get these "*Ma Wi Jung* codes" out of John, whatever those were, meant all this might end with Oaxyctl dead anyway.

He sighed. The gods, an invasion army, and who knew what else were destined to destroy the Nanagadan's last enclave within two weeks anyway.

What could he do against that?

Nothing.

The smart man played as best he could. That was all Oaxyctl ever did. Even though the luck had never come to him, he'd survived longer than anyone had thought he would. There was only one way to survive.

Oaxyctl cleared his throat. "Just get these items, please."

"I will. Stay here, and I will return." Cipactli turned off the light and walked up the stairs, leaving Oaxyctl to brood in the dark.

Oaxyctl's eyes adjusted to the dark. A small, painted-over window in the far corner yielded a tiny stream of light. In between small naps Oaxyctl watched it go from pure white to orange to nonexistent by the time Cipactli returned and flicked on the electric light.

The canvas bag he carried clinked when he set it on the ground.

"Everything?" Oaxyctl asked.

"Everything."

Oaxyctl smiled. The end was in sight. "I will need help. A few people to subdue this man and maybe bring him back somewhere like this. I act tonight. I can't risk any more waits, it is stressful as it is making these sorts of gambles."

"There is a problem." Cipactli looked far more solemn than he had earlier. "There is a curfew. It started now, with this sunset."

"Okay. We wait for the sun to rise—"

"No one of Azteca origin can be out without an escort. Anytime."

"Then I leave now." Oaxyctl picked up his atlatl and spears and walked forward to pick up the canvas bag.

"There are other ways to help you, they will just take some time to put in place."

"No, no waiting," Oaxyctl said. "I leave now."

He brushed past Cipactli and up the stairs. The Capitol City *quimichtin* followed him up and let him out a side door.

Oaxyctl did not look back, but melted into the shadows.

It wasn't jungle, but Oaxyctl was still good at keeping out of sight. He only made a few wrong turns that left him dry-mouthed until he regained his bearings. He was almost back before someone spotted him.

A mongoose-man yelled at him to stop, and Oaxyctl froze against the wall. He'd had to get out of the alleys to cross toward a street.

Oaxyctl waited until the mongoose-man was just behind him and pushed his sleeve up to show the tattoo. It hadn't worked before, but it was still worth getting the mongoose-man to come within range.

"I am a mongoose-man."

"Right," the man said. "But Tolteca mongoose are in Tolteca-town to help patrol, which is where you should be." Oaxyctl tensed as the man looked at the tattoo. "Look good. Not many Tolteca there. I respect that. Now, if you hold on, me partner pissing just around the corner. We can escort you back to Tolteca-town."

"Why don't you just let me continue on my own?" Oaxyctl asked, smiling. He turned to look the mongoose-man in the eye and faced a young man. He kept his hip turned, put his left arm into his pocket, and gripped the handle of a knife.

"I can't do that." The mongoose-man smiled back. "And why you alone? Where is *you* partner?"

"Oh." Oaxyctl leaned forward. "He's just—" He grabbed the young man by the shirt, twisted him around, and slit his throat.

The mongoose-man burbled blood and clutched his throat. Oaxyctl guided the mongoose-man gently to the street, rolling him over onto his back, and looked into the glazed eyes.

Then he glanced up and down the street, wiped his knife and hands clean on the mongoose-man's shirt, and ran off before the other mongoose-man could walk around the corner.

CHAPTER THIRTY-FIVE

Capitol City's roots lay deep in the solid rock of Nanagada. Honeycombs of sewer systems, access tunnels, and large caverns lay beneath the streets. Pepper had been though them before, though this time they looked more decrepit and encrusted with age than when the city had first been built.

To get to the sewers Pepper made his way over a few more hundred feet. Then he could watch the waters standing, instead of hanging like a damn monkey from the pier cracks. He'd done that for a few hours.

But now he was back up in the pillars still waiting for the Teotl to show itself.

"Easy, man, watch where you going."

Pepper froze.

Outlets poured wastewater, city water, toilet water, and excess air back out along the sides of the walls that ran along the ocean. All of this was designed to continue running without machinery, though the constant sound of moving and pouring water echoed everywhere. Pepper struggled to locate the direction of the voice.

Someone swore. The voice echoed.

"Nothing. My net dry."

Pepper moved over to one of the massive pillars, trying to keep even closer to shadows.

"How come you ain't bailin'?" Another distinct voice complained.

Here all the trash in Capitol Harbor came. And now it looked as if it was being scavenged. Small figures in rotting boats rowed through the brown water. Pepper relaxed, using two hands to hold himself up instead of keeping one near his gun.

"What? That water nasty."

"Treo. Pick up the bucket and keep we from sinking and swimming in it already."

The sound of water tossed over the side of a boat echoed around.

Pepper let go to hang by one hand, muscles straining against their locked position to hold him upside down from one single handhold. He moved over and grabbed a rusty piton hammered into the side of a great pillar, one of many that allowed the scavengers below him to string nets to strain the harbor water.

Easier to hold.

One of the small boats shipped oars and glided underneath him. They were children, Pepper saw. Bony children at that.

One of them in the boat beneath him leaned over and pulled a net up out of the water. A brown fish struggled. The urchin caught it with deft hands and tossed it into the bottom of the boat. "A fish!"

"Find some more, get we some lime to soak he in, bread it up, go be a good one."

They continued picking at the net while Pepper waited.

"Uuh." The smaller kid to the back of the boat waved his hands. "What that?"

"It a body!" The two moved over.

Pepper squinted. Pink flesh bumped against the small boat's transom. The kid used an oar to poke at his nets, and more pink rolled up. Translucent eyepatches gleamed in the dark water.

"Shit. It a Loa."

"What?"

"I telling you, it a Loa."

A tip of metal crowned a stubby tentacle in the water.

The kid with the oar looked around. "We need go. Everyone, we need leave," he yelled out loud to another boat. "Quick!" His body language showed he suspected they were next. He looked around, at the water, and then at last, in slow suspicion, up.

His eyes widened when he saw Pepper hanging ten feet above him. He fell back, grabbing for oars, mouth wide.

Pepper made a decision. They would help him. They knew the area, they might be able to spot whatever had killed the Loa. And if a Teotl were hanging around, these children were dead. Some might die if Pepper used them as bait as he intended, but at least with Pepper they had a chance.

Pepper let go, stopped his fall by grabbing another piton, then dropped into the aft of the boat in one smooth, quick motion. The boy held up an oar, trying to protect the smaller kid behind him.

"Easy." Pepper spread his hands out.

"Look." The boy's hair was starting to dreadlock, his hands calloused from rowing. Dirty, holed clothes, tattered and held together with net and fishing wire, Pepper noted. "We ain't see nothing, we ain't telling nothing. Let we go. Please."

"I didn't kill it." Pepper leaned over and glanced at the Loa. "But I know what did." He pushed the Loa over and pointed at the claw marks and shredded flaps of skin dangling from the Loa's torso. "Teotl did this." Pepper held up a hand. "See, I have no claws."

The boy shivered. No doubt Teotl had once been a tale told to make him behave, Pepper thought. When he'd had parents.

A second rowboat rounded the pillar. The boy on the bow carried a spear he aimed at Pepper. "What you name? If you touch any of we, I go strike you down," the boy shouted.

"I wouldn't point that at me," Pepper warned. He turned to face the boy in front of him. This was, he discerned, the closest they had to a leader. Pepper took a gold tooth from his pocket, a fleck of brown blood still on the root side. He handed it to the kid, who snatched it.

"I'm Pepper. What is your name?"

"Adamu," the kid said. Which would make the small kid he tried to protect Treo, Pepper thought, filing their voices from what he'd heard while on the pillar. "What you want from we?" Adamu asked, suspicious.

"I want you to help me catch the Teotl."

Adamu looked Pepper back in the eye. Brave. "How? We small."

Pepper nodded. It was best to be honest. Too many people used these kids, then discarded them. They deserved his honesty.

"I need you to be my bait."

Treo leaned forward and grabbed Adamu. "Please don't do it. It dangerous."

"I have more gold." Pepper patted the pocket of his trench coat.

Adamu looked down at the dying fish in the bottom of the boat. "No. We go help."

"Good," Pepper said. "Who are you all?"

"We the posse," Adamu said.

"Posse?"

"Just a name." Adamu shrugged. He looked up as the second boat hit them. The kid with the spear jumped out, jabbed it at Pepper.

Pepper yanked it away and snapped it in half. He took a broken end and hit the boy in the ribs with it.

"What is his name?" Pepper asked Adamu.

"Tito."

"Okay, Tito," Pepper said as Tito, curled up in the bottom of the boat, gasped for air. "I said don't point that at me, and I meant it."

Adamu bit his lip and put his hand in his pocket, fingering the gold. Another few teeth, Pepper knew, would change their world, and Adamu knew it.

If they caught the Teotl, Pepper would make them rich.

For a few days. Because once the Azteca came to Capitol City, chances were it wouldn't matter.

First, Pepper needed them to find their target.

"What we looking for?" Tito asked. His mouth remained set, his eyes slit. But gold was gold. He would do what Pepper said.

"Something under the water. A submarine," Pepper said.

"Like the metal one up in the museum?" Adamu asked. "They dig it out of the harbor. No one know how it work."

"Maybe." Pepper shrugged. "But I'll bet this one is made of wood."

"Wood?" one of the posse asked.

Pepper nodded.

"What about protection?" Adamu asked. "Them look like sharp claws, whatever rip up that Loa."

A smile.

"The safest place for any of you is right here." Pepper blinked. "Now come, we have to get moving."

Adamu sent the two boats to pick up spare nets. Ten minutes later they had rigged them with silt weights to drag the bottom.

Pepper watched, then got in Adamu's boat.

Treo stood up. "Take me back. I want go back into the sewer, get out. I scare."

"Treo," Adamu said. "I don't want you out alone, getting eat by this thing." Treo considered that for a moment, and stayed put.

Adamu started rowing, Treo huddled in the front of the boat.

"Where the Teotl now?" Adamu asked.

"Probably watching us," Pepper said. Treo whimpered. "Don't worry. It won't do anything yet. Not until we find its vehicle."

Pepper hunched over in his seat and bundled his long coat around him. He looked around the boat and whistled to himself.

Come out, come out, wherever you are, he sang to himself.

Come say hi to Pepper.

After three hours of slow sweeping, Tito stood up in the other boat and threw his oar down. It clattered between the wooden benches.

Pepper looked around at them all.

He took another gold tooth out from the trench-coat pocket by his chest and held it over the side of the boat. He opened his hand, and it plinked into the water.

The tiny waves smoothed out.

They went back to sweeping.

"Hey!" The shout echoed around them, bouncing around and skimming over the water.

"Yeah, yeah, this it." The boats slowed down, the net wrapping around something large under the water.

Tito stood and waved an oar triumphantly. The net wrapped around a twenty-foot-long curve of smooth black wood that broke the surface of the water as they tugged the nets up.

Pepper stood up and shrugged the trench coat off. He pulled the shotgun strapped to his right thigh free, letting his eyes go combat and talk to the gun.

Colors fell away, replaced by a wash of night-vision greens.

His skin crawled. His heart doubled speed, his extra veins sang.

Pepper balanced on the transom of the boat, shotgun aimed at the smooth black wood in the nets, hardly swaying as Adamu jerked the boat forward.

When they bumped against it, Pepper sprang into the air and landed on top without a sound. There was not a visible joint on the black curves, until Pepper leaned forward and found a lever.

He pushed it in with one hand, then pulled. The hatch opened, and Pepper ducked over it, shotgun aimed down in first, trigger almost all the way down.

Back again.

The kids stared at him. The speed was inhuman, and they were probably wondering what the hell he was.

"Nothing in there," Pepper said.

"We sink it?" Adamu asked.

"No. I want it." Pepper looked around at the rows of pillars and dark water. It was out there.

Now left. Be careful, he told himself. Maybe he could take the creature alive.

Get information out of it.

"The Teotl can swim?" Adamu asked.

"Maybe this one flies," Pepper said. "Maybe it swims. I don't know. They come in many different shapes and sizes. Depends on what they were bred for." Some even went back into pupation to change later in life.

There was a distant splash, one audible only to Pepper's ears.

"It's coming." Pepper raised a hand. "Move your boats behind me."

They hustled to ship oars and move.

CHAPTER THIRTY-SIX

Fifteen minutes of silence on the porch passed for Dihana. She heard her name being called farther down the corridor and ignored it.

Not right now. Another five minutes, she thought.

Haidan threw the doors open. The glass pane on the right-hand one shattered, the pieces falling and bouncing off the stone.

"Haidan!" He froze in place. Dihana folded her arms. First piece of information first. "Anandale and Grammalton aren't responding to any messages. I think they've been cut off. You said we had over a week before Anandale was invaded."

"I hadn't heard that yet." Haidan grabbed the doorframe. "You sure?"

"I can reach Harford. That's it."

Haidan bit his lip. "You know my estimate on when they would arrive was a guess. They probably using airship, dropping warrior off in the bush outside them town to cut off the wire."

"But do they have enough warriors to attack those towns? Or just cut them off."

"I don't know. I don't know." His boots crunched over the glass as he walked over to the railing and swept a hand out at the city. "I want to talk about this curfew you put up."

"Bombs, Haidan. They're trying to take our airships, our food."

"I know that. But you compromising things. I have agent there. You asking me where the Azteca is and if they can take a town, but the Tolteca won't tell me nothing now. We blind and deaf in Tolteca-town. So don't be surprise I can't tell you nothing. And by the way, you enjoy telling me mongoose-men what to do too much."

"I had to do something. And for all the agents you have, we were still getting hit hard. All those lost airships will hamstring us. And the grain silos they've destroyed . . ."

Haidan sat down and rubbed his eyes. "Maybe I wrong to be so vexed. But things is hazy. You want know how many Azteca marching for we? You want know what kind? The food they carry? Until you shut down Tolteca-town, people there was telling me all that. Now they don't trust me. We can't afford this, Dihana."

"I know. They'll hate me. Xippilli won't talk to me."

"Curfew everyone," Haidan said. "Already I lose one mongoose-man in this. Tolteca and city people beating each other up."

Dihana stepped closer to him. "I'm sorry."

He bit his lip. "Curfew for everyone," he repeated. "Not only Azteca-looking saboteur out. You know this, you see who kill the council-them back at that warehouse."

Dihana blinked. He was right.

She sat down on the ground, away from the broken glass, her back against the wrought-iron curlicues. "Full curfew," she said. "Full curfew. No one out at night unless accompanied by ragamuffins or your men. No matter whether they are Tolteca, Hindi, Nanagadan, or Frenchi. Patrols during the day as usual to try and catch anything."

"And hope we still trust enough by people-them so any strange thing get report."

"Yeah. Hope." Dihana sat for a long second. Hope. "I read those letters you sent."

Haidan walked around in front of her. "Interesting piece of history," he said softly. "What you think?"

"Your plan north?" Dihana got up, walked over to the railing. The sun had just set and the sky glowed orange. Lights started to turn on all over the city. "Those letters tore me up, Haidan. I understand what you're pushing for. But you and I both know we just can't cut our hands off to do this, Haidan. Three airships . . ."

Haidan stood with her and looked down at two mongoose-men guarding the doors. The grass had trampled sections on it from the regular patterns they walked around to make sure the building was safe.

"I ain't go haggle," Haidan said. "I ain't go ask for two airship, then one. Forget any airship. What if I say I got a backup plan?"

"A backup?"

Haidan looked over at her with a smile. Of course he would. It was Haidan. There would be plans within plans, no doubt.

Dihana rested her hip against the wrought-iron patterns. "What is it?"

"The steamship you told me I could have, the one out in the harbor." He smiled. "I help all your Preservationist build it. Been hoping to use it to head up coast, spy on Azteca. We design the hull flat, so it could get into shallow water. But, that same hull, I bet you, work real well in the ice."

Dihana shook her head. "I'm not surprised. You thought about using it to go north before?"

Haidan coughed into the arm of his shirtsleeve. "Got a few modification I want make to it, thing to help it when they get into the snow. Thing I been thinking about since the last expedition came back from the north sea and I talked to them all. Could be expensive."

"As much as an airship?" Dihana asked.

Haidan shook his head. "Manpower. I go need to take some of the Preservationist away for a bit." He grimaced and cleared his throat, dabbed at his lips with a handkerchief that Dihana had been noticing out more and more. "Go remake the ship so they can add treads, crawl over the ice. I seen something similar use up in a lake once, been hoping to make a big one."

"Still a big gamble, taking away resources for something so uncertain."

"Uncertain?" Haidan grabbed her arm. "The Loa love the idea. They know something up there, always have. Now they scare. Azteca coming, and Tetol coming with the Azteca, and that mean them Loa staring death in the eye. Whatever lying north, whatever this *Ma Wi Jung* is, it a sure thing, and the Loa know it go help, or they wouldn't be trying to help we any. Maybe it a weapon of some sort, the Loa ain't saying nothing yet. But we need this *Ma Wi Jung*. Our old-fathers needed it in the past and couldn't get it. We need it now."

Dihana grabbed his arm. "Okay. Do it. Get crew. Try to find anyone willing to go that far north and you've got half the battle won. I've spent at least two meetings trying to talk scared fishermen back out to sea because they think the Azteca are hiding everywhere."

Haidan let go of her and folded his arms. "Don't you worry. I got a whole other surprise for you there."

"What?"

He shook his head. "Later. When thing settle and for sure. Seen? For now I must send message. Make sure me mongoose ain't go get ambush out on the tracks. Make sure they get those two bridge between the Azteca and here destroy. You tell everyone you can reach they *have* to leave them town for the bush."

Dihana didn't answer, and he didn't wait for one. The door remained open, the shattered glass twinkling from Capitol City's lights.

They looked like stars scattered on the ground to her.

*   *   *

Emil found her after the glass had been cleaned up, stopping her in the corridor with a concerned look on his face. Another Councilman hovered at the end of the passageway, waiting to hear her answer.

"Prime Minister." Emil's voice strained from the pleasantness and familiarity trying to be injected.

"Coucilman."

Emil kept his distance and cocked his head. "We have a request, if you have a moment to discuss it?"

Dihana looked down the corridor at the other Councilman, who avoided her gaze. "What do you need?"

Emil spread his hands. "We want to be able to move about."

"Can't risk it. There is a curfew at night as well, just in case you were thinking of sneaking out."

She watched his reaction, a slight opening of the mouth and glance back to the other Councilman. So they were sneaking out of the building. She wondered how. Bribing ragamuffins? She'd have to follow up on that.

The secretiveness, again, irked her.

"We're setting up a mission to the north," she told him. "A place called Starport. You know where that is?"

Emil folded his hands. "An old, old memory. That is where we had come down to Nanagada. I was just a child." He closed his eyes.

"We are going for the *Ma Wi Jung*."

"You *know*," Emil whispered. "You know about that?"

Dihana smiled. "The Loa are also interested."

"Don't matter." Emil shook his head. "No one alive who could work it. Not on this planet. Certainly not you Preservationist, they know nothing. Is just a ship. A ship like the one we come down to Starport on. Nothing special, they say, except that the Loa help we make it. But *there none of we that could make it work now*. The last one done dead. You understand? We done dead. I got to go." His voice was soft. "We preparing for the worse now. We know this time might come, but we had always hope not, you know?"

Dihana let him walk past. "Emil."

"Yeah?" He kept walking, his back to her.

"Don't leave the building. It's dangerous."

He turned the corner.

They seemed broken, Dihana thought. They'd seen everything fall as far as it could. From before the time of legend, to the fall of Mafolie Pass, to seeing Capitol City come under direct attack. They were facing their own mortality, something they hadn't done in a long time.

She could feel sorry for them. She could lose a bit of the bitterness she reserved for them.

Dihana left them to send a message to the Loa priestesses, explaining Haidan's new twist in his planning.

CHAPTER THIRTY-SEVEN

John had not returned yet, so Oaxyctl washed his hands, threw away the slightly bloodied shirt, and put on his spare shirt. Then he wrapped the ends of a length of rope around his hands slowly, as if he had weights attached to his fingers, and planted himself just by the door.

He took several deep breaths.

Several minutes of waiting later, a hard knock on the door rattled it in its hinges. DeBrun wouldn't knock, Oaxyctl thought. He unwrapped the rope from his hands and slid it between the limp bed mattress and the boards underneath.

Three men stood at the door when he cracked it open.

The silver-dreadlocked man in front, a handkerchief held over his mouth, coughed. He folded the piece of cloth back up and put it in his breast pocket.

"Where is John?" he asked. "John deBrun?"

"He isn't here," Oaxyctl said. "I can take a message for you."

"No, that's okay." The man's eyes narrowed. "Maybe we can just wait for him?"

"There isn't much space in here," Oaxyctl mumbled. His throat constricted, he could barely breathe.

"That's okay. I could come in alone."

One of the two men behind him put out an arm. "Haidan . . ."

Haidan. *The* mongoose-general. Oaxyctl looked at the two mongoose-men. He didn't stand a chance. His world crumbled. The atlatl was too far away, the odds against him. The mongoose-men sized him up as well. Their rifles lay cradled in the crooks of their elbows.

"Yes, why don't we all squeeze in," Oaxyctl said.

Everyone hesitated a moment. Then Haidan walked in and the two mongoose-men followed. Oaxyctl closed the door behind them.

Haidan smiled. "So here we all are. And who are you?"

Oaxyctl didn't reply. He raised the corner of his shirtsleeve and showed the tattoo. The two guards nodded, but Haidan's eyes remained neutral. Feeling another slight seed of guilt for again abusing this brothership of the mongoose-men, Oaxyctl walked into the washroom, calm. He turned on the light and closed the door behind him.

Inside the cupboard lay his tools, the ones he'd just now unpacked from the canvas bag. Serums, scalpels, knives, Oaxyctl packed them all tightly into a small leather bag. Then he sat on the privy and took more deep breaths.

He might have to kill all these men to get John. He might die trying. They might just leave. Or not. But his god had given him a quest, and that was to get the codes to the *Ma Wi Jung*. This he had to do, any way possible.

Oaxyctl was nervous. If he did die, he would have failed the god . . .

To go to your death is a release, he whispered to himself. To meet your gods is an honor. To give your body to the earth is your destiny.

At least, that is what they say. Oaxyctl was more worried about the things the gods could do to him while still alive, and *would* do, if he failed.

The door outside creaked open, muffled from Oaxyctl's position inside the bathroom.

"John," the mongoose-general said.

"Haidan?" Oaxyctl heard John reply.

Oaxyctl took one final deep breath and opened the door.

All eyes fastened on him for a second. John put down a paper bag of groceries. A wad of celery stalks tied with blue string stuck out of the top and leaned over.

"What's going on?"

Haidan walked over. "We need you, John."

John sat on the bed. The boards underneath it creaked and settled. The two mongoose-men moved back to stand by the sides of the door. "I'm not flying to the northlands. I'm staying to fight."

Oaxyctl sat down at the small table.

"It most likely you go die," Haidan said. "Eventually. You ain't that good a fighter, you only got one hand."

"Then I will die," John said.

"Come, man," Haidan hissed. "You ain't one to give up. You a fighter. I know this. I seen you push through the jungle before."

John shook his head. "That was a different time."

"You scared?"

"Scared?" John raised his hook and looked at the light playing off it. "No. Tired, lost. My family is dead. And I left them there." He hit his chest with the side of the curved steel. "Haidan . . . there's nothing left for me."

Haidan sat on the bed next to John. The boards protested as the cheap bed pushed down. Oaxyctl held his hands steady over the table, but every muscle in his body tensed.

"John." Haidan pulled out the stained handkerchief from his breast pocket and held it out. "If anyone go die here, it go be me. You and I know I been sick ever since you pull me out that swamp in Hope's Loss and this here damn cough had start." Haidan dropped the rust-colored cloth to the ground. "I need someone who ain't go give up now. I need someone strong. I need you to go all the way north for me. I know you can lead men. I had talk to sailors who you lead back to the city. You the man for this. I know it."

Haidan stood up, and Oaxyctl let out a held breath.

"John," Haidan said. "You want revenge? You want to make Azteca pay?"

Oaxyctl scratched at his left index fingertip.

"Them bastard kill you family, they kill Shanta," Haidan continued. "They kill we friend in Brungstun. You want blood, I go give you blood, man: *Ma Wi Jung*."

Oaxyctl jumped in place, startled. Those words. Did these people know about his god's quest?

"Leave him." Oaxyctl's voice broke. "He's been through enough."

"Why you test me?" Haidan asked, turning around. "You mongoose, true, but I don't know you, and you tattoo new. Don't cross me."

John stood up between them. Oaxyctl kept his hands still on the table's rough wooden surface. If he shoved hard enough, he could feel a splinter poke into his palm. The pain helped center him.

"Give him slack," John said.

Haidan coughed. Blood flecked his lips. He wiped at it with the back of his forearm.

"Fine. Listen, John, I could get you the greatest revenge. You want bust the Azteca back? Then you go north. You go north and you find something, something from we old-father time, and you use it to smite the Azteca. That is *true* revenge. I can give you this."

John's back slumped forward. "Tell me more." It was an act of surrender, Oaxyctl realized.

"By steamship, with you the captain."

"With some ragtag crew? Made of fishermen, right? I did that once before." John paused, and everyone in the room hung on every movement of his back, his shifting feet, a sniff. "Maybe. If I captain the boat."

Haidan nodded. "Then I say you the captain."

"Who are the officers?"

"People I go choose."

"Good people? I'll need some mongoose-men who'll follow my orders."

"If you agree to go, I give up my best mongoose-man," Haidan said.

John looked around the room. Then he looked at Oaxyctl. "Will you come aboard with me?"

Oaxyctl pushed the palm of his hand farther into the splintered piece of wood. "What do I know of boats?"

"I will teach you," John said.

Haidan said, "I want this expedition launch within the week, before any spy in town realize what happening and try to stop it, and well before Azteca arrive at the city wall. I want momentum, I want it now."

Oaxyctl pulled his hand up from the table, the splinter breaking off inside his hand. "I will pack my things." Even to himself he sounded distant.

Gods, what a disaster.

Ma Wi Jung. What else could he do but follow them there? The group assembled outside the door of the small apartment, John with his single bag of groceries, and nothing else to his name, and Oaxyctl with his atlatl and bundle of spears, a small bag in his left hand.

On his way out, Oaxyctl ground the bloodied handkerchief Edward had dropped onto the dirty concrete floor with the heel of his ragged boot.

Born under the sign of Ocelotl, he said to himself.

Certainly.

CHAPTER THIRTY-EIGHT

For several minutes Pepper stood and listened to the water. He heard the creature come up, expelling air, watching them as the boys moved their boats around, drawing attention to themselves. Pepper motioned Adamu closer and got back in the boat.

The water remained calm for a maddeningly long time. Tiny waves lapped against the pillars. The city pipes trickled, emptying water out nearby.

Right there. Pepper saw the dimmest of shapes beneath the water by Tito's boat. Pepper pointed, and Tito picked up a spear from inside the boat. Like a tiny harpoonist the boy balanced on the side of the boat and slung it.

The shape darted underneath, and Tito's boat splintered. Water splashed out from the inside, and the kids leapt into the water.

"Stay close to the submarine," Pepper warned, not wanting Adamu to row them away.

The floor underneath erupted, and Pepper stepped back. Gray skin pushed through the floor planks, and a smooth, skeletal face turned his way. Adamu bent over the oars, his back to the creature, and shivered.

Eyelids blinked at the pair of shotguns Pepper had pointed at it.

Treo, in the front of the boat, screamed. One snap of the razor-sharp claws later and Treo's throat erupted blood.

Adamu turned around, the beginning of a scream on his lips. Pepper shoved him aside with an elbow and smashed the guns against the Teotl.

The claws turned his way.

He couldn't avoid them, but embraced them, firing the shotgun and throwing it aside to grab the creature's head and head-butt it. It tried to retreat back into the water, but Pepper hung on, ripping at its eyes with his fingers.

Three more shots later, Pepper managed to get the net around it. He was losing blood as fast as it was losing ichor, clear ooze making it slippery to drag the creature out of the boat up onto its own submarine.

Pepper threw it down the hatch, dizzied and burning hot with combat fever. He stopped a second to grab his trench coat before the rowboat sank, leaving the kids treading water or scrambling up onto the submarine. Then he followed the Teotl down.

He slid a knife out from his ankle strap and regarded the Teotl in front of him. Its legs were finlike around the shins and calves, but it still had feet. The hands were deadly.

Now the screaming could begin, Pepper thought.

He took the knife and made a few selective cuts, then pulled the claws free. The wailing deafened him.

And that was the beginning.

Pepper could hardly understand the creature's language. He could hardly understand its physiology. Only with that understanding would he torture something, so he could tell if that thing was lying to him.

It took time, many hours, but eventually Pepper understood the creature enough to make it cry, and then confess. It managed the spies in Capitol City. It told them what to destroy and when. And it was also hunting for John deBrun.

It thought John was alive and well, and in the city.

They knew about John. They knew about *Ma Wi Jung.* It had tortured the dead Loa to find out that John was on a mission to go to the northlands on a steamship.

There were Azteca warships at sea north of the city. They were ready to stop the journey north and capture John. In case John used an airship, saboteurs waited with bombs to destroy the airship.

This had been well worth the danger.

Pepper finally moved the submarine next to the sewers so that Adamu and his "posse" didn't have to hang off it. When he climbed out of the hatch five hours later, he stank of Teotl ichor, and one of the boys gagged and threw up when saw Pepper.

He was covered in his own blood, ribbons of shredded flesh, and bits of Teotl. Pepper, wearing the trench coat again, pulled it closer around him, ignoring the pain of cloth rubbing exposed wounds.

Adamu and Tito dragged Treo's body out of the water into the sewer and looked back up at Pepper with tired eyes.

He squatted next to the tiny body. Treo couldn't have been more than seven. "I'm sorry."

"Sorry. That how it is for you kind," Adamu said. "You ain't the one that find him last year, tie up and . . . bloody, left to die on a street up above." Adamu looked up at the stone overhead. "So now you give us more gold and escape in that submarine, right? I wonder why. I hear the Azteca coming. You go make a quick escape or what?" Adamu's lips curled with distaste. Pepper said nothing. "That how it is, right?" Adamu sniffed. "You didn't shoot that thing, you wanted it alive. The price of one boy, some boy you know nothing about, acceptable. You just like anyone else, we nothing to you."

Pepper took a small bundle of cloth from under his trench coat and threw it to Adamu. "It's all gold. Melt it down before anyone sees what it all is, or they will ask questions and take it from you."

Adamu opened it. A crown with a panther. Jade hammered into anklets, and wristbands. All Azteca. He looked back at Pepper. "How you get all this? Who you is really?"

"The Azteca a scary night story, right?" Pepper asked.

Adamu nodded.

"Well, I am the Azteca's scary story. I have been that for a long, long time. They marching toward Capitol City. They will be here soon." Pepper winked. "Take the gold. I don't need it anymore. But don't waste it."

Adamu swallowed.

"I'm sorry for everything." Pepper walked back onto the submarine. When he crawled into the hatch, he paused and looked back at Adamu. "When the Azteca come, stay inside here, stay quiet, and don't go topside. Anyone else coming down here doesn't understand the tides, or the sewers. They'll drown, you'll be safe. Use the gold to get as much food and stores as you can this week."

Adamu quivered as Pepper stepped farther down. "Just leave us, please," Adamu said to Pepper's face, all that was visible now.

Pepper climbed down and did so.

That was almost all the gold. And no matter how much he would have given them, he knew, it wasn't enough. It was never enough.

He looked down at the Teotl. Time to dump the body, clean the submarine, and hide it somewhere. Then go get cleaned up. Eight hours of recovery and as much as he could eat to get the repair processes in his body working overtime.

After that, find John. Who was alive and here, it seemed.

But first, a brief bit of rest.

CHAPTER THIRTY-NINE

John stood at the apex of Grantie's footbridge. This was the northernmost edge of the city, a tall arch that curved over the harbor entrance. It was the farthest point of land on Nanagada, and the ocean stretched underneath out to the horizon unbroken.

Two days of preparing the ship and he still wondered if he should slip out of Haidan's grip and join the mongoose-men on the wall of the city to fight the Azteca when they came. It looked like the Azteca had taken Anandale and Grammalton, which meant they would be on the Triangle Tracks soon. Even Haidan admitted he didn't know how much track had been destroyed, or if his men had been able to destroy any bridges leading to Capitol City. They'd be coming soon. Weeks.

Haidan would find out quickly enough if he left and joined the mongoose-men. How many one-handed men with hooks were in Capitol City?

Haidan had worked hard to dispel all of John's doubts, showing him how they would convert the ship to drive over the ice. Haidan had designed it so that the ship could travel over reefs using metal treads that ran off the steam engine, thinking he could use it to get mongoose-men into Azteca lands by sailing around the Wicked Highs to approach their coast. The ship had yet to be finished when the Azteca had come over the Wicked Highs. There was even a new compass and sextant, along with his new charts for the trip. Haidan had thought of everything possible.

A beacon ship at anchor outside the arch flashed its steady pulse out into the murky gray expanse of ocean.

Should he do this? Captain another mission to the north when the last had failed? Haidan was persuasive. When you were with Haidan. When John wasn't checking the steamship over, getting acquainted with it, he was left with his doubts.

He felt as if he were running again. He'd run from Brungstun, and he felt like a coward for doing it still, even though he had had no other choice. Now he was choosing not to fight the Azteca in battle, but skulk away up north to find some mystery device.

Where to turn? John couldn't talk to Haidan, he was too busy supervising everything under the sun in Capitol City. Oaxyctl was crew now, and that shouldn't have made a difference, but something funny was in the air when John tried to talk to him.

He scratched under his wrist where the buckles irritated his skin. A faint blotch of rust scarred the tip of his hook. He hadn't been taking good care of it, oiling it every night and drying it off.

John turned his back to the ocean and rested his elbows on the rail and looked out over the masts in the harbor. A small dory tacked in toward the smaller docks off one of the piers. Several fires glittered on the piers, illuminating tent cities that grew larger every day.

In the center of the harbor Haidan's steamship rode at anchor. Long, sleek, it had three raked-back boilers. No paddle wheels. Haidan used a copy of a propeller dug out of the bottom of the harbor by one of the city Preservationist teams.

The ship had enough coal to make the journey. Even now a small flat-bottom skiff lay next to the ship, unloading food supplies.

John gripped the rail. They needed cannon. They needed more guns. A larger contingent of mongoose-men. And more training. John and Haidan had found all the spare fishermen and Frenchis living in town they could. He had the old deckhands drilling the green ones, showing them the ropes. Including Oaxyctl. Everyone but Haidan and John remained on the ship, ready to drop and leave at a moment's notice.

Some in the crew were already grumbling, missing family and women who were just within sight.

Not a good start.

It would have to do. Just in the two days since John had agreed, Edward had showed him pictures taken by courier airships of the Azteca pushing up the coast toward Anandale.

Two days was no length to plan an expedition. But Haidan had anticipated much of it already. And what was the alternative? Wait until the Azteca arrived?

John took a deep, salty breath. *There is a plan, a mission, something to do.* It isn't a direct fight, he told himself, but maybe in the big picture this will hurt the Azteca.

That made him feel better about himself. But it didn't go far enough in filling in the hole ripped out of his center.

Sometimes he wondered how much more he could endure.

John sighed. Edward had also done John an extra honor, trying to help John cope with the loss in Edward's own way. He'd named the steamship *La Revanche*. The Revenge, in one of the old languages that Haidan said had died out right after Hope's Loss. A way to get John's full support. John knew Haidan was manipulating him, but he embraced it. He wanted, deeply enough, revenge.

So *La Revanche* she was. His revenge.

The town clock, housed in the belfry over the Ministerial Mansion, gonged that it was five. He had to leave for a meeting.

The footbridge's grayed planks flexed.

"Afternoon." Someone walked forward. John half-turned to his left. The tall man, with straggly, wet, shoulder-length locks and a tattered coat, looked right back at him. "Mr. deBrun." The man smiled. He looked like a mongoose-man.

Maybe. A tiny pinprick of recognition stirred in John. "I'm sorry"—he frowned—"I don't . . . really know who you are."

The man stopped. John felt that the man was a bit stunned, but nothing in the man's face, or eyes, confirmed that. John let his hook drop to his side. This man *felt* dangerous. Yet John felt he wasn't *in* danger. Be careful, he told himself.

"You're telling the truth," the large man said. "You don't know who I am."

"How should I know you?"

"It was a long, long time ago." One of the man's eyes looked translucent and rheumy. A torn piece of his coat flapped in the wind.

John stiffened. This *was* someone who'd known him before he had lost his memory. *And he'd recognized him first.* Just a tiny prick of it, but something, nonetheless. This was new.

"Who are you?" John stammered, not sure what to ask. This was the biggest clue to his past life ever, just standing in front of him.

"Incredible." The man laughed.

"How did you know me?" John wanted to seize the man by the large coat. "What was I? You must talk to me."

The man shook his head. "This changes just about everything. You really don't remember anything?"

John rifled through his head, hoping for a name to go with the feeling. Nothing came. It had been there once though. It was like something on the back of his tongue.

"Please, can I buy you a meal? A drink?" John asked.

"This was not quite what I had planned." The man folded his arms. "You are a planning a trip. A northerly one. I could help you."

Suspicion crept up on John. He'd felt this man to be dangerous at first. It was gone now, but he should still trust that instinct. Some people would try to sabotage their expedition: Azteca spies and sympathizers. An industrious person could have found out John had amnesia when he'd washed up in Brungstun easily enough, and be using that to manipulate him now.

If John's past included Azteca, who knew what might be happening here? What was a faint memory of feeling, or whatever it was that had happened when he'd seen this man at first, when compared to everything else he had just been through?

"What are your sailing skills?" John asked, trying to get the man to speak more so he could recapture something, anything, that would help him figure out how to better handle this encounter.

"I'm good in the cold. And I fight very well."

The back of John's neck prickled. "I'm sorry." John made another hard decision and hated it. He raised his hook, readying himself for anything. "I am just advising an old friend on outfitting a ship. I think you heard wrong, there is no trip north, whatever you may have heard. But if I hear of anything, I would like to help you. What did you say your name was?"

"Pepper."

"If you left me an address, I could get back to you. I want to know about my past. If you knew me before I lost my memory, you can help me . . ." If Pepper wasn't a spy, this was a big risk, turning away what might be an old friend. John's heart thudded. He couldn't believe he had to do this. Turn away a clue to his past for fear of disclosing this mission north. But the Azteca who'd killed his family must pay first.

He *was* committed to going north. Something deep inside him felt that it was the best course of action. But then, he'd pushed himself north before, following some forgotten ancient impulse within himself.

Pepper shook his head. "That won't work, John. I know you're leaving very soon, so now you're playing with me. Risky on your part, but I understand your caution. Let's deal anyway. You bring me aboard *La Revanche*, and as we sail, I tell you more about your past."

John bristled at the manipulation. Pepper could read him well.

"You could be lying," John said. If Pepper had met him any other time but right before the invasion, right before the trip north, everything would have been different. "You could say anything, and how would I know?" John ground his teeth. "I'm very sorry I don't remember you. I want to remember who you are, but I can't."

Besides, what if Pepper got him alone in some room in Capitol City and tortured him for information about *La Revanche* instead of giving him information about his past? John couldn't take that risk. Just hearing that he had been alone on Grantie's Arch would have made Haidan angry.

"So am I, but don't worry about it too much." Pepper reached out his hand. John shook it. "I'm going to go now. To better times?"

"To better times," John echoed, puzzled.

Pepper turned around. He limped back down the footbridge the way he had come.

If he had been an old friend, then John had done the man a disservice.

Maybe turning him away had been a mistake.

John looked reluctantly down at the timepiece on his waistband, a present of Haidan's. Damn. He was late.

When he looked back up, Pepper was nowhere to be seen.

That was when John realized that Pepper had spoken in the same accent that John did.

Alone on the bridge, John punched the empty air and swore.

CHAPTER FORTY

John watched Haidan cup his chin in his right hand, elbow on the chair's wooden arm, and sigh. The windows had been pulled shut. Only a series of electric lights in the middle of the table lit the area.

"We close," Haidan told him. "*Revanche* stock. Got enough food for there and back." He cleared his throat. Moving the hand under his chin away, he laced his fingers together to look over the top of his chapped knuckles at John. "How you feeling?"

John changed the subject. "Prime Minister Dihana will christen the boat tomorrow?" She was out meeting a group of refugees, trying to bring order and get a census of how many lay in the city's streets and in the tents in the piers.

"And you leave the next day," Haidan said. "Everything, charts, copies of the documents I want you to read, are in you cabin, sealed."

"Thank you. What about you?"

"What about me?"

"Aren't you coming? Who knows this plan better?"

"I have to stay." Haidan put the palms of his hands on the edge of the table and drummed his fingers. "I visible. The whole city know me, know my skill for leading the mongoose. If I leave, what they go think? DeBrun, you the best sailor Capitol City ever see. You and I both know you can figure that map out and navigate that boat."

"This is that important?" John dug the tip of his hook into the table and broke off a small piece of wood.

"The Loa think so. I believe it. Dihana believe it. We got three of the city best Preservationist ready to get on you ship. John, man, I ordering my best mongoose-man out with you: Avasa. And his best mongoose. I can't give you anything more without hurting us here in the city bad. You understand how important I think this may go be?"

The door opened. A mongoose-man walked in and whispered into Haidan's ear. "Okay," Haidan said as the man left. "They here."

Haidan let go of the table. The table lights lit him from beneath. His dreads cascading down out of seemingly nowhere.

"A Loa join we now." Haidan leaned forward, more of his weathered face coming into the light. "They insist on it, just as they had insist on the journey. See what I mean about how important this is?"

A strange tickle ran down the back of John's spine. Would Loa be on his ship? A strange reversal from the last expedition, a journey the Loa had protested, priestesses denouncing the attempt throughout the waterfront. The Loa themselves even came out of their six streetside buildings to stand on balconies and show their displeasure.

"This Loa tell me that it go help you. We really need that."

"Okay," John said. "Where the priestess?"

Wheels squeaked. A divan poked forward through the door into the electric light. A Loa's comma-shaped body lay on the couch: a wet, pink silhouette on the purple plush. Its steel-tipped tentacles dragged on the floor, pushing it forward.

"This isn't the same Loa we speak to earlier," Haidan noted.

"I have not the need of a translator," the Loa hissed at them. The sound sent shivers down John's shoulders. "My helper stays in the corridor." The door shut. "Nor do I want any other than you to hear my words." Clear eyes squinted in the light. The creature looked around the room by shifting its thick upper body up onto a tentacle to regard them.

"The *Ma Wi Jung*," it rasped. "The location coordinates you have are correct. And you surmise that it can be used to stop Azteca correctly."

"Good to know," Haidan said. "But what is it? How can we use it to stop the Azteca? And which Loa are you?"

"The one you spoke to is dead," the Loa said with a sigh. "It is unimportant. This expedition faces an obstacle. You must realize that you are not capable of using the *Ma Wi Jung*. Your technology, even if closely guided by us, is hundreds of years away in such regards. But my kind has an item that can be of assistance. So we must work together."

It held up a silver cone in one of its tentacles and set it on the table. John picked it up and turned it over. "How will this help us use the old-father artifact?"

"If you follow the coordinates exactly, and dig through the ice to get to it, the entrance to the *Ma Wi Jung* is an oval door, and on the left is a square box. Place this on the box. It will take a week, maybe two, but it will be able to open the *Ma Wi Jung* to you," the Loa said. "It will inform you when it is able to open the ship to you. You can then tell it to open the ship to you."

"But then what?" Haidan asked. "How they go use this thing? What it go *do*?"

"I have not finished," the Loa said. "The *Ma Wi Jung* will need more than just you can provide it to create a powerful weapon. Our device will follow your commands. You must tell it to force the *Ma Wi Jung* to come to Capitol City. Tell it, 'Khafou, fly this device back to Capitol City coordinates.' You must use that exact phrase. It has been precreated for you to tell it to do that. Do you understand?"

John and Haidan nodded.

"Please repeat the command phrase," the Loa said. John repeated it. The Loa settled farther into its couch. "Good. Make sure you stand inside the doors when you say this. You will return to the city where we can share the power of the *Ma Wi Jung*'s functions with you." It shifted its flabby body. "Remember, you cannot control the *Ma Wi Jung* without us. Only together can we use *Ma Wi Jung* as a weapon. If you try to do this by yourselves, or hide *Ma Wi Jung* from us, you will certainly suffer."

Haidan leaned forward again. "The Councilman Emil told Dihana *Ma Wi Jung* is a ship, one that can fly up past the sky," Haidan said to the Loa. "I listen to you speak, and it sound like you believe the same thing. Is that what this thing is?"

The Loa shifted. "I think so."

"Then how it go make a weapon?"

"If you had something that could take you anywhere in the world in minutes," the Loa said, "how would *you* use it as a weapon?"

John leaned forward while Haidan thought about that. "What exactly is this?" John held up the cone from the table.

"I was born to be master of languages for my kind and nothing more," the Loa explained, almost out of breath with the sentence. It spoke as if it was not accustomed to so much effort. "My memory dims with the years, but I remember almost three hundred years. Some of us were grown for the purpose of breaking into ancient machines and controlling them. They are the Kha. That was in the long years before I was created, when there were machines to be controlled, and fought, and used. But no one has ever needed Kha since then, and so they died. Only our master breeders kept the templates, in case they were ever needed. We have nourished and raised this Kha ever since the old prime minister died. We teach it what little we know, we expose it to the ancient ones among us who still remember things. It will crack open the *Ma Wi Jung* when you arrive using old memories we have kept for it. It will let you in."

"And bring the machine back to the city?" Haidan asked.

"Yes. Then we can study and use this machine to save us. We will do this together. We must examine this machine together. You must use the Kha to bring it here, or we will all die when the Teotl attack. And you must do this soon. Already one of us has been killed this week. It is untenable."

The tentacles stirred, their metal tips clinking against the cement floor, and the wheeled chair rolled out of the room.

"Something ain't right." Haidan leaned forward in his chair to look closer at the cone of metal in John's hand. "They been fighting metal technology for as long as anyone can remember, now they want help us bring it back. Strange change of mind."

"I imagine they want to survive." John had been transfixed watching the Loa. A second memory returned to him. Distrust. It sat ugly in the pit of his stomach. "They're staring death in the face."

"Yeah. And they refuse to let us guard them. Something up."

"They've been part of Capitol City for as long as anyone can remember." John puzzled through the question himself. "You might disagree with their advice, but haven't they always helped the city?"

"Common interest," Haidan said. "The Loa don't want be invade and that's the only thing I can pin them down on. True, they ain't like we, and we don't know what they thinking, and we need be careful out there, but they still want the Azteca away from the city. I think that the only thing we can trust from them."

"So this is probably genuine." John stood up. He wanted to get out to the ship, check it over, make sure all was well. He needed to hide the Loa's Kha somewhere safe with the other papers he would use to guide the mission north. And he wanted to get in motion before his own doubts and second guesses could begin. "We should get moving, then."

"Yeah."

John reached out with his good hand, keeping the Kha in the crook of his elbow. Despite the metallic sheen, it felt as warm as his own body. "You're right though. If the Loa want this that bad, it probably is going to be one hell of an adventure."

Haidan stood up and grabbed John's good hand. "Good. I need you navigation and captain skills. You the best. We lucky you made it to the city."

"The north won't be an easy place on men." John let go of Haidan's hand and gestured at his hook.

Haidan looked at the leather straps. "Neither was Hope's Loss when you and me had pass through there. I lucky to still be alive."

They looked at each other, remembering others who had died in the jungle from whatever it was they had walked into.

Only John hadn't been affected.

"At least," Haidan said thoughtfully, "we got a chance now. Before I were spitting in the dark, hoping this would help we. Total long-shot plan. Now I know for sure it a good thing. You could make all the difference, John, if this thing go let we hurt the Azteca something good."

CHAPTER FORTY-ONE

Far above Jerome the booming of waves against the rock was a distant and constant sound that permeated every conversation, whisper, and sound in the underwater caves. Sometimes the water flowing by the entrance to the cave would cool, and fog would creep in over the sand. Jerome would huddle in a pit of sand close to the rocky walls. There he could feel the thud of water against the small of his back.

The week went on, and Jerome realized how long they would be here for. Troy and other men came and went, diving out with scudder-fish to scout.

So Jerome explored the back of the large cavern while Troy was gone. He did it cautiously, scared of being yelled at. But no one did. Far from the fire and the green waterpool they couldn't see him.

With his hands Jerome felt his way around the walls, waiting for his eyes to adjust to the dark. Within several minutes of walking around the cavern, farther and farther from the flickering orange of campfires and the steady babble of hushed Frenchi voices, he encountered several large lumps of metal sticking out of the rock. Flakes of corroded metal fell off when he brushed his hands over them.

"What you doing?" Sandy whispered.

Jerome leapt up, his heart thudded. "Why you following me?"

"Sorry. I just see you going off, so I thought I come over keep you company."

She moved between him and the light and made a silhouette.

"I looking around. You know what this is?" Jerome took her hands and placed them on the metal lumps. Her fingers scratched over the metal and flakes dropped to the sand.

"It old," said Sandy. "We don't have much time to explore when we does come out to the cave, usually."

"So you never been here long?"

"Actually"—Sandy shifted, her silhouette sitting down—"I never been in here in this one. There some other small caves us children learn to dive into, but this one supersecret."

"Oh. Then you know as much as me about this place."

"I guess."

Jerome moved along the wall again. Sandy kicked sand around as she stood up to follow him. "You didn't seem surprise," Jerome said. "About the rusty metal."

"Nah. That in all the cave them I see. I don't know what they is."

Jerome walked along. "Who made these?" he wondered aloud.

"The old-father. A place to hide from the Azteca, deep below. Some say these thing go deeper and stuff. No one really know. Is called Tolor's Chimney. Is why we live out on the reef, ready to break down and go under any moment."

She grabbed Jerome's hand. He stopped and turned toward her shadow. "You should talk to Troy. He know all this stuff good."

"Okay." Jerome turned to pull away from her, but Sandy held on.

"Jerome?"

"Yeah."

"No one here can see us."

Jerome's mouth dried out, and he stepped from foot to foot. Sandy stood right in front of him, her long hair framed in dark shadows.

"You ever kiss?" Jerome asked.

"Yeah. One of the other boy them."

"Oh."

Jerome kicked at the sand. "Don't mean I don't want kiss you, though."

She leaned forward, and Jerome brushed her lips with his, the puzzle of the rusty metal lumps forgotten.

The sound of a woman yelling startled them. Dinner was ready. Now. She sounded impatient, and Jerome knew that if he missed eating now, he would not get anything later.

They both paused for a second, looked at each other, then ran across the dark sand toward the flickering fire.

Jerome soon realized that the old ladies *were* keeping up with him. Every half hour they would step around the camp with a good idea of who was where. And if he was missing, out in the dark edges of the massive cavern, they would give him a stern sermon. "What you doing over there, boy? You ain't scared the dark or nothing? Stay close to we fire so we see you. We go cook up some hot soup for all of you."

So his expeditions were quick, and hurried. But Jerome found that each of the metal lumps was spaced several feet apart. There were four of them at the back of the cavern, and if he spread his arms, he could reach two at the same time.

There were no buttons or levers on them. Nothing but featureless lumps of metal. He wished he had a torch.

On many of his excursions he waited for Sandy to catch up to him. They had ten minutes before the old ladies would check up on them, calling out their names.

It was enough time for him to discover a great deal about kissing.

On the tenth day since Brungstun fell, Jerome sat on a chair of sand by the edge of the water. A smaller fire crackled next to him, and he sat with a stick poking at it. Fog rose off the water.

"You been exploring?" Troy asked. Troy sat cross-legged across from him, back from scouting. "Around the edge of the cavern?"

"Yeah," Jerome admitted. "So what them thing is? The metal thing?"

"Mmm." Troy poked at embers, stirring up pieces of ash that flew around in circles and landed in the sand. "Not any of the Frenchi remember what it really is; they think this a secret place to hide." Troy got up. "Come with me."

He walked across the sand, into the dark, without even a light. Jerome struggled to follow him.

They reached the wall, and one of the metal humps. Troy placed his hand over it. It glowed, and the rock in front of them scraped aside. There was dark now, but not the darkness of rock. An unlit passageway inside the rock. A tunnel.

Troy walked forward. His voice came from in front of Jerome, who could hardly see. Troy grabbed his shoulder. "Come, child, I ain't go do nothing to you, but I have to show you something."

Jerome stepped in—and jumped as the rock closed back behind him.

Eerie green lights lit up along a floor, and he could see Troy standing in front of him. Troy's eyes were all gray for a moment, a trick of the light, Jerome thought, and then Troy blinked.

They walked a good hundred feet, and then into a room. There was a desk and two chairs. Troy walked over and sat down with a sigh.

"I come every year." He motioned for Jerome to sit. "Make sure everything work still."

"What is this?" Jerome asked, still in shock. He sat with a thump. The chair wasn't too soft or hard. His spine aligned just right.

"Protected bunker," Troy said.

Jerome looked around. "For the old-father them?"

Troy nodded. "For me. I am a old-father."

"But . . ." It wouldn't take that long, Jerome realized, to become comfortable with that idea. He'd met Pepper. The idea that men like this existed was becoming a part of Jerome's new understanding of the world.

"I almost four hundred year old," Troy said. "I come to Nanagada. To retire. Pretty land, good fishing, some garden. They tell me I could have any land anywhere. I choose to settle down near other Caribbean people-them."

"The Frenchi don't know you a old-father?"

"I change me last name, claim to be me own son. There always a Troy here. Plus, the Frenchi is the Frenchi because of me."

"What you mean?"

"Most of the Frenchi me descendant, from a couple wife me first while here. That why I single now. Can't marry me own family."

Jerome looked around. It was incredible. "Why you tell me this?"

Troy leaned on the desk, and Jerome looked down at it. There were screens of glass in it, he noticed for the first time.

"Because of you father, Jerome. He like me. He old-father."

"No." Jerome shook his head. "My dad can't be that," he protested.

"Think about it. In all you life, you ever see you father age? You see any picture of him when he first came here? He look exactly the same. But you mom, Shanta, you see the gray in she hair?"

Jerome sat there. "If you know them thing, you been lying all along." He looked up at Troy. "You could have help him. You could have show him all this. Why wait? He hurt so much, not having he memory!"

Troy avoided Jerome's accusative glare. "I make a choice, Jerome. I can't give he he memory back, all I could do is tell him thing. And getting tell thing ain't memory. I could have been lying for all he had know." Troy took a deep breath. "You father did something, something really, really hard to do. I think the memory of it, it probably almost kill him. I believe for himself to survive, he forget it all. A way of defense. And you think I could force them memory back without something bad happening? No. I stay quiet, watch him, and make sure that if them memory start coming back, I would be here to help." Troy leaned back in his chair. "But maybe I was mistake. I done sneak into Brungstun for a night, and I can't self find him. And even he make it out and head for Capitol City, I still worry about him. Some of the Councilmen in Capitol City does know he still alive, and they might try and tell him thing that go bring back he nightmare-them."

Jerome shifted. "What nightmare? What go be so horrible?"

Troy looked across the smooth, shiny desk at him.

"I four hundred year old, Jerome. And I had spend most of that time free. I had come to Nanagada and were able to do anything I want. Even after Hope's Loss, when most of all we technology and machine fall and stop, even then, I could still live here in the island. But imagine if you was trap, trap somewhere for most of all that time, and you was awake the whole time. Can you imagine being in a small room like this here for three hundred year, or even something smaller?"

Jerome looked around. Just this time in the cavern had been hard for him.

"Imagine hundred and hundred year of being trap in a small thing, not much larger than this room. That is why you father don't remember nothing. And I wouldn't either, if I were him."

Troy got up. "I have more, Jerome. But not now. I go let you have this time to adjust, seen?"

"Seen." Jerome nodded, shaken.

Everything around him was changing. His perception of his dad, something that had always been unshakable and set in stone, was now shattered.

"Okay, good," Troy said. "Now, put you hand here, on the desk."

Jerome did so. The desk flashed and blinked a green square.

"Now, if Azteca find we, and you need to escape, put you hand on the panel out there, like I had done, and it go let you in now. It didn't before, but I told it you allowed in. Understand? I want you to stay safe. There a whole bunch of passage in here, place for you hide and escape, okay?"

Dad was old-father. Dad was hundreds of years old.

"Okay," Jerome said.

What did all this mean?

CHAPTER FORTY-TWO

Oaxyctl scrambled up a set of ropes, not daring to look down. The steady pace of a blimp was preferable to this. The rope netting under his feet swung loosely, and the whole boat pitched.

"Hurry, hurry," the man at the top yelled down at him.

They said the steamer needed sails to help it along. He didn't understand that; either they had an engine or they did not. Oaxyctl saw sails and masts only as another mess of lines to trip over.

"Look him go!" Someone cackled from the other mast. "Slow like the turtle. Be steady, you might win the race yet!"

Oaxyctl looked down at the deck far beneath him. His feet slipped and he dangled in the netting.

At this rate he was going to die.

What else could he do but this? Oaxyctl thought about that question on a number of different levels. He had to stay by John deBrun's side. This time if a chance presented itself, he would strike. He could spirit John away in a lifeboat, though Oaxyctl knew nothing about sailing.

The luck of the Ocelotl had struck him with a vengeance.

Oaxyctl closed his eyes. The ropes burned into his wrists where he hung, and the sun blazed down on his neck.

"You all right?"

Someone scrambled down next to him. Another set of feet shook the ropes, and hands grabbed him from either side. Oaxyctl opened his eyes. The man in front of him winked. "We here to help."

"Thank you." Oaxyctl was lifted up. He grabbed the netting, balancing his feet, free once more.

"No," said the man. "We here to help *you*." He let go of Oaxyctl.

Oaxyctl understood. The man didn't look Tolteca, but maybe he'd been raised on the other side. One didn't have to be brown-skinned to believe in the gods. "How do you know?" Oaxyctl asked.

"Several god came to the city." The man pointed at the harbor water. "Came for we. Told we, 'Be ready, to join this expedition.' Some of we couldn't get through, some did. Like you, we ain't leave the ship since joining. But we was waiting for you. Yeah. We know who you is."

"Thank you." Oaxyctl's heart dropped. A god? Here in Capitol City? Were they everywhere?

Any thoughts of trying to give up on his responsibility, even though he was trapped on this boat and almost powerless, dissipated. He was still trapped, he still had the god's bidding to follow.

"Hey," the man said. "What a *tlacateccatl* is?"

"A leader of men," Oaxyctl said. "Like a commander."

The man nodded. "That good. I go be a leader of men, with much gold and women for me, when this all done." He grinned. Oaxyctl wanted to ask his name, but he jumped up the rigging away from him toward the top.

Oaxyctl followed with a lighter heart. He had hidden allies on board. How many, he didn't know. Now he had to be aware, come up with a plan, and figure out who was who aboard this ship.

When Oaxyctl reached the top of the mast, three men lounged around the steel crow's nest. "You make it."

"Come in."

As Oaxyctl crawled over the strips of metal, he saw a skiff approaching. It was decorated with ribbons and bright yellow and red paint. "What's going on?"

"I think it getting time for we launch this boat for real," they said. "That the minister boat."

The man closest to Oaxyctl, the same one who had helped him up, looked out over the water. "Look at them." He pointed with his head.

Oaxyctl followed the nod, puzzled. A huge flotilla of dinghies, small sailboats, and barges filled with people were approaching them.

"Who are they?"

Everyone shrugged.

Below them Oaxyctl saw the minister getting out, a lady dressed in red. Behind her others climbed out, including John deBrun. John deBrun wore a new blue uniform, had an extra step in his stride, and his hook had been polished so that the sun seemed to strike it and flash at every opportunity.

He was in John deBrun's world now, Oaxyctl realized. It would be a hard journey.

But Oaxyctl had the gods on his side, he realized, looking up at the sun and the man by his side. And he was a strong man. He would triumph here, and honor the gods.

He would obtain the secret codes from John deBrun. He could still do this and bring them back to the god.

Oaxyctl believed it. He hung on to it.

CHAPTER FORTY-THREE

Dihana accepted two crewmen's hands to help her up to the ladder and small stage floating by the steamship. *La Revanche*, she whispered.

"Are all these boats out here for the christening?" she asked.

"I don't know," Haidan replied.

John, looking every bit the captain he was, walked down the deck, inspecting everything, nodding at various crew who stood to attention.

Just over twenty years ago she'd first met John deBrun when he'd headed off to the northlands. He'd even made land, before being forced to turn back for lack of food and supplies. He'd left with two hands and returned with one. He left Capitol City for Brungstun after that to rest and recover and never came back.

"Wish I was going," Haidan grunted. He wore a beige trench coat that flapped in the wind. Dihana noticed the pair of guns in leather holsters on each hip. "You know I put my best mongoose-man on this trip?" She chose not to say anything. "My notes. My expedition. Hard to let go, you know?" He spit over the side, then wiped his lips with a handkerchief.

John walked back down toward them.

"What exactly are we doing today?" Dihana asked.

"We have a quick affair." John grinned. "Haidan objected to the long one. Too many people off and on the ship."

"We should proceed, then," Dihana said.

"Yes, let's."

John walked aft to where the steering wheel loomed out of the deck. A protective wall of wood and steel boxed in the area, though she noticed holes had been set at the bottom to allow water to drain.

Three men circled him. John introduced them in turn. "Barclay, my commander." The tall man in a blue uniform nodded and shook Dihana's offered hand. "Harrison, lieutenant commander." Dihana shook another hand. "And our mongoose major, Avasa." Avasa, a thin Hindi, gave a short bow. Haidan spoke highly of the man's fighting skills. He would lead the fifteen mongoose-men aboard.

A lot of shouting ensued, from all sides. John started, the crew took it up. People moved ropes and the three stacks belched smoke. The moorings were tossed away, with sailors keeping a careful eye on where the ropes floated.

For these few moments Dihana was just an observer. No one even looked at her; everyone had their own duties to take care of.

She watched them all get the ship under way. It picked its way around the harbor, dodging anchored fishing vessels and large, bobbing mooring balls.

Haidan walked up the side and sat far up toward the front of the ship. Dihana walked along the deck, careful not to let her feet hit any of the menacing toe-height cleats on the deck. She grabbed the railing, the varnished wood smooth under her hand.

"Amazing ship," she said.

Haidan looked out over the shiny rail at the harbor water.

"Hopefully amazing enough," he said.

Dihana sat next to him on the roof of a cabin, not far from a large hatch and set of stairs built into the side of the cabin.

"It isn't our only hope, Haidan. We have defenses, the city walls. The Azteca will die of disease in their camps. It will take a year for them to breach the city."

"We just buying time. Maybe if we hold out long enough the Azteca go give up. But if they never gave up trying to get over the mountain-them, what make you think they go give up here? How many will they sacrifice to wait we out?"

Dihana folded her arms against the faint wind and concentrated on the quiet feeling of *La Revanche* moving forward with a faint shiver. Then the boat's motion changed.

Haidan cocked his head. "We reversing."

Screams came from the side, and three shots. Haidan stood up and moved in front of Dihana to protect her. He looked over the rail.

"They everywhere," he shouted.

Dihana pushed past him to look down.

A flotilla of small barges, dinghies, people in kayaks, and rafts had assembled in front of *La Revanche*. People with bags by their sides waved. Mongoose-men stood along the side of the steamer, weapons drawn.

"Take me with you," an old lady cried, a small chest by her feet. "Please don't leave all of we, Minister. Them Azteca go kill we."

The silence broke. The flotilla threatened, pleaded, demanded, begged, to leave Capitol City. Some cursed them for leaving, and some sat and stared at her with empty, hopeless eyes. Dihana stood at the railing in front of hundreds of Capitol City people looking to flee.

"This is no good," she told Haidan. "Give me a bottle of wine to smash against the bow. Let us christen this ship now. Tomorrow morning, early early, before the sun rise and anyone realize what happened, the ship must leave."

"Seen." Haidan's locks swayed and he turned around to find a bottle of something for her to smash. The ceremony would be done quicker than anyone had planned.

"What a mess." Dihana wanted off the boat, to show the people of Capitol City she wasn't running anywhere. She grabbed her skirt and grabbed one of the thick ropes hanging from the mast. With a grunt she pulled herself up to stand on the rail where everyone could see her.

"What you doing?" Haidan asked.

The boat, not ship, she told herself, rocked. Not enough to drop her into the water as long as she kept a good grip on the rope.

"We ain't going nowhere," Dihana shouted as loud as she could, changing her speech to address the large crowd. It was like being a young girl again, when she had made the rhythms of her words sound one way for her father, and then another for her friends she met in the Ministerial Gardens. "No one going nowhere!"

The flotilla quieted down.

"This ship here a *fighting* ship," Dihana yelled. "Ain't no running ship. You hear? Ain't no one running here. When Azteca come, I go stand up on the wall looking down at them me-self, just like any of you.

"Azteca looking for living sacrifice for they god-them. And I don't intend on letting them walk into Capitol City.

"So don't be ganging up on this ship. If you want leave, the gates of the city out there." Dihana pointed back inland. "Or through Grantie's Arch yourself, on any of you boat. But not on this one. This boat already got a mission."

She turned and held out an empty hand.

"Hand me the bottle," she demanded. Haidan stood under her, a small smile cracking the edges of his mouth anyway. He handed her a cheap green bottle of ale.

"Here," Dihana shouted. "I christen this boat *La Revanche*. They tell me this name means 'revenge' in some old language of the old-father. May it live true to its name then, and help all of we bring fear back out of Capitol City to the Azteca." She smashed the bottle against the rail, covering Haidan in cheap alchohol.

When she clambered down, Haidan took her arm. "You remind me of you dad. Decisive leader. Never someone to cross."

Dihana stepped over broken glass. The last thing she wanted today was to be compared to her father. He had known about *Ma Wi Jung* for all she knew. He must have needed something important from the Loa to not try to get to the north.

Maybe something like what the Loa gave John for his journey. Haidan told her John had it in a safe in his cabin, and that none of the crew knew about the device that would get the *Ma Wi Jung* to work. But if the Loa had been getting this device ready, maybe her dad had not been so misguided as she had thought.

This possibility shook her a bit.

"Come, we need to head for shore." Dihana gathered herself. "Get as many boats to follow us in as possible. Haidan, get your men out there to sign up fighters from the men on these boats. Any of these people could help us fight the Azteca."

Haidan pulled the collar of his coat up. "Well, for better or worse we commit now."

Dihana looked him straight in the eye. "One man who has been north. One gift from the Loa. It only takes one thing, Haidan, one thing."

Haidan nodded. "I know."

Just before they left, Dihana slowed down to meet John deBrun one last time. She shook his good hand. It was anyone's guess as to what would happen next, she thought, on their rocky voyage. But it was out of all of their hands. They had a city to defend now.

"Good luck, Captain," she said. "You're on you own now."

"Thank you, Prime Minister," John replied.

And then she was helped back over the side of the boat, to the cheers of the ragtag armada all around them.

CHAPTER FORTY-FOUR

The warm hues of the morning sun lined the edge of the eastern ocean's reflections, while in the other direction the world remained dark as they left. Grantie's Arch slipped past *La Revanche*, and the crew spoke in tired morning whispers, going about their duties. A small cooking fire spread the smell of coffee around the deck.

This was the best time to leave, John thought. He stood off in the corner of the rear cockpit, watching the two helmsmen pull at the wheel.

John held a cup of coffee in his good hand and kept his hook tucked underneath his other arm, yet still visible. It gave him credibility among many of the fishermen sailors that crewed *La Revanche*. He liked that.

The steamship was fast. The deck thrummed under his feet as they surged out from Capitol City's watery gates.

They cleared the breakwater walls, a jumbled pile of rock protecting Grantie's Arch from the worst of the Northern Sea weather. *La Revanche* began to pitch.

"Sails," John ordered. "Full canvas!"

The word passed down in scratchy voices. Three teams leapt up the netting to unfurl the sails. The canvas dropped down with a pleasant scratching sound, then a snap as the booms bounced at their end.

"That's better," someone muttered. The ship's bucking steadied into a slow swaying as the sails filled and the rigging creaked tight. John took a sip of coffee. Already Grantie's Arch looked just large enough to walk through.

A few small fishing boats bounced near mooring balls of different colors, pulling up wicker fish traps. The fishermen waved at them.

Even in the face of impending war, some things went on.

After several hours of clipping along, the walls of Capitol City slipped beneath the horizon. By that time the cooks had served a late breakfast for several sailors. Most of the mongoose-men lined up against the rails, hung on for grim life, and puked their guts out.

This was not the heady adventure of his last trip over two decades ago. A lot of time lay between here and then; six years of marriage to Shanta, and thirteen years raising Jerome. The memories threatened to overwhelm him. John looked at the rolling waves and pushed it all away.

He wondered if that passage of time had matured him for this second attempt or made him too soft to pull it off. He knew the dangers of the ice and the cold this time.

This time the stakes were higher than he could ever have imagined.

CHAPTER FORTY-FIVE

A ragamuffin woke Dihana at sunrise to tell her the Councilmen had fled. She ordered him to find Haidan. She wanted a squad to hunt them down.

By the time she was having a midmorning breakfast of sausage, eggs, and some fresh milk, Haidan had the Councilmen rounded up.

"They was in Tolteca-town," Haidan said.

Emil was bound with rope. He sat down at the table across from her, and Dihana put her fork down. The other Councilmen stood outside in the hallway, sullen, mongoose-men with guns eyeing them.

"Get up," she snapped.

Emil did so, with a startled look.

"Take them out to the gate," she said. "Walk them out into the jungle, and leave them there."

"Dihana." Emil started a plea.

"To you, I am *Prime Minister.* Or *Miss Minister.*"

Someone coughed.

Haidan stood still and looked at them. "You want know what they was doing? We find them . . ."

Dihana shook her head, picked her fork back up, and sipped from her glass of milk. "They are no use to me. They don't understand the old-father's technologies. They barely understand the history that got us here, from what the Preservationists who talk to them have said. They hide what little they know from me." Dihana shrugged. "Therefore they are useless."

"You got to understand." Emil put his hands down on the table. "We were trader. Nothing big. Some of we was just young then. None of we was in charge, or in the military fighting the Tetol. We was just here, in the city, when it all happened. And we had never leave."

"Tell Haidan what you were doing, maybe he'll have the heart not to throw you out of the city."

Haidan glowered at them.

"We talk to some Azteca spy here," Emil mumbled. "Give them information for the guarantee that we ain't go be sacrifice when they come." He held his tied hands up to his face and scratched his nose.

"What information?" Dihana asked. That they had betrayed everyone like this did not surprise her. They had already shaken her once before, she refused to let them affect her again.

"We tell them you set up an expedition north again."

Dihana finished her eggs. "You're traitors." She put down her fork with a clink. "Now you tell me how much of a traitor you are? What do you expect to get from me?"

"No, look," Emil said. "We had talk about it a long time. We refuse to give the Azteca anything that go make the city fall. That way, if the city win, we okay and helping it. But if it fall . . . You see? So the first thing we had tell them were about this trip north. It probably go fail like the other one. It were no big secret. Only one trip ever make it, and that were because—"

"DeBrun captained it," Dihana said. "He also captains this one."

"What?" The shock in Emil's voice was genuine. It made Dihana flinch. The other Councilmen swore.

Emil's knees buckled, and he leaned against the table. "DeBrun alive," he whispered. "He alive!" Then he looked up.

Now Dihana was interested. "What is this all about?"

"John deBrun were the leader of the fight against the first Teotl. When he came to Capitol City, twenty year ago, we thought we was save. Until we find out he have no memory anymore. Nothing since he wash up in Brungstun. We thought him going north would help him get he memory back, but the mission fail." Emil looked frustrated. "Maybe this would have help him with he memory. But now he in trouble."

Dihana stood up. "Lock them up," she told Haidan. "Just get them out of trouble."

Late last night Harford and Malair had gone silent. The Azteca were on the Triangle Tracks. Now this. She walked out to her balcony, looking down the street toward the harbor. She could just see Grantie's Arch, and through that, she could see a sliver of the ocean. We're tearing ourselves apart back here in the city, she thought, and the Azteca haven't even gotten to within firing distance of the walls.

Good luck out there.

PART THREE

THE NORTHLANDS

CHAPTER FORTY-SIX

They had sailed for just over a week already. *La Revanche* plunged forward, taking the northern seas wave by pounding wave. The ship lurched every few hours when a large wave smacked her from an odd angle, but the bow, again and again, ripped out the other side of a wall of dark wave, and water would race down the decks and drain off.

It was a rhythm, though John wished he could speed it up. Every week was a week that the city faced the Azteca without him.

It took two days before the most vulnerable, the mongoose-men, gained their sea legs. Another day had passed before the last of them stopped throwing up. By that time the salt in the air coated everything. The fine patina of crystals made a scraping sound whenever someone ran their hand down a rail.

By now everyone had an inkling of what long sea voyages were about. Bad weather, incredible drenching seas, and storms. Dried foods, weevily foods, and bilge rat patrol. Cockroaches, canned vegetables, and one orange a day, just in case. The ocean killed here, no longer a friend like behind the protective barrier reefs just off Brungstun.

John stood on a cabin top, the steamship pitching slowly under his feet. Oaxyctl walked up the deck and stopped next to him.

"How are you taking this?" John moved over next to him at the rail, which John walked up and down, up and down, every day. It had been a sudden decision to ask the mongoose-man to come, but John remembered the way Oaxyctl had been treated on the street. That would not be repeated on this ship. Oaxyctl had saved his life, John owed him as much as the man would accept.

"I don't think my stomach will ever forgive me."

John flexed his knees to stand straight in respect to the horizon and smiled. *Revanche* gimballed under him. "Give it another week . . ."

A small rogue wave broke the ocean's rhythm, slapping the ship's side and throwing up spray that struck them both. The water dripped from John's waterproofed coat, but a small rivulet snuck in under his collar and trickled down his back.

"Gods." Oaxyctl gripped the railing. "Another week."

"You'll get used to it." John folded his arms. As long as one didn't think about all the time they were using up.

"What do you to pass time?"

"Knots."

"Knots?"

"Some men can afford books to bring with them and trade them once they're read," John said. "Others learn crafts. Knots are a good start. Whittling fish bones into naked women is another."

Oaxyctl snorted. He looked at John and let go of the railing with one hand and swayed with the boat a bit, trying to imitate.

"I guess this isn't too different than some of the long shifts in the lower mountains," Oaxyctl said.

"At sea you are your own worst enemy."

"That is the way it works anywhere." Oaxyctl shuffled his feet as he lost his balance. He looked through the scuppers at the shifting landscape of water. "I'm far from home, John. Far from home."

"Lonely?"

Oaxyctl nodded. "I feel like I have no friends, no family, no one who cares if I were to fall off the side of this boat."

"It's a ship," John corrected him. "But, yes, I understand." Out here it was like an alien land where the horizon never ended and the land constantly shifted and broke over itself.

Alien world. That impression bubbled right up through John's subconscious. It was one of many different images and feelings that had been surfacing since the voyage started. He resented them, though. He'd been trying to hold pictures of Shanta and Jerome in his head. The weird feelings stirring in his gut scared him. He hadn't had such distinct feelings since washing up in Brungstun and waking up with nightmares. Why now?

Every night the memories of Shanta and Jerome grew softer, shattered by the still-striking nightmares of images that had once haunted him before his family had come to him. Images of the spiked egg dripping water were John's most prevalent dreams.

It was that, and a constant feeling of being alone with dark nothingness around him for unimaginable distances, that woke him up sweating in the night now.

"Oaxyctl, be honest with me. What will happen to my family in Brungstun?" John asked.

"Your wife, if she is lucky, will be working as a servant." Oaxyctl lifted a hand to brush away one of his dark bangs. He blinked. Another wave slap and he lost his balance, sitting down roughly on the deck. John crouched next him. "I do not know what they will do with your boy, as there are several . . . festivals to the gods that approach."

John leaned his head back against the cabin and sat down completely. "Festivals? They sacrifice people for these, right?"

Oaxyctl didn't reply. But the silence meant assent.

John ground his teeth. "Why?" he demanded. "Why the blood?"

"It isn't that we, they, hate life. They adore it. They treasure it. It is the holiest gift of all."

"So why . . ." In the distance, from under the decks, a faint yell.

"What would you offer your god?" Oaxyctl asked. "The mud from the bottom of a river? Or the holiest gift of all? I have seen verses that say the gift of human life is a holy deed. Is not that one of the tenets of the christians who live on this side of the mountains?"

"That is a perverse comparison." *La Revanche* changed her heading, John thought. The rolling felt different. He stood up.

"Perverse?" Oaxyctl raised his voice. "No more than any other religion. What religion doesn't have a strong connection to blood? The Vodun and christian faiths ask for blood in one way or another. You have others as well. What god do you worship? I am sure you will find some strange, if not horrific, practice there."

"I don't worship any gods." John stepped forward down the deck and looked around, trying to see through the boom and sails in his way. Something was wrong. A random wave struck the side and *La Revanche* leaned far over. Things slid and banged around. Down through one of the hatches, sailors swore and things broke.

Oaxyctl looked around. "What's wrong?"

An explosion ripped through the rear hatches from inside. John ran forward to the nearest hatch, conversation forgotten. He leapt down the companionway, shoving aside a mongoose-man at the bottom.

Smoke billowed forward at him. Hadley, wearing nothing but pants and carrying a pistol in his hand, grabbed John's arm.

"I think I catch the man who done this," Hadley reported. "A stowaway. But the explosion kill three crew."

"We can't steer, and we taking on water serious," someone yelled from in the smoke.

Sabotage.

"Keep all the hatches open." John coughed, eyes watering from smoke. "Let me see who did this."

Two bulky fishermen in dirty coveralls pulled what looked like a mongoose-man with long dreadlocks forward. "I know you!" John grabbed the man's chin and stared him in the eye. "At Grantie's Arch, on the footbridge. Pepper?" John tried to recall all the impressions he had gathered that night for some sort of conclusion.

"Good afternoon." Pepper pulled at one of the fishermen, forcing them to stagger. Hadley raised his gun in warning. Pepper looked at them. His face was black with cordite, his dreads singed. He'd been lucky to live through the blast.

He's holding himself back, John thought. He could see it in the body language. Pepper was dangerous.

But he already knew that. He didn't have to look for it, John had known it the second he'd first seen Pepper. It sat with certainty in John's gut. "Get him tied up and locked away. We'll deal with him later." They didn't have the time right now. They needed to fix the damage quickly, get back under way. Then they could think about that.

Pepper stared at him.

"Should kill he dead now," one of the fishermen said.

"Don't do anything stupid, John," Pepper said, his voice icy.

"I'm not sure who you are, exactly," John snapped. "So don't call me by my first name." To Hadley he said, "Put him in the brig, we have other things to worry about first."

"A brig?"

Hadley and John stared at each other.

"Lock him in a room. Anywhere. You have a place like that?"

Hadley nodded. "A brig," he repeated, rolling the word around.

It was a word that came easily to John. It mustn't be used much in the northern parts, John thought.

"Come." Hadley kept the gun aimed at Pepper.

John walked past them into the slowly clearing smoke. Near the rear of the hold, water rushed in, creating puddles he stepped in. Two men lay bloodied and dead on the ground, one missing a face, just a pink, shredded pulp of a skull facing the hull.

"Who can hold their breath?" John yelled back at the smoke. They would have to repair this now. A sheet of metal welded on and some struts, but first they had to pull something over the cracked hull on the outside, some watertight canvas. John hoped the explosion had not damaged Edward's machinery for the treads they would need to travel over the northern ice.

And Pepper.

He would talk to him later, after this crisis was taken care of.

CHAPTER FORTY-SEVEN

Two mongoose-men hastily cleared a sail locker to the fore of the ship, then ripped Pepper's coat from him, throwing it aside. They yanked free any weapons and knives they found including his binoculars. Then they tied his wrists behind him with rope and pushed Pepper into the locker. They put a lock on the slatted wooden door and took up positions on either side to guard him.

Annoying.

Pepper watched through the gaps in the wooden door as men ran around. *La Revanche* pitched madly until John ordered a sea anchor, a large canvas parachute with spars that forced its throat open, thrown off the back of the ship. That got the ship facing downwind with the waves.

Two men with ropes tied to their waists leapt over to guide ropes and canvas to seal off the leak.

Pepper flexed until the rope around his arms popped. With his arms still behind him he dug his fingers into his forearm. He could feel skin resist, but he forced his thumbnail down until warm blood dripped onto the coils of salt-crusted rope and spare sailcloth underneath him.

He kept digging until he found a sharp edge and pinched it between his thumb and forefinger. He pulled out a slender tube.

Pepper kept it, still bloodied, in his left free hand, waiting. His right boot rested against the lower lip of the door, ready to kick out outward.

The real saboteur would have to come and try to kill Pepper. The crude dart gun ripped from under his forearm would take care of any unwanted visitors. And from the brig Pepper had a good view of the entire deck.

The hours passed. It didn't look as if *La Revanche* was sinking, though Pepper could hear the thrum of the pumps sucking water out over the side and the spitting of welding. The sea had calmed, and they drifted into the evening. Pepper remained alert, peering out through the slats, ready.

The figure that came up the deck wasn't the saboteur, but John deBrun, easily recognizable due to his hook. John squatted near the edge of the sail locker. "You say you didn't do it. What proof do you have?"

"What proof do you have that I *did* sabotage your ship?" Pepper said. "No one stopped to ask this." Pepper had been hibernating in the bottom rear of the ship in a storage area, near the rudder cables, when one of the crew had snuck back to attach something near the rudder and hull.

"True." Through the slats this close, Pepper could see only John's eyes. "But *you're* the stowaway."

Pepper shifted, right boot on the door, dart gun in his other hand. The blood on his arm had dried and clotted. The skin by the gash quivered, repairing itself. "John, you've got worries. You're worrying about me, but I'm actually the least of your many issues. You have people aboard this ship who don't want it to reach your destination. And there's an even bigger problem about to bite your ass."

"And what is that?"

"There are Azteca ships out here hunting you. The bomb wasn't supposed to go off for another couple of days, when we got closer to the Lantails." Pepper had woken up, groggy, and surprised the first crewman. He'd killed him, but didn't get to the second until he'd triggered the bomb. The concussion still hurt. And now Pepper's life was even more complicated. That annoyed him even more.

"Azteca don't have ocean-worthy ships," John said.

"They do now," Pepper said. "The Teotl have helped."

"And how do you know this?"

"Bars."

"Bars?"

"Bars are your first avenues of locating information, John. You know this. With my ears, I hear all the gossip, the truth, the confessions made into rags and beer mugs: there are two deep-ocean fishing boats missing in the Lantail Islands and one sighting of a strange new-looking ship by city fishermen. They've petitioned for protection, but no one believes them. And then there is the matter of the Teotl I happened to catch and torture in Capitol City that told me there are three big ships out here, John, waiting for you."

"You're trying to get us to turn around and give up."

"If I'd wanted that, I would have killed everyone on board during any of the first few nights at sea and burned the ship. You might not remember things, but listen to my voice and tell me I wouldn't have." John was quiet. "About those ships," Pepper continued. "When they try to stop us, you should let me out. They won't sink this ship; they'll try to board. They want to capture you."

"I'm not letting you out."

"Okay. I've spent lots of time in confined spaces . . . and getting out of them. Just make sure to feed me well."

"Where do you remember me from?" John asked. "How do you *really* know me?"

Pepper put a finger through the slat and wiggled it. "Your reaction to that information, without your memories to guide and back you up, would get in my way. You'd call me insane. We've got enough difficulty here as it is, why add to it?"

What would he say? Hi, John, you're hundreds of years old. You once navigated between the stars, now you're mucking about on a steam-powered toy boat on a small planet cut off from the rest of the human race.

Better to wait.

"How did you get aboard?" John crossed his arm and hook over each other. "We had guards and ships cordoning *La Revanche* off."

"I swam." Pepper had left the Teotl's submarine on the bottom of the harbor to sneak up the side of the ship.

"What makes you think I don't already believe you're crazy?"

Pepper pulled his finger out from between the slats and rearranged the ropes behind him so that he could lean back comfortably. He could see John's arms through the slats as John turned to walk away.

"By the way, John, Jerome is safe."

John turned and pointed his hook at Pepper. "If you're—"

"He's with the Frenchi. He'll be safe." Pepper settled back farther in the darkness of the locker.

"And Shanta?"

"Your wife? I did not meet her. Sorry."

John walked over to the rail, his back to Pepper. "If you're messing with my head, Pepper, I swear I'll throw you overboard."

"Okay."

John let go of the railing and walked away. Pepper leaned back for a short nap, but as always, half of him remained alert. John deBrun had no memories, Pepper thought as he drifted. It made sense that John might have done something drastic like that.

Pepper had spent almost 298 years trapped in a near-dead escape pod before landing on Nanagada. Both he and John had expected the pulse that had shut down civilization. It was that or let the Teotl own them. They had also expected it would be a decades-long journey back from the destroyed wormholes in tiny, barely functioning vehicles that they'd hardened to survive the pulse. But things went wrong, and instead of decades, they saw centuries. They both had the modifications, and the pods the recycling equipment, needed to hunker down for that kind of time, though.

It had almost driven Pepper mad. Apparently John suffered as well.

Pepper spent months after arriving on Nanagada catching up on the changes and trying to hunt down John. He'd thought he was close when he'd arrived in Brungstun, but the Azteca invaded. He'd thought he was close in Capitol City, when he tracked John down, but John didn't remember a thing.

Now he was on a steamship with John going north, but John didn't have a clue as to why this was all so important.

Apparently the Loa remembered the *Ma Wi Jung*, though, and had ordered an expedition. That they'd chosen John to lead it meant they knew something about his past. The Teotl knew something about John. Pepper knew a lot about John. Everyone knew something about John's past except John.

Damn annoying that he would find John alive and that John wouldn't even know who either of them was.

Still, the right people were going to the right places. So Pepper was content to doze off on the bundle of ropes and see what happened.

CHAPTER FORTY-EIGHT

Haidan walked with Dihana down the dirt road toward one of the great arches leading out of the city into the towns and forests around Capitol City.

"When I was just a little girl," Dihana said with a sweep of her hand, "I used to sneak away to explore it all. It's beautiful."

Haidan looked around. "They was putting up a new iron mill," he said, a twinge of sadness in his voice. "Now it on hold, they coming in behind the walls and getting ready for the Azteca."

They had argued about such progress before the Azteca threat. Dihana had been excited to see the city spill out beyond the walls into the land of the peninsula. Haidan loved the jungle and worried about how to defend the settlements outside city walls. But now Haidan was interested in seeing more airships launched into the sky, and he wanted to observe tests of the wheeled guns on the great walls. He wanted the gunners to have the Azteca in their sights when the fighting began. He wanted Dihana's factories to build more guns, more bullets.

The land outside Capitol City's walls had taken on a nightmarish quality. Men worked in shifts to pull down trees and give an unobstructed field of fire around the walls for defense. Arced trenches inched their way out around the walls. Haidan had created three zones of alternated trenches, then fire zones lined with explosives and flammables between them. Long fences of barbed wire sagged everywhere between large pointed stakes in the ground.

Caravans of Nanagadans trundled through the defenses on roads manned with mongoose-men and spiked gates to seek safety inside Capitol City. Thousands every day. And whenever Haidan doubted more could be fit in the city, Dihana managed to find ways.

"How many gates are shut?" Dihana asked.

"We got half of them," Haidan said. Mortared over, guns and bombs ready to defend them. "By the end of today only two will remain open." The northernmost gate, a small road-gate, would allow defenders out in the trenches. The southern one was riskier, a full railroad access gate; it would allow trains in and out of the city under heavy guard.

"How long will it take for them to get the gates?" Dihana asked.

Hard question. Haidan looked out over the mongoose-men's battle plans made real, carved into the landscape. "A month if everything go right, and they go lose a lot of men," he guessed. "We retreating, and losing men, but here we ready." The Azteca would come in along the north rails, and Haidan intended for them to stay there. In addition to the trenches, he'd flooded the land between the north and south rails and put men all along the southern rail to keep it in the city's control. The strong guard along the southern rail and the flooded middle area should convince the Azteca to continue to funnel themselves along the north rail, and Haidan would make good use of that. And having the southern rail kept open meant that they could still receive volunteers, and more important, any supplies, from southern coast towns such as Linton or Hawk's Nest.

The best minds in Capitol City had considered how best to defend the city walls. With Dihana and Haidan leading them, they had made sure many Azteca would die trying to cross the ground in front of Capitol City. If Haidan could juggle this battle just right, he could drag it out for the Azteca much longer than just a month outside the walls. Maybe two or three. And once they camped along the walls, it would be a waiting game. Who starved first?

Haidan worried about the threat from above. Massive numbers of Azteca airships had come over the mountains to fly with the moving army. They supplied it and guided it over the land, sped up the invasions of towns along the way. His airmen spoke of a miles-long line of gaudy Azteca airships coasting over columns of Azteca along the Triangle Tracks near Petite Mabayu, halfway along the Tracks to Capitol City. They could fly over Capitol City's walls and bomb it. They could get warriors into the city later into the battle by air as well. Haidan tried to compensate for that with what few igniting shells they had on hand. He'd also armed their own airships with weapons.

"We lost a lot of men in the retreating. They still in the bush, hiding. Lot of them dead most likely." Dihana walked with him under the thick walls. "It make me crazy trying to think of every way they could get in," Haidan said.

"Yeah," Dihana agreed.

"Someone say we need extra gun up on the wall to defend the harbor."

"The harbor?" Dihana shook her head.

"I doubt we need anything there. No one ever hear of any Azteca ship. Still, I have some smaller weapon mounted out there." Haidan kept walking. "If it happen, we can wheel gun out there."

Dihana nodded. "I could get some lookouts there, just in case."

"That good." Haidan pulled out a handkerchief and started coughing into it.

Dihana paused with him. "You okay?"

Haidan stopped, wiped his lips, and continued on. He didn't want Dihana to know how bad the cough had gotten. He stayed up later and later, pushing himself to plan for as much as he could think of. And he tried to delegate it so that if he died, he'd have done as much as he could have.

"Yeah."

By sea, by land, by air.

The hardest part was the waiting. The tense expectation in the air, the worried and weary looks on everyone's face. Haidan saw the occasional nervous look back to the edge of the jungle from random people in the street. And in front of the jungle a whole mile of stripped, brown earth.

The best thing, Haidan knew, was to keep busy.

CHAPTER FORTY-NINE

John sat with Oaxyctl at the rear of the steamship. The moon remained covered by threatening clouds. A lantern swung on the mizzenmast's boom overhead, throwing its light around in time to the gentle swaying of *La Revanche*.

"Marlinespike," John said. More knots, trying to tie away the time that slipped past them every day. He wondered how much closer the Azteca were to Capitol City. "Sailors been tying knots for centuries and centuries. On all different worlds." He held up a six-foot length of half-inch rope. "Or so they say." Just floating here, waiting for the repairs to finish, caused his stomach to knot with impatience.

"I know some knots." Oaxyctl held up his piece of rope.

"But do you know many knots used on a ship?"

Oaxyctl shrugged.

John held up the end of his rope in his hand. "This is the bitter end of the rope."

"Bitter end. And the other end?" Oaxyctl pointed at the part by his feet.

"Standing part."

"Bitter end and standing part." Oaxyctl looped the rope over itself and tied it. "There is a good knot."

"A square knot. A child's very first," John chuckled. "You can tie your shoe with it, but that isn't the most useful on a single line, but for tying two lines together."

"Oh." Oaxyctl looked down at the knot as if it were about to bite him.

"Here is a knot you should know." John held out his hook arm. He took the rope and laid it over his arm, brought it back around in a loop toward himself, then crossed over the first loop and back under itself. He snugged it tight around his arm. "Clove hitch."

"They taught me that for the fenders we had over the side when we were in harbor." Oaxyctl lashed his piece of rope to the nearby rail.

"Glad to see you quickly learning things out here." John untied the rope from the rail. "This next one is a sailor's favorite knot." He held the rope in his hands for a second. He'd never even got to teach this one to Jerome. He should have. Too busy sailing about, having fun.

He looked up the deck toward the brig. Was Jerome really safe?

"You okay?" Oaxyctl asked.

"Yeah." John looked back down at the rope. He pinched the burned end with his fingers, running a thumb under the smooth nubbin. "Yeah. I'll do this one-handed. You take the end and make a loop overtop, then come back around under and through the loop, dip under the standing edge, and come back into the loop." John held the loop with his hook and cinched the knot tight. "Makes a fixed loop. Good for anchors and towropes. The reason we like it is"—John tugged the knot and it fell apart—"because it doesn't bind itself so tight you can't undo it."

"I see."

"That one was called the bowline." The rope draped over his hook like a pale, limp snake.

Oaxyctl copied the moves.

"Make sure the bitter end goes back in—yeah, like that." John watched.

Barclay, his blue uniform scuffed and wet, squatted next to them. "Marlinespike?"

"Yeah." John nodded. "Bowline."

"That the good stuff there." Barclay smiled. "Mr. deBrun, we got the patch welded on, and we already pull up the canvas."

"Right, right," John said, excited. "And it's holding?"

"Yeah. We add some crossbeam, the spare boom, to push against it."

"Good. And the rudder cable?"

"Fixed. And it go hold."

John clapped the commander on the back. "Then let's get back in motion. Now. Waste no time." Barclay ran off and John walked back from the aft rails toward the cockpit. "Get ready to sail!" he ordered. Crew napping by the rails or on cabin tops stirred and sat up, rubbing their eyes. "Bring in the sea anchor. Move everyone, move!"

They were moving forward again. That was good. They didn't have time to waste.

Much later, once John had men up in the crow's nest with binoculars to comb the horizon, he sought out Oaxyctl below in the crew quarters in the forward cabin. He passed the galley and gimballed stoves. The rank smell of pea soup clung to the heavy belowdecks air.

Dodging swinging hammocks of sleeping men, he found Oaxyctl sitting under his limp hammock. "Hey." John lay down and rested his head against the hull as Oaxyctl put down the piece of rope.

"I'm sorry about being short, when I talked to you about Azteca." John could feel the ship flexing as it moved over the waves. Everything creaked in time to that rhythm. "We've been on the run since the invasion began. I've had no time to stop, or think."

Oaxyctl folded his hands and looked at John.

"I'll be honest," John said. "I know . . . some things about Azteca. Assumptions. Rumors from other people. But I have seen and known Tolteca. And you. So I know there must be some way to talk through this. We must have some common ground. Right? It's just the mountains that divide." John shifted to lean on his good arm and looked at Oaxyctl. "What's it like on other side of the mountains, Oaxyctl?"

"It is the land of the gods." Oaxyctl spoke softly, and slowly, deep in the ship's hull, surrounded by sleeping men in their hammocks. "They carry them through the streets in full procession, with finery. All the way up to their pyramids, where the steps flow with blood in their honor." Oaxyctl leaned his head back and closed his eyes. He smiled. "Where the people are all bronze and almond-eyed. Smooth-skinned, and well-toned. You know, I even miss the ladies of the night chewing chicle by the lake-street side."

John shifted quietly, trying not to break Oaxyctl's attention.

"Capitol City is in fear," Oaxcytl said. "They should be, because the priests have already arrived and demanded the city's surrender. Soon the first waves of warriors will arrive to capture as many Nanagadans as possible to be their servants, and the most honored prisoners will be sacrificed. They will capture Capitol City. With these new sacrifices, the sun be convinced to rise again, and the crops will be full and good."

"Do you think they can take the city?"

"Yes." Oaxyctl's eyes remained closed, his mind in another country.

"Why?"

"Because they are the best. For hundreds of years they have fought each other in the Flower Wars. All of the seven kingdoms do this. Over and over. We capture the priests, show whose god is more powerful, and take the prisoners to the altars to offer blood, or to our homes as servants. And all seven of these kingdoms march towards Capitol City now."

"But why now? The Flower Wars, are they not enough for the gods? What have we done to provoke this?"

"The gods command it," Oaxyctl said. "That is all."

"Which gods? The ones you say are captured during Flower Wars? What happens to those? Are all the gods united in purpose? How do they rule? How do—"

"Mortals don't question the gods. They talk among each other. The gods decide our fate." Oaxyctl's voice quavered. "That is the land and the people"—Oaxyctl opened his eyes and looked around—"that lie on the other side of the Wicked Highs. That is how it is like."

"Once your land," John said. "But no longer."

"Right. But I still miss it."

John reached out with his hook and tapped Oaxyctl's shoulder. "That must be very hard."

"It is. It is very hard."

"But at least you have a life to remember. I don't have anything to go back to when I lie awake at night. And the life I made for myself now has been taken away from me."

They fell quiet. *La Revanche* pierced the waves and drained seawater back into the ocean through the scuppers on her sides. The clouds eventually hid the moon giving them light through the portholes. Everything became swathed in pitch-black.

CHAPTER FIFTY

The swells calmed. The steamship no longer plunged its bow into the troughs of the vicious north seas, but cut its way through a small white chop that sprang up with a strong wind. A lone seagull swooped down into the small waves by *La Revanche*'s side. It plunged its beak into the water to pluck out a struggling fish that glinted silver in the sun.

"I see reef." John held a brass spyglass to his left eye, balancing it on the end on his hook. He handed it over to Barclay.

Barclay stared through it. "Yeah, that look right."

"Good, good." John smiled. Barclay's blue uniform looked ragged and unwashed. "You ever navigate the Lantail Reefs before?"

"Once I see them, I know the reef."

"Then take the helm. Put us right through the middle channel." If they skirted the islands, there was always a chance of hitting hidden offshore reef thanks to faulty charts. The islands and the channel were well-known, a safe bet. "I'm going up the mast." John walked down the deck, pulled himself up onto the rail, and took to the ropes to clamber up and join the men in the crow's nest. They watched him use his hook to maneuver up through the ropes and gave him a hand getting in.

"It a nice view from up here, eh?" John stood up with them.

"Yeah, but it look like a lot reefs is around."

They could see the craggy hills of the Lantails, and the water brightened from a dark blue into an aquamarine as the water got shallow. John shared the nest with his men until they passed through the worst of the reef, barking down warnings as they sidled too close to the brown patches of coral and rock.

The islands loomed up on either side as they went up the middle of the channel.

The Lantails. It meant they were over a third of the way there. They were making good time.

When John was navigator on the outbound expedition, the Lantails had been the edge of the map: the place where the largest fishing vessels stopped and turned around. The reefs extended outward for miles and miles, notorious for sinking explorers this far north.

Before they passed out from in between the hills of the Lantails, John had another decision to make.

John crawled out of the crow's nest.

When his feet his the deck, he walked forward toward the bowsprit. At the wooden, slatted doors of the sail locker the two shirtless mongoose guards got up and saluted him.

"Pepper, you there?" John hit the slats with the palm of his hand. "Pepper?"

"I'm here," Pepper said.

"We're at the Lantails."

"Not bad."

John crouched by the door and looked in. He could only see dark shadows between the tiny pieces of wood.

"So what am I supposed to do with you?" John asked. "You say you aren't the one who blew up the back of the boat, you know my son is okay, and you seem to know a lot about what is going on." John looked around. "Should I leave you here on these islands?"

"That wouldn't be good. Your survival depends on me."

"Really? Do you have another trap waiting for us? Will it go off if you aren't appeased?"

"John." Pepper sighed. "I'm not that kind of person."

"Maybe, but I can't really be sure, can I?"

"That's true. Let me out, I'll find who your saboteur is and save you all sorts of trouble."

"No."

"Come on, John." Pepper's eyes appeared between the slats as he leaned forward. John wondered if Pepper would be able to survive on the rocky Lantails, and if it was fair to maroon any man on mere suspicions.

The steamship rocked some as it encountered choppy water. They would be rounding the cliffs and heading back out toward open water. John had twenty minutes to decide whether to throw Pepper into one of the skiffs with enough food to live on the Lantails until the next fishing boat came out.

Which might not be for months.

"Hey!" The two men in the crow's nest shouted. "Them boat!"

John jumped up. A faint boom reached them on the deck. He scrambled up to the railing and looked out in front of *La Revanche*. A geyser of water erupted just off the bow. He raced over to the other side. A large green ship with full canvas bore down on them. It had been hidden by the cliffs and islands. Damn it. Damn it. They'd have to turn and run, skirt the islands and reefs, lose time.

A second shot from its bow gun whistled overhead.

"A trap," Harrison shouted, coming up from belowdecks. He had his shirt in his left hand and a rifle in his right.

"Get your rifles!" John yelled. "Uncover the deck gun."

"John," Pepper said from the sail locker. "Don't forget the other two ships."

Right. John ran down the deck, dodging ropes and tackle, crew and hatches. He stopped amidships and leaned back to shout at the crow's nest.

One man had crawled out and clambered halfway down the nets.

"What the hell are you doing?" John shouted.

"I coming down."

"The hell you are. There might be two other ships out there. Find them and tell me where they are."

Another shot landed fifteen feet short of *La Revanche*'s side. The spray drifted over the rail. John took a good look at the Azteca ship. It was sail-powered; he couldn't see a smokestack anywhere. They could outrun it if they lasted through the shelling. He walked down the deck to Barclay.

"In all of this time the Azteca never make a ship. We ain't really made for fighting," Barclay said.

The deck gun was being uncovered from its waterproof canvas by two mongoose-men. A third mongoose-man stumbled up from under the hold with a single shell. Another came behind him with another, and two more struggled topside with a trunk of ammunition.

"We'll improvise," John said as they swiveled the barrel to face the Azteca ship. "Get everyone armed. We going as fast as we can?"

"As fast as we go get without busting something," Barclay said.

Harrison walked up to them, pulling on his shirt. He looked at the Azteca ship. "Ten minute before she catch us," he estimated. "I say turn around, skirt the island."

La Revanche steamed straight north, and the Azteca ship came down at an angle off the starboard bow.

"Reef on either side," John said. It'd be hard to dodge the other ship. He looked down the channel they'd steamed their way up. Harrison was right. He opened his mouth to give the order.

"Them other two ship behind we" came the word from the crow's nest. John reached for Barclay's spyglass and took a look. The other two ships Pepper had warned him about rounded the channel behind them. They couldn't catch *La Revanche*, but they had cut them off.

"What we go do?" Barclay asked.

John looked at the large, yellowed sails of the Azteca boat. Another boom and puff of smoke from the front of that ship, and this time they heard a whistle close overhead, twanging some rigging. Everyone ducked. The shot landed fifty yards on the other side.

"We go forward. Faster," John said. Barclay opened his mouth and John kept going. "Tell your engineer to go *faster* or we all die."

"Okay." Barclay ran down to the nearest companionway. He grabbed the wooden trim, his fingers scraping the edge, then disappeared below with a jump.

John ran midships as he watched the progress of the Azteca ship long enough to make sure they would intersect *La Revanche*.

"What that on them sail?" someone behind him asked. John frowned and looked at the image on the advancing ship's full sails.

"A lady's face." The face in question had tassels hanging down from either side, and blue and white shapes decorated the edges.

"Chalchihuitlicue." Oaxyctl leaned against the rail next to John. He held his atlatl in one hand and throwing spears bundled in the other. "Jade Skirt Goddess, She Who Was the Water. Those are her symbols."

Appropriate for Azteca sailors, John thought.

La Revanche's gun fired. A cloud of smoke floated out over the rear cabin. Mongoose-men lined up on deck and checked their rifles.

Harrison joined them. "They go ram we?" he asked.

"They might. All they have to do is stop us, and then wait for the other two ships to pick them up if they sink," John said. "They can afford to lose a boat."

"If she bow got good wood, or some metal in it, it go tear we side up real bad."

"True." John watched. Another shot made everyone on deck flinch. An upper boom cracked and fell down into the rigging. *La Revanche* responded with a shot of her own.

"We have more maneuverability and speed," John said. "We need to use that." He walked back down toward the helmsman, dodging a pile of rope. *La Revanche*'s gun fired again, deafening him.

The Azteca ship fired back; it sounded louder now that it was closer. Small pops carried over the foaming water; Azteca rifles. The mongoose-men returned shots, but Major Avasa shouted for them to wait. The Azteca ship was still too far away.

"Here's what we're going to do," John yelled at the helmsman, standing so he could talk and watch the Azteca ship. "Wait until the last minute, then turn hard right to try and get around him. We don't want him to hit us. We need to hit him while getting around him. Understand?"

The helmsman nodded. The Azteca ship came from *La Revanche*'s northeast and *La Revanche* steamed straight north. The Azteca had a sail ship; it would take a while for them to turn and keep *La Revanche* boxed in. *La Revanche* could steam north hard, wait until the last second, then turn hard east and get around the Azteca ship. But it would be tight with the reefs on either side.

La Revanche fired. The men on the gun cheered as they hit something.

"And have someone bring up your replacement, have him lay low, in case you get hit."

The helmsman's eyes widened. The Azteca ship fired back. A whistling sound snapped through the air, and the sound of exploding wood made everyone jump. The middle of the starboard rail sagged. Three sailors lay in a bloody heap on the deck, one moaning. John's heart raced.

"I go do that." The helmsman turned and yelled at one of the sailors on deck to come be his replacement.

"Barclay," John yelled. Barclay had come back up topside. "We're going to turn hard right in a minute and try to go behind them."

Barclay actually grinned. "I see. Engine full astern for the turn, get back up to speed. I like it."

"I'm going forward."

John walked forward. This wasn't Capitol City, but they were going to face Azteca. It almost felt good, being forced into this trap. The wind kicked up, tussling John's hair and the edges of his shirt. It gave the Azteca ship more speed, and the Azteca sailors used the opportunity to try to put their ship almost dead in front of *La Revanche*.

"Shit." *La Revanche* fired again.

"Here." One of the mongoose-men handed John a rifle.

"Everyone move to the port side," John yelled. "That's where they'll hit us." Mongoose-men moved to the left side of the bow, though the Azteca ship was off the starboard bow and they couldn't shoot their rifles at it now.

John put his hook into the trigger guard but behind the trigger and let the rifle dangle as he continued toward the bow. The Azteca's sails loomed, the larger-than-life caricature of their water goddess looking down at them. It closed in fast, sail canvas taut with the wind, and *La Revanche* strained forward through the water to meet her.

The Azteca's guns kept firing, smacking into the metal sides, tearing at the rigging, and exploding into the water around them. The mongoose-men kept *La Revanche*'s single gun firing.

John looked back at the helmsman. "Hard starboard," he shouted. Sailors repeated the shout down the side of the ship. The steam engine beneath vibrated the entire hull as they started the maneuver, engines churning in full reverse. *La Revanche* turned east and the two ships faced each other bow to bow.

La Revanche kept turning. Now the Azteca ship was off the port side of the bow, not the starboard.

"Now!" Avasa yelled. The mongoose-men fired their rifles in series.

"Go, go, go," John screamed.

La Revanche surged forward. The Azteca ship let its sails flutter in the wind as they tried to turn in and still hit *La Revanche*. John had them steaming for the reefs, but the Azteca ship was still trying to turn into their side and ram them. They hadn't dodged her yet.

The mongoose-men kept up the volley of fire. John could see the Azteca on the other ship running to switch sides, shouting at them. Several stumbled and fell to the deck, dead by mongoose fire.

La Revanche was turning north again, squeezing by reef and Azteca. John's hope was that they would strike the other ship hard, and their momentum would carry them right past and out into open ocean.

"Watch for grappling hooks," John shouted. "We're going to hit." He grabbed rigging.

The two ships closed and struck. John swayed but held on. *La Revanche*'s bow raked down the Azteca ship's port side. Azteca leaped aboard, several missing and falling into the frothy water between.

Three hooks with lines landed on the deck and began to scrape along until they snagged something. Sailors ran with machetes to chop at them. One rope snapped into the face of the man chopping at it. Azteca swarmed aboard *La Revanche*, swinging by ropes or jumping aboard.

John got his balance and raised his gun to his good hand. He fired at the first warrior in padded cotton armor and a feathered mask. The man fell back over the rail into the sea.

Another dodged a mongoose-man with a well-placed knife and rushed John with an aimed pistol.

John struggled to aim the rifle with his hook.

Several feet behind him, the locker door erupted in splinters that rained down around John's feet. A small dart struck the Azteca. The Azteca fired and fell forward. John's left thigh exploded with pain. He fell to the deck.

Pepper crouched over John. John groaned and clenched his eyes. Pepper pulled him back into the locker, ripped off his shirt, and handed it to John. "Hold that on the wound. I'll be back."

Pepper stepped out of the dark locker into the light and noise of the deck battle. John closed his eyes, but not before he heard the screaming begin.

Fifteen minutes later Pepper shook him awake. Barclay stood next to him, looking on.

Pepper's skin dripped blood. His own and others'. Slashed pieces of skin hung from his arms and chest. A bullet hole in his shoulder oozed blood.

"I don't guess medicine is too highly advanced here," he said. "Your injury could be very bad."

"We get around that ship. What should we do?" Barclay asked. "Turn and fight? Go home? They could catch up with we when get to ice."

John shook his head. "Keep going north. Outrun them."

Barclay nodded and backed out of the sail locker.

Pepper picked John up, and John passed out again as he was lifted off the coils of bloodied rope beneath him.

CHAPTER FIFTY-ONE

The Loa dragged the metallic tips of its pale tentacles over the floor and wheezed from the effort of moving as it came into Dihana's office. She stood up, surprised to see it alone.

"This is the last time we speak," it said.

"Is there something I have done?" Dihana had been good to them, accepting, including them in every update and discussion about city defense. And they had offered nothing, just listened, since the ship had left for the icy north. That was all they had wanted. They didn't seem to care about anything else.

"No," it said. "We have seen the information, we know the odds. Even with the mission to the north, with the man deBrun, the assembly met and decided we should not stay in sight or risk capture. It is time for us to hide and let things happen as they may without our presence."

"Let things happen," Dihana snorted. "What is it you want from us? Why should we allow you to live among us?"

The Loa considered it, then said, "If our memories are correct, faded though they are, then the Teotl and my kind are both from the same stock. We were ambassadors to this region, and we disagreed over how to deal with the human problem. Our cousins still walk the faraway stars. If the Teotl win domination of this planet, they will recommend subjugation of your kind when my kind return in great numbers. We prefer subtler methods of manipulation that do not involve needless force. However both our efforts to aid you technologically and bring you to self-sufficient military strength have failed disastrously and led to all this. So, we hide, deep in the shadows. We hide and hope that we can survive and still influence things once the rest of our kind come through the wormholes."

In the face of all that information Dihana had one question. "Hide? Where can you hide? The Azteca have Limkin, only three towns stand between them and our walls now. And what if the expedition returns with the *Ma Wi Jung*, how will you help us with it?"

"The expedition has one of our own on it, waiting until you get to the north to assist your expedition. It will come out of hiding to reveal itself when you arrive, and when the expedition returns, will contact us. If we told you where you could find us, you might betray us." The Loa rustled around in the wicker chair and pulled something out from a pocket along the arm's chair. "We have something for you, though. We have spent a few generations creating something for this instance."

It placed a small gourd on her desk, with a wax-sealed top.

"What is this?"

Tired eyes looked at Dihana. "When all hope is lost," it told her, "when there is no other recourse, release this into your water supply."

"What will it do?" Dihana looked down at the being in the chair.

The Loa sighed. "It will kill everything. A plague that spreads swiftly through your packed city and beyond. The death will spread all the way back over the mountains when the Azteca try to retreat from it. It will spread through them, eat them alive. But more importantly, it looks for the Teotl and will eat them as well."

Dihana looked down at the gourd and swallowed. "How can you expect me to kill my own people, the entire city? This whole world?"

The Loa took a deep breath. "It is a last measure."

"You have no cure for this? Even for yourselves?"

"No, we do not. That is why we hide now. Take this if you will. Or do not. It is your choice." The Loa turned the wicker chair around. As it squeaked out of the door, Dihana held up the gourd.

"It shouldn't have been my choice. You are just too cowardly to make and face this decision yourselves. You leave to hide from it all."

Could she get mongoose-men to stop them? What would happen if she tried? Revolts? More trouble in the city than she was already managing?

She couldn't.

A word struck her: *generations.*

"Did my father know of this?" Dihana walked out into the corridor after the Loa. The Loa continued scraping down the corridor. "Answer me, or I will call the guards and you won't be able to join your friends in hiding."

The Loa paused. "Yes, Dihana. Your father knew of these things."

Mother Elene ran to the Ministry building. She stopped when mongoose-men aimed rifles at her. By the time Dihana came down to the lawn, Mother Elene had collapsed on the grass.

"They gone," she cried. "They leave."

Dihana crouched next to her. "They didn't warn you?"

Mother Elene shook her head. Her silver earrings danced with the motion. "Where they go? You know?"

"They wouldn't tell me."

Mother Elene wrapped her arms around her knees and sobbed. A priestess whose gods had left her. "Mother Elene." Dihana put a hand on her shoulder and moved around in front of her. "Did they leave you gourds of any sort, with instructions?"

Mother Elene nodded. "There are three of them."

"I know this is a bad time, but you must give those up to me. You understand? I know the Loa have given up, but we haven't. We *can* fight the Azteca. Please do as I say." Dihana stood up and pointed at two mongoose-men. "Follow her back, make sure she brings the gourds back. Make sure I get all three."

Dihana walked back toward the doors, wondering how many gourds were scattered throughout the city as gifts from the Loa.

"Prime Minister," Mother Elene called out. "What we go do without the Loa?"

Dihana paused. "The same things we were going to do with them."

She walked up the steps.

CHAPTER FIFTY-TWO

The dreams came back to John. A spiked egg dripped water from its sides as it rose from between the waves. The giant metal bird returned and flapped toward him. Dark seas tossed and turned all around him.

John's own face loomed out of the liquid metal that coalesced above the bird's neck.

Pepper stood next to him dressed in gleaming metallic armor. A gun the length of his body attached to his hip. He winked at John. "Keep her steady, deBrun, I'll be right back."

Now John was trapped inside the egg. There was nothing anywhere, he was going to die in it. Stale air and stench made him gag.

It cracked. Ocean and fresh air rushed inside, choking him. Steam rose up around the egg. He burned his fingers on the inside edge of the crack as he floundered out into the water.

The egg sank behind him. He was alone in the ocean. He didn't know who he was. Broken pustules on his arms hurt. Blood ran down his head and out his nose.

Were there sharks in this ocean? He couldn't remember. He couldn't even remember what sharks were.

John woke up on the surgeon's table. A small kerosene lantern swung overhead, lighting up the room in random half-shadows and patterns. Pepper sat in a chair watching John from the corner of the small room, bundled in heavy clothes.

Tight bandages wrapped John's left thigh. His pants had been cut away.

"You did this?" John asked, resting on an elbow.

"No. Mongoose-man surgeon. I watched." Pepper stood up. "So you will keep me aboard then?"

John nodded, still half-awake. The sound of Pepper's voice felt familiar and comfortable. "If you wanted to kill this expedition, you could have killed me. There is something else going through your head." John wanted to know what the hell Pepper was thinking of next.

In time. He gingerly swung his leg over to get off the table. Pepper's mind had always been something of a closed trap.

That was a memory. John froze in place, and the familiarity fled.

He was alone, on the boat again, and the man in front of him wasn't a friend, but a stranger to him again. Pepper.

"Wait," Pepper said. "We need to splint that before you get moving." He walked to the door and bellowed for the surgeon.

John observed a strange thing on deck. The way in which the crew looked at Pepper. Conversation dropped around him. They looked nervous around him.

Respect or fear?

Obviously Pepper had killed Azteca, brutally. He must have, to have been covered in so much blood.

Even Oaxyctl fell silent and shifted from foot to foot.

After a morning of limping around the deck, John sat down with Oaxyctl facing the rail by the side of one of the cabins. Oaxyctl had a new set of knots to practice.

"What did he do?" John asked.

"Who?" Oaxyctl concentrated on joining two lines together with a sheepshank knot.

"Pepper."

Oaxyctl finished the knot. He held it up. "He killed the first man with his bare hands." Oaxyctl pulled the knot apart. "Took his gun. Killed the second man with that. A third by bashing his head in with the barrel. A fourth tossed between the hulls. And many others after that. Then they say he jumped between the boats and killed Azteca there, then leapt back over before we pulled away."

"Did that really happen?"

Oaxyctl shrugged. "As far as I can tell."

John looked down at the knots. "Shit."

"He's a scary man. You keep strange company."

John shrugged. He saw Barclay at the center mast balancing and taking a sighting. "It's more like strange company keeps me."

"That will get you killed one day."

"Keep with the knots, they come in handy." John stood up and limped back down toward Barclay, using the rail to help take the pressure away from his leg.

He waited until Barclay had done his calculations, then took the piece of paper. "I'll go and look at the charts," John said.

"I can handle plotting them," Barclay said. "I familiar with this. If you will let me see the chart."

"I know." John frowned. "But I would rather keep the charts with just me. That was what was asked of me before we left." Neither the minister nor Haidan wanted the coordinates to their find being given to anyone. Not unless it threatened the mission because John was dying would he give anything up just yet. Then John would have to give somone the coordinates, and the strange artifact the Loa had given him.

Oaxyctl? He had saved his life. Barclay? Barclay was already thinking about it, trying to get in to see the final coordinates and chart. Or Pepper?

Pepper? The thought had bubbled up to his surprise. It didn't make sense. That wouldn't work at all.

Barclay's curiosity about the maps made him nervous.

"Barclay, please." John held out his hand. "The sighting. I am sure it is accurate, and I already know you can use our charts well."

Barclay handed over the slip of paper.

Later, when Barclay was not around, he would have to find a way of double-checking the sighting.

Just in case.

John limped over to the nearest companionway. One of the crew helped him down the stairs.

Down at the chart table in his small room John wondered if he was being paranoid for no reason. One explosion and the three Azteca ships made him think otherwise.

The world was turning upside down, he thought, taking out a pair of walking rulers. A little paranoia is needed. John marked their location on Edward's chart.

Everything looked good.

Harrison knocked at his door. "A problem," he said.

After locking his room John hobbled after Harrison to the hold near the front of the ship. John leaned against a bulkhead, his thigh throbbing to the point he felt dizzy. "The freshwater?"

"Yeah. It were one of them Azteca ship point-blank shot." Harrison opened the door. "Aiming for we waterline no doubt."

Shattered water casks dripped their final drops onto a waterlogged floor. The hole in the side of the hull had been patched over with another metal sheet. They were lucky it hadn't been lower. The Azteca might have sunk them.

"What we do now?" Harrison asked. His face looked yellowed and tired in the weak electric light coming from the small bulb at the top of the hold.

"We just need to make it there." John had no intention of turning back since the attack. The Azteca were desperate to stop this expedition. He understood that now. He could hurt their plans with this expedition and he felt more committed to it as a result.

"We won't have the water to make it back." Harrison moved aside to let somone past with an armful of broken casks.

"Plenty of fresh water where we're going," John said.

"Maybe we don't got enough for that."

A pump, connected with pneumatic hoses to the engine room, hissed away. One hose snaked down into *La Revanche*'s sump through an opened hatch, and the other led out and up the stairs onto the deck, spitting the salt water over the sides.

"Make some new casks. Take them to the center of the ship. Gimbal them so they don't splash. And get some rubber, or rubberized tarp. Then get any big pots we have and fill them with salt water to boil," John gave directions, and Harrison smiled.

"A still?"

"Yeah." John shuffled his straight leg over with his good hand and leaned his shoulder against the doorway for balance. "Freshwater still." He grunted. "And while you're at it, have them make me a cane. Do it now before people start saying we don't have water. Get them to help you."

"Right." Harrison still hesitated. "There something else you go need see first."

John watched a crewman in the far corner who hadn't moved yet. The man stood still, watching them. "What?"

Harrison walked over through the undamaged water casks. He looked back. "Close the door," he ordered. "And you two by the pump, leave."

When the door closed, Harrison and the other crewman pulled the sides of a cask off. Shaggy fur spilled over the cracked wood and snapped metal.

"What the hell?" John limped forward.

Harrison grunted and pulled the creature out of the cask. It flopped onto the floor, a thick hand lolling out from its body. The face of the thing had been blown off, leaving a messy stump on its shoulders.

"What kind of god you think it is?" the sailor asked, crouching next to it. "Teotl, or Loa?"

John looked at the jagged claws on the heavy, padded hands. And muscle. Even beneath the fat and blubber he could sense this compact creature could have killed anyone who had found it alive in the blink of an eye.

"Could be anything," John said. "Wrap it up in something and throw it overboard."

"Suppose it a Loa?" Harrison asked.

"Suppose it is," John said. "What else can I do? Keep it to rot? Give it a burial?"

Harrison looked down at the deck. "No. You right."

"Get the still going." John walked out of the locker. "Clean this place out. I need to go rest." His thigh ached. A small spot of blood stained the front of the bandage. John avoided looking down. He'd lost a hand to the saw the last time he'd made this journey. He did not want to undergo another amputation. It gave him chills just thinking about it.

Best not to.

Better to hope, look forward, and plan. Keep moving.

CHAPTER FIFTY-THREE

A faint frost had formed on the rigging. Oaxyctl pressed his fingers to a railing and let the cold seep into the palms of his hands. His fingernails were black and he stank. Black grease and dirt clung to his clothing. He'd been in the deepest bilges of the ship, moving pump hoses around to suck water out. They kept taking in water from leaks. Leaks from the shot taken to the front of the ship, and the explosion in the rear. Even the massive stuffing box where the propeller came in through the hull had started to leak.

Now he had a moment to rest, and he chose to clamber up the deck to the bowsprit. He shimmied out along the long pole and dropped onto the netting just below it.

Hard work was good. It had kept him from thinking about the attack. It had shaken him. He still wasn't sure if it was an attempt to capture them all or kill them all. Remember, he told himself, your god seems to think different than some other gods.

There was a thought that could keep a man up late into the night.

And it was best not to think about.

So the work was good, it kept his mind away from such things.

The sea remained calm tonight. The days had been getting shorter, it seemed to him. The moons seemed to be out more often. And the air was getting colder.

It was like climbing a mountain. The higher you got, the colder it got. And this was the second week of it.

Oaxyctl lay back in the netting and watched the stars, occasionally catching a bit of lighthearted spray on his back as *La Revanche* pushed farther north on the large, almost infinite ocean, until the last faint bits of orange evening succumbed to the gradual night.

How could someone obey the gods when the gods themselves couldn't agree with one another?

Oaxyctl held up the bight of a line, the loop flopping over, and tied a sheepshank.

"You still know your other knots?" John asked. He limped over with the aid of a cane. Oaxyctl noted that the bandage around John's thigh was stained with blood from his injury, and John winced in pain as he moved.

"Yes." Oaxyctl pulled the knot apart and demonstrated the bowline, the sheepshank, a simple square knot, and a sheet bend.

John grunted and sat down next to him. He set the quickly cut wooden cane next to him. "Isn't there enough land on the other side of the mountains? Why do the gods think the invasion is necessary?"

Oaxyctl looked down at the rope between his hands. "They do not do this for land."

"Then what for?"

John was looking for answers. Oaxyctl could hear it in his voice. John will die, he realized. That bullet wound, it was a killer. Not then, but in the near future. And John wanted answers before he died.

But *when* would John die? Oaxyctl wondered. Before or after they found what they were searching for? The mythical *Ma Wi Jung* that all seemed to desire. More important, could he get the codes out of John before that time?

"They need more blood. They need more land. More servants. They tell their people, go here, move over the mountains. Most cannot make sense of these orders. But gods are gods, and who are we to know what they direct in the long run?"

John rapped his hook against the deck. "I don't believe in gods."

The declaration didn't surprise Oaxyctl. He'd been around Nanagadans too long, he thought. Too many different ideas, religions, and peoples.

The thought of living a life without the threat of sacrifice seemed pleasurable. Though he'd once thought dying for the gods the greatest honor, at the gut level dying still scared Oaxyctl. He'd confirmed that heretical survival instinct to himself, shaking and scared in the mud, on the outskirts of Brungstun.

But then, without the direction of the gods, how could someone live his own life? There would be no certainty in anything.

It was just as scary as facing the eagle stone.

"How can you not believe in gods?" Oaxyctl asked. "You see them walking the ground! The gods of Capitol City are there for any to see."

John pulled his good leg up to his chin. He looked tired. "If I were the only black-skinned man to appear in Aztlan, and no one had ever seen such a thing, and I called myself a god, would you believe me?"

Oaxyctl shook his head. "You would have to prove it."

John smiled. "Your priests. They have a lot of power?"

"They control all. It is the greatest position in society." Oaxyctl cocked his head. "Why do you ask?"

"Because." John looked through the scuppers at the sea. "After this, we will have to go into the heart of Azteca land and stop this at the source." His face hardened. "One must understand the enemy to effectively combat him."

It sounded both like John, and unlike him. The man was changing. All this stress. Before he seemed content to follow, and now he was thinking of other things.

"Am I your enemy?" Oaxyctl asked.

John shook his head. "You are a friend." He craned his head back. "It is getting very cold. Look." He exhaled; a faint puff of his breath hung in the air for a second.

Oaxyctl nodded. "I think soon we will see . . . what is it called?" He struggled to translate the words for a second. "Crystal rain?"

John smiled. "That's a nice description. It is snow. Not a word we use often at home, but you see it in books sometimes. Stories. Tales of brave fishermen going far north, some disappearing."

Oaxyctl leaned back and exhaled to see his own breath. "Yes, sometimes you can see it on the mountains. At their very tops. I've seen it a few times, when out scouting."

When he stood up to help John struggle to his feet, the wind shifted, and it blew right through his clothes. It was cold enough to make him shiver.

Like going up a mountain, he thought.

A faint tapping woke him up. Oaxyctl blinked, looking for the source. His hammock shook as someone brushed against it.

"*Quimichtin?*" a voice asked.

The word made Oaxyctl shiver. Spy. He swallowed. If he answered yes, would he die?

"Azteca-man, you here?" the voice whispered.

"Yes," Oaxyctl said.

The sailor he had met in the rigging looked over into his hammock. He looked scared. "Come with me." The man carried an old, hooded electric lantern. A small, single beam of light broke the darkness, then flicked off again.

"It came aboard during the attack," the man explained. "Them attack, just a diversion to place it aboard. Seen?"

Oaxyctl didn't. He hesitated, not sure what the man was talking about. The man grabbed Oaxyctl's hand. It was slimy, greasy with bilgewater. The faint smell of decay reached Oaxyctl. A familiar smell. Rotted flesh.

Together they moved down through the holds of *La Revanche*, careful not to wake anyone. The man popped open a hatch. Oaxyctl smelled dead flesh and heard water slopping around below.

"Come."

Oaxyctl lowered himself into the brackish sludge, holding his nose. It came up to his knees. The water shifted around as the ship plunged into the rough waters, and tiny wavelets splashed the nasty water up against his crotch, making his privates shrink behind his cotton pants.

It was ice-cold enough that it hurt to breathe while wading through.

He bumped against the back of the man. The lantern flicked on, its single, concentrated beam flashing against dull, pitted metal and slimy water.

The beam of light rested on a giant lump of egg-shaped, black flesh hanging from the side of the hull.

"It speak to me," the man said.

The egg stirred. Oaxyctl thought he could just see through it, to some familiar-edged shape beneath.

His heart almost stopped. He dropped to his knees, ignoring the pain of cold water around his waist.

"It tell me," the man said, "we close to the northern land, where *Ma Wi Jung* lie. It say it waiting for you to deliver it the code because it changing for the cold weather. It waiting. If you do the job before it finish it change, it go reward you. If you fail again, it say you go suffer like you never suffer before and it go get the code anyway."

"I understand," Oaxyctl said. Either this was his god, and it had followed them all the way here, or it was another that knew about Oaxyctl and the plan to get the codes.

"Soon it go be free from it recovery here. So waste no time."

Oaxyctl stood up, water draining from his pockets. "I will go at once."

"Good. We done. Come." The man shut the light off, plunging them back into the dark. The hair on the back of Oaxyctl's neck rose. He struggled to turn around, leaving the god behind him. He rubbed his throat, remembering the feel of the claws around it, not so long ago.

Before they climbed back out of the hatch, Oaxyctl grabbed the man's arm. "What is your name? I need for you to do something."

"What you need?"

"We need to take control of this ship. We need to get John deBrun to ourselves."

The man thought about it. "Okay. One of we high up in command here. We can throw enough doubt to turn this ship back around."

"Who?"

The man sighed. "High up enough. Don't ask."

"Why not?" Oaxyctl asked, frustrated.

"The less who know, the better. I ain't taking no chance."

The man moved again. Oaxyctl took one last look at the dark water beneath the hatch, the ship's bilges, then walked away. Behind him the hatch closed, squeaking as the wheel tightened it shut.

Still not enough metal between him and the incubating god. Oaxyctl would not be able to sleep knowing what rested in the lowest depths of the ship. You cannot escape the gods, he thought to himself.

CHAPTER FIFTY-FOUR

Someone considered killing Pepper. Half of Pepper's conscious mind heard them walk toward his hammock, then pause. Pepper waited, welcoming the attack, his nerves fired, senses tuned to every clink and squeak.

Then the would-be assassin changed his mind and ran.

Pepper let the rest of himself come up out of the resting state. The steamship was taking a pounding. His hammock swung from side to side and someone mewled and retched, scrunched up against the side of the flexing bulkheads.

Pepper crossed his arms over his chest and dropped back down toward sleep. His steely eyes could see his warm breath in the air, though no one else could discern anything but the failing oil lantern swinging at the center of all the hammocks.

Three days of this storm. A break before that. Another storm. They were crossing out of the warm waters into the cold. An abrupt and miserable transition.

The moment of alarm had passed. Pepper returned to his half-sleep without further thought, conserving energy for whatever lay ahead.

Today the storm blew itself out, passing them by with ominous low-sweeping clouds and explosions of lightning that sizzled and exploded into the waves in front of them.

Crew and mongoose-men alike crowded the decks, dressed as warmly as they could, carrying picks and tools to scrape at the elaborate formations of ice that clung to every surface of the ship.

Pepper joined, his fingers numb as he pried sheets of ice away from the rigging. Right now they treated it as a joke, a novelty, taking their time. By tomorrow, Pepper realized looking around, the ice would begin to weigh down the ship. Then it would become a matter of scraping ice or drowning in the cold water.

He kept scraping. Everyone gave him a wide berth. Which was just how Pepper wanted it.

During a break in the scraping Pepper sat at the aft railing, watching the water and small bits of ice churned up by the propeller. To the starboard a large iceberg floated by, reflecting the sun off its clear sides. Mongoose-men and sailors thronged to the side of the ship to watch it and marvel.

John limped to his side. Pepper regarded the bandage around John's thigh with suspicion. "You're going to lose your leg." John grimaced and gripped the aft rail with a gloved hand. The hook rested by his thigh. "Speaking of which," Pepper continued, "why the hook? I spent some time in Capitol City before stowing aboard. They have the means to make a mechanical hand. Couldn't you afford one?"

"No, I couldn't." John looked down. "Not with a family." He turned his back to Pepper, watching the iceberg. "We'd better slow down at night, shouldn't we? Do you think we can afford losing that time?"

"We're close to land." Pepper flicked a stray piece of ice over the side with his forefinger. "The icebergs calve big. Better to slow down."

John nodded. "At least we'll have access to freshwater soon."

"And then?"

"Then we have a lot of work in front of us."

"You up for that?"

"The sooner we find this device, the sooner we can figure out what the hell it does, the sooner we can return and use it against the Azteca." John crouched in front of Pepper. And for a brief moment Pepper saw a bit of the old John that he knew, in command, fire and purpose in his eyes. "What is the *Ma Wi Jung*?"

Pepper smiled. "If you truly don't have any of your memories . . ."

"Try me."

Pepper thought about it. "I can use words, and make analogies, but they don't really matter. It is technology. Advanced technology."

"Everyone wants it. The Loa certainly want it, or control of it. Haidan thinks it might allow us an edge. And you say even the Azteca gods wish to stop us from getting it. Or want it themselves."

"And you?" Pepper asked, curious.

"Can we attack the Azteca with it? Is it really a weapon?"

"Not really the weapon anyone thinks it is," Pepper said, half-lying. It made him nervous. John might have amnesia, but was he still good at ferreting out lies? Pepper didn't want to undo any of the trust he'd built with this new John in front of him.

"Then I'll drag it from the ice by my own hand," John said. "If it helps us push them back over the mountains and helps me find my wife and son, then I'll deliver it to Capitol City."

"Strange. I still can't get over it. John deBrun, settled down, raising a family. That's certainly not the John I knew."

John stood up. A loud crack split through the air, and the sides of the iceberg they had passed slumped into the water. A small, frothy wave washed toward them.

"That John is gone." He pointed his hook at Pepper. "You're the only one who remembers him, and you hardly speak to me about it."

"Those things will come back, John." If John had blocked his own memories, then Pepper wouldn't force anything.

Too dangerous.

There was no context, no way he could even begin to draw a picture, unless John was a willing participant. Pepper wasn't willing to risk doing anything damaging or dangerous by forcing out things the block was there for. "And nothing is gained by my telling you things right now. I will tell you what you need when the situation calls for it."

John changed the subject. "You asked me why I want the *Ma Wi Jung*. But a better question is, what do you want it for?"

The steamship rocked as the wave slapped against the stern.

"You and I shared goals and concerns once," Pepper said. "No doubt, when I help you get your memories back, we'll share them again. Listen." Pepper stood up, almost dwarfing the tired, anemic-looking John. "I can still see you, John. Some things don't change. And one thing is that, even now, you're the most dangerous man I ever met."

He could see John calculating what to do with him still. And without the memories . . . Pepper knew he was an unknown. And a potential liability.

"You can't throw me off the boat," Pepper said. "You've seen me in action. The cost of life is too high. All you need to know is that I am an old acquaintance, and that you should keep me around. I will protect your life. What greater bargain is there?"

"*Acquaintance?* An interesting word choice."

"We weren't bosom buddies, John. People who do what we do don't have that to spare."

John shifted on the deck. Pepper saw the pain from walking. A sure sign the wound in John's thigh was not getting any better.

John sighed. "Will you be able to help me find my family? Push back the Azteca?"

"I can't guarantee anything, John." Pepper looked around at the sea, at the coils of ropes on the deck, and not into John's eyes as he thought for a moment. "But I will say there is something I *can* give you."

"Yes?"

"Your old life back." Pepper met John's eyes. He kept them level, meeting John's in a silent deadlock.

"You'll give me my old life back, but not talk to me about my past?" Pepper nodded. "If you were the closest thing I had to a friend, Pepper, I don't know if I want this old life back without my memories. I can see what you are, and that is just plain dangerous. And I don't like it."

No threats, no power games, just the truth, Pepper thought. "You're right. For now I can't remember your past for you, only you can do that, so you're a player in a game you don't even know the rules of. But if we make it to the *Ma Wi Jung*, you will be given your memories back. I will make it so. Then you will have your old life back, and you will know who you are, and you will know what to do."

"Suppose I die rather than follow this 'old life'?"

"I doubt that John. Die, and leave your family? You're not that kind of coward." John stiffened, and Pepper bit his lip. Bad choice of words. "Besides, I can't let you do that."

"Why?"

"You're the key to the *Ma Wi Jung*. You are the only person on this planet that has the code to get in." When Pepper had first stowed away, he'd searched John's cabin, trying to figure out how they were hoping to get onto the *Ma Wi Jung*. He'd found an artifact from the wars, a device the Loa used to get in and take over ships. But not even that ancient device the Loa bred, and John was hiding from everyone else, would work quickly enough. It would take the Loa several weeks to take over, and even then, then it wouldn't be of any use to the Loa who'd given it to John. *Ma Wi Jung* had been made for humans, and only humans, to use. That had been the agreement all those years ago when the Loa helped build the ship.

"Why am I the only person? Wouldn't others have had the codes?"

Pepper cleared his throat. "*You're* the code. Your skin, your blood. Your voice, your eyes, your fingerprint, your face, and most importantly, your heartbeat." Because John had to be alive, and not coerced, for the ship to open up to them. And he had to grant Pepper permission to board. John was the only living human Pilot on this planet, and he didn't have the capacity to realize it. "You're it, the only person that can save this world."

John looked at him with obvious incredulity. Pepper shrugged, long and languorously, his shoulders bunching. "Anyway, right now these things don't matter. We must first survive to get to the *Ma Wi Jung*."

He stood up and walked away. Enough conversation. Verbal games annoyed him. It would have been a lot easier to grab John, and for Pepper to put the tip of his right index finger against John's temple, then link up and shove the information down into his brain.

But that would kill John. The block on his memories would make sure of that.

Another iceberg approached the ship. Pepper watched it from the side rails, alone on the busy deck as people chipped at the ice still accumulating on the ship.

Later that night something else came to his attention. A hatch had opened somewhere, and he caught the faintest whiff. A faint smell. One he was surprised he hadn't noticed before. Decay.

Teotl.

Pepper left his hammock and followed it. Several times he doubled back, losing it, but found himself moving down into the ship until he came face-to-face with a closed bilge hatch.

He opened it, carefully, quietly, then stopped. He sat next to it for a long minute, holding an internal conversation with himself that even he didn't recognize.

A casting of the odds.

Would he live if he crawled down into the water?

Not sure.

A Teotl was down there. Damn creature. Probably waiting in molt, growing into a more focused hunter-killer.

The creature's casing at this stage would be impermeable to gunfire or spears or anything Pepper could muster just now, unless he provoked it into coming out. He didn't have the tools to pull it off the wall, either.

It would have the advantage, knowing he was there, waiting until he tired before it emerged. Then Pepper would be the one on defense. And he didn't like that, not at all. Not in this small space.

No, he decided. Better not to let it know he was here. Let it make its move. He'd been lucky back at Capitol City, with the kids to obscure the fight and confuse the Teotl; he might not be so lucky now.

Better to kill it when it was out of the case, more vulnerable, not aware he was out. Pepper always looked for advantages going against the Teotl.

He hadn't lost a fight with one yet, but that didn't mean anything.

They were efficient adapters, and dangerous enemies.

Pepper closed the hatch and dogged it back, aware that the odds of survival had just dropped.

CHAPTER FIFTY-FIVE

The Azteca armies arrived on the peninsula and the mongoose-men retreated before their numbers. Haidan's men slowed the Azteca down by destroying train tracks and food warehouses as they retreated. Several large explosive traps closed off hill passes.

The brilliantly colored Azteca horde continued forward after clearing them and unknowingly followed the path Haidan hoped they would. Every hour the leaders of the mongoose-men sat with Dihana to update her on what was happening.

Until this morning. They told her there was no more information to give. The airships spied on the Azteca, and the city waited for the siege to begin.

Dihana left the Ministry building to find Haidan.

He stood on one of the walls, looking out over the empty villages and depots around the city's walls. The fringe of jungle green lay beyond a wasteland of barbed wire, trenches, troops, and brown earth. Dihana imagined the shadows of Azteca creeping through it.

"What about their airships?" she asked.

"We can hold most of them with what we got. We got explosive shell we can fire from these wall. And we own airship go battle them down if they come too near. But they can still fly in the distance, watch the battle, try to look inside the city."

Dihana allowed him to take her in hand and tour the rest of the walls, where men grimly manned guns of all sizes, machetes strapped to their sides. Most of the defenses on the wall weren't useful until the Azteca broke the outer rings of trenches and came much closer to the wall. "Haidan, what could we have done to prevent this?"

"I don't know. More spy in Azteca land?" He'd been up for nights in a row, overseeing every possible detail, hounding his men. It showed in his puffy eyes and gravelly voice. He leaned against the wall and put his head in his hands. "If we still alive after this, we go have to change things. Bigger forces, more villages. More cities. This entire land go have to be powerful, dynamic. We can't wait, can't be laid-back. There a thousand things we need."

Dihana nodded. "We will have to be the ones on the move, not them. No more defensive waiting."

"That too." Haidan stood up. "We still can't find any Loa."

"Where do you think they went?"

"Deep under the city?"

Dihana nodded. "They give you a gourd? One with a plague in it?"

"We could fire it into the Azteca when they attack our walls," Haidan suggested. "And hunker down. Maybe we won't catch it?"

"I think the Loa would have suggested that if it worked, don't you?" She walked with Haidan back toward one of the heavy platforms on the edge that would lower them to the streets.

"I collected all the other ones, the ones the Loa left behind for the priestesses, the one they gave the Councilmen, and the one they gave me, in a locked vault. I want yours there as well."

Haidan helped her onto the platform, the wood squeaking under her feet. "You think you go use them, if it get to that point?" Haidan asked, his teeth bared in what wasn't a smile, but not quite a grimace. "Destroy everything, so no one gets anything?"

"That would be like Hope's Loss. For us to point our own weapon at ourselves, just like our ancestors destroyed all of each other's machines so no one would have anything. So many died then, Haidan. How could I do that?"

The platform jerked. The steam motor powering it hissed as it let the brakes go, and she dropped down toward the ground. "You hope you die with it all," Haidan said, "and never get held responsible for such a thing."

"The Loa are hoping to hide this one out and come back up when either their disease has claimed everyone, or we survive by some miracle. Maybe that was what the old-father thought they could do. Wait it out. They could have just been trying to buy some time."

Haidan chuckled. "All that had survive of the old-father were the Councilmen them. Not so good, eh?"

The platform slowed and stopped at ground level.

There were more meetings to be had with the people in the city. No one knew how long this would take. Food and water supplies were critical, and meting them out meant dangerous decisions. No one was sure how long they could hold off an Azteca attack, but with so many people behind the walls, Dihana didn't think it was long. A couple months? Maybe more if the fishermen kept their larders full.

Dihana wondered how much longer she could hold up without sleep. As she stepped into a waiting vehicle, she mentally set aside time in the afternoon for a nap.

Later in the night she awoke to a series of deep thuds. When she walked over to her window, she heard people shouting in the street.

Up on the walls of Capitol City, flashes of gunfire lit the night sky with stabbing orange streaks. A cloud of eerie-colored backlit powder floated in the air. Below the clouds seed-shaped figures coasted over the city, dropping flares.

Dihana leaned against the windowsill and cried.

The Azteca were here.

CHAPTER FIFTY-SIX

La *Revanche* landed three days into the third week. Pepper stood on deck along with the other crew, all shivering, frozen, but awed at the majestic mountains covered in snow. All around them the staccato snaps of breaking ice and swoosh of calving icebergs filled the air.

It took another day before they were stuck in ice. The crew grew nervous, but Pepper saw from John's calm that this was something John expected.

The bottom of the steamship was shallow and curved, not the sharp cutting shape of the traditional sail-ship. John explained that he'd seen shallow skiffs survive the freezing ice in his previous trip with that design and seen deeper-keeled skiffs staved in. Pepper watched over the next night, his eyes piercing the dark, to see unstoppable sheets of ice push against the sides of *La Revanche,* then slip under the hull and lift the boat up onto the ice.

La Revanche was shaped like the fishing skiffs that could be pulled up onto ground and float over shallow reef water easily. John was right. As a result, the ice could push up without damaging the hull.

Pepper smiled and explained it to several of the mongoose-men milling around, expecting the sides of the ship to be stove in, waiting for the announcement of their deaths.

The mood brightened somewhat. The land was alien, dark, like something out of a nightmare, but at least they still had the ship around them.

Preparations began in earnest. They pulled the ballast out of the bilges of the boat. No one found or said anything about the incubating Teotl, Pepper noticed. He helped with moving ballast and made his way through bilges, looking for it.

He only found a patch of clean hull in the grime. Presumably where the creature had attached itself to cocoon. Pepper looked around. The Teotl would have left the ship in the night, crossing the ice.

It was out there somewhere, watching them.

Sailors yelled at him to get moving. Great lead weights and blocks of stone had to be lifted out by yardarms and lowered over the ship's side onto bright red tarps so they could locate them when they returned and put the ship back into the water. It was hard work.

Several men spent full-time shifts boiling and making clean water to replace their stores. Food was inventoried and split: half on the tarps, half in the ship. All spare supplies were set in the snow with the ballast and marked with tall flags.

They were lightening the ship. The Teotl could poison or get rid of the stores they'd left behind if they got free, but it was a nonissue. All Pepper had to do was get to the *Ma Wi Jung.*

The next surprise for Pepper came when massive axles were pushed out of the sides of the front bow and rear stern. Then tiny additional axles where welded to the sides of the hull. Wheels were mounted, and then several hundred feet of tread threaded on by grunting mongoose-men, their sweat freezing to their eyebrows.

In just a little over a day, they had converted *La Revanche* to a giant snowtank. The mongoose engineers spent another day in the boiler rooms redirecting the gears from the ship's propeller to the axles. Their shouts drifted up from the ship's hatches into the crystalline air as they worked at getting the ship converted.

Pepper walked along the length of the tread. He'd been somewhat dubious, but the more he examined it, the more it looked as if it would work. Several small, additional wheels had been mounted along the hull of the ship, on upper and lower tracks, to keep the tread taut and provide some suspension.

Stars filled the sky, and for a moment Pepper enjoyed the mass of constellations, many still unfamiliar to him.

Something ahead made his nostrils flare, and he crouched to the ground.

Blood.

He found several scarlet drops on the ground, pockmarking the snow with their warmth.

Several more feet ahead a whole pool of fresh blood lay around the ripped furs of a mongoose-man. Pepper bent over and looked at the wounds. A cut to the throat had cut the man's vocal cords, and then numerous nasty jabs to the stomach, chest, and groin had caused the blood loss.

Teotl. It had escaped. This poor mongoose-man had spotted it and paid as a result.

A spotlight struck Pepper and he tensed. Men rushed to the side of the deck, murmuring spreading around, looking down at him.

"You have got to be kidding." Pepper turned and looked into the light. His eyes adjusted, and he made a note of every face on the deck, every expression, to analyze later.

"Is he dead?" someone asked.

Pepper nodded.

"You killed him," someone else said.

John's haggard face appeared on deck. He looked over and frowned. With his Aztecan friend's help he walked down the gangplank to the snowy ground and crunched over to the scene.

The two men stood looking at Pepper in the glare of the light.

Pepper looked at John. Come on, man, he thought, you can't believe this shit. But Pepper could tell it was futile.

"I didn't do this," he said.

John didn't answer, but looked down at the dead man. Oaxyctl, Pepper noticed, never bothered. Instead the Aztecan stared Pepper down. Something was going on, behind those brown eyes and the frozen fringe of jet-black hair.

"We can't be sure if he did this," Oaxyctl said. "But we saw him in action at the battle. He did fight for us. But we know he is very capable of this sort of butchery. And we still don't know what he is doing here. We must lock him up. For our own safety."

Now Pepper knew who at least one of the enemy was. Pepper focused on the sweat frozen to John's forehead. John was not doing well.

Oaxyctl hovered by him like a buzzard. John nodded, almost absentmindedly, considering Oaxyctl's words. "Yes, yes, I think that is best for right now." He looked at Pepper, met his eyes. "Just a precaution."

Again, Pepper saw a glint of the familiar John: calm, calculating, scheming. This was the easiest way to calm the crew. Have some faith in him, John's eyes seemed to say. Even without his memories, John knew what he was doing. Pepper didn't move as more men came down the planks and surrounded him. Several stayed far back, guns pointed at him. He could have killed them all. Instead he let them lead him back on board.

The sail locker they had locked him in the first time still had no doors, so they chained him between two sturdy posts.

Just temporary, he thought. John is taking the best gamble. And he couldn't leave John here alone. John was Pepper's only way into the *Ma Wi Jung*.

Don't hold it against him.

Arms draped at his side, rattling chain, he sat cross-legged, ears perked, flicking as sounds reached him from the gloom of belowdecks.

*   *   *

After a few hours, movement started up again. People thudded around on the decks. The boilers in the engine room hissed steam, and men shouted instructions back and forth, reading off dials.

The crunch of gears being engaged shuddered through the hull. Pepper shifted as the steamship lurched forward, almost stalling as even more screaming came from between the bulkheads, the three engineers demanding more fuel be fired.

Not far from the hull Pepper listened as the treads thumped and creaked past. *La Revanche* moved forward. Men shouted as they clambered up from the slow-moving treads back onto the ship.

There was more conversation. Ahead of him on the other side of a bulkhead, in the hammocks where the crew slept, Pepper listened to someone breathing heavily. Pepper focused on the sounds, tuning his hearing up to unnatural levels.

Someone spoke.

"Can we trust him?" The voice sounded nervous, but a fake nervous.

The heavy breathing stopped. Someone dropped a spoon to the floor and fumbled about for it. "He the captain, he know what he doing."

"He know where we even going?" The second person's voice took on a tone of incredulity.

"Someone say he have map." Defensive.

"You see it?"

"Uh-uh." The hammock creaked as someone got off it. "What you saying?"

"That we can't self trust that."

"Look, we can't turn back. The mongoose-men ain't go stand for that. This dangerous. But think back on what we done escape. Azteca."

A long pause. Pepper tuned out the sound of treads to focus on the almost whisper that came next.

"What if I say some of the mongoose-men nervous as well? They think a run to Cowfoot Island would save all of we."

The heavy breathing came back, along with footsteps that moved away. There was no answer, just the faint static of whispers that had moved out of his hearing range.

Mutiny, Pepper thought.

CHAPTER FIFTY-SEVEN

Five Azteca airships moved in with the clouds. They dropped several bombs before turning around and leaving. They had flown too high for any of the guns on Capitol City's walls to reach them, and they had left by the time any of Capitol City's airships took to the air. They'd been doing that all day.

Haidan had finally gotten a series of patrols in the sky to try to keep the Azteca airships at bay.

He walked down the street toward his house. He was tired, his cough had flared up, and he found himself perpetually out of breath. Three mongoose-men moved with him. One caught his arm when he stumbled over an uneven flagstone.

"I sorry," Haidan said. "Let's pause." He leaned against a brick wall and caught his breath. Too many late nights, going 100 percent with no rest. The Azteca bombing airships had arrived, Firstop had fallen quiet, and the first Azteca warriors trundled in large cannons to open fire on Capitol City's trenches. They'd been funneled right into the area of the peninsula he wanted, but they were testing his defenses, and waiting for the rest of the Azteca to catch up with them. And now his sickness had caught up with him. Haidan needed to rest as the siege began.

An armed squad of grim-looking Tolteca walked by and nodded.

"Where they headed?" Haidan asked.

"Outside the wall to fight. They volunteer."

"I wonder how long they go fight their own kin," Haidan said.

"You don't trust the Tolteca," the other bodyguard said. "How come?"

"Is not the Tolteca I worried about." Haidan put his hands on his knees. "It all the Azteca spy who hiding in the Tolteca who volunteer to fight."

The two bodyguards shrugged. "Too late to worry now."

"It never too late to worry."

"That's true."

They stood and looked at each other for a while. Then Haidan looked at the band of Tolteca marching to protect the city. "Either way, it damn good to see so many mongoose-men out," he said. A high-pitched whistle filled his ears and the world exploded around him. The wall he had been leaning against crumbled. The bricks struck him. It all slumped on top of him, blacking everything out. Haidan coughed as he inhaled dust.

The roaring in his ears stopped.

He stirred.

He hurt all over. In several places it was more than the press of brick, but the pain of broken bones. Haidan moaned and tried to push the heavy weight off him, but he was too weak.

Voices filtered down to him. After several minutes large pieces of wall were dragged away from on top of him. One of the bodyguards and several Tolteca scraped away the rubble and pulled him out.

They strapped him to a piece of board and carried him down the street. Every few seconds a concerned face would look down at him and ask him if he was okay.

He tried to reply, but his voice croaked, and there seemed to be a lot of blood everywhere. He'd planned. He'd planned enough that it would go on, he told himself. No matter how tiring this was, no matter how he was hurt, the city would fight without him. Dihana and his men would see to it.

Far, far over the city, he watched a pair of airships crash into each other and burn.

Haidan was relieved to close his eyes, black out, and finally get some rest.

CHAPTER FIFTY-EIGHT

The icy lands stretched out around them. Fast winds bit into the sides of *La Revanche* and made the rigging sing. Anyone not on watch huddled below near the ship's kitchen fires or in the boiler rooms.

On the second day word spread throughout the ship as they passed between two great mountains of snow that something wondrous was to be seen from the decks. Through clear sheets of translucent ice, great slabs of silvery metal flashed back at them.

Buildings, hundreds of feet high, had been caught in the ice.

John stood with several mongoose-men at the ship's rail. Someone asked the inevitable question.

"What are they?"

"Things left over from the old-fathers," John said. Great buildings, leaning over at strange angles as they were swept away in slow motion by the blocks of ice. A great city had stood here once.

Welcome back, he thought. Yes, this was . . .

Oaxyctl walked over to John. "They are made of a metal?"

"It glints like metal," John said, losing the feeling of another fleeting memory. "But there is glass as well." He pointed. The buildings had rooms, and they could see furniture inside. It made John shiver. It was as if he were looking at a perfectly preserved piece of time.

The familiar feeling came again. John let go of the railing and turned to walk away, but his wounded leg buckled under him. Oaxyctl grabbed his shoulder and held him.

"Buildings by them god," someone marveled. "No man could make them thing."

John shook his head. "The old-fathers made Capitol City." The sailors didn't look so sure. "They were powerful men. Not gods. Men."

"How long before we arrive?" they asked.

"Three days." John leaned over and looked at the deck, almost talking to himself. "Just outside the city."

The name on the map said this was Starport. It echoed around John's head for a while. Stars. The old-fathers launched their great ships all the way to the stars from here.

"Whoa," Oaxyctl muttered, catching him again.

John's leg would not cooperate. Frustrated, he hung from Oaxyctl.

This was no way to lead an expedition.

"Take me to my cabin. Get the mongoose doctor-man," John ordered.

Oaxyctl helped him hop over to the nearest companionway and struggle down into the ship.

John began sweating. The humid belowdecks, dank and dark, set something off in him. He fought off a touch of claustrophobia. The bulkheads loomed in on him, and his vision blurred.

It was too close, too dark. He'd spent an eternity in dark, cramped spaces, and he was sick of them.

"I don't feel so well," he said as Avasa walked into the cabin and Barclay came close behind.

"Sir," Avasa said. "If that the case, you should hand over the chart. Let we navigate. You need to stay below, stay warm. Rest. Don't use your foot."

And maybe Avasa was too helpful, John thought. What happened when he handed over the map to the thin mongoose leader?

He couldn't be sure. Or maybe he was paranoid.

Barclay leaned against the doorjamb with his hands crossed over his chest. "Ain't no matter." He shrugged. "When food get half out, we turn back. Right?"

John wiped his forehead with a sleeve. "We run out of food in ten days with no rationing. We have plenty of time."

"Then no worry," Barclay said. "We got four day to search for this . . . thing, we should do okay."

"Maybe," Avasa said. "But not if it buried under the ice."

John began unwrapping the bandages around his thigh with his good hand. The strips of gauze were sticky and wet. The faint smell of decay made his heart sink. "You're right, Avasa. But now is not the time." John regarded his thigh with disappointment.

Avasa's surgeon walked in. "What happen?"

John pulled off another bandage. He met the surgeon's eyes. "Everyone out. Leave." John waved them out. Parasites. Expecting him to die. Or turn around. He couldn't. Pepper had told him Jerome was still alive. He didn't know where Shanta was.

They were far, far from here.

He'd be damned if he died so far from them. Damned if he didn't finish this mad attempt to turn the scales back on the Azteca.

John looked at the surgeon. "No cutting. Not yet."

"The longer you wait, the more likely you go dead." The mongoose-man looked at John as if he were crazy. "It smell infect. Gangrenous."

"You can't operate," John said fiercely. This insistence made no sense, but he did know that for some reason the idea of someone cutting into his leg scared him almost more than the thought that there might be someone on board the ship trying to sabotage the mission.

He had to rely on his instincts. Here, they were all he had.

The surgeon sighed and opened one of the cupboards near John's desk to fetch more gauze.

After enduring more bandaging, John dismissed him and pored over the map, trying to memorize what was blank white past the coastline.

He would get them there yet and still remain in command.

John woke in the middle of the night. Feverish. Pepper sat near his bed, watching him, and John wasn't surprised.

"How are you feeling?" Pepper asked.

"Not so well." John looked around, eyes barely focusing. "They want to cut my leg. I won't let them."

"Good. It isn't like your hand, clean separation. The leg will have more mods. Don't want those cut, now do you?"

"What are you doing here? How'd you escape?"

"There are men among the crew who're going to mutiny." Pepper shifted. He hadn't shaved in days, and John could see a patchy beard beginning to grow in. Pepper's eyes reflected a random piece of light.

"What are they saying?" John asked.

"They say that you don't know what you are doing. That we are chasing a bush tale. That we should head for Cowfoot Island and hide from the Azteca there."

John sighed. "I just have to hold it together for two more days. That's all. Then we will see if Edward and the Loa were right about the *Ma Wi Jung*."

"We're close, John, but we may not have that long." Pepper moved over and sat on the bed next to John. Clumps of ice slid off his coat onto the bed.

John looped his good arm around Pepper's arm. He still didn't understand what Pepper's goals were, but for this shadowy moment, he felt an unspoken brotherhood with the man. "You shouldn't be out. The crew will kill you if they realize you've escaped."

"Doesn't matter." Steps toward the cabin door prompted Pepper to stand up. "I have to go, John." He pulled his coat tight around him. "It's hard to see you like this, man. You and me, we were just about the most dangerous things out there. Now here we are, messing around on this small little world, facing death. Unknown. Insignificant." Pepper walked over to the rear porthole and opened it. A blast of cold air made John shiver. "Now we're just alone." Pepper slithered through the porthole, twisting and contorting to fit through a space that John didn't think anyone could have fit through.

"Where are you going?" John asked as Pepper dropped out of the porthole.

Pepper's hands grabbed the lip, and he looked into the cabin. "Out. Off this contraption. But I will be close by, John. Always close. If anything happens, strike out into the snow, quick. I'll be there soon enough. Hear?"

John nodded, and a hand knocked at the door. Pepper closed the porthole behind him and disappeared into the night.

"Come in," John said.

Barclay strode in. "We got a problem." His mouth etched out a grim line, his eyes narrowed. John didn't know Barclay well, but he could see the anger in Barclay's tense posture. "We missing food."

"Help me up," John said. "How much are we missing?"

"What we going do?"

"How much are we missing?" John repeated.

Barclay slammed the palm of his hand into the desk by the door. "Half." He looked at John and nodded. "Enough to get back, seen? Someone plan this real careful."

John balanced on his good leg. "Call everyone topside, awake or asleep. We give orders. Half rations."

"They ain't go like it. Not a bit."

"I know. But what's the alternative? Our only hope is this damn machine everyone wants, you know that. Or do you think we have enough men in Capitol City to hold off the Azteca?"

Barclay shook his head.

"Do it," John ordered. "Get someone to help me up the companionway." Damn it, they were so close!

Barclay walked off, shoulders slumped over. John hobbled over to the steps that led up into the dark, cold air. He could see stars just past the rails that led up.

He shifted the crude crutch. Things were coming to a head, he realized. And a stubborn part in the back of his brain told him that there was no way he could back down. Some old part of him, long since forgotten, insisted that they find this machine. No matter what the cost. John's breath steamed the air as he thought about how to get the sailors to find that same determination.

CHAPTER FIFTY-NINE

So now what, John? he whispered to himself when Oaxyctl helped him out of the companionway and onto the deck. He wobbled for a second, the skin on his face crinkling as the cold wind brushed at him.

Far in front of *La Revanche* great jagged edges of metal and ice grew out of the snows. They looked like shark fins. The landscape had changed from the natural to the unnatural. The graveyard of the old-fathers, John thought. Their ancient ships, their buildings, stuck in this snowy waste.

La Revanche lurched to a stop, and John toppled forward. He braced against the fall with his arms, then struggled back to his knees. All twenty sailors stood on deck, and the mongoose-men lined the rails, shivering.

"What the hell is going on?" John snapped.

Barclay walked forward and John's shoulders slumped. He could tell. Something in Barclay's walk alone. He hadn't kept control. "You?" John asked. "You're turning the ship around, aren't you?"

"Sorry." Barclay looked down at John. "I had tell you we only had half we supply. But I lie. I'd hope you would have turned back when I told you this. But instead, you want push on."

"So you think we chasing a fairy tale?"

"We think we lucky if we make it back alive."

"Back where?" John yelled. "Capitol City? Or you go hide in the bush, on Cowfoot Island? Where?"

The sailors muttered when they heard Cowfoot Island.

"Already one of we lose they finger to the cold," Barclay said. "This ain't right. This weather, this place. We ain't supposed to be here. If we leave now, we could hide on Cowfoot Island, build more boat, build some weapon. If we turn back now, we could fight."

"How long you think you can stay on Cowfoot Island?" John grunted and pulled himself up to stand on one leg. "Weeks? Months? Then the Azteca come and wipe you away when they realize people hiding there."

"Then we hide in the jungle," someone yelled. "At least we live."

John walked forward. "This is foolishness." He took another half step forward and Barclay pushed him. John flailed over backward and the side of his head hit a cleat. He bled onto the icy deck.

Several mongoose-men stepped forward and the sailors produced spears and guns. An uneasy silence settled across the deck.

"So what are you going to do with me?" John asked, looking straight at the forest of boots shuffling on the deck. Pepper had told him to go out onto the ice. But John didn't have the strength to stand. The dizziness threatened to overwhelm him.

"Lock you up, take you with us," Barclay said.

"Why don't you leave me here." John coughed and pulled his cheek off the cold deck. "Leave me here with food, water, let me try to find the machine myself."

Barclay shook his head.

"He go die anyway," someone shouted. "Toss him."

"No," Barclay said. "If we amputate him leg now, rest him up, keep him warm, he go live."

"They don't want that," John said. "What do you do with me anyway? Maybe I'll tell others about your treachery. Suppose I wander around, saying that you had a chance to save Capitol City, their brothers and cousins, from being sacrificed, or spending their lives as slaves?"

Barclay looked around, judging the air for himself.

"If you leave me," John said, "you won't have that on your conscience. You can still say you left me out here, and that if I didn't find the machine, it was because it didn't exist. Or it didn't work."

"Okay." Barclay swallowed. "You stay." He looked around. "Get him supplies."

The sailors spread out.

"Who will go with him?" Oaxyctl asked, still standing behind John. Barclay paused. "He can't walk. And there are people on this ship who don't want to turn around."

"Go with him, then, Azteca," Barclay said. "Who else?"

Avasa stepped forward. "I will go." The long line of mongoose-men stirred, but he flicked his finger. He turned and pointed at two more mongoose-men. "As will they."

"You have twenty minutes," Barclay said. "Then *La Revanche* steaming back to the ocean."

John dug the tip of his hook into the deck, splintering wood as he ground his teeth. He'd said he would get to the *Ma Wi Jung* and bring it back any way he could. Pepper had told him he was the code.

He would get the *Ma Wi Jung.*

"Oaxyctl," he whispered. "There are maps in my cabin."

Barclay heard him and shook his head. "We need the maps to retrace the route, deBrun. You on you own."

John nodded. He had it memorized anyway. Instead he told Oaxyctl where to find the device the Loa gave him in Capitol City. Just in case.

Twenty minutes later Avasa and Oaxyctl helped him into the snow. The cold seeped through his clothes. Two sailors hopped down after them, silently agreeing to become part of the marooned group.

La Revanche left the pack of seven a skiff and a pair of axes. Oaxyctl wasted no time in hacking the small boat apart to make a crude sled for John. Once done, the six men grabbed the ropes and pulled.

On the sled, John and several bags of supplies moved forward toward the massive scythelike fins in the distance.

"I hope," Avasa said, "this thing we are searching for will be able to save us now, or we will die in the ice."

Oaxyctl, John noticed out of the corner of his eye, said nothing. He just looked back at the ship with dread in his eyes. It was as if he expected it to come bearing down on them at any moment.

CHAPTER SIXTY

Oaxyctl was convinced he would die in the cold. The bleak, colorless hills of snow stretched and stretched until they either hit small mountain peaks in the distance or disappeared into the gray haze that hung over the land. Each step into the deep snow, almost halfway up his thighs, seemed to bring more numbness. And the constant struggle through the powder exhausted him.

Hopefully he could do what he was commanded before the god caught up to them.

Sweat froze. First it trickled down his back and sides. Then it froze. Sometimes the beads of sweat would unfreeze again, and trickle farther down until his clothes caught it.

On the pallet they pulled through the snow, John lay in a slight fever. At least that was small consolation. Oaxyctl had been told Barclay would try to jail John, so that Oaxyctl could torture him for the codes, but it had also been understood that Oaxyctl might have to leave the ship with John to get the codes.

If he could return to *La Revanche* quickly enough with the codes, he should be safe. But even if he didn't, Oaxyctl's friends had told him that the god was out on the ice now, and it would catch up to them one way or another.

If he got the codes first, then they could return to the ship, Oaxyctl imagined. He would have done his duty to the gods.

Oaxyctl wasn't sure what John dreamed or hallucinated now out in the cold, but he couldn't imagine John would live long. And he needed the pass codes John had in him before John died.

Where was the god? Oaxyctl wondered. Close?

He wondered if he was supposed to kill John right after obtaining the codes, to seal them away for good. It seemed that the gods might want that, but Oaxyctl wasn't sure he could do it. He'd spent too long in Nanagada and been through too much with John. He viewed John and his men as just that, men, like him. And they did not deserve slow deaths any more than Oaxyctl did.

Coward, he told himself. That is all you are. At one time he would have been glad to offer himself up as a sacrifice to the gods.

But now he no longer believed they were gods. Just that they were more powerful creatures than him.

All these thoughts swirled around his mind as he trudged along the icy wastes. But the one image that sat foremost in his mind was that of the glistening, black cocoon ensconced inside *La Revanche*.

Oaxyctl wondered what form the god would take to track them through the snow.

The great fins towered a few hundred feet overhead, blocking out the strong winds that seemed to whip the cold right through them. Avasa agreed that they should rest in the shelter of one, away from the ten-foot-long icicles that had developed on the ledges overhead.

Oaxyctl sat close to the fire and listened to the snapping sound of ice. Avasa huddled close to him.

Times like this seemed surreal. They were so far removed from the things they considered normal that they began to lose themselves.

"Do you miss your wife?" Avasa asked.

Oaxyctl looked at the man. They both had dark skin, brown compared to the darker skin of the average Nanagadan. In the cold it seemed to turn gray. Avasa's mustache drooped tiny icicles that moved as he spoke.

"I barely remember her," Oaxyctl said. "Does that sound bad?" Over to his left John stirred, wrapped in blankets, only his eyes visible. "I'm so far out from anything I consider normal, I don't even understand things. I just keep going."

Avasa nodded. "I'll miss seeing my wife again."

"What makes you say that?"

"Kali's infinite eyes stare back at me in this desolate shitland," Avasa said. "I know I'm going to die of the cold here. Look." He pulled at his gloves, tugged at them, until the stiff piece of clothing pulled off. The edges of his fingers were black. "I can't feel them." Avasa's voice broke. "The cold is eating me away at the edges."

He solemnly held the damaged hand close to the fire.

Oaxyctl looked down at his boots. He'd stopped feeling the stinging snow around his toes at midday. He wondered what his feet looked like.

"So why do it?" Oaxyctl asked. "You could have stayed on the ship."

Avasa looked at him. "I've seen the plans to keep back the Azteca. We stand no chance. This long shot John chases, that Haidan came up with, it's the only hope I have of saving my family, my children. One must do whatever they can, even it means one's life, understand?"

Oaxyctl squinted at the dancing fire. Thinking of John's struggle, he said, "Yes, I understand." He huddled into his clothes as best he could. The wind whistled nearby, broken by the great slab of metal at their backs. He'd been right. Capitol City could not stand. There was no place that he could hide from the gods.

Their will demanded to be obeyed. He had no choice.

The other men glanced at each other, grim, quiet, mostly trying to catch sleep. Oaxyclt nodded at the two sailors who'd volunteered to come.

One was the man who had led him deep into *La Revanche*'s bilge to meet the god. The man nodded back.

Oaxyctl stamped out the fire. He looked at the last embers wistfully, recalling the warmth and already missing it. The fierce, constant wind kicked up snow, making it hard to hear anything.

"My name Lionel." Oaxyctl turned around toward the accomplice who was yelling at him over the wind, the sailor by his side. "I never introduce myself before." Lionel nodded over at the other sailor. "He name Vincent. He with us."

"Okay." Oaxyctl pulled Lionel close and whispered, "Your task is the two mongoose-men. Get them out of sight, kill them."

"Yeah."

They crunched over the ice away from each other, breath puffing out in front of their faces.

John's fever had let up again, Oaxyctl noticed. John craned his head back and looked up at the great fins of metal around them all. "Oaxyctl, are those letters?"

Oaxyctl looked up the sides of a large fin across from the party.

"Yes." Faint shadows of symbols could barely be discerned.

"Read them to me."

Oaxyctl squinted, but couldn't read the faded shapes. "I can't."

"Damn." John struggled around a bit, then stopped. "I don't know where my spyglass is."

"We left it on the ship."

"Oh."

Oaxyctl walked out toward the end of the rope, taking his place next to Avasa and Lionel. The two mongoose-men walked out in front, scouting the way. They'd found the ice to be treacherous, filled with crevasses. They walked with splintered lengths of plank to stick into the snow every other step to search for lethal gaps.

"Oaxyctl," John called out. "I think we lost my leg."

Oaxyctl said back over his shoulder, "I know." He picked up the rope, then he and Avasa began to pull. They weren't as fast as the ship. And *La Revanche* didn't fall into crevasses as they might.

Three, or four, more days of this hell.

It didn't help Oaxyctl's nerves that at any moment he knew something horrible could burst out from the gloom. The god was out there, tracking them by now.

He felt it.

Lionel's attack came three hours later. The mongoose-men and the two sailors left to explore up ahead. They were out of the great forest of fins into gentle hills of snow.

Oaxyctl heard a scream, and then another.

Lionel returned alone, fifteen minutes later. He looked shaken, a good actor. "A big crevasse," he panted. He shook his head. Looked at Avasa with a tired expression. "My man Vincent dead. And you two mongoose-men."

Avasa dropped the rope, calm. "My two best men?"

Lionel nodded. "We go need avoid that area."

Avasa walked over to him. "Those men never made mistakes like that. Not ones *you* would have been able to walk from."

"What you saying?" Lionel asked.

"We keep going. Straight. I want to see what happened for myself."

Lionel hesitated, but Oaxyctl took up the rope. "Let's keep going."

Avasa circled the scuffed marks in the snow and squatted. Oaxyctl stood next to him. The crevasse, he thought, was a few feet away. If he just shoved and kicked Avasa in, he could be done.

But he could see a wariness in Avasa's posture that told him otherwise.

And even if he didn't see it, he wasn't sure he could do it.

Coward, he berated himself again.

"They fought," Avasa said. "I don't know about that man Lionel. He is lying. He killed my men."

"Maybe the other man, Vincent, did something," Oaxyctl said.

Avasa shook his head. He pulled a gun out and trudged over to Lionel.

Oaxyctl pulled the ax out of his belt and followed. "Listen, there is no need for any of this!" He tried to get closer to Avasa.

Lionel stood up and pulled a long knife out from his boots. He and Avasa circled each other. The sound of a shotgun being cocked stopped them all.

John sat upright, shivering in his blankets. "No one kills anyone. You all stay right in front of me. You all put your weapons on the sled, slowly. Then we continue on."

The silent face-off continued until John fired a shot between the three men. Snow spray kicked up into the air.

"Now."

They complied. John sat upright, shotgun cradled under his good arm, watching them with a strength none had suspected he still had.

Oaxyctl began thinking about the sign of Ocelotl again.

CHAPTER SIXTY-ONE

Pepper trudged his way through snow. To any other eye, the constant white sleet would have rendered them lost. Even as Pepper moved forward, his footprints disappeared.

But he kept tracking John, as he had promised.

The cold numbed him. Pepper increased his body temperature. He'd lose some body mass. It would impede his ability to survive more than a week out here, but that didn't matter. If he didn't survive the week and find the *Ma Wi Jung*, he was dead anyway. Why prolong it?

A faint change in the wind.

He sniffed the cold, barren air and paused.

Snow crunched far to the left, and Pepper realized he wasn't the only one out among the featureless hills and sudden crevasses tracking prey.

The nearest snowy hillock exploded. Pepper planted his feet and turned to face the Teotl.

CHAPTER SIXTY-TWO

John's leg stopped throbbing. Chill crept throughout his whole body. He wasn't too sure if his left hand was a hook. He remembered both that it was a hook, and that he had once had a hand and that was new. He hadn't remembered what it was like to have a hand for a long, long time.

And Starport: he saw a map of where they sat in his head. He spun it around a bit, rotated it, then pushed it away.

He had a kid. Jerome. He remembered a wife. Shanta.

Interesting. When had that happened?

"Johnny, Johnny, what the fuck is going on?" he chattered.

He'd fucked up something serious. Left himself bits and pieces.

Gonna have to amputate this soon or die. Only an ax around, strapped to a bundle of canvas. Ax wouldn't do the job. Kill him quicker. And the three men standing at the edge of the rope looking back at him might do the job even sooner.

John didn't trust them. Couldn't trust the motivations. Several things were in the air.

Emergency, man. Focus on the necessary. Discard excess.

You're dying, he told himself. By the way, if you amputate, you're going to have to cut through some stuff in your leg tougher than bone. Don't forget that you're not all natural.

What?

He tried to make sense of the new memories bubbling out from behind the brick wall of his mind. The memories weren't specific images, or anything swirling out like a dream. They were just things that happened to be there when he turned his thoughts different ways.

For example, the name Starport felt familiar. He remembered being there before.

One of the men walked back toward John. He held the rifle up. Focus on the moment. "I'll shoot you if you don't get back out on the rope," John growled. It was in his eyes. This one was bad news. Oaxyctl, it was familiar to roll that name around in the back of his mind.

The fever, the shock, must be shaking old memories loose, he thought. I finally remember myself. And all it took was getting shot, gangrenous, and half frozen to death.

He laughed, and they looked back at him.

John gestured with the rifle. "I'm fucking serious."

Of course, he thought, he needed them to pull him, so he couldn't shoot them in the legs. If they rushed, he'd wait until he could hit an arm. They could still pull him there with a shot arm.

Some of them wanted him dead. Or needed something from him.

They were so close to the dockyards, he thought, leaning back and drowsing off. He could feel the *Ma Wi Jung* calling him.

The man called Lionel stood overhead, blocking out the sun.

John placed the end of the barrel against Lionel's chin. "I'm napping."

Lionel scrunched back to the end of the rope and joined the two waiting men.

How long would this last? Wasting away, almost at the end. The memories he'd grabbed during the last wave of semiconsciousness fled again.

Where the hell was Pepper? He'd have to get the man's attention.

John fired the shotgun into the air three times, fumbling to reload, then leaned back. Let them think he was mad. That would keep them back for a while longer.

He was kidding himself. He was too tired. Whom could he trust out of the three men? Oaxyctl had saved his life before. John relaxed, called him back.

"I can't do it any longer." He handed Oaxyctl the shotgun. "I'm too tired. You protect me. Keep us moving."

Avasa walked up behind Oaxyctl and whispered. Oaxyctl nodded.

"John." Avasa leaned down next to John. "John. Your leg is gangrenous, and you're hallucinating. We need to cut it off now. We're trying to save your life." Avasa cut and pulled away John's trousers. John protested weakly. The numbing wind crept through the rest of his clothing from the inside out.

"Here." Avasa held a bottle of rum to John's lips and grabbed his good hand as warmth spread. "I'm sorry, John, but I have to cut."

"Please don't," John whimpered as Avasa unwrapped one of the packages lashed to the sled and unwrapped a saw. "Too dangerous."

Avasa picked up the long saw and positioned it above John's knee, his back turned to Oaxyctl. Oaxyctl raised the shotgun, aimed it at them, and fired. The back of Avasa's head exploded over the snow in front of the crude sled and John's bare leg.

"I don't understand." John blinked.

"He was trying to kill you." Oaxyctl walked away, head down, shoulders slumped, shaking his head. Lionel sat next to John. The sled creaked down into the snow.

"We need the code," Lionel said.

"What code?" John stared at the pieces of gleaming skull fragments on his boots.

"The *Ma Wi Jung.*" Lionel dribbled more rum down John's throat, then leaned down and pulled a long knife out from his left boot. "The *Ma Wi Jung,*" he repeated. The rum's warm calm fled. Lionel was the fucker trying to get something from him. *"Ma. Wi. Jung."*

Lionel slammed the knife into John's kneecap. On the good leg.

John screamed.

CHAPTER SIXTY-THREE

Dihana ran along the great wall of Capitol City toward the gates. Gordon saw her and waved her over to a small wooden platform.

"Why isn't Haidan here?"

Gordon handed her a spyglass. "He hurt. Airship drop a bomb near him."

"Oh, no." Dihana's stomach clenched. Not Haidan. That meant Gordon was the new mongoose-general in practice, and the only friend she felt she had lay hurt somewhere. Dihana closed her eyes a moment, clutching the spyglass.

"They already drown a few thousand marching to take the flood area," Gordon said. "Been watching them all morning. But they keep coming."

Dihana raised the long brass tube up. Mud, twisted wire, and bodies leapt into focus. "So many." The Azteca seemed to be everywhere she looked, as far as she could see. "What does Haidan think? Will I be able to go see him?"

Gordon looked down. "He still out, asleep, or unconscious, something. He ain't responding."

"But he's alive?"

"Yeah."

They watched the mud and trenches for the next hour. Watched more Azteca struggle through the flooded area between the tracks, then begin to use the drier ground north of that, pushing up against their fellow warriors already coming up along the northern tracks.

The front of the line faltered as mongoose-men opened fire from the trenches farthest out from the city. Then Azteca cannon fire blew gouts of earth into the air among the mongoose-men trenches. Dihana winced.

"We have Haidan's plans, we know what happens next," Dihana told Gordon.

The mongoose-man nodded. "I know." He turned and gave orders. Mongoose-men scurried off to small stutter-stations along the wall, and minutes later Dihana saw one of Haidan's surprises lumber down the northern tracks. He'd left a one-mile stretch still down. An armored engine chuffed along it, gaining speed. Two mongoose-men jumped out of it, and others pulled gates and wire out of the way to let it pass through the zones.

It picked up speed, barreling toward Azteca who jumped off the track to get out of its way.

Gordon leaned forward. "Right now."

The train exploded, metal and fire ripping out into the Azteca warriors nearby. They were blown away from the explosion like so many colored feathers, Dihana thought.

"And again," Gordon said, as a second train gained speed and headed toward the Azteca. It was the first of many surprises for the Azteca.

"We might break them here," Dihana whispered. Who could lose thousands a day and recover?

By midday the Azteca advance faltered. Hemmed in by the coast on their left, the flooded areas on their right, and the press of their own advance behind them, they chose to pause and began digging in.

Heartened, Dihana left the walls to return to her office but was intercepted by a breathless ragamuffin.

"Minister," he gasped. "We have a problem." He took a deep breath. "Tolteca-town in revolt. Three hundred Tolteca take over a barrack. They have rifles now."

Gordon swung around. "There mongoose in the barrack?"

"No, no, they just holing up. Maybe sending out the word to other Tolteca. They already kill anyone they pass up in the street."

"How'd this happen?" Dihana fought not to yell. "I thought we had enough mongoose-men keeping Tolteca-town hemmed in?"

"Haidan and I move a bunch of them out past the walls. Bad thinking." He looked out over the city. "The Azteca ain't pressing the south rail. Take five hundred mongoose-men from there, go back, and take care of this, Dihana." Gordon whistled a mongoose-man over and repeated his orders. "You know," Gordon said, "this probably wouldn't have happen if you hadn't work so hard to keep the Azteca in the city."

Dihana said nothing in return. She took the three mongoose-men with her and ran with them along the wall toward the south rail gate. It beat arguing over something that couldn't be changed. And it was doing something.

A trio of commanding mongoose-men met them above the south rail gate. Someone grabbed her arm. "We lost contact with the southern towns."

"What?" Dihana pulled away. "Are you sure?"

"We just send an armor train down to see about it, they still gone. We think the Azteca either split they forces, or an Azteca scout party cut the wire."

They couldn't withdraw so many mongoose-men from the southern line if Azteca were coming up it now. And—Dihana felt despair—that would mean they'd lost their ability to get resupplied by the southern towns.

"Somebody send an airship along to confirm this, and see if we can spot Azteca." This was out of the plan. She missed Haidan.

"What do we do about them men from Tolteca-town?" they asked her.

Dihana stood there. "We need to get back to Gordon." She couldn't make a decision like this on her own, but she knew they were going to have to withdraw the men along the southern rail. They'd lose their ability to compress the Azteca into their killing field.

By sunset mongoose-men trooped back away from the southern rails, and the first of a second wing of Azteca arrived on the southern edge of the peninsula.

The Azteca attack began again in twilight, this time from two sides, as mongoose-men inside the city hunted down the Tolteca traitors and killed them to regain the barracks.

When Dihana saw Gordon again, he pursed his lips. "They force us," he said. "We could have hold the southern track or take care of the Tolteca in the city."

The boom of Azteca cannon fire threatened to drown their conversation out. A line of airships in the distance drew closer.

"We still hold the outer trench line," Dihana said. "We're killing so many of them."

"Not much longer," Gordon said. "I giving the order to fall back so that the attacking Azteca within range of the wall guns. We killing them, but for every one we kill, two more standing behind the one that fall."

Later that night the mongoose-men fell back and long trenches of fuel burned in the night to make a barrier between the Azteca and the mongoose-men. It added to the Azteca casualties, they saw, but it didn't stop them. Out of the smoky veil over the land when the flames dwindled, the Azteca came onward. Dying, but inching ever closer to the walls.

They didn't have a chance of breaking the Azteca tide. They could only slow it.

CHAPTER SIXTY-FOUR

Lionel repeated the same words over and over. *Codes. Ma. Wi. Jung.* Each punctuated by the impact of the blade. Foot: through the boot and into the cartilage and flesh, twisted to emphasize *Jung.* Calf: through the legs of the trousers that soaked the blood up. Arms: slicing John's forearms. Chest, stomach, Lionel remained patient. "Give me the codes, John, or it will get worse, you'll die slowly, so slowly, in so much more pain. I'm just getting started."

Then Lionel stabbed John's left thigh and the blade tip snapped off just under the skin. Lionel tried again, and again, and then John sat up, covered in his own blood, and grabbed Lionel by the throat to pull him close. He remembered he once had the strength to snap Lionel's neck with just that same amount of effort. "Look, fucker," he growled. "None of you get it. Pepper was right. There are no codes. Just me."

Lionel responded by slamming the knife through John's shoulder and he dropped back down to the sled. A shotgun fired. Lionel fell to the snow in a gout of his own blood.

"Gods!" Oaxyctl yelled. It sounded as if he was talking to someone John couldn't see. "This man was torturing John while I was away. I don't know why."

John's vision stopped working, but he felt large hands yank the knive free and pick him up. Pepper. Too late, too late.

Time passed. He wasn't sure how much, and then Pepper's familiar voice punctured his trance. "John?"

"Torture," John whispered. Everything hurt so much that nothing hurt in comparison, and everything felt sticky or crusty or still bloody. He couldn't hold out much longer. Not in this cold, not with these wounds. He would die. And soon.

John fell into a deep sleep. He dreamed of flying.

CHAPTER SIXTY-FIVE

Pepper used a spare ax to chip out the blocks to make an igloo, while Oaxyctl watched, not sure what Pepper was doing. His muscles ached from the last day of wading through snow and the encounter with the Teotl that still hunted them. Pepper threw Oaxyctl the other ax.

"Get to work. Make ice bricks. You can see what I'm doing."

Hacking the ice into bricks, chipping them into the shape. The first few rings grew up out of the ground, rising and falling in on themselves to begin the dome. Pepper sensed the pressure dropping, the wind increasing. He chipped the bricks into accurate shapes as Oaxyctl handed them to him. When Oaxyctl fell behind, Pepper made his own.

The upcoming storm he sensed might last only the night, or a few days. They had supplies, but every day they dallied increased the chances of failure with John's death. And damn it, Pepper hadn't gotten there in time to save John from being tortured. The whole damn situation balanced on a knife's edge.

He wasn't even sure what role Oaxyctl had played in the torture, as Oaxyctl claimed that he had left to look for a sheltered area and come back to find Lionel torturing John.

Pepper didn't believe him.

These ignorant idiots didn't even realize that there was no code to be dragged out of John deBrun. Even the Teotl chasing them, old enough now to have hazy memories of those times, thought the same.

This wasn't, Pepper thought, like the cave in *A Thousand and One Nights*. Nothing like the *Ma Wi Jung* just opened for the right words. The ship had to *know* for sure whomever it let aboard was legitimate.

Since the day the Teotl had captured the wormholes and trapped everyone in-system, Starport, with the help of the Loa, had thrown its men into building a long-range ship that could launch from the ground and travel the distances between the stars. It could repair itself after great amounts of damage and help keep the humans in it alive for insane lengths of time thanks to the Loa's contributions.

It would eventually have brought them help.

The Teotl had almost won, so there was one last assault on the holes to destroy them and cut the Teotl off from their endless stream of reinforcements, as well as cutting Nanagada off from all the other worlds. The backlash of the weapons used to collapse the wormhole destroyed the ships in that attack, most satellites in orbit, and many orbital habitats. Almost anything with a chip in it died.

Survivors of the destruction unleashed their worst remaining weapons on each other, and Pepper had listened to the survivors destroy each other with nuclear and antimatter weapons in a matter of days. Some in hardened life pods survived thanks to the combination of organic Loa technology and protected circuitry. That left a small constellation of floating, powerless survivors in space waiting and listening for rescuers who never came. Most suicided after the first hundred years.

The *Ma Wi Jung* was designed to take that kind of abuse in her long trek across the stars, just as the pods. Pepper knew the initial burst would have quieted the ship. But it could recuperate.

A combination of hardening, shielding, and recuperative organic technology the alien Loa had given them meant that the *Ma Wi Jung* would be the best candidate for a surviving ship.

Not just any surviving ship, but one giving him a chance to finally go home.

He'd been trapped in this system for 350 years. With most of those centuries spent inside a damned escape pod. Pepper would do anything, let nothing stand in his way, to end that sentence.

Lionel's almost headless body had frozen solid. Pepper hefted it like a massive log and walked over to a pit in the snow he'd dug.

He dropped the man in and pushed snow over.

Oaxyctl had done him a favor. But Pepper would have prefered taking care of Lionel so that he could get some more information.

And he wondered where the Teotl was. He'd have expected another attack, but the alien seemed reluctant to leave the perimeter of *La Revanche*. Was it waiting for something?

Maybe it hadn't realized that its prey was not on the boat.

"Come on," Pepper said, returning to the igloo. "Get inside."

Oaxyctl obeyed.

Inside, Pepper started a fire. The warmth creeped over him, welcome. Pepper removed his clothes, and Oaxyctl gasped.

"What happened?"

The claw marks across Pepper's chest were deep, and still oozing.

"I met one of your gods," Pepper grunted.

"Is it . . . did you . . . ?"

"A draw. We both live." Pepper grimaced as he pulled out spare clothes from the tightly packed sled. They'd built the igloo around it rather than leave it outside. "Shame."

Oaxyctl swallowed. "Are you a . . . Loa?"

Pepper laughed. "I might seem inhuman." He grinned. "But Loa, no." He spat the words. "Nor Teotl. None of those bastards." He turned to Oaxyctl. "Strip."

"What?"

"Take your clothes off and give them to me." Oaxyctl hesitated, and Pepper grabbed the shotgun leaning against the wall behind him.

Oaxyctl stripped. His ribs showed against gray skin, abused from the cold. Inside the igloo a half-blue light dappled around them, reflecting the fire. Smoke swirled up toward the small exhaust hole. Pepper doubted that it was visible in the storm, but just in case . . .

He picked up Oaxyctl's clothes, glanced at the tips of Oaxyctl's frostbitten toes. "Get in with John. You'll keep him warm." Oaxyctl obeyed. Pepper tossed the man's clothes behind him, with the shotgun. He continued to dress himself with the new set of clothes.

He'd lost fat, he noted, and some muscle. Body cannibalizing itself for fuel.

"Will you sleep?" Oaxyctl asked.

Pepper smiled, rooted through their supplies for jerky, or anything to fill up on, then stamped out the fire over Oaxyctl's objection.

"No more fire, we don't want to get spotted." Once Pepper had enough to eat, he warmed up with a simple stretch. Reached his toes. Touched the ceiling. All night long he moved, keeping limber and warm.

The movements calmed him.

Eventually Pepper slipped down into sleep and left only the right half of his brain awake to perform the movements. After several hours, he switched, and by morning, before Oaxyctl stirred awake, and John began coughing and hacking blood, Pepper was rested, awake, and ready.

The storm, thankfully, had subsided in the early-morning hours.

CHAPTER SIXTY-SIX

John struggled up and looked out around him at the endless white. Two men in front pulled the sled over a small hill, and the sled sped up. Oaxyctl ran back and grabbed the front to slow it. The impact shook John.

"You're awake?" Oaxyctl gasped.

John's eyebrows crinkled when he blinked. "How long have I slept?" The pain came in waves from all over his body.

"All day today at least. How do you feel?"

"Not so good." John shivered. "Did Pepper kill Lionel?"

Oaxyctl tucked the edge of John's hood in. "I did. Once I saw what he was doing."

"He was a spy." John tried to scratch his nose, but he realized he was strapped into the sled, and he didn't have the strength to pull his arms out from beneath the ropes. "For the Azteca."

"Yes."

And John still couldn't decide what he thought about Oaxyctl.

Pepper yelled. Oaxyctl turned around. "I must go. This madman is making me pull you through the storm."

John wriggled. "Be careful." The talking exhausted him. He closed his eyes. "Pepper is dangerous."

"I know." Oaxyctl walked back behind the sled and pushed.

The slow trek continued. As John faded out again.

He still couldn't help. But the fever had broken. The pain ebbed, somewhat. John watched the broken ice around them pass, and Pepper bearing them on. The man was a horse. He pulled without a grunt and ate enough food during their breaks to raise Oaxyctl's eyebrows.

They untied John's arms and had him try to sip a bit of warm broth, but he threw it back up.

"We just need to get there." Pepper saw Oaxyctl's worried look. "I won't eat your food. No worry." He stamped out the fire, lay John back down carefully, and leaned close. "Keep strong," he told John. "I know you're in bad shape, but you can handle that kind of pain. It's the infection that's most dangerous."

He stood up, walked away, and soon the sled was on its way.

"We're close, aren't we?" John asked Pepper during another break.

Pepper nodded. "I think so. I saw the coordinates you tried to hide."

"I can feel her." John felt unease at the pit of his stomach. A prickling in the back of his neck. A shape under the snow nearby. He remained focused, alert through the haze of continuous pain. He must hang on to life. There was Capitol City, and his family, later, but right now his sole focus was survival.

He thought about Shanta. Often. He wondered if she was hanging to a thread, somewhere far south of him.

At least Jerome lived, he consoled himself. Pepper had seen this.

They were close. Every image in John's head told him they were right where they needed to be.

"Look." Pepper pointed to a glazed mound of snow three miles away. "Something is under there. The snow is piled around it, but it looks like it was warm, and then refroze."

"Ma Wi Jung?" John whispered.

"Maybe. It could be the top."

Pepper found more energy. He bounced toward the rope and picked it up. The sled jerked forward, and Pepper forced through the snow with determination.

John felt the movement before he saw anything. The sled rocked and a hunched shape leapt toward Pepper. John caught the blur of a muscled humanoid shape with white, shaggy fur and long blades on each finger.

He shouted a warning, but it came out as a croak.

Pepper spun, kicked up snow with the back of his boots, and squatted.

He fired twice before the mass of muscle and hair struck him dead-on. Without a sound they both rolled, locked together, deeper into the snow. Chunks of ice flew with them.

Oaxyctl pushed the sled on.

"We have to help," John said.

"Do what? You have a gun? You can't even stand," Oaxyctl huffed. John leaned back with a groan. His head upside down, he looked at Oaxyctl's wide eyes behind him.

"You're scared."

"God of gods, yes!" Oaxyctl snapped. He battled for footing and slipped when he pushed the sled too far in front of him.

John mustered his energy and leaned to his side. Snow kicked up into the air as Pepper and the Teotl wrestled. One of them started snarling, an eerie sound that floated toward the sled.

Another pair of shots ended the struggle.

Pepper loped back over the snow. John saw blood dripping from his elbows, staining the snow as he caught up. Pepper's forearms flapped ribbons of loose flesh.

The air around the man steamed.

"Move!" Pepper growled. He spat a tooth out. It bounced off the edge of the sled.

"Is it dead?" Oaxyctl demanded. "Is it really dead?"

Pepper scowled at him. "Dead? No. Slowed down. Best I can do right now. I blew off its head. It'll take a while for the eyes to grow back."

What the hell? John coughed as he tried to form the words.

"Here." Pepper shoved the shotgun in under the straps holding John in and took over pushing the sled. His clothes dripped sweat, water, and ice.

They moved closer to the mound of ice.

Over the whip of the winds a steady wailing from the Teotl began. Oaxyctl swore something in his language.

The ground transitioned abruptly from snow to ice and the sled got free, skittering forward and turning in a lazy circle.

Several hundred feet behind them the Teotl, shaggy and covered in snow, trotted in circles. It's large, padded feet kept it on top of the ice; it moved quickly, patting the ground in front of it with its clawed hands until it found their tracks, and it paused.

Then it turned straight toward them and sprinted.

Pepper skidded up to the sled and pushed it out toward the mound with another good shove. Oaxyctl stumbled behind, alternating a half-run with an all-fours crawl to get across the ice.

"Where is it?" John asked, his throat on fire. "How do we get to the *Ma Wi Jung?*"

Pepper ripped the shredded remains of his overcoat off and threw it aside. "Keep moving," he yelled at Oaxyctl, and guided the sled while Oaxyctl slipped and pushed. The Teotl's wailing warbled as it hit the ice and skittered out at them. Oaxyctl muttered to himself.

"I don't know what to do," Oaxyctl said at last.

"What?" John asked.

Oaxyctl sat down. Pepper looked back at him. "Get back up!"

The Teotl stopped wailing.

Pepper got down on his hands and knees and peered through the sheet of ice. He smiled. "Here it is, gentlemen."

He punched the ice with a fist. The thin sheet collapsed, taking Pepper with it. He landed on his feet five feet down in a large hole, next to what looked like the beginning of a tunnel.

He grabbed the sled and pulled it down with him, grunting, and John looked into the tunnel. Beams of light lit up the smooth, translucent walls that ran for a few feet. A large metallic, oval door waited for them.

"This it?" John asked.

Pepper walked forward. "Yes. Looks like the ship is operational and has been keeping this area warm and the outer air lock accessible. Now relax and let me help you sit up." Pepper walked around, helped John up, and pushed the sled forward toward the door.

John struggled to remain up as a blue beam of light appeared and moved toward him. He tensed, but when it touched him, it felt warm. The light flicked off. A small console, the size of John's hand, pushed forward out of the metal and lit up.

"Here's the hard part, John, for you." Pepper pushed the sled right up to it. "I'm going to have to hold you up, and you're going to place your palm on that pad and tell it you are coming in, and you would like us to come in with you. It's going to hurt when I pick you up. You ready?"

"I think so." John bit his lip and steeled himself.

Pepper nodded. "Just make sure you really want to go aboard, and that you want us with you. If you don't give the ship assent, if you don't trust us, the door remains closed." He unlashed John's legs from the sled and grabbed his chest. "Here we go."

Pain exploded as Pepper carefully pulled John up out of the sled, holding him under the arms. Pepper held John's legs an inch off the ground so he wouldn't have to put any pressure on them, but just the weight pulling at his kneecaps made him want to scream.

John leaned forward and put his good hand on the section of metal jutting out by the door. It felt warm, despite the cold.

"These men are coming in with me," he hissed. "Now what . . ." John coughed and fought dizziness. Something wriggled under his fingers. He pulled his hand up. Long strings of gooey black stuff came with it. "Oh, shit."

"Keep cool," Pepper said. "Just security."

The black stuff writhed, then hardened. It turned to dust and wafted away. With a low whine the door rolled aside. Pepper walked inside, still carrying John, but with only one arm. Oaxyctl followed with the sled.

"Okay," Pepper breathed. He tapped a sequence on the panel next to the door and it rolled back closed. Pepper leaned against the wall, still holding John, and chuckled. "Nice job, old friend. We made it after all."

John cracked a faint smile through the haze of pain, catching the enthusiasm. The Teotl couldn't make it through the door. They were safe.

It was warm.

Oaxyctl pulled the shotgun out of the sled. He chambered two rounds and cocked the hammer. "Don't move. Either of you." His hands shook. He blinked at them.

"Oaxyctl?" John bit his lip. Not Oaxyctl.

"You must press that thing to open the door again," Oaxyctl said. "It's coming. We must let *it* in before you escape. I have no choice."

John felt Pepper's arms tense. Then Pepper threw John at Oaxyctl's feet. John screamed as his legs erupted in waves of pain. He passed out for a second, opened his eyes again, silent tears leaking to the floor. Several of his wounds opened, blood trickled down his stomach and arms. He started shaking. His lip bled from where his face had hit the grated floor.

"I don't think so," Pepper said. The two men squared off, Oaxyctl pointing the gun, Pepper leaning against the wall with arms crossed.

"Open the door." Oaxyctl shifted from foot to foot.

John used his hands to pull himself slowly, painfully, a little closer to Oaxyctl's feet. Oaxyctl continued trying to stare Pepper down.

"You're not thinking clearly," Pepper growled. "Letting that thing in is a death sentence for you, just as surely as it is for us."

"That . . . that isn't the point," Oaxyctl rasped. "I have to. I can still let it in, deliver it the *Ma Wi Jung,* and then it will be over."

John freed his hook, poking it through the edges of his sewn-up sleeves, and slammed it down into Oaxyctl's foot. Oaxyctl screamed, and Pepper launched himself off the wall and threw Oaxyctl onto the sled.

Oaxyctl hung on to the shotgun with both hands as Pepper grabbed it with one hand and yanked the struggling Oaxyctl back up. He tapped out the open sequence with his free hand, overriding the air-lock protections.

John wrapped his arms around himself, shaking in pain, unable to stop.

The door whooshed open, and Pepper threw Oaxyctl out still clinging to the shotgun. Pepper picked up the sled, supplies and all, and threw it at the man. Oaxyctl screamed, trying to stop the blow with his arms.

Pepper tapped the panel and shut the door again.

"He'll die." John mustered the words against chattering teeth, wondering if, despite Pepper's promises, he would die aboard the *Ma Wi Jung* anyway.

"That would never have bothered you before this mess," Pepper said. "Let's get to business. If you want to recover, you need to tell the ship that I have authorization to control all other functions so I can save you."

"Speak it out loud?" John whispered. Pepper nodded. "Ship." John swallowed, blinked, felt himself passing out again. "This man has full authorization."

"Confirm this," Pepper said.

"This is confirmed," came a voice from inside the walls. John looked around, dazed.

It was starting to feel okay, as weird as it was.

Pepper leaned over. "Neither of us are in good shape, but you need this first." He picked John up.

John gritted his teeth, unable to find the energy to scream, and they hobbled down the corridor to the next door. It opened onto a small circular room filled with ghostly lines of light that hovered over the floor.

Pepper paused, turned around, then found what he was looking for. A clear glass pod recessed against the wall.

The glass cracked and opened with Pepper's palm print. "Get in."

"What is this?"

"It will heal you." Pepper laid John in. "Relax. Don't fight." He smiled. "We made it, John. You'll be back. I'm giving you everything you wanted."

John dropped his hook between the glass container and the lip to stop it from being closed. "I can't fight you, Pepper, but please, don't."

Pepper shook his head. "I need you back, John." John saw for the first time that some of the dreadlocks on Pepper's left had been sliced off in the fighting.

"Please don't take my memories. Of Shanta. Of Jerome."

Pepper pushed John's hook back in and folded his hand over his chest.

"Trust me on this, John. You'll be okay. You'll have all those memories still, and more. It's this or death. You can't hang on much longer like this. We all need you."

John saw the open need on Pepper's face.

"I don't think," he said, thinking of all the times the feelings had drained out of him, that he'd iced out when things got tense, "I don't think I might like the old me."

Pepper didn't reply. He shut the pod door and knocked the top twice.

A thick goop trickled down around John's back.

The air in the pod tasted sweet, erased the pain, and lulled him to sleep. He stopped fighting the darkness.

CHAPTER SIXTY-SEVEN

Pepper let go of the medical pod and stood up. He checked the diagnostics, tapped in a sequence, then walked forward into the tiny cockpit. The soft seats embraced him. It felt disconcertingly comfortable to do that. Sleep threatened to overwhelm him.

"*Ma Wi Jung?*" Pepper called out.

From the left of his shoulders came the ship's soft voice. "Yes."

"I'm in slight danger of hypothermia and your cabin is cold. Adjust this cabin's internal temperature to eighty degrees. Do this in slow stages."

"Adjusting," the ship confirmed.

"Do you have anything to drink?"

"There is water aboard, and tea. The holds are not fully stocked."

"Good. I'll have some tea." Pepper stood up again. A good cup of tea, then he would make a tour of the ship to see if it was ready to fly. No sleep yet.

That would take a few hours.

He needed to power the ship up fully, bring everything online. Things John could do better than he could, but John was in the medpod until at least much later in the day.

Pepper walked around the cockpit and stretched.

"Something is trying to board the ship," *Ma Wi Jung* said. "It is using acid to try and eat through the hull."

"Show me." The front of the cockpit lit up to show a blue tunnel of ice, and the Teotl's fuzzy face dripping acid against the side of the hull. "Is there any way to stop it?"

"I have no weapons. My fitting was never completed. But I do have stabilizing jets near this location."

"Fire them," Pepper ordered, and watched. The scene didn't change for several seconds. Then a wall of steam exploded through the tunnel, blowing the Teotl with it. "Did the creature damage the hull?"

"No. The hull remains unbreached."

Pepper walked out of the cockpit. "Where is the galley?" His tea would be the first small luxury in a long time. Then it was time to try to make the *Ma Wi Jung* fly. Pepper wasn't a Pilot, just impatient.

"*Ma Wi Jung*," Pepper asked. "Do I have the authorization to fly?" He walked into the small galley and opened the cupboards until he found a mug snug inside a bracket.

"You do not have the necessary implants. You are not authorized."

Pepper sighed. "What about automatic pilot?"

"This ship will only fly within planetary atmosphere by automatic pilot. The human pilot in recovery is required for any orbital or extrasolar activity."

Pepper smiled. That would do.

CHAPTER SIXTY-EIGHT

The first thing Oaxyctl did was grab the sled on his way out. The shotgun could serve no purpose. He couldn't shoot the *Ma Wi Jung* with it, he didn't even know where under the ice to shoot the ancient machine. There was no game that he knew of on this icy expanse to shoot, but Pepper had let Oaxyctl grip the shotgun when he'd thrown him out the door, so Oaxyctl pushed the weapon under the sled's supplies. Oaxyctl limped with the sled out onto the ice and slid around as he pushed with his good foot, the whole time glancing over his shoulder, waiting for his death to come.

After several minutes of slipping around, he paused and looked back at the mound.

An explosion of steam blew out of the ground. Oaxyctl dove for cover, expecting more displays of power from the device they had found.

He waited for the next ten minutes until he realized more explosions wouldn't come, then he pushed the sled out over to the hole to investigate.

It didn't take long to find his god. It lay on the snow, mewling, fur burnt off and sheets of skin red and blistered.

Oaxyctl sat on his sled and watched it squirm.

This thing had remade itself into a shape that could live on the snow. Large, padded feet, fur, and blubber. Blubber that had been fried and smelled like meat.

He watched it heal itself.

The process looked almost as painful as the burns. The skin cracked and tried to reform. Goop spilled out onto the snow. It looked clear after several minutes that this god would not be able to heal itself. It didn't seem to have the energy.

It stopped mewling and stiffly turned its newly grown face toward him, a fleshy stalk of eyes and nose.

Oaxyctl thought about Pepper's and John's unconcern about his heresy. He thought about the gods differing with each other on what to do, and the fact that they depended on men to do their bidding. If he was going to die, he was going to try something first.

Oaxyctl pulled the shotgun out and aimed it at the Teotl's head.

He pulled the trigger, wincing from the loud sound, and watched the Teotl's head explode. It dropped to the snow. Oaxyctl fired again, wiping ooze off his cheeks that had splattered back on him from standing too close. Then he went and looked for the ax.

He doubted the god could regrow itself after being hacked apart.

The job wasn't easy. The creature had bones of metal, and parts that shocked and sparked him. But he kept at it until he could throw pieces of the god out into the snow as he worked.

When he was done, Oaxyctl packed the gun and ax back on his sled.

Covered in the blood of one of his gods, he pushed off the ice and into the deep snow.

The mound behind began to snap and crack. Oaxyctl turned to watch. A five-hundred-foot length of silvered metal broke free of the ice. It looked like a sleek bird, with great wide-open mouths around each of its sides facing eagerly forward into the air.

The *Ma Wi Jung*, he thought.

It rose, hovering with a great rumble that shattered the silence in the air. Then it flew over Oaxyctl, casting a big shadow over him. It sped up until it was no more than the size of his fist, his fingernail, a dot, then gone.

Oaxyctl turned back to trudge through the snow.

He had enough supplies to last for almost a week. Pepper had built shelter out of the ice a little over a day's walk away. He could live this last week well.

Death didn't scare him. Nothing scared him anymore.

Oaxyctl walked across the snow, a small dot in the almost infinite expanse. He knew he was trapped in the ice and would die here. *La Revanche* was too far away by now, using its steam power to trundle away from him faster than he could walk. He'd known it the second he was thrown out.

But he still felt a tiny bit exhilarated, free, and a little bit relieved.

CHAPTER SIXTY-NINE

A simple question: Who am I?

"You are John deBrun."

What is a John deBrun? What does that mean? What's happening?

"You are being repaired. You've suffered extensive trauma, frostbite, and cognitive impairment: a retrograde amnesia."

How? Why?

"You ordered it. Your low-level personal nano is being stimulated back online."

What?

"You will understand in half an hour. Exedyne Bio is not liable for any psychosis or personality fragmentation that occurs as a result of this procedure."

John lay in a thick soup of some sort.

"Do you remember the last time you were in a medpod?"

The block removed itself. The sensation of being suspended by chemicals, tiny machines roving throughout his body to stitch it back together, returned. Radiation damage reversed, trauma reversed. Saline feeds. Yes, he thought. This is familiar. I've done it before.

A survival pod. Extended periods . . .

"How long?"

John accessed that memory.

He smashed his fists against the pod window and screamed. He heard nothing, fluid filled his mouth and lungs.

He knew why he'd buried those memories.

"Please Mr. deBrun, let me help you. Relax. We will help you manage this."

His muscles sagged, his throat collapsed.

That's right, John, let the nice machine help you, he thought. When it's done, we can get out. We're not trapped. We're not in space. We're still in the *Ma Wi Jung* and Pepper is just outside.

This will only take a few hours.

Not centuries.

He relaxed. A bit. He was a strong, mean little shit. Fuck claustrophobia, he thought. I can handle it just a little more. But someone would pay for all this. Pay hard. He wanted people to hurt, and hurt bad, because that's what happened when they screwed with him.

No, no, that wasn't it. He wanted to get back and find Jerome. That was it.

Who?

My damn son!

John lay there, his mind split and groaning under a new, and far more ancient, load.

CHAPTER SEVENTY

Commotion spread through the cavern. Jerome watched several women run to the edge of the water as men broke the surface with scudder-fish.

"Granpa Troy!" someone shouted. "No, no, not him."

Jerome ran across the sand, water sucking into the spaces of his footprints. The Frenchi men stood around Troy, whom they'd pulled onto the sand.

"You should have seen he," the nearest said. "Them Azteca were burning the house, and he left the water. He had fight them with he hand. He were fast. So fast you could hardly see."

Jerome saw at least ten bullet holes. Slashed flesh was everywhere he looked, peeking through ripped clothing.

"He insist on coming back."

"Hey," someone protested. "Get the child out of here."

With dark looks the women surrounded Jerome, but Troy raised a bloody hand. "Bring Jerome here," he hissed.

Jerome swallowed. Troy wasn't like the mongoose-man he'd seen on their table when he'd fallen out of the tree. Troy was still speaking and moving.

People muttered as Jerome stepped forward and sat next to Troy.

Troy grabbed his neck. Water and blood dripped down Jerome's shoulders and collar.

"You . . . you like Pepper," Jerome said.

"Something like him, yeah," Troy said. "Only Pepper heal, and I don't." Troy leaned his head back on the sand. "Remember what I tell you?"

"Yes."

"Everything I know about we history, it in that desk I show you. Just take John, you father, to the desk and have him talk to it. And remember this, the wormhole is being fix. And them Teotl, they ain't just coming for this world. They coming for all the world-them that have people living on it. You understand? Tell him the wormhole go be fix."

Jerome looked down at Troy. Blood leaked out of the corner of the man's mouth. "I think I understand."

Troy didn't reply.

Jerome waited another few seconds until the men pulled him away. He sat in the corner of the cavern, away from everyone, quiet. So much blood, he thought. Everyone dies, even the powerful ones like Troy and Pepper.

Was no one safe? Even the old-fathers?

Suppose Dad was dead? If Troy died, what chance did Dad have?

Jerome cried into his knees, muffling the sound so no one could hear him or come find him in the dark.

CHAPTER SEVENTY-ONE

Three mongoose-men guided Dihana through an underground sewer filled with dirty, wet women and children huddled around each other. They piled quietly up against the sewer walls, shoved aside by the mongoose-men as they tramped down the middle. A mongoose-man ran forward, peered around a corner, then nodded. They followed it around into more ragged-looking refugees from the streets, climbed up rusty iron stairs, and Dihana broke to the street level back into hell.

Spotlights lit up the sky over Capitol City, stabbing out in search of Azteca airships making bombing raids in the dead of night. One by one the Capitol City airships had gone up against the Azteca, but there were just too many, and now only a few struggled to keep the sky over the city safe.

"This way, ma'am." A gentle tug on her elbow. Dihana walked swiftly with them down the alleyway toward a makeshift hospital. They were out near the harbor, she could smell the salt on the air. They were near the wall, but apparently the Azteca hadn't bombed this section much.

Moaning wounded filled the portable cots that lined the alleyway. The sewers were too dangerous, unpredictable tides swept them clean, and large enough buildings for this many wounded were targeted by Azteca bombs. The alley was the best they could do.

A woman with her head bound in bloody rags shuffled out of Dihana's way, but didn't seem able to focus on anything. Two small children huddled next to her.

A round whistled far overhead and struck a building. The children flinched at the sound of the impact, and the rain of broken brick afterward.

Someone's steady sobs carried over the cobblestones.

The mongoose-men conferred with a nurse dressed in a long and shabby beige dress. Splotches of blood darkened the plain material. The nurse pointed. "He just down here."

Dihana walked past the rows of suffering. Nine rows down she kneeled next to Haidan's cot and took his hand in hers. He opened his eyes.

"Edward." She used his first name, and he smiled. "I came the moment I heard you were awake again. We really need you." She stroked Haidan's cheek. The Azteca had pushed the mongoose-men, and any volunteers willing to pick up a gun, back to the last ring. Several times it had looked as if the sheer mass of Azteca warriors would break over the last line, but the mongoose-men held. And they were paying for it.

And so was the city. They had been naïve to think that the walls alone would save them. The Azteca airships constantly tried to fly over the city and drop bombs. Something hit a house several roads over, the ground rumbled. Azteca flares floated down through the air, giving the night an eerie red glow that flickered in the corners and crevices. They were trying to see what damage they might have done.

Dihana looked up the tall expanse of the city wall, stories over her head. She could see the dim shapes of soldiers moving around, reloading, resting.

"We go fall soon, right?" the nurse asked.

"No," Dihana said, defiant. "The city can hold."

"We hope." The nurse set a bowl of fresh bandages by the bed.

A fourth mongoose-man ran up.

"The boat ready?" his companions asked him.

"What boat?" Dihana asked.

"Gordon says you should run for Cowfoot Island," the nearest soldier explained. "You could try and regroup people there. The Azteca ain't as good with boats like they are with weapons."

But the fourth man shook his head. "Azteca have some boat outside Grantie's Arch. We moving men and cannon out to face the sea."

"And besides, the airships can reach Cowfoot just as easily as a ship can." Dihana clenched the edge of the cot. The city was now surrounded in every conceivable way. She looked at the mongoose-men assigned to protect her. "Go," she ordered. "Get on the walls. And the boat you would have me run away in, use it. Get guns on it."

"We suppose to protect you. We can't just leave."

"There might be nothing to protect come morning. Go."

The four mongoose-men broke and left. Dihana took the bandages and helped the nurse lift the sheets from over Haidan. She winced when she saw the bloody, seeping wounds on his stomach.

He squeezed her hand and drifted away again.

Hang in there, she willed. Please wake back up. She wanted to talk to him at least once more.

CHAPTER SEVENTY-TWO

The pod released John just as the sun dimmed and night fell. Pepper watched John groggily walk into the cockpit and sit down, frowning when the cushions adjusted themselves around him.

Did he have his memories back? Was he fit? Pepper watched John's every movement.

"Where are we?" John asked.

"Over sea, circling, letting *Ma Wi Jung* fly herself. She isn't fully online, so we can't skip out of the atmosphere just yet. Plus, it needs you for that sort of thing. I can only access autopilot for nonorbital flight." Pepper smiled. "John, how are you feeling?"

"You son of a bitch." John put his head in his hands. "Asshole."

"Maybe. But only you can pilot this thing out to the next star system with a wormhole. I want to go home, John. I miss Earth."

John looked up at him. The pod had given John a shave, repaired his thigh, and given him a new hand. As far as Pepper could tell, John didn't seem to be paying attention to the change.

"You've brought it all back. I have memories." John sniffed and cleared his throat. His eyes wrinkled. "I considered killing you for this. I don't need this shit."

"You were wandering around being a little Pollyanna," Pepper said. "Oh, look at me, I'm different without my memory. Oh, I have feelings. Oh, I forgot I helped pull the trigger on an entire damned solar system. It was time to set your priorities back in order."

"That's what I didn't want to remember. I didn't want any of that back. I didn't want sitting in the pod back. I certainly didn't want you back."

"That's a shame. John, I need out of here." This conversation was going nowhere.

John shifted in the seat, brushed his hair back, and stared at his new hand. "You're right."

Pepper nodded. "Better."

"You *were* right. This ship isn't the weapon they had hoped for back at Capitol City. But we still need to help them. Capitol City can't hold out long. You *know* that. We can't just leave them to the Teotl and Azteca."

Pepper sighed. "I have done more than my bit here, John. I was there as protection with you when they terraformed. I was with you when the first Teotl came through, I helped create a defense. I was with you when we realized there was nothing we could do against them. And, John, I helped destroy the wormholes to gain us time to stop the Teotl. You know where that got me? Over two hundred and ninety-seven years of drifting in space." Pepper threw the teacup by his elbow at John, a snapping motion so quick his hands blurred.

John caught the cup with his left hand. A few small drops struck his dirty shirt. A few more stained the carpet, then faded.

With a faint smile, John looked at the teacup and his new hand.

Then he set it on the floor by his feet.

"Two hundred and seventy-one," he said.

"What?"

John blinked tired eyes. "When the wormhole was severed, I floated for two hundred and seventy-one years before the pod could eke its way back to Nanagada. I've been living in retirement for twenty-seven years. Six years in Brungstun, sailing, two in Capitol City and sailing north the first time, and nineteen married to my wife. I have a son, Pepper, that kinda shit changes people." John grabbed the malleable cushion on either side of his thighs with fists. "I'm still here, with the old memories coming back now that you 'healed' me, but I know more things about life, Pepper. Twenty-seven more years' worth than I had before. I can't get rid of those, and they're giving me one hell of a headache I can't ignore."

Pepper stood up. "What do I have to do to get you to fly us home?"

"Home. To get home, Pepper, we will have to fly almost thirty light-years to reach the nearest wormhole. Even there no one lives to help us, it is just a random dead system, a transit point. How long will that take in this ship? More hundreds of years? I know your body will last that long, and the recycling in this ship will handle it just like our pods did. But can your mind?"

"Yes. Just because you snapped and blocked those memories doesn't mean I will," Pepper snapped. "There are ways. I can edit. I can loop, I can learn, I can be entertained. I've done it once already. I'll do it again." The sheer dreadful passage of time in a pod was a horrible, mind-altering thing. Doing it in a ship designed with that in mind would be easier.

Space travel was a long affair. Humans had met other races, and the men who traveled space adopted life-extending technologies to manage journeying between stars where there were no wormholes to help them.

"Yes. Ways." John reached down and picked up the teacup with his new hand. "Some Pilots were willing to suffer those years in transit when the Teotl took the wormholes and blockaded us in this system. But we need this ship for something else now, so it won't happen just yet. I'm the Pilot. This is a ship. You can't even get into a simple orbit without me. I say we're going to Capitol City. We will not let the Teotl win here, on Nanagada. Not after everything I've been through."

Pepper struck the chair nearest him. It slowly moved forward, then pulled back to its position after absorbing the strike.

"*Ma Wi Jung* has forward shields to stop dust punctures. It's just an electromagnetic umbrella, though, we can't protect ourselves from crude artillery fire, or anything of the sort that the Azteca will have at Capitol City. This isn't a magic bullet."

"It doesn't need to be." John handed Pepper back the teacup.

"You have a plan?"

"I do. And if you help me, I'll do you one better than taking you back to Earth. I'll make you a Pilot. We have a medbay for the alterations, we can train you. You can return to Earth on your own. You don't have a choice. I'm back, Pepper. You did this."

Pepper blinked. "Back to Earth. If it's even there anymore." He sat back down with the empty teacup as John grimaced. Humanity scrabbled for survival among the intolerant Gahe and Nesaru since being given political freedom by the Maatan in the days after the pacification of Earth.

Messy times. Times that had created men like Pepper and John as the Gahe and Maatan fought over the remains of the solar system. Immigrants and whole societies had tried to run and hide deep in the tortuous mazes of wormholes, out of reach on new, undiscovered worlds.

The immigrants had run into something worse. Teotl and the Loa, creatures embroiled in their own struggle for survival.

John and Pepper started out running the Black Starliner Corporation to profit as they moved paying minority populations to safety, away from the dying mother planet. The immigrants contracted them to provide security on the newly terraformed world against the aliens, and suddenly it became a war of survival. One so bad that the only choice was to collapse the wormholes and spark off a round of final destruction.

"Okay," Pepper said. "I will help you." He rubbed the edge of the teacup with a thumb. "But, John. Remember this: you started it."

John bit his lip. "I have a plan. I'll be in the pilot's cabin. Call me when we approach Capitol City." He walked off. Pepper noted the slump of his shoulders. John once again carried the load of a world on them. Old habits die slowly.

Pepper leaned back in his chair and threw the teacup against the wall. He watched the composite accept and absorb the projectile, then gently slide it down to the floor.

He should never have let John talk him into coming to Nanagada 354 years ago.

Pepper would never forgive him for it.

CHAPTER SEVENTY-THREE

Dihana watched the sun rise and fill the inside of Capitol City with amber light. She sat in a boarded-up house near the waterfront, listening to the murmur of her guards in the nearby room.

Harbor waters lapped at the new high-tide mark cut into the stone of Grantie's Arch. Just beyond the harbor walls Dihana watched three Azteca ships tack into the wind. They turned their sides to the city's seawalls and shattered the morning calm by opening fire.

A full previous night of shelling showed its effects on sections of the seawall. Pockmarks, gaping holes, and chips on the edge could be seen along the full expanse. Bodies littered the seaside footpaths, volunteers caught by Azteca sharpshooting last evening when the ships had sailed toward Grantie's Arch.

The three ships formed a wedge and made another run for the harbor's entry. For several minutes the two ships in the rear would sail forward, split out and turn their sides toward the city walls, fire a broadside, then turn back in to follow the lead ship.

Newly moved guns on the walls kept a constant rate of fire, hoping to push the ships back out to sea again.

Four small fishing boats with cannon aboard loitered on the inside of the arch. If the Azteca ships came in, they would ambush them, though they knew it was a suicidal task.

The Azteca ships continued forward, catching the full wind, coming in on the tide. They almost entered the harbor when the middle of Grantie's Arch exploded, and the structure slumped into the sea.

Dihana covered her mouth. The mongoose-men had blown up the arch to stop the ships from coming in.

After several seconds of commotion the two covering Azteca ships turned away and managed to tack out. The ship in front struggled to turn, but came through the remains of the arch. Chunks of rocks still dropped into the sea, and onto its deck.

The Azteca ship ground to a halt with a loud scraping, stuck in the one opening to the harbor.

Mongoose-men fired down into its mast, threw flaming pitch onto the decks, and dropped bombs. Dihana walked up to the window to close it and not watch anymore. But she paused. A high-pitched roar shook the sky. People paused and looked up. A silvery winged machine swooped out from over the water, headed straight for the city.

The incredible craft slowed down until it floated leisurely over the harbor. It dropped slowly down, kicking up a furious amount of spray and water.

It edged itself next to the docks and dropped into the water with a deep sigh, not fifty feet from where Dihana stood, frozen at the window. A fine coating of salt drifted up and covered her face.

Then it just sat still for several minutes, thrumming the deep hum of a content beast.

Was this the old-father machine from the north? So soon?

She turned to the nearest mongoose-man. "Get a wheelchair. Bring Haidan from the cots."

"Prime Minister, he still very ill."

"He'll want to see this."

The mongoose-man nodded and ran out of the room.

CHAPTER SEVENTY-FOUR

John leaned against the wall of the bathroom with his eyes closed and remembered the first time he'd wrangled his way aboard a combat ship. The surgery alone had bankrupted him: backup high-g hearts, neural taps, remapped cortex, and two years of training his mind in simulators.

The moment he'd slaved into the ship, though, he'd been both a god and a tiny speck in the middle of vast space. A gratifying experience.

Then he remembered his own son being born, something even more impressive than the light-years crossed, the scams pulled off, the adventures he'd been in, and the things he had seen on other worlds.

Pepper opened the door, and John blinked away unexpected tears, holding a washcloth up to his face. He hoped Pepper hadn't caught that.

"There's a crowd up on the docks," Pepper said.

"Yeah." John placed his palm on the diagnostic tab next to the washbasin. The readouts returned all normal. Nothing wrong with him at all. His dizzy spell after landing the *Ma Wi Jung* had just been disorientation.

Twenty-seven years of divergent memories and actions had to be sewn together. Couldn't happen without some bumps.

John wondered if this would happen again. Could he count on himself to hold up through the next few hours? And if Pepper doubted John's ability to pull this off, he would find a . . . creative way of getting what he wanted.

John was under no illusions as to who or what Pepper was now. His earlier suspicions had been correct. Pepper was dangerous.

Then again, John remembered, flashes coming back to him, so was he.

He watched his new hand as if it belonged to someone else. It twitched. Nervous. John forced it to stop and faced Pepper.

"Let's not keep them waiting." John dropped the washcloth. It swirled down the drain, followed by a squirt of water.

Pepper put a hand on John's shoulder. "I know you enough to want to watch this happen. It's good to have you back, John. Even if you are twisting my hand."

Memories of a bar popped into John's mind. In this memory, he sat next to Pepper, watching women walk by in loose silk. A pair of guns pushed against his ribs beneath a shabby uniform. Good to have you back on board.

Honey-coated almonds.

Beer and piss.

John remembered a handshake. Dead men. Blood pooling on metal corridors. And Pepper's half-grin beneath the dreadlocks. A friendship born in violence. He remembered Pepper's surprise when he'd first met him on a small island, on a world not unlike Nanagada.

They were both islanders. That was the real thread. Both from Earth. Which is how they'd struck up a friendship. Two native sons on an alien planet, far from home.

John was piloting a freighter full of stolen goods for some moron of a fence and wanted the best protection aboard and that had been Pepper. They'd never drifted apart after that.

"Let's go." John looked at Pepper. "We flew over. You know Capitol City is close to going under."

Pepper shrugged.

"Don't tell me you've grown so cold," John said, "that you would see your people wiped extinct?"

A single blink. But John felt triumphant to get it.

"John, boy." Pepper leaned down and got level with him. "The reason I followed you all the way here on this fool venture was because you said the same thing years ago. And now I have fought that fight, and lost. Capitol City *went* under, for all intents and purposes, a long time ago. My only goal here is to leave." Pepper walked out of the cabin.

The *Ma Wi Jung* rode centimeters from the edge of the docks, and several men stood there with ropes. Several others with rifles. Pepper followed John out of the hatch and they both stood at the top of the starship, on the port wing.

"You John deBrun?" someone yelled.

"Yes. I'm going to come ashore." John walked down the slope of the wing and jumped ashore. The first time he'd jumped on these docks they'd been freshly extruded. The chief architect and city programmer had toured him around the frame of the city with pride. Technically, the man had said, using nano to build a city out of the bedrock was illegal, but they were far enough from Earth, so who would care? Besides, the Loa were helping with the templates.

That was before the war. When having Loa help just meant business. And John was part of the traders and terraformers hoping to make a buck off the creation of a new human world and civilization.

Pepper landed next to John with a hop.

The rifles remained pointed. The mongoose-men among them looked grubby and tired. The nearest nodded at John's hand. "You was describe as having a hook. What happen?"

"Now I have a hand." John waved the good hand back at the expanse of silvery metal. "I also just landed in a large ship made by the old-fathers, so you'll have to give me the benefit of the doubt." He smiled. The word *old-fathers* produced another small skip in his balance. A part of him didn't recognize it or at least felt amused by the fact that he was an "old-father." The other part let the word slip off his tongue. A word he had used often. Nothing more.

A few more rifles lowered. Then a shout from a window nearby caused the rest of them to lower. Two mongoose-men pushed Haidan, wrapped in a large blanket, out of a door. They crossed the small street and stopped in front of John. Haidan looked up and grabbed John's shirt.

"Haidan, are you okay?" John asked.

"I can't self even believe me eye," Haidan croaked. "You dropping out the sky. Returning." He gave a weak grin.

A wedge of soldiers developed around them, protecting them. Despite the rubble-filled streets and the tension in the air, a crowd had still developed. Old ladies, and a few children, watched as Haidan was pushed down the street with John alongside.

"If you have something to save we," Haidan said, "you come just in time." He glanced down at the bystanders. "We holding the wall, but just barely." He looked at the two of them. "Where the rest of you?"

"Ah, yes," Pepper said. "Them. There was a mutiny. They might be heading to Cowfoot Island, if things go well for them."

Haidan turned, grunting in pain, and frowned at him. "Who you?"

"That's Pepper," John said. "He'll help. He's very good at what he does."

"And what is that?" Haidan asked.

"Killing people."

Haidan stuck out a shaky hand. "Welcome."

Pepper gently shook it.

In the middle of the eastern wall road in a tent with wheels on the wooden platform floor, Haidan struggled with a leather bag of photo plates and laid them out on a picnic bench. An air of urgency settled over them.

Pepper turned his head and pushed his foot against the wooden floor.

"We keep it moving," Haidan said, not looking up. "Five other duplicate looking like this one run up and down each side. They more or less safe from the shelling. Azteca can't quite reach the middle except by airship. We keep them confuse enough."

John pored over the plates, his eyes hunting for particular shapes among the hacked-down-forest clearings and encampments. He took a closer look at a line of artillery guns. Most likely the ones pounding his eardrums at this second with steady, distant thumps.

"The minister being moved from house to house now to keep she safe."

John scanned the rear of the camp and found what he was looking for: a round eagle stone and several lines of people in front of it. A large square shape just to the right of it.

"Tell me." He pointed at the rear of the hundreds of tiny black and white tents, fuzzy triangles on the delicate plates. "Are these the priests?"

Haiden looked at the tiny area John indicated. He used a pinkie finger and traced it along what looked like a line of ants.

"The priest by a wooden pyramid, and a round stone. Them lines you see is people waiting to be sacrifice."

John sat in a canvas chair. "That is their weakness. Haidan. Your best men. Find them. I want you to get pictures, get some Tolteca in here to draw pictures if we need, but we have to show your men what the high priests look like." Haidan grabbed the edge of the table. Sweat dripped from his forehead. John got up and squatted next to him. "Haidan . . ."

Haidan waved him away, took several deep breaths, then slumped back into his wheelchair. "My best men?" Haidan grunted.

"Your best," Pepper said. "There is only one chance against the tens of thousands of Azteca at your walls. You can't hold them off."

"What you plan?"

John picked up the plate and pointed at the sacrificial areas on it. "They depend on their priests and gods. We capture or kill them, the Azteca have been practically trained to give up." John set the plate back down. The pictures were burned into the back of his mind. He'd match them up in the ship with other instruments.

He remembered lessons from three hundred years ago. Everything Oaxyctl had ever told him on the decks of *La Revanche* reinforced what John knew of the Azteca. The original Azteca civilization had perfected the art of the Flower Wars. The highest of Azteca fighting involved the capture of slaves and sacrificial victims, not the killing of enemies. And the Teotl, John almost laughed, the goddamned Teotl had been using Flower Wars for the past few hundred years to perfect their human soldiers.

Generations of Azteca had clashed on the other side of the mountains, getting better, training for a final war against all the humans on this planet. And no doubt the Teotl had been hoping to wipe out the Loa and capture the *Ma Wi Jung* so they could return to space and find their kind.

Here they all were, all gathered around the city.

John knew the Teotl had one gaping weakness he could exploit. John deBrun would drop a Flower War on them unlike anything in Azteca recorded history. If the Teotl could use human foibles and traditions against the city, John could reply in kind.

The question was, which was more powerful, the tradition of the Flower Wars, or the orders of the "gods" when they realized their own tool was back-firing on them?

"Oh," John said, as if an afterthought. "Make sure to equip them with nets. Weighted nets."

"Nets?" Haidan asked. "Like for fish?"

"Like for big fish," John said. "And, Haidan, we need to get you fixed. You aren't in good shape."

Haidan shook his head. "We don't have time. You need go now."

John looked at Pepper.

"You're not thinking right," Pepper said. "But if you're going to do this, I want ammunition, guns, and a good trench coat. I want to guard the ship."

John put a hand on Haidan's shoulder. "There are things I can use to help you when I get back, okay? So hang in there." John knew now what ailed Haidan on top of his wounds. Cancer, developed from the high radiation of Hope's Loss where old reactors had plunged back to the ground. John's own body could handle that, but now, with those gut wounds, Haidan had a few days left at best. He was up and about now because he was too strong, too stubborn, to give up.

Haidan nodded and leaned back in the chair. Mongoose-men sur-rounded him.

"We'll get everything you need together. Leave him be for now. We need let him sleep some. This tire him a whole bunch," one said. "He get hit by a whole wall, and he already sick."

John nodded.

*   *   *

Overhead a wedge of red Azteca blimps fought to get over the city. Four small, more agile, Capitol City blimps converged on them, firing their guns with random popping sounds. Grapelike clusters of bombs swayed from the Aztecan undercarriages.

A Capitol City blimp exploded and fell out of the sky. Men jumped from it, clothes on fire. They fell until they disappeared in between the buildings.

John watched the last of fifty men walk aboard *Ma Wi Jung*. They climbed up the wing, looking around nervously.

Another detachment of mongoose-men stood on the docks, guns ready.

Clusters of bombs exploded in the streets. An Azteca blimp caught fire and headed back out to the forest. It blazed its way down over the walls.

Several permanent stacks of smoke hung over their heads. Two of the small Capitol City blimps dipped into the smoke to hide and wait for the next Azteca wedge to bomb the city.

John stood up from the wing.

Time to pull his plan off.

John walked forward to the tip of the wing and addressed the mongoose-man on the dock who had rounded up the men inside the ship. "Your men know that I, and only I, command this? You told them what they might have to do if I need help?" The mongoose-man nodded. "Then good luck holding the Azteca back."

John walked back up the wing.

Pepper waited inside the cockpit. He pulled a large canvas trench coat on and strapped knives next to either boot. "I want to repeat to you that I'm not going in, John, I mean it. I'm staying here to make sure no Teotl gets aboard and kills your fool ass, you understand?" All fifty mongoose-men lined the corridor under the top air lock, crammed shoulder to shoulder.

"I understand. We dust off now," John told him.

"If we wait until night, they can't hit it with artillery. If we go right now, they will harm it, John. I doubt she'll be able to repair herself, or if she can, it might take many, many years for her to recover. We can't take this risk."

John sat down on the main couch. It canted itself into a takeoff position. "They might fall today yet, Pepper."

Pepper grabbed a fistful of John's shirt and pulled him out. "Think straight, John,"

John snapped his fingers. It was echoed by the sound of fifty gun safeties releasing, then the sound of fifty guns cocking. "Fifty crack jungle warriors, Pepper, in close quarters with guns aimed at you. You have a good chance, but so do they."

Pepper dropped him back into the couch and punched the wall. It rippled. A display several inches away shattered and rained to the floor.

When he pulled his fist out, the imprint remained.

Pepper sat down on the adjacent couch and put his head in his hands. "Go."

"Hang on," John yelled to the mongoose-men. "It'll be bumpy. There should be handles in the wall. Safety your weapons."

The *Ma Wi Jung* rumbled.

"You are using a delicate interstellar ship as a cheap troop transport," Pepper growled.

John leaned back into the couch. Somewhere in the back of his head he began to make a link with the ship, the half-living computer inside it. His visual cortex lit up with an imposed world of information. This was what he did. He was a Pilot. Only John was built to interpret this complex brew of information.

He shut his eyes and pulled *Ma Wi Jung* out of the harbor water. On the outside left-down camera he could see water streaming down and soaking the docks.

Facing forward, he saw three blimps. Capitol City. Their heat signatures still stood out in the heavy smoke.

In the far distance, a wedge of five Azteca blimps moved leisurely forward.

John raised *Ma Wi Jung* up even farther, moving past the Capitol City blimps like a silver ghost breaking through the smoke.

Then with a grim smile he jacked the ship forward, ignoring the ping of bullets fired from the ungainly, red airships in front of him, and flared upward at the last minute.

Behind him the Azteca blimps popped like soap bubbles from the punch of *Ma Wi Jung*'s engines, while, inside, the mongoose-men hung to the walls as they shook and rumbled.

John let the ship spin as he scanned the barren landscape around Capitol City's walls, then found his target.

Now he would bring revenge to the people who had invaded his land and broken his family.

CHAPTER SEVENTY-FIVE

After several seconds of flying, John's eyes flicked open. Despite the medic pod's reconstruction, Pepper saw one overriding look on John's face: tiredness. Lines etched the corners of John's mouth, layered on top of the clenched lips. "Show them all the exits," John said.

He flew in figure eights. Pepper felt the motion through his feet. Keeping Azteca artillery interested, and their attention away from Capitol City.

"Okay." Pepper stood up and massaged his fist. He'd pounded his knuckles into powder with that frustrated punch. They were beginning to heal again, but that was a dumb move just before action. "There are four ways to get out of this ship. Cargo's the biggest, top air lock, and two front air locks." He pointed directions out and walked forward. "You five, to the top. You should remember the way."

Five mongoose-men walked back down the cramped corridor and climbed up a floor. Their feet echoed off the ladder. Pepper grabbed five more, stationed them at the right front air lock, and another five on the left. The rest he took with him down into the cargo bay.

John looped them around the sky some more, shoving them against the floor at times with acceleration as he needed.

Then they dropped. Pepper's stomach flip-flopped. A hard jarring sound shook through the hull. Contact. "The more feathers, the more colorful, the better," Pepper yelled. They'd all been shown pictures, told what to do, shown the layout of the sacrificial area. But a last impression before they jumped out would take their minds off the ship and back onto fighting. "Bring as many back alive as you can. John'll be waiting in the sky." The cargo bay opened, and the three nearest men slid down onto a broken tree log a few feet under *Ma Wi Jung*.

A mongoose-man threw a rifle at Pepper, and he caught it with his left hand. The man cocked his head out the door, asking if Pepper was going.

Hours ago he'd thought he was home free, giving John his memories back. He'd been dreaming of accounts he held in NovaTerra and Earth with interest still ticking, hot baths, and candy bars with names he recognized.

Now he was back where he had started.

Pepper looked down at the gun. He reached under his jacket with his other arm and pulled out the handgun Haidan had given him. It hardly matched the Ruger taken from him up north, but it was deadly enough.

Enough to ruin any Azteca's day.

A mongoose-men held up a net for Pepper, but he shook his head.

What was it John had said? He killed people. How many could he kill before some random Azteca sniper dropped him with one in the head? Or would he be quick enough, lucky enough, coolheaded enough, to make it through this next one?

Fuck it. Pepper sighed and jumped down into the bush. This needed to be over, one way or another. Two hundred and ninety-eight years of waiting to go home had eroded his patience.

Pepper watched the *Ma Wi Jung* explode back up into the air as shots followed it. Each one made Pepper wince. The loamy ground sprung underneath him, making each long stride easy. Mongoose-men crunched through around him. Pepper kept each one in track as he scanned.

Long, drooping palms struck Pepper in the face, and then he burst out into the clearing. The smell of blood hung humid in the air. Hundreds of tree stumps lined the perimeter, but closer to the great wooden pyramid the ground had been cleared.

"Who goes?" cried a voice in Azteca. A priest, a low-order acolyte judging by the scraggly feathers and lack of blood.

"I do." Pepper dropped his voice down until the words rumbled.

"Are you a god? Do you come for blood? I will guide you, good sir."

Pepper hardly slowed as the young man realized his mistake and raised his mace. Pepper dodged the blow and struck the acolyte in the face with the same force and frustration he had struck the bulkhead.

He shook his hand free of skull and brain tissue and kept moving. He circled the pyramid, a half-mile dash, running so fast he could feel wasted energy rippling out of his body in the form of heat.

Then he turned toward the pyramid.

Guards moved forward. Pepper shot one with the rifle the mongoose-men had given him, used the butt to stave in another's chest, and picked up the mace thrown clear as the man clutched his wound.

The third guard reached for his gun, abandoning any idea of trying to take Pepper for a prisoner. So Pepper shot him first.

A hundred Azteca priests of the highest castes milled about, not sure where to run. Mongoose-men finally caught up with Pepper and burst out into the clearing.

Now the priests bolted, running toward Pepper as they tried to escape the wide crescent of fifty silent mongoose-men with nets and guns.

Pepper waited, chest heaving overtime as he pulled in enough oxygen; too much, he felt dizzy.

He shot the first priest in the thigh, and the man fell forward into the mud. The one next to him slowed, and Pepper shot him in the foot.

They wielded knives slick with the blood of Nanagadans' hearts, and Pepper took those same knifes out of their hands and hamstrung them. Others he knocked out, smashing their faces in enough to let them live, but never forget.

When calm, planned actions resulted in nicks and cuts on his arms and chest, Pepper cut loose. Sizzling with energy, he thrashed through the crowd and cut the legs of anything with a high enough rank. He was a silent, methodical blur amidst the colored confusion.

Acolytes simply died, not worth the energy of saving.

Pepper killed and maimed and cut and slashed until all he was left with were shapes in the bloody mud, shapes that groaned and cried out to their gods.

He looked like one of them, now. Blood ran down his shoulders. His shirt dripped with it. It streamed off the edges of his trench coat and matted his hair. He couldn't blink through the gore on his face.

The mongoose-men stood and looked at him.

"Fire the flare," Pepper ordered. "Bag them."

They had mere minutes before the warriors came. He could hear them. He blinked, blind, as the actinic green of a flare filled the clearing.

Ma Wi Jung banked out of the sky and flew in over the treetops, making them shake so madly it looked as if they were dancing. The starship dropped over the pyramid, smashing it with shrieks and groans, and opened the bay doors.

Half the mongoose-men dragged priests unceremoniously to the ship while the others brought up the rear.

Pepper stalked back toward the *Ma Wi Jung.*

He looked around, suddenly aware that hundreds of eyes watched him through the bars of the pens erected around the pyramid. Nanagadans waiting to be sacrificed.

Thirty seconds before the first warrior burst out at them.

Pepper looked over at the mongoose-men. He could see some sidling toward the pens while trying to cover their comrades hauling half-unconscious priests.

"Open the pens," he said. "I'll cover."

He reached under his sticky trench coat for more rounds and reloaded the Nanagadan handgun. He'd dropped the rifle somewhere.

Once loose, the Nanagadans would be slaughtered by the Azteca. But they didn't have room for them in the ship. Maybe some would survive, and at least they would die on their own terms, not at the hands of some priest with a knife. Better to go down fighting than be slaughtered like a cow.

In the forest several Azteca arrived. He could see body heat signatures in the cool, dark jungle, waiting to gather enough numbers to attack.

"Gentlemen." Pepper picked up a mace slick with fresh blood from the nearest mud-caked body and walked toward the forest.

CHAPTER SEVENTY-SIX

As the Azteca pushed into the clearing, John watched Pepper sprint back into the *Ma Wi Jung*.

John shut the doors and took off.

He flew the *Ma Wi Jung* around the peninsula over the water and landed in Capitol City. They disgorged their bloody, half-unconscious cargo onto the wharf without even landing.

From outside it would look like a miscarriage from a giant, silvery bird.

Inside the ship Pepper forced his way through the wounded mongoose-men into the cockpit to face John. The stench of death on him was overwhelming. He looked horrific. His bloody footsteps meandered back down the corridor.

"How many more of these trips do you want, John?"

"As many as we can," John said.

When he dropped them off on the second one, John circled around and kept a camera on the scene. He saw Pepper moving around the pyramid clearing and cutting the priests off again.

The flare went off after three minutes. John dropped down again. Again the mongoose-men dragged bloodied priests into the hold.

This time Pepper came with a net of his own. A large grublike figure struggled inside.

"Teotl." Pepper dropped it at the mongoose-men's feet. "Adapted for non-physical activity." He smiled. "Helpless." And he winked at John. Just like the old days. Blood in the air. And something in the back of John's mind almost had him wink back.

John closed his eyes to it all and took off again, dodging around the sky, watching the blimps in slow motion, and dropped off the captured cargo.

He opened his eyes again as they touched down onto the wharf. Pepper had lost forty or fifty pounds easily. His face looked thin now. He didn't loom over the other men. He couldn't keep that up much longer, John thought, dropping in for attack number three.

The cargo bays dropped open, John took the *Ma Wi Jung* back into the sky.

They were doing what they did best, what they had modified their bodies to do. John flying, his mind interfaced wholly with the ship, Pepper an efficient killing machine on the ground.

Just like the old days.

* * *

John came in carefully, watching the trees in all spectrums. The ground crawled with Azteca. The dark forest lit up with the firefly blinks of muzzle flashes. The hull was pockmarked with bullets.

He dropped into the clearing. This time only thirty-nine mongoose-men climbed back aboard with their cargo. Pepper leaped into the right front air lock at the last minute.

Cameras picked him up, half-naked, bullet holes oozing blood. The blood on his skin sizzled like a grill. Pepper grabbed the wall to keep his balance. "Water," he demanded.

John gained altitude, paused to reorient the starship, and the whole craft rang like a bell.

Smoke poured into the corridor, and emergency foam followed it. They lurched back toward the docks as John coerced the ship to tell him what damage they had taken. It didn't respond. John got the sense it was focusing all its attention on trying to repair itself.

He wobbled them down toward the docks and waited for Pepper while some of the mongoose-men unloaded more bloodied nets of Azteca priests. Two mongoose-men sat in the cockpit, holding their guns nervously.

Pepper stumbled forward to John. "We're hit." Pepper had lost even more weight, burning it up as fast as he could speed around and kill. John could count his ribs. "That is it, now. We can't risk any more damage. Let it go repair itself. We're done."

John opened his eyes, losing in his head all the ship's visions of the world around it. "One last compound."

Pepper sipped more water from a tin flask, trying to cool himself down and recover lost water weight. The leather strap dangled around his forearm. "They're wise to you now. I'll bet they have more artillery than that last one in place over the sacrificial areas. *Ma Wi Jung* will get hammered. She'll be far from spaceworthy."

"One more," John said.

Pepper broke the straps off the flask and leaned closer.

"Stop him," John ordered.

Two mongoose-men leapt on Pepper. The first smacked him in the face with the butt of his gun, the other slipped a noose around Pepper's feet and yanked him onto his side. All three fell to the ground, struggling. A third mongoose-man in the corridor ran forward and put a knee to Pepper's chest and a gun on his neck.

None of this could have been done without Pepper's being weakened by the fighting. John was relieved when they stood up with Pepper between them bound in ropes. The alternative, if Pepper had not fought and weakened, would have been to surround him with guns again. A second showdown that would have ended in many dead.

"Take him out on the dock. Keep him secure and feed him as much jerk chicken and water as they can spare."

Pepper would break out quickly enough. But not soon enough to stop this last foray. John avoided Pepper's eyes as the mongoose-men dragged him away.

What a mess.

John closed his eyes as they dropped Pepper onto the ground. He watched the thin trail of smoke coming out of the rear of the ship and checked over the numerous holes in the ship's side, trying to remember if there was anything critical nearby.

The more priests they had, the more likely they could force the Azteca to turn around and go home. Just one last run.

He closed the doors in the belly of the ship and took to the sky.

John angled the ship down, dropping toward the trees. But even as he did so, he knew he was in trouble. Several large guns had been towed into place, and they caught him in cross fire. He dodged below the Azteca artillery and to the ground. As he looked up, he knew getting back into the air would be expensive.

Azteca waited on the ground for his thirty-nine mongoose-men.

Without Pepper they would face a slow, desperate fight.

John gunned *Ma Wi Jung* just over the ground ahead of the mongoose wedge at the Azteca. He dropped her belly to the ground and scraped it toward the gathered enemy.

Tortured metal screamed back at him. The ship hopped into the air again, and he repeated, feeling the bay doors buckle and fall off.

Three guns on wheels were pulled around the side of the sacrificial pyramid. The first round knocked *Ma Wi Jung* sideways a whole foot.

John dragged the ship on toward the priests, gritting his teeth. Mongoose-men ran around him with nets and began capturing priests, but only a mere handful before John shouted at them over the external loudspeakers.

They had ten high-ranking priests when they flew back into the cross fire. One priest for every mongoose-man left.

Ma Wi Jung barely made it to the docks. Smoke poured out of every opening as John made his final drop. He shouted instructions to the mongoose-men as they left.

He wondered if Pepper could see the sorry shape of the ship, no longer a sleek traveler between suns, but a casualty of war. He could see a fire raging down in the rear areas where the engines struggled to power them back into the air.

John raised the *Ma Wi Jung* up over the harbor, just getting it over Grantie's now broken arch. He flew east away from the peninsula, away from the Azteca ships and out of sight, before he nosed it into the water. They would never know that Capitol City couldn't raise *Ma Wi Jung* at any time.

For a while the ship floated, while John tried to get a response from it.

Would the ship be okay? And if so, how long would it take to mend the damage taken? John got a glimmering of an answer through his connection: fifty years.

Water rushed in through the broken bay doors and filled the ship. Several air-lock doors snapped shut to preserve airspace in critical areas.

Choking in the smoke created by the doused fires, John fumbled his way to the upper air lock. He yanked open a locker and pulled out a life-raft packet.

Then he paused.

Ship, are any first-aid kits available?

The location came to him. John fumbled his way down, still holding on to the bulky raft packet until he found a storage cabinet and opened it. Water threatened to sweep him away, rising to his chest. He grabbed the floating bright red box with the white cross on the side and stumbled back toward the air lock with each item under his arms.

Two hands came in handy now.

He threw the life raft out the air lock and clambered up after it.

When he cleared the hatch, he took several deep breaths of fresh air, grabbed the life raft, and ran down the length of the wing into the cold water.

He pulled the rip cord and the packet inflated itself into a full raft. John climbed in, found the collapsible oars, and began to paddle his way toward Capitol City. It would take a day to reach it. John knew the currents that he had to take to get to the city's harbor, avoiding the jagged reefs and rocks around the peninsula.

John turned and watched the *Ma Wi Jung* slip beneath the waves. He marked the location in his head.

He was a Pilot. He always knew where he was. He could find her again, in fifty years. If Pepper wasn't angry enough to kill him first.

The whole way back, John thought about Haidan lying in the wheelchair.

Hang on old friend. I may yet help you again.

CHAPTER SEVENTY-SEVEN

The mongoose-men had moved Dihana again. She'd ordered them to take her to the walls with Haidan. When he'd wake, she'd tell him what she knew of the battle outside the walls. When he fell asleep, she'd watch and listen to the battle and do what she could to ease his pain.

Haidan sweated constantly and had taken a turn for the worse after John had left. She had the feeling he'd been holding on until then, but now felt he could let go. He barely remained lucid. The mongoose-men seemed to think he wouldn't last the day. They'd drugged him to ease the pain of his wounds.

"He bleeding inside," they told her. "Nothing we can do but wait."

One of the wall runners came up with the news that the Azteca had fallen back. The distant shelling didn't let up, but the warriors on the ground no longer advanced.

She'd been hoping the attack by the ancient flying machine would have had more of an immediate effect, like the Azteca leaving. But now it had been almost a day since the raid, and John deBrun had disappeared out to sea with the flying machine.

Things had gone from hopeless, to hopeful, to uncertain, within the last day.

One of her ragamuffins came up in the late morning as she ate some stale bread. "John deBrun here. He want to see you."

"Well, bring him." He'd survived. But where was the airship?

Several minutes later John arrived, surrounded by mongoose-men. Seawater dripped from his wet clothes. He set a bright red box with a cross on the ground next to Haidan's wheelchair.

"I'm going to need a table to lay him out on," he said.

"You a doctor now?" Dihana asked. John wiggled his two hands in the air, and Dihana blinked. "Okay," she said. "What you need?"

John shook his head and opened the red box. "Anyone know if that man Pepper is around?" Several small metal machines gleamed inside. John surveyed them, then chose one. It was nothing more than a rounded cylinder with black tips and textured surface.

"He escape. He somewhere in the city, no one know where."

John nodded, not surprised. Behind him the mongoose-men cleared a table. Four of them picked Haidan out of his wheelchair, pulling the blankets away and letting them drop to the ground, and laid him on it.

"You need to get rid of he clothes to operate?" they asked.

"No." John took the instrument and box up to the table. Haidan moaned and moved. John put the box on the table and leaned over Haidan. He inserted the cylinder into Haidan's mouth and let it go.

The cylinder slid down, then stopped. The black end unfolded and planted small arms on Haidan's bluish lips. The textured surface writhed, and the rest of the cylinder moved down farther.

Haidan gagged, his eyes flickering open. The cylinder hissed, then pushed down even farther.

John sat down and touched the lid of the box. Text appeared on its surface, and John began reading it. Occasionally he tapped the surface and read more. A minute passed. The cylinder hummed, the arms retracted, and it slid the rest of the way into Haidan's mouth and down his throat. The mongoose-men looking on swore, and John looked up.

"He's okay. That should be it," he said. "Now we wait. Don't disturb him. By morning, he'll be a whole different man."

Dihana looked at John. "Do you have any more miracles up your sleeve? They're still shelling us out there."

John looked in the direction she pointed. "No. I want to wait out the night until we get Haidan back. We'll need him."

"I'll wait with you." Dihana sat down in a nearby chair.

It was a long night. Dihana spent it wondering what the machine inside Haidan was doing.

When the sun rose and the men drank coffee with John, Haidan sat up and groaned, clutching his lungs and grimacing.

Dihana smiled and sat next to him.

John looked up, then walked over with coffee. "We have priests and Teotl. Now we need to force the Azteca to talk terms to get them back and I need your help."

Haidan nodded. He looked at the coffee. "Could I get some of that? And food. I wicked hungry."

CHAPTER SEVENTY-EIGHT

Smoke roiled across the trenches in front of the great walls of the city. Mongoose-men and city volunteers occasionally popped their heads over the edges, looking out over pits of never-ending smoldering fires and barbed wire for the next wave of Azteca.

Two men covered in days of mud, bags under their eyes, and dreadlocks dripping with sweat, helped Haidan down a long tunnel. He could run with the men. It was exhilarating feeling confident enough to be running. He was healed thanks to John. And John's ship had given them an upper hand. They had priests, a god, and a mystery weapon, though the weapon had been ditched in the sea. But the Azteca didn't know that.

The mongoose-men paused twice to disarm traps in the ground meant for incoming Azteca.

If they were going to see an end to this, Haidan knew it had to be quick.

Occasional craters steamed from recent explosions, and several bodies had been stacked up like sandbags outside a trench. Three mongoose-men stood around a warrior-priest who'd walked over the trenches to their side with a white flag. A puffy, bloodied face looked up at Haidan.

"He refuse to go any further," one of the mongoose-men grunted. "We had try and make him."

Haidan squatted in the mud face-to-face with the Azteca. "What you want?" The chance for a truce, or withdrawal, made him hopeful. But whether this Azteca was here to advance it or not he didn't know. If this priest wasn't here to start that process, Haidan had plans for forcing them to the table anyway.

"A stop to fighting," the warrior said.

"You have authority?"

"Do you? You do not much look like a priest or a leader of any sort."

Haidan grunted. The warrior looked thin and hungry. The Azteca hadn't been resupplied. The mongoose-men had done an able job on destroying anything of use on the route the Azteca had used to get to Capitol City, and Capitol City was a long way from the Wicked Highs.

The mysterious ship from the sky must have been a hell of a blow, Haidan thought.

"We got one of you god," Haidan said. "We could come back for more."

"Cenhotl." And the Azteca listed the names of the captured priests. "Many of our leaders abducted. There is chaos among the remaining."

A fine rain pattered in. The night would be a muddy, sloshy one.

"We need meet and discuss we do next," Haidan said. "If you don't start this, I go drag you god to the city wall and torture him."

The Azteca paled. "If you are interested in bargaining, then we are. That is why I came here. May I return?"

Haidan nodded at the mongoose-men. The warrior-priest got to his feet and staggered down the trench. They helped him into the maze of barbed wire, and with a few grunts the Azteca made his way back toward the Azteca line.

"You think he serious?" one of the mongoose-men asked.

Haidan shrugged and kept walking back toward the city walls. "We'll see."

A few distant thuds indicated Azteca artillery starting a new barrage.

The nearest mongoose-man looked up. "Ain't a good idea for no general be out here—"

The air above them whistled and the side of the trench exploded.

Haidan blinked and pulled himself off the ground, a whole half a minute gone from his memory. Blood leaked out of his ears and he had trouble focusing on anything in front of him. In the distance he saw mud flung high into the air from more explosions. Concussions ripped through the ground, thudding his chest, but he heard nothing.

Someone grabbed his arm and pulled him along. They were yelling at him, but Haidan pointed at his ears.

Hearing came back as they passed through the tunnel again, the mongoose-men disarming traps. Dirt swirled in the dark air.

The Capitol City response was an equally deafening thunder from weapons in the trenches and high up on the city walls.

"A trick?" someone asked.

Haidan shrugged. "Maybe they really confused and fractured," he murmured. He needed a moment to sit and sort himself out. "Try to keep any of them asking for truce alive."

The shelling got worse, forcing him to hunker down in the tunnel and wait it out with several other mongoose-men. Haidan ate hard, stale bread and drank weak tea and waited while the mud dried to a crust on his boots and pants.

*   *   *

Haidan was back in Capitol City before the sun kissed the horizon, and by the time half the sky was purple, he had given his orders. He waited on the outer edge of the city walls, looking out over the muddy trenches and craters he'd spent the afternoon in.

One Azteca priest, groomed, washed, and in full finery, was dragged out along the city wall. His ankles were bound several times over with rope. Several men checked it over, while the priest looked at them all.

The mongoose-men lifted the proud, defiant Azteca, tied the rope off on a cleat by the walkway, and threw him over the side of the wall.

Haidan leaned over and watched as the priest reached the end of the rope and recoiled part of the way back up with a scream. He bounced off the walls and swung wriggling in a wide arc from side to side, twenty feet below Haidan. His clothes and feathers hung toward his head, leaving him naked around the waist and legs.

Men laughed, some spat, others just shook their heads.

"Wait three hour," Haidan ordered. "Then throw the next one over."

He left the walls.

It was midnight, and three Azteca priests hung from the walls when the Azteca guns felt silent. They wouldn't kill their own priests. Haidan smiled.

By the early-morning hours several of the remaining Azteca leaders had sent notes with runners to the Capitol City trenches asking for a truce.

Haidan handed a mongoose-man his own prepared letter, with a time, a meeting place, and agreeing to the cease-fire.

He was tired and hungry. He crawled onto his cot for a brief respite.

At least it was quiet out. Quiet enough for a somewhat restful sleep. His chest and throat still hurt from whatever John deBrun had done to heal him.

PART FOUR

THE BITTER END

CHAPTER SEVENTY-NINE

Dihana faced the enemy on the other side of her conference table.

The enemy dressed in feathers and padded armor, the makeup on his face smeared from sweat. His arms were wiry, and a dark fringe of hair hung almost over his eyes.

His name was Cotepec. The provisional leader of the Azteca forces, he was a man in a tight spot. It was true he had a larger army, but his men were almost out of food. Haidan's mongoose-men had done their job well and kept supplies away from the Azteca. His leader was captured, priests were captured, and one of his gods captured. He could press on hoping for victory and face starvation if that gamble failed. He risked the god's death, and his own priest's death if he did so.

He could take the town if he fought just a bit longer. Both Dihana and he knew it. It danced in their eyes when they squared off across the table. But if he allowed his god and its priests to die, he would have failed as well.

Dihana felt no empathy when she laid those items out in a flat, precise manner.

He looked up at her. "My people in this city said you would be hard to bargain with." He wouldn't meet her eyes. Maybe, Dihana thought, he expected her to be a hard bargainer . . . for a woman.

"You expect any less?" Dihana handed him the papers. "You invaded the land, besieged the city."

Cotepec read the documents with care, putting aside each page as he read it. When he finished, he gathered the ten pieces back up in his hands. "You have the upper hand. But we are not defeated. I agree, in principle, that I will take Azteca back to other side of the mountains for the return of our god. But you say you will deliver the god to us when we return to Aztlan. How can you guarantee us this?"

"You have read the terms, Cotepec."

He raised a hand. "What if you keep our god anyway?"

"We will not."

"The Others will want to kill our god. How can we allow this?"

"You mean the Loa?" Dihana asked.

"That is what you call them."

Dihana took a sip of water, then refilled her glass from the pitcher on a bronze tray on the side of the table. "By airship," she said.

"You could crash the airship and claim it was an accident."

"How do you suggest we do this exchange?"

Cotepec laid the papers down. "We understand you already know about the tunnel through the mountain." Dihana nodded. Haidan had found this out, and John had told her as well. "We will make the switch at the tunnel. It easy for you to defend, and we can take safe control of moving our god back across to Aztlan."

Dihana thought about it. "Okay."

"Please make the changes." Cotepec handed her a pen. It was, Dihana realized later, the first compromise of many. Fourteen more points and adjustments had to be made before Cotepec would agree to begin decamping and returning through the jungle to get back on the other side of the mountains. It was the final item that shocked Dihana.

She stared at Cotepec. "I can't do this. Those are people's lives. You've captured thousands. Their lives are not yours to use as you see fit." She almost yelled.

He folded his arms and leaned back in his chair. "It is the only way I can get my priests to agree to return. They want what they already have. They have to return somewhat victorious, with some honor. It is that or they die here."

Dihana felt sick. A dizzy, stomach-clenching sick that made her wonder if maybe dying at the table would be best. "You must give me time to think about it."

"I will leave here before the sun sets." Cotepec tapped the papers. "We either have an agreement then, or I return and restart the siege."

"You will starve, your god will die, your priests will die."

Cotepec shrugged. "That is not as bad as returning empty-handed for all the other gods. So that decision is not mine to make."

"I can't. God, no, I can't." Dihana picked up the papers unsteadily as the Azteca stood up.

"You save many more than will die here if you agree."

Dihana closed her eyes. Clot you, she swore at the Azteca in her head. You and all your bloodthirsty gods. She grabbed the pen and dropped the final page to the table. Her signature was shaky and done quickly. "There." Her voice cracked.

"All these points are satisfactory," Cotepec said. "I will, then, return with one of the priests you hold captive now. We will make preparations to leave."

When the door closed behind Cotepec, Dihana slumped against the table and cried. She gave the papers to the ragamuffin outside the door and ordered copies made.

It was all she could do to get to her own room and sit on the chair by her desk. She called for a glass of spiced rum.

The ragamuffin who brought it up handed it to her, and Dihana downed the glass in a single gulp. "Bring a whole bottle."

As the ragamuffin returned to set the bottle on her desk, he asked, "Minister, are you okay?"

"No. No, I'll never be okay after what I just did." She shoved him out the door, locked it, and set to drinking herself into a troubled sleep, glass by burning glass.

CHAPTER EIGHTY

At the top of the Capitol City wall facing the Azteca, Haidan sat with Dihana in the dark night. Overhead Capitol City blimps made patrol circles and flicked spotlights at the ground outside the wall.

Earlier in the week it had been covered in Azteca tents and warriors. Now the battlefield was quiet.

Another blimp left the city, flying out into the darkness to follow the long trail of Azteca retreating back toward the Wicked Highs.

Down along the wall Dihana heard the clink of pots over fires as men heated tea. Laughter and conversation drifted in the air.

People had returned to the streets. Market reopened tomorrow, and Dihana had lifted all forms of curfew.

Haidan sipped a cup of maubi. "It go take almost a month to get them back into they land. But they truce holding." Haidan shook his locks.

"Haidan, do you think I made the right choice?" Dihana asked.

He took a deep breath. "I think you make the only choice you could have make." He took another sip.

"When the city finds out, they will come to tear me from limb to limb."

"I protect you."

Dihana wrapped her arms around herself. "I don't think I want to be protected, Haidan."

He looked at her, surprised. "What you saying?"

"I don't want to do it anymore. Running the city. No one person should ever have to make the choice I made in that forsaken conference room, Haidan. How many mistakes did we all make, acting alone? Haidan, I've done the most horrible thing a Capitol City person has ever done." She pushed her head into his arm.

He held her shoulders.

"Come, girl." This time she let him call her that. "When I general, I have men to support me, understand what I asking. You got nothing. You gone through more, with less, than I can imagine, being in control the whole city. What you done for all of we amazing. You done good."

Haidan hugged her and she hugged him back. It was comforting.

"I made my own share," Haidan said. "I left Mafolie weak, concentrating in the wrong area. Maybe is time both of we take some rest for a while."

Things were going to have to change, Dihana knew. Let the unionists duke it out with each other. Let someone else meet every week, give them a taste of the hell she'd endured for the past several years.

Dihana was going to step down from it all.

"Yes, I am over. Done for sure." The sudden resolve lightened her. "It is time for a rest."

"And what you go do?" Haidan asked.

"I want to find the Loa. That's first. I want their knowledge. I am going to join the Preservationists."

"Good." Haidan put his cup down. "You will do well leading them."

Dihana looked at him. "What about the gourds? Do we destroy them, or keep them around just in case?" They'd talked about sending them over the mountains and releasing the plague into Aztlan. Dihana had felt queasy just thinking it. There was no guarantee it wouldn't cross back over to their side of the mountains and kill them all as well.

"Destroy them," Haidan said.

"That's a good choice."

"Let we hope everyone else keep making good choice. The Loa would kill the world with those gourd. Whoever come after you, however we rule we-self after this, they need make some good decision."

Below them, inside the thick walls, Capitol City settled down for a trouble-free night. In the weeks ahead Dihana looked forward to turning the city over to parliament, and Haidan would transfer the gods and priests over to the Azteca by the mouth of the tunnel. He would stay there to watch it destroyed by dynamite after that. And Dihana would prepare herself to explain to the city that she had allowed cousins and distant friends to be taken back with the Azteca in bondage.

Nothing in Capitol City would ever be the same.

Nobody would ever be the same.

CHAPTER EIGHTY-ONE

Azteca lined the mouth of the tunnel in full Jaguar scout finery. New feathers had been glued to their masks, and the scouts lined the rocky, carved walls like brightly colored statues. Dull mongoose-men uniforms mingled outside, a full force with rifles ready for any movement.

Haidan watched his men trundle forward the wheeled cage that held the Azteca god. The Jaguar scouts murmured, stirred, but held still.

A line of Azteca priests in loincloths followed the cage.

The handover occurred smoothly, though the mongoose-men spat with anger. They wanted the thousands of Nanagadans already on the other side of the tunnel freed.

It couldn't happen.

Yet.

Haidan ground his teeth and watched the last of the priests disappear into the dark of the tunnel. The Jaguar scouts surrounded their own, turned their backs, and walked down the tunnel. Fifteen minutes later all that remained was dark shadows.

Haidan waited another hour, then gave the signal.

Thuds rippled through the ground, up his feet, and into his chest. Deep inside the tunnel the charges went off. A wall of dust exploded out of the mouth, and the sides collapsed in.

When it settled, only a wall of rock remained.

Haidan relaxed.

Mafolie had been handed over earlier in a similarly tense exchange. This was the final part of the truce.

Now the rebuilding began. Of all the cities raided. The mongoose-men. Their future. There was almost no food across the land, but crops would be planted and grow soon. Fishermen in Brungstun and Capitol City would bear the weight, and so many had died it would be easier to spread what they did have. The forest would provide wild fruits and berries.

Most would live. They'd made it. They had a second chance.

CHAPTER EIGHTY-TWO

One day the Azteca left, the Frenchi told Jerome. A huge trail of Azteca came from the north and they all walked out of town. They left some people in chains, took others, and retreated to the mountains.

The Frenchi men all went into Brungstun. Carefully at first, then brazenly when they realized all the Azteca were truly gone.

Airships no longer flew overhead.

All the Frenchi women and children returned to the village, though it was burned to the sand it stood on.

Rebuilding began.

Jerome was allowed to play outside in the sand with the other children, but got in trouble for getting into fights for no reason. The anger just exploded out of him. He even once pushed Sandy down, for arguing with him, and they'd stopped speaking since.

At night, the thought of Teotl, scary monsters, streaming out of the stars down toward his home to kill them all kept him awake.

Eventually Jerome played alone and talked to no one.

After a few more days people from Capitol City arrived. Mongoose-men sailed out to the village to talk to them.

"The mongoose-men say they defeat the Azteca, and the Azteca retreat back to the other side of the mountain," someone explained at a bonfire. "The Azteca had come through a large hole they dig in the mountain, is what they say. It take them many generations to do this, but the mongoose-men say they go dynamite it. But the threat still there. They want volunteer to become mongoose-men and learn to fight the Azteca."

Several men volunteered. And Jerome held up his hand and stepped forward.

They shook their heads. "You too young," they said.

"I want kill Azteca," Jerome insisted. That was where the anger came from, he had realized.

They got angry with him, though. The mongoose-men left without Jerome with the recruits who would learn how to kill Azteca and defend the land. And that made him even angrier.

*   *   *

Three days later a small boat landed and his father got out. Jerome watched from the distance, hiding by a palm tree, as his father spoke to the people.

Jerome saw his dad put a hand on one of the men's shoulders.

A real hand.

This couldn't be his dad. Could it? Jerome stood stiffly by the tree. But when his dad came over and picked Jerome off the sand in a crushing hug, Jerome broke down and cried into his dad's shoulder.

"I couldn't do anything," he sobbed. "I could only run from them Azteca. I don't know what happen . . ."

"I know," John said, and hugged him harder. Jerome hung on tight until his dad pulled him free and looked him in the eyes, sadly. "When we go back, we're going to stay with Auntie Fixit, okay?" His dad swallowed and bit his lip. "Uncle Harold is dead. And so is Mom." His dad sniffed, and Jerome began to sob. "Auntie Fixit has some stuff of your mother's she kept while the Azteca were in Brungstun. We will take that stuff back to our house."

"What happen?" Jerome asked through tears.

"I don't like telling you this."

"Please," Jerome begged.

"They sacrificed her. Along with many other women in Brungstun. Auntie Fixit saw it all. She was with Shanta until the very end. They buried her in a big pit."

Jerome grabbed a handful of his dad's shirt. He cried, but inside he also raged.

CHAPTER EIGHTY-THREE

Several months passed for John before Jerome calmed down. They were long months of fights with his son about his hand, where he had gone, what had happened to Shanta.

Each one wearied him more than he thought he could handle.

And there were all these memories sitting in the back of his mind, waiting to explode at the most inopportune moments. Memories of the dark, black emptiness of drifting in space that woke him up screaming at night. The guilt of all the people who had died as a result of decisions and actions John had made. Actions several centuries ago, and actions just months ago. Some days he could hardly function. His mind felt as if someone were poking holes through it and letting out molten, confusing images.

Jerome had lost his childhood and had been forced to grow up to the toughest realities of a harsh world. In some way he couldn't express he resented it, and John understood.

So he spent time at the beach, or at sea, trying to bring Jerome back some measure of normality.

But at night they both sat at the table, not able to find words. Sometimes John found Jerome in a corner crying, and sometimes Jerome found John staring off in the distance with wet eyes.

One of those lonely nights Jerome had found John on the porch, staring into the distance. "You missing she?"

"It hurts I miss her so much," John said.

"I know." Jerome sat on the chair next to him and stared into the same distance.

The days passed, some better than others.

One day Jerome pulled himself together and told John everything that had happened. Troy, the passages, the people he'd seen dying.

John could only hug him.

It was a breezy day on the beach just out by town when Pepper found them. Jerome ran into waves and laughed loudly, bringing a grin to John's face. John leaned back against a palm tree, with a quick glance up to see if any loose coconuts hung above him.

Footsteps crunched through the sand, and Pepper crouched next to him. His dreadlocks swayed across his eyes.

John couldn't look Pepper in the face, but kept an eye on Jerome. From the corner of his eyesight it seemed that Pepper had all his bulk back.

"You know, I find it funny that I still don't know you as anything other than Pepper, even with all my memories back." Pepper snorted at him. "I'm sure you've thought about many different ways to kill me," John said. "All I can say is that I'm sorry."

"We all do what has to be done," Pepper said. "And maybe you should realize that just as you were changed down here with your family, I was changed after spending so many years drifting with nothing but my own thoughts." One of Pepper's hands remained behind his back. A gun? A knife?

John looked straight at Pepper. "You weren't going to let me do another run."

"You had enough priests. The Teotl I caught you was alone a good bargaining chip. You went too far. Too driven, John. Should have cut your losses."

"Maybe. The ship will repair itself eventually. I know exactly where she is."

"And I'm stuck on this planet until then, John. I think, maybe in some lower area of your tactical, ever-scheming mind, you wanted that."

John didn't reply.

Pepper pulled his arm out. He held the Loa device John had hidden in his cabin on *La Revanche*. It glinted in the somber evening rays. An icy sensation ran up John's neck. Pepper had the ability to take over the *Ma Wi Jung*. There was a threat there. Pepper was telling him he could take the ship back, at any point. If John ever deceived Pepper again, Pepper could take the ship and find a way to use it. Maybe with the help of the Loa, or maybe with enough time . . .

John remembered how damn effective the tiny Loa probes were. They'd been spit out into deep space to hijack Nanagadan ships during the first few years of contact, before the Loa began to work with humans instead of pressganging them into service fighting against the Teotl between wormholes and planets.

"The Azteca are still out there," Pepper said. "They'll attack again. And since I'm stuck here until our ship heals, I will work to stop that."

Jerome dove into another wave and resurfaced several feet away, spitting water out of his mouth. John still kept his lips pressed shut.

"There is something else only you can appreciate," Pepper said. "The Loa all came out of their hidey-holes after the battle. They're trying to help the inventors and engineers. They're pushing for larger armies, a navy, and more aggressiveness against Azteca."

"I'm sure the Teotl are doing the same on the other side."

"We're being manipulated by those damn creatures again. Huge searches for lost technology, reverse engineering, that is okay. But behind it are the Loa and Teotl, which means more war. More death."

John listened to the sound of the palms shifting and rustling. The top layer of sand, so fine the wind played with it, danced and swirled down the beach.

"I could use your help in stopping the Teotl," Pepper said. "There are some other tricks I have up my sleeve. Hardened bunkers I could search for weapons. Come with me. We'll make Nanagadan history again. You and I will make our own war on the Azteca until it's time to leave."

For a moment John was tempted. There might be a suit of reactive armor he could climb into to kill Azteca with. Some Azteca had stayed on this side of the mountains to become Tolteca. He knew these deserters could come in handy. He could run them back over the mountains as spies. Plans began forming in his head.

But Jerome ran out of the water and started climbing a pile of boulders at the corner of the beach.

"I can't." John pointed his chin at Jerome, jumping from rock to rock. "Jerome, he's shaken. He needs me more than anything right now."

The thirst for revenge died in the face of his son's pain.

Pepper stood up. "When he is grown, will you fight with me?"

"Look for me then." John stood up with him. They faced each other under the shade of the palm tree.

"I think you have the right idea, John." Pepper smiled. He put a hand on John's shoulder. "I'll see you again."

Pepper turned around and walked up toward the dirt road leading into town. He was headed straight for the Wicked Highs, no doubt.

"Pepper, there is on last thing," John said. Pepper paused. "The Spindle." They both looked up. "There are working instruments in Tolor's Chimney that say it is being stabilized and opened up again. They will come through again, in numbers." There were maybe thirty Teotl on this planet. But through the Spindle and the destroyed remains of the wormhole, there were billions of Teotl.

"How long?" Pepper asked.

"It'll take at least a hundred years." The computer in Troy's desk predicted two hundred years for them to stabilize the wormhole.

"Then we should get busy."

"The ship will be ready, Pepper. I'm no fool. If we don't get help, if we don't warn other worlds, the Teotl will wash over all the worlds like the tide."

They had thought a single system, with all of its defenses aimed at a wormhole with the Teotl on the other side, could hold the Teotl off.

It hadn't worked. All they'd done was buy time.

"I'll be back then," Pepper said. "We'll get the word out with the ship. We'll be waiting for them when they come through."

He turned and walked off down the dirt road leading to the beach.

Jerome ran up. "That was Pepper?"

John nodded.

Jerome watched Pepper walk down the turn in the dirt road and disappear. "I want to be like him when I grow up."

"No, you don't, Jerome. Trust me." John put an arm around his son.

They stood there for a while.

Jerome looked up at John. "How did you meet Pepper?"

John laughed. "That isn't a story for young men. I'll tell you when you grow up, okay? We should go home now."

He walked down the dirt road and Jerome followed.

When Jerome grew up. Ten years from now. What could he do to help Nanagada while he remained in Brungstun? He wasn't sure, but he was thoughtful as he led Jerome back home.

It was dark when they got there and lit the gaslights on the porch. Electric lights wouldn't be coming out from Brungstun for a long while yet. Both moons were behind the horizon. The great Spindle hung in the sky, along with all the other stars, and for the first time in twenty-seven years John could trace the patterns in the sky and name the twinkle in the sky he'd come from. There was Earth. Home, in a way. Though not as home as Nanagada was now. John marveled at the sky.

Then Jerome offered to make dinner. John smiled and went inside. He helped him while he thought about what needed to be done outside. The garden needed to be plowed and replanted. And then he needed paper, lots of it, as he would put down on paper everything he could remember that would help them build bigger cities, better weapons.

Could he get them to rockets in fifty years? A lot could happen in fifty years before Pepper demanded they leave in the *Ma Wi Jung*.

Tomorrow he would do all these things.

Tomorrow would be another day on Nanagada. A new day. But for now, Jerome peeled potatoes for soup, and John picked up the badly cut chunks of potato and laughed. After a few seconds Jerome laughed and slowed down, taking the time to slice only the skin off the potato.

Till Jerome grew up, John thought with a smile.

EPILOGUE

It was rainy season in Anahuac. The floating gardens on the lakes were ripe with vegetables and fruits, and the cornfields grew strong. The back of the village bordered on the jungle that led up to the mountains.

The priest had chosen several lucky children all at the same height as the corn to offer to the gods. The whole village of Anahuac gathered by the center of the town to watch the priest with his blood-matted hair offer the children to secure the health of the corn crop. Much to the shame of some parents, the children cried, gathered in a small group near the top of the village's small pyramid.

This was a special day, for a god had come in a divan to bless the offering. It remained under the curtains, away from the harsh sun, but the villagers were excited and honored to have it.

A priest with a flayed cape of skin grabbed the first child. He held the knife in the air, the jewels along the hilt glittering, and pulled the child up to the center of the pyramid. Everyone grew quiet in anticipation. The bustle of those selling things alongside the street fell as all eyes looked up the steep slope of the pyramid at the priest.

An explosion rocked the pyramid right under the priest's feet. The knife he held shattered from a single, expert shot. The priest clutched his bloody hand in shock. He clambered off and fell down the black stones toward the ground, as if a sacrificial victim himself.

Everyone turned around in confusion.

The god's divan flipped over. A horrible squealing deafened those standing around it, and several shots ended the sound. Everyone watched in horror as a curtain flipped open, and a black man with knotted dreadlocked hair and gray eyes stepped out, guns in either hand.

He turned in a smooth circle and shot the four warriors standing by the side of the divan. He looked at the throng of people around him and they stared at him, shocked.

He smiled.

"Who are you?" the priest lying at the foot of the pyramid demanded, struggling to stand up and hold his wounded hand.

The man did not answer. He walked through the villagers, his long, tattered coat swaying with him, and ran up the pyramid. Without any effort he picked a kid up under each arm, still holding his guns in his hands, and walked back down the pyramid.

He stopped by the edge of the flagstones, near the trees, and turned around. "I am Pepper," he told them. His deep voice echoed in the village square. "I am the man your gods will have nightmares about for the next fifty years." He put the children down and pointed off into the jungle.

The children looked back at the pyramid, then ran.

He shook his hands, and clear, sticky fluids splattered down onto the flagstones by his mud-encrusted boots.

Warrior-priests gathered at the edge of the square with atlatl, but the black man moved like a cat, his sinewy muscles exploding with energy. He ran for the jungle before a single dart was thrown.

The bushes rustled where he disappeared. The priests' darts clattered to the ground hitting nothing.

All that was left of the man was a wicked laugh.

ACKNOWLEDGMENTS

They say no man is an island unto himself, and so while I'm excited about having written *Crystal Rain*, I had a community of friends who critiqued various versions of this novel and who cheered me along. I owe them all a debt of gratitude.

My thanks to Mary Turzillo, Rebecca Carmi, Geoffrey Landis, Darrin Bright, Pat Stansberry, Bonita Kale, Marie Vibbert, Paul Melko, Jerry Robinette, and Mark Siegal (who, sadly, passed away before I returned the favor) for critiques early in the process. More big thanks to the 2003 Blue Heaven crew who all critiqued my first fifty pages (Chris Barzack, Roger Eichorn, Karin Lowachee, Paul Melko, Nancy Proctor, Mary Rickert, Ben Rosenbaum, James Stevens-Arce, and Amber Van Dyk) with superspecial thanks to Charles Coleman Finlay and Cathy "Chance" Morrison for detailed critiques of the whole novel (and a shout-out to Robin and Marvin, our magnificent Blue Heaven hosts; if you ever have a chance to stay at the Eagle's Nest or Himmelblau on Kelly's Island, you won't regret it). I also owe Ilsa J. Bick and Karin Lowachee thanks for being "writing buddies" and egging me on through various drafts.

I am lucky to have a great agent, Joshua Bilmes, who believed in this project and me enough to ask me to write the whole thing. Thanks to all the wonderful people at Tor, and particularly to my editor, Paul Stevens, for shepherding me through to the final draft.

And lastly, many thanks to my wife, Emily, both for being my first reader and for putting up with me during many late nights and much absentmindedness as I blundered through the creative process.

Without you all, I would never have been able to do this. Thank you.